D0210025

WITHOUT RESTRAINT

ANGELA KNIGHT

BERKLEY SENSATION, NEW YORK

**BERKLEY
SENSATION**

An imprint of Penguin Random House LLC
375 Hudson Street, New York, New York 10014

WITHOUT RESTRAINT

A Berkley Sensation Book / published by arrangement with the author

ISBN: 978-0-425-25114-0

PUBLISHING HISTORY
Berkley Sensation mass-market edition / August 2015

PRINTED IN THE UNITED STATES OF AMERICA

10 9 8 7 6 5 4 3 2 1

Cover art by Don Sipley.
Cover design by George Long.
Interior text design by Kristin del Rosario.

Penguin
Random
House

For Michael, my real-life cop hero.
I've lost track of the number of times
you've saved my life, my soul, and my heart
over the past thirty years.
None of it would mean a damn thing without you.

And for America's law enforcement community,
who risk their lives to help others
for very little in the way of pay or respect.
They make the world a better place every single day,
whether the rest of us know it or not.

A lot of people made this book possible. First I'd like to thank Dr. James Hunter, Oncologist, whose swift action and skill helped me survive ovarian cancer while writing this book. Dr. Hunter, along with Dr. Sarah Tillman, and his office staff registered nurse Lynette Kemp, Sara Camp, and Tiffany Shelton, were endlessly kind and patient with my questions and fears. I could not have been in better hands.

As always, I would like to thank my beta readers and critique partners, Joey W. Hill, Shelby Morgen, Kate Douglas, Diane Whiteside, Camille Anthony, Marteeka Karland, and Virginia Ettel, aka Bookdragon . They have always been willing to read my work, often at the last minute, flagging typos, errors in logic, and at times utter stupidity. They're dear friends and wonderful writers.

And I would like to thank my editor of more than a decade, Cindy Hwang. She has always been patient, but I was never more desperately in need of her understanding than during this book, when I struggled with first a broken leg, then cancer, then surgical complications. Thanks also to my agent, Jessica Faust of Bookends, who dealt with my drama without turning a hair.

And thanks to personal trainer Cory Matheson of Gold's Gym, who has helped me gain new physical strength after this year's adventures. I wouldn't have bounced back from cancer so quickly without his help.

CHAPTER ONE

Bruce Greer had always had a talent for breaking and entering. Of course, it had been years since he'd done it—he'd been walking the straight and narrow for almost a decade now. But after what he'd done six weeks ago, that was over and done.

Besides, he was really pissed.

The lock was a good one, but he'd learned to break into houses at his daddy's knee. Steve Greer's interests had been too expensive to fund on a mechanic's salary, so they'd had to find other sources of income. Daddy was so good, the cops never caught them. Otherwise Bruce wouldn't have his current job.

He used the picks with delicate skill, ignoring the sweat cooling on his face in the October air as he sought the familiar click and give of the lock's pins. *I've got plenty of time. The bastard won't be back from the gym for another hour.*

Good thing his target was such a creature of habit. He'd had the man under surveillance for weeks since he'd learned what they'd done to him. How they'd lied to him.

Especially Alex.

The thought of her betrayal sent a hot knife of anger slicing into his heart. He'd loved her since they were kids, and she'd done nothing but lie. Only pretended they could become lovers again.

All a <u>lie. She</u>'d been laughing at him the whole time.

Nobody laughed at a Greer.

There had to be an accounting. By the time he was done, they'd all bleed. Her. Her family. Her friends.

They all owed him blood.

The lock clicked open beneath the delicate manipulation of his picks. He lifted his bag, opened the door, and walked into the house.

October 20

Alexis Rogers had never been this turned on in her life. Especially not from watching somebody else have sex.

And how the hell did Frank turn swinging a bullwhip into a sex act? Not just a kink act—something that aroused you if you had a little twist in that direction. Which admittedly, Alex did.

The big man used the lash with sensuality, as if he were eating out the blonde lying across the spanking bench. Plump, pretty, and naked, Tara merely groaned in woozy pleasure.

The overhead spotlight caught the wet glisten of her rosy vaginal lips. She lay with wrists and ankles cuffed to the bench's legs, the wedge-shaped custom padding raising her hips higher than her head.

Forty people surrounded Frank and the girl in the house's sprawling basement dungeon, watching the scene with rapt interest. One of them was Tara's husband, who leaned a shoulder against the nearest oak support column. Roy was a wiry Dominant with thinning blond hair and a long bony face. His hazel eyes were fixed on his wife with protective intensity.

Though he loved bondage and emotional domination, Roy often said he couldn't bring himself to hurt his masochistic submissive. Rather than deprive her of what she needed, he liked to arrange for someone else to provide the impact play Tara craved.

Apparently, Frank had volunteered to provide the foreplay this time. And foreplay was all he'd be getting out of it; Tara and Roy never had penetrative sex with anyone but each other.

Alex intended to make it up to Frank—and God, she couldn't wait. Captain Kyle Miller, host of tonight's party, had been singing the big Dominant's praises for years. She gathered they'd served in the Navy together before Cap retired and returned to Atlanta with his wife, Joanne.

Now Frank and his bullwhip had moved to the area, too. Alex looked forward to sampling his skills. If Cap was to be believed, Frank was the Dom of her dreams. Alex believed him, since the Millers took their kink seriously.

Just look at their basement dungeon.

Running the whole length of the huge brick colonial, it was a suitably menacing space with cement block walls painted flat black, recessed lighting, and square oak support beams, also painted black. Home dungeon or not, it was as well furnished as any upscale New York sex club, with spanking benches, St. Andrew's Crosses, stocks, cages, manacles, and just about anything else horny kinksters could use in pursuit of an orgasm. Cap had built the majority of the equipment himself; he was, according to his wife, good with his hands. She usually leered cheerfully when she said it.

At the moment, several pieces of that gear had been shoved aside to give Frank room to swing his whip. Tara lay at one end of that space, spread wide and chained down in all her glorious submissive nudity.

CRACK! The popper—the fringe at the very tip of the bullwhip—struck her reddening ass. The lash ought to sting like a bitch, but Tara seemed to feel no pain. Just the reverse, judging by her pleasure-drunk moans.

He'd built the intensity slowly, starting with a spanking, then progressing through two different floggers—the first deerskin, the second with thinner tresses that left thin red lines against her creamy skin. The blows he'd given her were just hard enough to make her squirm, pant, and occasionally yelp. Only when he judged her properly warmed up had he brought out the bullwhip.

A single tail could cut like a meat cleaver if you didn't know what you were doing—or inflict nothing more than a sharp sting if you did.

Frank knew what he was doing, and he was careful about doing it. He had to be. He was a Dominant, a practitioner of BDSM—a blended acronym for Bondage and Discipline, Dominance and Submission, and Sadomasochism. It was too easy to hurt somebody badly if you were careless playing BDSM's edgy sexual games. No orgasm was worth that.

Still, for people like Alex and Frank, sex was an extreme sport: at its most exhilarating when spiced with danger.

Between clusters of strikes, the big Dom caressed Tara's pussy and reddening ass. The combination of pain and pleasure had sent her flying into what the community called "subspace," a high caused by a combination of endorphins and adrenaline. Pursuit of the floating euphoria drove subs to seek out Dominants like Frank. Skilled, a little sadistic, with a keen understanding of a submissive's sexual needs.

The whip cracked into another hissing arc. Frank watched Tara as if savoring every twitch of her lush ass and flex of her fingers, every heartfelt plea and whimper. As he moved, he swung the whip with a bullfighter's elegant grace.

Alex figured him at 6 feet 5 or 6 inches, maybe two hundred and forty deliciously muscled pounds. Frank's shirtless torso was brawny enough to make Michelangelo's *David* grit his marble teeth in envy. Adding to his erotic appeal, his long legs were clad in faded jeans tucked into polished leather riding boots. God, she'd always had a thing for riding boots.

He had the perfect Dom's face, handsome but intimidating. His nose was just short of hawkish, while his broad jaw had a strong cleft chin. He wore his black hair in a military cut that emphasized the angularity of his features.

As if to belie the stark male aggression of the rest of his face, he had a dreamer's mouth. Lower lip plump, upper with a pronounced bow, it looked soft, deliciously kissable.

Alex couldn't wait to kiss that mouth—and work her way down the rest of Frank's glorious body to the erection bulging behind his fly. Sweet Jesus, it looked like he'd stuffed a rolling pin in there.

Patience, Alex. Captain Kyle, their kinkster matchmaker, had promised to introduce them after the scene.

CRACK!

Powerful muscle rippled along Frank's right arm as he popped the whip against Tara's ass. The sub caught her breath, then let it out in a long, erotic groan.

"Rate it," he ordered. His smoky voice seemed to curl around Alex's aroused body like sandalwood incense.

Tara moaned something that definitely didn't sound like pain. He strode around the spanking bench, wrapped a huge fist in her cascade of curls, and jerked her head back with a Dominant's showy snarl. "When I ask you a question, you damned well answer. Talk to me!"

"Uh . . ." The girl panted. "I don't . . ." Yeah, she was definitely flying, as stoned on endorphins as a Woodstock hippie on a joint the size of a redwood.

Frank glanced toward Roy. Tara's husband nodded and picked up the blanket and bottle of water he'd had waiting for this moment. The physical aftereffects of subspace could include a drop in body temperature and blood sugar; a responsible Top came prepared.

Crouching by Tara's head, Frank began talking to her in a low voice as her husband joined them.

"I've always thought you can tell the most about a Dom by what he does *after* he puts down the whip," Calvin Stephens commented from Alex's right. He was a tall young man with the build of a marathon runner, flamboyantly displayed by a submissive's leather harness and snug black shorts. "An asshole would walk away and let Roy handle the aftercare. Frank's doing his part, which says something about his sense of responsibility."

Cal turned to the man next to him with a wicked grin on his narrow, clever face. His white teeth appeared to glow against his dark skin. "You give great aftercare, too, sir."

Ted Arlington snorted and folded his arms. His black tee revealed impressive biceps. He had a broad, intensely masculine face with a wide mouth, a round bulb of a nose, and a thick blond mustache. Though a head shorter than his lover, he was all muscle and power. Anybody who tried to target Ted in a game of "beat the cop" soon regretted it. "You're just saying that because I always give you cock as part of the package."

Cal grinned wickedly, dipping his dark gaze to the zipper of his Dominant's black leathers. "And what a nice package it is, sir."

"Suck-up."

"But you like it when I suck."

"You're pushing it, subbie."

"Every chance I get, sir. More fun that way."

As her friends flirted, Alex's gaze slid across the basement in search of Frank.

He'd helped Roy unbuckle Tara from the spanking bench so the two men could wrap her in the blanket. Roy half-carried her to one of the couches that stood against the walls. Pulling what was probably an energy bar from his pocket, Frank sank down beside the couple to unwrap it for her. Meanwhile, Roy helped her with the bottle of water she was too buzzed to manage on her own.

"Cal's right, Frank does look like a good Dom," Alex said, with a nod toward the trio. "I'm impressed."

Ted eyed her, a blond brow lifting. "That's not saying much. Hell, *Gary* impressed you."

Alex forced a smile to hide her flinch. "Well, Gary was very pretty."

"So's a coral snake. I still wouldn't fuck one."

"Sir," Cal put in, "you do know gay men are supposed to be sensitive, right?"

"Sass me one more time, subbie, and you'll be sensitive for the next week."

Cal sighed under the weight of world-weary skepticism. "All I get are promises. Sad, empty promises."

"You do know your ass is getting more stripes than a zebra?"

"God, I hope so."

Ignoring that, Ted turned to her. "As for you, I want to talk to this Frank before you traipse off to scene with him. You ain't getting hurt by another Danger Dom on my watch."

"Ted, Cap wouldn't fix me up with somebody like that."

"I somehow doubt the Captain has ever slept with Frank, much less subbed for him."

"You're not mistaken, sir," Cal assured him. "Cap definitely doesn't bat for our team."

"And how would you know?" Alex narrowed her eyes in mock suspicion. "Been flirting?"

"With the Captain?" He recoiled in mock horror. "God, no. He scares me. He looks like Captain Picard's bigger, meaner brother."

"You are such a nerd, Cal."

"Hey, my mom's a fan. She raised me on reruns of *Next Gen*."

"Your mom," Alex drawled, pumping skepticism into her voice. "Riiiiiight. Tell it to somebody who doesn't know you and fellow fanboys. I've heard y'all argue Kirk versus Picard on the Captain Coolness scale too many times."

"I've said it before, I'll say it again—Kirk is much cooler. Take how—"

"I'm serious, Alex," Ted interrupted. "This Frank guy makes Gary look like the 'before' fatty in a Bowflex ad."

"Don't worry, Dad, I'll be careful."

"None of your lip." He glowered at her. "Don't think I won't whip your little ass as hard as the subbie's."

"Better watch out, PoPo," Cal put in, using the slang term for police he'd made her nickname. "He means it."

"Yeah, okay, I hear you." Her gaze slid back toward Frank again.

Ted turned to his submissive. "I just wasted my breath, didn't I?"

"Might as well try to blow out a forest fire like a candle on a cake. She's completely under his evil spell." Cal's voice turned dreamy. "His muscular, towering, evil, evil spell."

"I am definitely whupping your ass."

Cal merely grinned, looking distinctly smug at the prospect.

The redhead was driving Frank Murphy crazy. Alex—they'd exchanged e-mails, but she hadn't revealed her last name yet—wore the proverbial little black dress that hugged some luscious curves. Throw in lace-stocking-clad legs in stiletto heels, and it was no wonder he was tripping over his tongue. Which was unacceptable, especially when he was providing aftercare to somebody he'd just whipped into subspace.

Focus on Tara, dammit. He'd told Roy he'd take care of his wife, and he'd do it if it killed him.

Be easier if he could throw a burqa over Alex, though. Those legs . . . God, the Leg Fairy had been good to the girl. Endless as a Fallujah patrol, with long, lean muscle in thigh and calf that flexed every time she twitched a do-me heel. He'd bet his Budweiser she ran every fucking day. He'd love to have her wrap his ass in those legs while he ground in nice and deep . . .

No wonder he had a hard-on up to his navel.

Tara, dammit. Get your mind back on Tara. Discipline usually wasn't this big a problem. Between Iraq, Afghanistan, and his mother—and all their respective IEDs, whether literal or not—Frank knew how to gut through almost anything.

Roy looked up at him over Tara's blond head. "I can take it from here. Go talk to Alex."

He stiffened. Was his distraction that damned obvious?

"You done good, Frank," the Dom reassured him. "It's going to take me three hours to pull Tara down out of orbit . . . assuming she stays awake that long. I only know about Alex because Cap's been planning to set you two up for months."

"Ah. All right. Look, thanks for trusting me to scene with your wife." Smiling, he shook Roy's hand as he rose to his feet. "You're a lucky man."

"Don't I know it." The blond Dom gave his wife a tender smile as she leaned against his shoulder. Tara sent him a slow, dazed blink in return. "See you later, Frank."

"Later." Starting off through the crowd, Frank scanned for his host, wanting the introduction Cap had promised him.

"Nice scene, son," a voice rumbled from behind him. "You flew that girl like the space shuttle."

He turned with a smile. "Not as high as you'd have sent her."

"Now you're just flattering an old man's ego." Captain Kyle Miller was a tall man, wiry and tough, with a fringe of gray hair around an otherwise bald head. That blue-eyed stare of his could make even Frank want to drop his gaze. His black slacks and navy golf shirt covered a build that was still respectable, though his SEAL tours in 'Nam were forty years in the past.

"Let's go get you properly introduced," Cap said, and turned to lead the way through the basement. Classic rock pounded in the background as people in latex, lace, and leather gathered around assorted bondage gear, preparing for their own kinky scenes now that Frank's bullwhip demo was over. "Y'all made contact yet?"

Frank shrugged, sidestepping a naked girl walking on a leash behind a short Domme in a green leather catsuit. "Exchanged a few e-mails, a photo or two, chatted on the phone a couple of times. Enough to know both of us have tested negative for STDs recently. I've been so busy getting all the requirements done for the new job—not to mention stuff with my mom—that we haven't managed an actual date yet." He frowned. "Alex hasn't told me much, beyond that she's not married."

Cap shrugged. "I'm not surprised. She's pretty deep in the closet, as far as the Scene goes. Most everybody at the party tonight is."

"Including me." Being known as kinky could get you fired or ostracized. People had even lost their kids over BDSM.

Which was why, as in the movie *Fight Club*, many kinksters never publicly discussed what they'd done, where they'd done it, or who they'd done it with. The price of running your mouth could be entirely too high.

As his attention focused on Alex, Frank put out a hand to stop his friend. "Who's the guy? The glaring blond fireplug with Alex and the black kid. I thought she wasn't involved with anybody." The man wore the leather pants and black T-shirt that was a popular uniform for Dominants. The kid—he looked to be in his mid-twenties—was dressed in an artistic arrangement of straps, the male submissive's answer to lingerie.

"That's Ted. He and the kid are a couple."

"So what's with the glare? They in a *ménage* with Alex?" Frank was the last man to poach. Not after Sherry.

"That'd be damned near incest, the way Ted is about that girl. You'd think he was her daddy, he's so protective." Cap grimaced, as if at an unpleasant memory. "The glare is probably because Ted absolutely hated her last Dom. Not that you could blame him. That one was such a prick, he should have worn a condom over his head as a warning to the rest of us." Correctly interpreting Frank's wary expression, he added, "Don't worry about Ted, I'll deal with him. You concentrate on Alex."

"Okaaaay," Frank said, dubious. He wasn't sure he needed any more drama in his life.

Alex turned toward him, pivoting on those incredible legs, gleaming red hair curling around her shoulders, her little black dress hugging bra-challenged breasts and curvy hips. When she saw him, a smile lit her face like a sunrise.

On the other hand, what's life without a little drama?

* * *

*G*ood God, he's huge, Alex thought, staring up at Frank Murphy as Cap performed the introductions. She wasn't used to being towered over, especially not in heels that had her scraping 6 feet 1. *If he got drunk and disorderly on me on the street, I'd have to shoot him. Otherwise he'd kick my ass.*

Of course, if she did shoot him, the rest of the female population would rise up *en masse* and lynch her. The man was even more mouthwatering up close than he'd appeared from across the room. His chest alone seemed to take up her entire field of vision. And she definitely approved of the view.

"It's a pleasure to meet you at last, Alex," Frank said, engulfing her hand in a big, callused palm and long, strong fingers.

"I can definitely say the same." His eyes were deep and dark gray, staring into hers in the kind of hypnotic Dom stare that made her want to give him anything he wanted. Especially if what he wanted was her. She suspected her smile looked besotted. Her nipples had hardened into tiny erections. His eyes flicked down to the tight silk bodice of her dress, then flicked up again, darkening hungrily. She swallowed. "Impressive flogging demo."

"You do seem to know your way around a whip," Ted said. The words were complimentary. The tone was dubious.

"I've sacrificed many pillows to the bondage gods." Dominants were often told to practice their whip skills on pillows until they could throw a lash precisely where they wanted it. It was a hell of a lot harder than it looked. "Damned near lost an eye once, too. You can bet I never forgot those safety glasses again."

"Good for you. Got any references?"

"Yes, and I already checked them," Alex told Ted, losing patience. He was deliberately trying to yank Frank's chain.

Cap moved up behind her friend and clapped a hand on

the shorter man's beefy shoulder. "Come on, Ted, I'll get you a beer."

"I don't drink when I'm sceneing," the cop growled, glaring at Frank like a protective father trying to warn off a Hells Angel.

"Then I'll get you a Coke." The ex-SEAL dragged him away. Cal rolled his eyes, gave Alex a wink, and followed them.

One dark brow lifted, Frank watched them head for the refreshment table set up beyond the bondage equipment. "Protective, isn't he?"

Alex sent a fond smile after her friends. "Can't seem to break him of the habit."

A woman yowled as her Dom barked a command over the classic rock booming from the sound system. At the moment, Jim Morrison badly wanted someone to light his fire. Alex had to raise her voice to be heard. "Want to step into the other room? We can't exactly talk in here."

"That depends. Will Ted feel driven to defend your honor?"

"I'll protect you."

He grinned at her, gray eyes crinkling over wolfish white teeth. "Got a deal. Want something to drink? I'm dry from that flogging."

"Sure." She followed him over to a cooler and took one of the canned soft drinks he handed her. Neither of them reached for a beer. Ted was right; only an idiot drank when he scened. BDSM was dangerous enough stone sober. Besides, the whole point of kinky games was the pursuit of a different kind of high.

Someone yelped as his Domme swatted his ass with her riding crop. Morrison was getting insistent about his fire.

Rising to her tiptoes, Alex called into Frank's ear, "Want to head somewhere quieter? There are a couple of private scene rooms across the hall."

"Yeah!" Frank called back. "I can't even hear myself think in here. It's for damn sure we can't negotiate."

Together, they wound their way through the crowd and out of the main dungeon into a hallway. Three smaller rooms and a powder room lay opposite, with the stairs leading to the rest of the house at the other end of the hall.

Two of the rooms were occupied, judging by the lusty sounds coming through their closed doors. Fortunately for Alex's frustration level, the door to the third room stood open. She threw Frank a questioning look. He shrugged. "Why not?"

Leading the way in, he flipped on the light to reveal a home gym instead of the pocket dungeon they were expecting. A treadmill, a small wall-hung flat screen, and a set of free weights shared space with a stack of padded mats that probably did duty during yoga or self-defense practice. Or knowing the Millers, sex.

"What do you think?" Alex asked.

Frank shrugged. "At least we can hear what we're agreeing to."

She closed the door, muting Morrison's wail. Frank was right—nobody scened without negotiating. There was a BDSM saying: once trussed like a turkey, you didn't want to discover your plans differed from those of the guy with the whip.

The skirt of her Little Black Dress was just loose enough to let Alex lower herself down on the stacked mats. Frank sat next to her, stretching his long legs out and crossing his booted feet at the ankles.

"Nice job getting Tara into subspace, by the way." She popped the top on the Coke and took a sip. "Not that I'm surprised. Both your references had good things to say about you." She might be an adrenaline junkie, but Alex wasn't stupid; she'd called his former subs. BDSM attracted its share of abusive assholes, as Gary had painfully demonstrated. "They said you play responsibly and have a chivalrous streak that's surprisingly wide for a guy who likes riding crops. And judging by the way Cap sings your praises, you may be his favorite person on the planet. Except for Mrs. Cap, of course."

"Cap's a hell of a guy. He taught me the ropes when I was just starting out on the scene." Frank eyed her over his Mountain Dew. "He thinks a lot of you, too."

"Really? Cool." She leaned back on her elbows, enjoying the way his gaze skimmed the length of her legs. "What'd you think of my limits list?" The question didn't sound quite as casual as she would have liked, though she hoped her tension didn't show.

He grinned, flashing white teeth. "I'm shocked—shocked, I say—by your wanton depravity. And I'm wanton to fuck your brains out."

She grinned back. "Smartass."

"You do know I'm going to have to punish you for that?" He delivered the threat in a velvet purr that made her want to squirm.

"Feel free."

"Mmmm." Frank gave her a slow, wicked smile. "Our tastes do seem to align pretty well."

Alex had thought the same thing when she'd read his list of hard limits—things he absolutely wouldn't do—soft limits—things he'd consider doing—and fantasies. It had read a lot like the one she'd written about her own tastes.

On the other hand, she'd thought she was a good match with Gary, too.

Sobering, Frank studied her, as if sensing the battle between her doubts and her desire. "Why don't we see how this evening goes?"

Alex blew out a breath. "That might be wise."

He started to lean toward her, only to stop. "May I kiss you?" A polite Dominant never touched a sub without permission.

Her heart began to pound. "Yes." She swallowed, cleared her throat. "I'd like that."

Hot approval flared in his eyes, and he lowered his head toward hers.

His lips felt just as soft as they looked, tasting of Mountain Dew and masculinity. One big hand came up to cup her cheek, his fingers long and strong and warm. His broad body curled around hers, making her feel sheltered and protected. It wasn't a sensation she was used to. She was surprised at how seductive it was.

She reached for him, feeling the hot flesh of his ribs under her palm.

And sighed, melting into him.

CHAPTER TWO

God, she tastes exquisite, Frank thought, his mouth moving gently, carefully, on hers. His tongue traced over the soft curves of her lips until they parted in a low moan of passion. He entered slowly, drinking in the sex and sin of her mouth.

Alex moaned, her body lithe against his, hands pleasantly cool on his bare chest. Her nipples felt hard as cherry stones beneath the snug bodice of her dress. His cock, already hard from the sight of those prima ballerina legs, jerked at the sensual promise in her kiss.

Before today's flogging demo, it had been a year and a half since he'd even spanked a sub. Between training for his new job and taking care of his mother, he hadn't had time to search for a lover. After what had happened with Sherry, he hadn't been in a hurry to look. At least not until Cap had started singing Alex's praises.

No wonder I'm losing it. I'm deprived. His lips twitched. *Or maybe depraved might be closer to it.*

She eased back a fraction and opened her eyes, vividly green, a little dazed. He reached up, unable to resist stroking a hand through her blazing curls. Her hair felt like cool, raw silk and smelled of pomegranate shampoo. "What do you want in a Dominant? What drew you to the scene?"

Swallowing, Alex licked her lips. He almost bent to take her mouth again. "I like . . ." She paused to consider. "Testing myself. Being tied up, helpless, while a Dom does whatever the hell he wants. The risk, the heat . . . It's sexy. Seeing how much I can take when he tests me, tries to drive me past my limits with pain or need."

He traced a forefinger across her lips, was gratified when her little pink tongue darted out to taste him. "And what do you want in a Dom?"

She lifted her gaze, met his eyes steadily. "If my Dom wants me on my knees, I want him strong enough to put me there."

He gave her a slow smile. Resisted the urge to flex. "I think I can manage."

Her answering smile was a wicked scarlet curve. "Oh, I don't doubt it." The smile faded into seriousness. "If you're looking for a twenty-four/seven sub to kiss your boots, I'm not your girl." Her gaze flicked down his legs. "Though they are really nice boots."

"You a brat?" He'd never liked brats.

"No, I'm an adult. I don't need somebody to spank me for being a bad girl. I've already got one daddy—two, if you count Ted. I don't need another."

"Then what do you need?" His voice sounded a trifle hoarse.

"A demonstration." She paused as if at a sudden thought. Her brilliant green eyes widened, and she grinned in delight.

Alex wasted no time acting on whatever idea she'd just had. Despite her heels and snug skirt, she rose in a smooth surge and skimmed the dress off over her head, revealing a long, strong, sweetly curved body clad in a lacy garter belt and stockings. Her breasts were lush as mounds of cream, topped by taut pink nipples. Her narrow waist flared into a gorgeous ass, then sleeked down into those dancer's legs.

As Frank stared in stunned hunger, she balanced on first one foot, then the other to slip off the fuck-me heels. "I want you to prove you can master me. Two out of three falls."

It wasn't that unusual for a sub to undress at a BDSM party; half the women here weren't wearing a stitch. But Frank hadn't expected Alex to strip before they'd even finished negotiating.

He watched hungrily as she rolled the stockings down the sleek muscle of thigh and calf. However he'd thought their first scene would go, this wasn't it. "Two out of three falls? Are you suggesting some kind of fight?" He didn't fight women. Not if he could help it anyway; sometimes the women had other ideas.

"More like a practice bout. No punches, kicks, or choke holds—you'd kill me." Alex sounded utterly matter-of-fact about the whole thing. "Just joint locks and throws. And pins. Loser taps out of the hold." She looked up from rolling the other stocking down her calf. She'd bent almost double to do it, making him imagine all the erotic possibilities of a sub that flexible. "Unless you don't want to."

His cock lengthened, on the verge of escaping his waistband. Frank ignored its dicky demands; he needed to know exactly what she intended. "So you're not talking about me actually hitting you? Because there's a big difference between flogging somebody with a deerskin cat and punching her with my fist."

She snorted. "I have no interest in trading punches with you, Frank. You're too far out of my weight class."

"Yeah, I am. What do I get if I win?" *When* he won was more like it; not only was he a SEAL, he outweighed her by a hundred pounds of muscle. She didn't have a prayer.

Alex grinned at him as if reading his mind and shifted her weight, calling attention to those lush female curves. "What do you want?"

"You." He bared his teeth and let the hunger show.

She smiled. "If you win, you get me." When his head tilted in question, she clarified. "Sex. With a condom. However you want it."

His smile broadened, and he started pulling off his boots. "I'll win."

"Maybe. I don't intend to make it easy."

"Good." After dropping his socks into his boots, he stood, barefoot. And looked down at her from his seven-inch height advantage. Her eyes drifted down his bare torso to the fly of his jeans, which bulged from the pressure of his erection. "Dicks are off-limits," he added quickly.

"Well, not completely, I hope." Alex glanced around before he could come up with a suitably suggestive response. "Let's put the mats out." Bending, she grabbed one of them to pull it into position in the center of the room. The sight of her round, perfect ass as she bent made his mouth go dry. Dragging his attention back to business with an effort, he caught the other mat and wrestled the bulky thing around beside the first one.

Frank straightened as she stepped onto the padded surface, falling into an easy crouch that did interesting things to her breasts. He moved to face her, his attention on those pale globes. Her nipples looked as pink and tempting as candy.

"What's your safeword?" He referred to the emergency code a sub used to let the Dom know something had gone wrong during the scene, whether physically or mentally.

"Red for stop, yellow for slow down. Green for okay." The stoplight system was commonly used because it was so easy to remember. "Stop," ironically, was the one word that was never used, mostly because some subs liked to scream it when what they really meant was *"Keep going!"*

When he hesitated, Alex smirked. "We going to go, or are you just going to stand there looking sexy?" She crouched like a knife fighter.

"Oh, we're going." Frank felt a hot smile spread across his face. He'd heard of a lot of inventive ways to play BDSM games, but this was a variant he'd never tried.

Eyeing her tempting curves, he lunged, meaning to trip her and pin her to the mat. *Shouldn't take long*, he assured his impatient cock.

Alex stepped to the side, smooth as oiled silk. Before he could whip around, she seized his wrist, kicked one foot out from under him, and fell backward, jerking him over. They landed on their backs, Alex at a right angle to his torso, his captured arm trapped between her strong thighs. Both hands gripping his wrist, she levered his arm across the fulcrum of her hips. If she chose, she could easily break his elbow, crippling him permanently.

And it hurt like a son of a bitch.

He tried to roll toward her, but she had his chest gripped in her legs. There was no way to reach her in this position, no way to fight her hold, despite his far greater physical strength. It was a classic *Juji Gatame*, a combination judo throw and joint lock, expertly applied.

"What *dan* black belt are you?" Despite the painful pressure she was exerting on his elbow, the sensation of her bare pussy against his trapped arm made his cock jerk.

"Don't have a black belt," Alex told him cheerfully. "I've just been studying *Krav Maga* with Ted for the past five years." The deadly fighting style was a hodgepodge of martial arts techniques from judo, Karate, and similar fighting systems. Unlike most modern martial arts, it wasn't a sport. Israeli commandos had created it for use against terrorists. If you studied *Krav Maga*, you weren't fucking around.

Alex cranked back on his wrist until the vicious pain nearly tore a yell from his throat. "Tap out."

He did, thumping the mat with his free hand despite howls from his male ego almost as loud as his elbow's. She released him. As he rolled to his feet, Alex did the same, meeting his gaze with cool, watchful eyes.

That was when Frank realized this was a test. "Smart. Better to find out if I'm a hot-tempered prick with twenty people ready to come running if you scream."

"Given the towering SEAL thing, yeah. I can handle most guys, but you'd take me apart."

That stung. "I don't hurt women." Honesty forced him to add, "Unless they want me to."

"Sorry, but my last master was an asshat."

"He the one that demanded you kiss his boots?"

"Among other body parts. I'm afraid I'm not real good at being anybody's slave girl."

Frank unzipped his jeans and stripped them off, freeing his cock to bob at her. Now as naked as she was, he gave her a slow, hot grin and gestured for her to come at him. "Let's find out what you are good at."

Anything you want to do, Alex thought, eyes widening. Naked, he appeared even more powerfully built, between brawny shoulders, narrow waist, and legs elegant and strong. The thick length of his cock jutted, its shaft curving upward above the furry, heavy weight of his balls. Gray eyes glinted at her, hungry and intensely male. His smile shone white and predatory as he spread muscular arms wide, hands flexed and ready.

Frank had underestimated her once. He wouldn't be doing *that* again.

A cautious woman would have hung back, forced him to come after her. Alex had never been cautious. Sinking into a combat crouch, she darted in, seeking a grip on his wrist. He knocked her hand aside, pivoting clear with fluid skill. They circled in a flurry of attacks and blocks, attempted throws and dodges. She was faster and a bit more agile, but he had the advantage in reach and strength.

Spotting an opening, he stepped in and hooked a foot behind her ankle and his arms around her waist. A twist of his hips, and she found herself flying, held securely in his grip. He hit the ground first, taking the impact of their landing before rolling over on top of her.

Now she was the one trapped. His long legs coiled around

her calves as he pinned her wrists to the mat. She bucked, writhing against his hold, but he was too just strong.

Bracing on his knuckles, he reared over her with a hot half smile. "Tap out."

His erection pressed into her belly, burning and hard. She swallowed at the raw eroticism of being helpless, the feral need in his eyes. "Why should I?"

"So I can put you down again—and fuck you." Leaning down, Frank kissed her, his mouth moving over hers in a slow brush of velvet and heat. His tongue slipped between her lips in an erotic thrust. When he drew away, his gray eyes gleamed. "Hard and fast and balls-deep."

Alex licked her lips. "Maybe I'll take you down . . . and fuck *you*."

"Well, as long as one of us gets fucked. Tap out."

Instead she writhed. Deliberately. Slowly. Mostly to stoke the heat in that wicked Dom stare, to feel his cock thrust against her belly. "Not yet. I want to see if I can get loose."

"You can't." He lowered himself on flexing arms until his mouth hovered a breath above hers. "I've got you. You're mine—if I decide you're worth keeping."

She bared her teeth. Snapped, just short of that taunting mouth. "You want me to tap out, I'm going to need a hand free to do it."

He freed one wrist, his gaze challenging. "So tap."

"Okay." Quick as a cat, Alex darted a hand between them and tapped his cock twice. It bounced against her belly, and she wrapped her fingers around it for a slow, teasing pump. His eyes widened. Glazed, just a little. "Well?" she breathed. "Think I'm worth keeping?"

Frank growled like a puma, a rumbling note of threat. Grabbing her hand, he pinned it to the mat and leaned down to seize her nipple in his mouth. He began to suck, drawing hard, his tongue lapping sensitive flesh.

Alex moaned at the sweet, swamping lust. "I thought . . ." she panted, "you wanted to take me down and fuck me?"

"I've got you down. Maybe I don't see any reason to wait on the fucking."

He claimed her other nipple, giving it the same head-spinning treatment as the first. She fought his hold, but he leaned into her, letting her feel his weight, his hot strength, the brush of his body hair across sensitive skin. His teeth closed on her peaked tip, and he drew back, raking gently, then swirled his tongue in erotic patterns across her areola.

Alex bucked against his grip, just to feel that implacable male strength, to savor the arousing power of it. Heat stormed her senses in a sweet flush that raced the length of her body. Still he teased her, teased until she twisted on the piercingly sweet barbs of lust and pleasure. "Oh, God! Frank, please, Frank . . ." She had no idea what she was begging for, was barely even aware of what she was saying.

Frank released her and shot to his feet in an abrupt male surge. Powerful legs braced on either side of her thighs, he stared down at her, breathing hard. "Get up. Get up so I can put you down again."

Panting, Alex crabbed away from him on palms and feet. He watched her stagger upright with a cat's predatory intensity. She felt like a particularly juicy canary, a helpless ball of fluff and feathers, plump and slow.

Frank lunged. She leaped back, only to realize from his wicked smile that it was only a tease. A feint, designed to tire her out.

I think I've bitten off more than I can chew. Never mind that this was only supposed to be a game, something to get the blood pumping with arousal and need. For the animal deep in each of them, it was a lot more than that.

In a real fight, there'd be things Alex could do—punches, kicks, head butts. All the dirty little tricks Ted had taught her for use against drunks and thieves. But she'd specified those things off-limits, knowing perfectly well she'd handed him the advantage.

Not that Frank needed it.

Even if she could use every trick she knew, he'd still be able to put her down. Yet somehow she sensed he'd never inflict real harm on her. Yes, he might hurt her, but only as a means of giving her a soul-searing climax. But her gut insisted he would never do actual harm in their games, though she had no logical reason for that belief. She barely knew the man.

She needed to be sure. Needed to know she could trust him. That he wouldn't abuse her as Gary had, fists and Gucci loafers striking her in a frenzy of jealousy and resentment and vodka. Shedding her blood to prove his dubious masculinity.

Instead, Frank came after her with carefully measured force, hands flashing, seeking out holds, joint locks, and leverage. She twisted away from his lunges, and danced over the ankle sweeps that would have taken her down. She made him work for it.

Until Frank snatched her right out of the air and tossed her facedown on the mat. Alex rolled, tried to scramble away.

Too slow. He landed on her, hot and hard and strong, one big palm thrusting her right shoulder flat on the mat. The other hand grabbed her left wrist and cranked it up between her shoulder blades. "Tap out."

"Fuck off," she growled, hoarse with lust and excitement. His cock pressed against the curve of her lifted ass. She rolled her hips against it. Teasing.

"Don't piss me off."

"Or what?" God, she was wet. Bondage games often had that effect on her, but this was even more intense than usual. "What will you do, big man?"

Frank rolled his hips, let her feel his width pressing hard against her cheeks. "Keep it up, and you'll find out."

"Maybe I want to know."

"Maybe you don't." Frank pulled her upright by her captured arm, gently enough to avoid causing true pain, rough enough to arouse. Pumping his hips, he slid his erection between her pussy lips, almost entering—but not quite. The smooth head of his shaft glided across her clit in long, luscious strokes. She gasped as he whispered in her ear like a demon tempting a sinner. "Maybe I'll ream your little pussy until your eyes cross. God, I want to. I want to impale you on my dick like a cocktail olive. Drive it in nice and deep." His teeth closed over her earlobe in a sharp bite. Released. "Grind."

Alex gasped as streamers of creamy need heated her blood. "Bastard."

"You're pushing it hard for a girl with such a wet pussy." His tongue swirled over her ear, making her shiver. "I'll bet you're tight. Are you tight?"

"Find out."

"Shouldn't tease me like that, baby. I could drive my cock somewhere you don't want it to go." Another thrust, this one bucking against her anus.

She shuddered at the velvet threat, imagining it. The merciless entry, his width working in, remorseless and thick. "I'll take my chances." Her voice rasped. Shaking.

"I ought to take you up on that." He cranked up on her wrist, taking it right to the scarlet edge of pain. His free hand teased her bare torso, stroking heated, hungry skin. Gliding down to her sex, then between the lips, pausing there to circle and dance in her cream, a fraction of an inch from her aching clit. "Ought to give that snug little ass a fucking you won't forget." His teeth closed over the straining cord of her throat. Bit. Released. "Make you love it. Every. Single. Minute."

He could do it. He could make me love any damned thing he did.

Big fingers stabbed up her cunt, ripping a gasp from her throat as he claimed the slick opening. "Good thing for you your pussy is soooooo wet. Sooo tight. I never could resist tight, wet pussy. Feels good gripping my dick while I slide in. And out. And in . . ."

He fucked her, fingered her, made her writhe on his hand, helpless and lost in animal lust. Until his hand tightened on her wrist, levering her back down on the mat in a helpless ball, ass lifted for entry. "Oooh, God!" she groaned, lifting her hips to grind against his, barely even aware of the pain he was inflicting on her twisted wrist. "Frank . . ."

"Do you want it?" He rolled his dick between her slick lips.

"Yes! Christ, yes!"

"Tap out."

Maddened, she banged her free fist down on the mat, once, twice. Surrendering to him. To whatever he wanted, however he wanted her.

He let go. Before she could protest, he grabbed his jeans and pulled out a foil packet. Ripped it open. Found the slick opening of her pussy with his long, ravenous shaft. And thrust, impaling her.

The bliss was brain-melting. Cock, so thick, so long, sliding into her cunt, filling her to the brim. He began to fuck her, his hips slapping against her helplessly lifted ass. "You like that?"

"Oh, God! Yes! Christ, don't stop!"

"That's what I want to hear." Shifting over her, he angled his shaft to rake right against her G-spot, grinding over her clit, sending pleasure stabbing through her in strokes of fire.

Alex panted into the mat, angling her ass up into his pounding. "More!" she cried out, the word all but a scream.

He swore, a hard gasp of pleasure as he fucked her.

The fire he'd been stoking built. Built. Exploded, a searing wave of it that tore a scream from her throat.

She heard him roar, a deep male bellow, a moment before he drove to the balls and stiffened, shuddering against her as he came.

Moments passed as panting gasps became hard breaths, heartbeats slowing from jarring thunder to a steady, banging thump. Frank's arms tightened around her waist, his skin damp against her own sweating flesh. He stroked a hand through her tangled hair. She sighed and closed her eyes a moment. "God, you're amazing."

"Mmmm. So are you."

Slowly, he sat up. "I can't remember the last time a scene got me that hard, that fast—and made me come."

With an effort, Alex rolled over. She felt delightfully sore, sated, all but purring. "I figured since you'd just finished doing a whipping demo, you'd probably enjoy something a bit different. I always love combat practice, so I thought, why not combine the two?"

"Yeah, well, it worked." Frank hooked a big hand around the back of her neck and swooped down for a kiss. She kissed him back, drinking in the taste of his mouth. With a groan of pleasure, he shifted his hold to cradle her face between his palms.

A damned promising beginning, Alex thought.

Frank and Alex got dressed reluctantly. "You sure you don't want another scene?" he asked.

"I would love another scene." She dug a brush out of her purse and whipped it through her hair. "I'd love to continue the last one. Unfortunately, Ted and I have to be at work on Monday, and it's a three-hour drive. We both worked third-shift Saturday, and I swore to him I wouldn't keep us out too late if we came tonight."

"Yeah, I have the same problem. Doubt I'd mind the missed sleep, though."

"Neither would I." Alex leaned in for another dreamy kiss, then murmured against his mouth, "Unfortunately, it's not up to me. Ted is my ride."

Frank stepped back and cocked his head, giving her a long look. "Not to be pushy . . . Oh, hell, who am I kidding? I'm a Dom, I am pushy. I want to see you again."

Pleased, she smiled at him. "I want to see you, too. You know, there's a munch next Saturday at two p.m. We can get together then." A munch was a type of BDSM social event held at a restaurant or other public venue, usually once a month. It was a vanilla way for kinksters to meet other kinksters in a nonthreatening, nonerotic setting. "I'll bring my own car next time."

He grinned. "You've got a deal."

Frank walked her across the hall, where they found Ted

looking mellow and Calvin moving as if his ass hurt. Which it probably did, in more than one sense of the word. No wonder he looked so pleased with himself. *I know just how he feels*, Alex thought, every bit as smug.

Next weekend would probably be even more delicious.

CHAPTER THREE

Cap joined Frank in accompanying Alex out to Ted's battered green Jeep, one of a row of kinkster cars parked along the curb in front of the house. Ignoring the glare he got from the driver, Frank opened the rear door for her, then pulled her into his arms.

The kiss tasted hot and sweet, her tongue stroking and circling his as he sampled the softness of her lips. His spent cock stirred as arousal slid lazily through him.

When they finally drew apart, Alex gave him a sensual smile and traced a finger over his bare chest. "I'm looking forward to next week."

"Me, too." Reluctantly, he stepped back to let her slide into the backseat. The vehicle was already running, a rumbling testament to Ted's impatience to be gone. "Take care." Frank closed the car door and stepped back on the sidewalk. Alex gave him a little wave as the Jeep pulled away.

"Judging by that kiss, it must have gone well," Cap observed as red taillights disappeared.

"Yeah. Alex surprised me. Subs don't often manage that."

"Did she?" They turned back toward the big brick Colonial.

"She challenged me to hand-to-hand." Reading Cap's lifted brows, Frank added, "No kicks or blows. It was more of a judo thing. Two out of three throws." He felt his mouth stretch into a wicked grin. "Winner fucks the loser."

Cap laughed as they walked back into the house. The basement soundproofing was good; no audible cries or thumps sounded from downstairs. "Sounds like you won either way. I assume you did win?"

"Oh, yeah. After I underestimated her on the first engagement and she put me on my ass. She's good. Got me in a joint lock. Could have snapped my elbow like a bread stick."

"I'm not surprised. She's been training with Ted for years."

"That's what she said. I gather he's something of a badass."

"Former Green Beret."

"I'll keep that in mind the next time I piss him off. He's pretty fucking protective." They passed through the living room with its stone fireplace and elegant fine leather furniture.

Just beyond that, the Millers' kitchen looked something out of the Food Network programs Frank had grown addicted to. White-painted cabinets piped in burgundy surrounded stainless steel appliances that testified to Joanna's love of cooking.

Cap walked over to the coffeemaker that steamed and burbled on the gleaming black Silestone counter. Frank inhaled appreciatively. The air smelled like fresh beans from somewhere they grew expensive coffee. "What's the story with this ex-Dom of hers?"

"Like I said, he was a dickhead." The old SEAL turned to the refrigerator and pulled out a tiny white pitcher of cream, then rattled around in drawers and cabinets looking for the sugar bowl, mugs, and a couple of spoons. "Most of us become Doms because it turns us on when a woman gives herself. Then you have your plain vicious bastards. It can sometimes be tricky for a sub to tell the hardasses from the assholes until things get the hell out of hand. That's what happened with Alex—fell in with a Dom who liked to use his fists even more than a crop."

"Her Dom *beat* her?"

"Once. Only once. And then she kicked his ass." He poured them each a cup. "That's why Ted kept giving you the stink eye. He feels guilty he didn't figure out what Gary Ames was before the prick started using his fists."

Frank swore viciously.

"Yeah, that's exactly what I said when she told me." He paused, doctoring his coffee as Frank did the same. "For what it's worth, Alex made ol' Gar pay, but the cocksucker did get in some nasty shots—including kicks—before she managed to put him down. He had thirty pounds and two inches on her, so she had to work at it."

"You and Ted bury him in the county landfill?"

"I was seriously tempted, but Ted convinced me jail would suck at my age. I hate it when Ted's the voice of reason. Sure sign you've fucked up somewhere."

"I admire your self-control."

"Wasn't easy. For what it's worth, Alex made sure the little shit was charged with domestic violence."

"Good for her. Did he get any time?"

"Probation. Apparently he'd never beaten the hell out of a woman before, so the judge decided to give him a stern talking-to."

Frank wasn't surprised. South Carolina law treated criminal domestic violence like one man beating another man in a bar, instead of the brutal act of betrayal it actually was. "So where does this future corpse live?"

"Sorry, 'fraid somebody beat you to it. Literally. Clubbed him like a baby seal a month ago."

"And you say he's not in the landfill?"

"Hey, don't look at me. Alex's daddy wasn't exactly a fan either. Luckily, we were all in Columbia with ten thousand of our closest witnesses." When Frank lifted his brows, he explained, "Her father's the Harrison High football coach. They were playing Irmo."

"Alex is Ken Rogers's daughter?" The man was practically a legend. He'd led the Harrison Hawks to four state championships and was universally worshiped by every man who'd ever played for him. In Morgan County, that seemed to be most of them.

"Yup." Cap bared his teeth over the rim of his cup. "As for the douchebag ex, his murder hasn't been solved. Hell, they only managed to ID him from his tatts."

"Sounds messy."

"Oh, it was. The killer did a really thorough job on his head with some kind of thick, heavy object. Flashlight or a rolling pin or something equally well deserved."

Frank toasted Cap with his mug. "Long may he rot."

"The world is a better place." A companionable coffee-drinker's silence fell. Finally Cap asked, "So you enjoyed your scene with Alex?"

"That's putting it mildly. Though she's not particularly submissive. Basically told me if I was looking for something twenty-four/seven, she is not my girl."

"No, Alex doesn't submit anywhere but the bedroom. But the question is . . ." Cap contemplated Frank, his blue gaze shrewd. "She may not strike you as particularly submissive, but is she submissive enough?"

Frank hesitated. "I don't know," he admitted. "But I do know she has my attention." *My complete, undivided attention.*

Cap smiled.

Alex leaned her temple against the cool glass of the left rear passenger window of the Jeep. Calvin was gossiping cheerfully in the front seat, something about another gay couple. She let his voice wash over her, her mind drifting to the pleasure of Frank's hips slapping her ass, his cock grinding deep and hard just where she needed it. There'd been a raw heat to the scene she'd never known with any other lover. Even—especially—Gary.

Cal looked over the seat at her. "PoPo, did you even hear a word I said?"

Ted spared her the embarrassment of a confession. "Hell, no. Bastard's got her halfway to subspace. I hope your ass is up to eight hours in a patrol car, Rogers, no matter how many stripes he put on it."

"Nope, I'm stripeless. We didn't do any impact play." Though "halfway to subspace" did have the ring of truth.

Calvin twisted in his seat, the better to peer. "Yeah, well, he obviously did something, PoPo, given the way y'all vanished for the better part of an hour. When you did come back, you looked dazed. Frank looked like a cat with canary feathers clinging to his muzzle." He gestured at her hair. "Red canary feathers."

"Canaries," she informed him loftily, "do not have red feathers."

"Tell it to the guy picking plumage out of his teeth."

"I told you, he didn't touch a hair on my head."

"Didn't say he got them out of your *head*, PoPo." They'd often seen each other naked, given the kind of parties they went to. He knew the carpet matched the drapes.

"Pig."

"Oink."

"So if he didn't beat your butt," Ted interrupted before they could really get going, "what did he do?"

She grinned, suspecting there was probably a feather or two in her own teeth. "We wrestled."

Ted took his eyes off the road just long enough to flick her a skeptical glance. "You *wrestled* the jolly Dom giant?"

"Two out of three falls."

Calvin looked at his Dom. "And she did the falling."

"Yeah, that's what I'm afraid of. Fell right for the fucker. He'd better not be another Gary, Alex. I came so close to putting a bullet in that bastard . . . If somebody hadn't done the world a favor, I probably would have. Assuming your daddy didn't beat me to it."

He wasn't exaggerating. Alex's father had hated Gary

with a burning intensity she'd never before seen the Coach display. And he hadn't even known the kinky details; Alex was definitely not Out to Daddy. "Gary notwithstanding, I am not in love with Frank."

Ted snorted. "Yet." His voice dropped to a muttered growl. "Fuckin' frogman."

Cal glanced at him in the dashboard light. "Frogman?"

"The original version of the SEALs. Specialized in underwater demolition during World War Two. When they started doing other kinds of missions in the sixties, the brass renamed them. SEALs—Sea, Air, and Land." Ted was a human wiki when it came to military history.

"Back to Frank . . ." Alex began.

"Oh, yeah, by all means, let's talk about your new crush."

"Jealous, boss?"

"I thought I whupped your ass enough tonight, subbie. Guess not."

Ignoring the byplay, she tried to put the night's experience into words. "Gary would be brutal, and I'd kind of like it. But Frank kept protecting me from getting hurt even by accident. And it was . . ." She broke off, remembering the burning intensity of the moment. "Incredible. I've never felt like that. Not ever."

Cal blinked over his shoulder at her, then looked at Ted. "Well, fuck."

The older cop cursed. "She is completely gone on the son of a bitch."

Alex supposed he had a point. *But the real question is, how does Frank feel about me?*

He heard himself roaring, deep-throated bellows of rage as his arm lifted and fell, smashing the flashlight into the man beneath him. Blood flew as he knelt astride his target, until his nose was filled with the beefy smell and his mouth tasted of copper.

All he wanted to do was punish the bastard for what

he'd said. For saying Alex had lied to him, played him. For saying Bruce could never give her what she needed.

When he finally stopped, he was too tired to lift the flashlight, and something gummed his lashes shut. Reeling to his feet, Bruce scrubbed his free hand across his eyes, blinked hard. Managed to clear his vision.

And froze.

The face of the man beneath him was no longer recognizable. His skull was shattered, jaw hanging misshapen and bloody. Broken. His arms were flung wide. The first blow had knocked him cold; he hadn't managed to fight back.

I murdered him. Oh, God, I murdered him.

Staggering, Bruce looked down at himself. He was covered in blood. His hands, his chest, his face.

Murder. I've committed murder.

There was blood on the floor, on the walls, on the ceiling. He whirled, stumbled one step, two. The scarlet carpet squelched underfoot.

His stomach rebelled, cranking his body double. He vomited until his nose burned, the taste and smell of blood filling his consciousness, making the sickness worse.

When he was done, he staggered out of the blood-covered living room, searching for the bathroom. He needed to rinse out his mouth.

He found the sink and turned on the tap as he grabbed the soap and began to wash his bloody hands. Lifting his head, he looked into the mirror over the sink.

His father's face looked back at him.

B ruce's eyes snapped open. Panting, sick, he stared into the darkness. *A nightmare. It was a nightmare.*

But not just a nightmare. Far too much of it had been real. *I'm a murderer.* Six weeks ago, he'd beaten Gary Ames to death.

Wiping his mouth with the back of his hand, Bruce rolled out of bed. At least the dream had done one thing: reminded him there was no going back. Being a hero in his mother's memory was no longer an option.

All he had left was serving as the instrument of his father's revenge on those who'd betrayed him.

S he dreamed of hard male hands and a rough voice crooning erotic orders.

Which was why waking up with a cat's ass in her face was so disconcerting. "Meow!" the ass said in a distinctly demanding tone.

"Jesus, SIG, get your butt out of my face." Alex batted the Siamese's chocolate-tipped tail away from her nose.

"Meow." SIG Sauer turned and rolled his fuzzy head against her chin.

"All right, all right, I'm up. Way to ruin a perfectly good wet dream, furball."

Tumbling reluctantly out of bed, Alex bent to pick up last night's dress and hang it up in the closet, as she'd been too pleasure-drunk to do the night before. Scratching her ribs through the black Morgan County Sheriff's Office T-shirt she'd worn to bed, she wandered into the bathroom, SIG bitching at her heels. She took care of business to the sounds of the cat's increasingly irate Siamese curses.

"Keep your fur coat on. I'll feed you in a minute."

There were only four rooms in the old house, not counting the bathroom her great-grandparents had built onto the back porch five decades before. Alex padded out of the main bedroom, through the den, and into the kitchen, avoiding SIG's affectionate attempts to trip her on the way.

In the kitchen, an elderly white refrigerator hummed and rattled across from an equally ancient electric stove. A rubber dish drainer sat on the counter beside the stainless steel sink, dark brown to match the wallpaper's crowing roosters. Yellowing lace curtains hung at the tiny window. The morning sunlight shone through them, casting golden light and lacy shadows on worn, brown-speckled linoleum.

But old though the house was, she didn't have to pay rent.

She'd inherited it from her grandmother, and had been damned glad to get it. Besides, she was doing good to afford cat food on a deputy's salary. Renovations were out of the question.

Worn linoleum felt cool underfoot as she got SIG a can of cat food from one of the cabinets. The can opener ground over the sound of his increasingly frantic meows. "Oh, for God's sake, you'd think you hadn't been fed in a week." Alex dumped the can into his bowl, and watched him plunge his head into it with a satisfied feline growl.

Which reminded her of the much deeper growl Frank had produced while plunging his cock into her helpless cunt. God, what an arousing scene. As she filled SIG's water dish, she tried to remember the last time she'd burned that hot for a man. And came up blank.

No surprise. If she'd special ordered her ideal Dom, Frank would have been it: towering, chiseled, and just sadistic enough to be interesting. The mere thought of him made cream flood her pussy until she gave serious thought to going in search of her vibrator.

Oh, why not? It was only noon. She didn't have to be at the department until five thirty, when everybody was supposed to gather for the sheriff's birthday celebration. There was plenty of time for a kinky fantasy and a nap before she had to get up again. Then she wouldn't have to actually be on duty until midnight.

Heat flaring beneath her skin, Alex walked through her home office with its laptop and treadmill into the bedroom. The house was too small for hallways.

The bedroom beyond was sunny, with a rocking chair in one corner and a queen brass bed she'd found tarnished and sagging at Goodwill. She'd refurbished it over several weekends, buying a new mattress and box springs before polishing away the tarnish, dreaming of cotton ropes and adventurous lovers.

Now it was covered with a wedding ring quilt her grandmother had made when Alex was a child, every stitch placed with loving, blue-veined hands. Rag rugs covered the hardwood floor, and lace curtains hung before the one tall, narrow window. The room smelled like dusty old house and the ghosts of mothballs past.

Rummaging in the mirrored vanity that held her makeup, Alex found her pink rabbit vibrator, Thumper. After stripping off her panties and Morgan County tee, she flung herself down on the bed, her mind already on Frank. The vibrator began to hum as she spread her vaginal lips and traced the toy over juicing flesh.

God, the look of him. So incredibly *male*, big, and brawny as he swung that whip in breathtaking arcs. The steady crack of the popper as it landed precisely where he'd intended, accompanied by Tara's erotic moans. Danger and seduction and dominance—everything calculated to strip a woman of her instinct for self-preservation.

She eased the vibe into her core, shallow thrusts at first, then deeper and deeper. Catching her breath as it filled her, its pink gel ears finally teasing her clit with delicious quivers of pleasure.

Alex gasped, imagining being tied and helpless while that whip bit her ass and straining thighs. Frank's feral gaze on her, hungry as the hard jut of his cock behind his blue-jeaned fly, accompanied by the click of riding boots. Building her heat until she thought she'd burst into flame from sheer lust. Until even he couldn't take it anymore, and his zipper hissed, loud in the gasping quiet, and he thrust deep, so deep, seeming to fill her all the way to her back teeth.

Her hips pumped helplessly, her mind leaped to the memory of the way he'd stalked her, that gorgeous cock swaying . . .

The first notes of the Beatles' "Let it Be" rose above Thumper's delicious hum.

"Oh, you have got to be kidding me!" Alex panted in frustration. She was so close . . .

And her mother would be so pissed if she let the call go to voice mail. Mary Rogers knew her schedule as well as she did. Jerking Thumper out of her frustrated sex, Alex switched the vibe off and tossed it aside. Scooping up her cell, she swiped a thumb across its screen, cutting off Paul McCartney in mid-*be*. "Hi, Mom."

"Hi, baby!" Mary said, her voice sounding so loving it was hard to be pissed even under the circumstances. "Hope I didn't interrupt anything."

Alex managed not to grind her teeth. Her mother could detect emotional nuances better than a homicide cop grilling a suspect. "Nah, just killing time. What's up?"

"Nothing, dear. I couldn't help noticing you weren't in church yesterday. Remember, I told you I wanted to introduce you to that nice boy I told you about. The electrician?" Anybody under forty was a boy to her mother.

"Yeah, sorry. Rough night."

"I really think you'd like him. He's so cute, and such a nice man!"

I don't want a nice man, Ma. I want a man who will beat my ass with a riding crop. Which was not something she could say to her mother. Ever. "I'm not looking for anything serious right now, Mom. I don't think it's fair to start a relationship I don't intend to pursue."

"You need to get back on the horse, honey. I know Gary hurt you . . ."

You have no idea. She hadn't told her mother what her ex-lover had done that last brutal night, explaining the bruises away as being the result of a fight with a drunk. Which had been perfectly true. She just hadn't told her mother who the drunk was. If she had, the sheriff would have had to charge her dad, her three brothers—and probably Mary herself—with first-degree lynching.

Hell, it had been all Alex could do to keep Cap and Ted from beating the fuck out of Gary, not that she hadn't been tempted to let them go to it.

Apparently he'd had that effect on somebody else. Someone who'd actually done it.

So now she said only, with perfect honesty, "I'm over Gary. I've been over Gary." *Since he stopped using a flogger and started using his fists.*

Though he still didn't deserve to die that way. She didn't grieve for Gary, but she did pity him.

"Good. You should be. I hate to speak ill of the dead, but your father and I never liked that man. I do not understand what you saw in him."

"In retrospect, neither do I."

Her mother, of course, pounced on the opening like SIG on a catnip mouse. "That's why I think you'll really like Jimmy. He really is a perfect gentleman. Why don't you come to prayer meeting Wednesday, and I'll introduce you?"

Oh, God, no. Trouble was, she hated disappointing her mother.

A flamethrower blast of guilt made Alex mentally writhe. If her mom knew what she'd done last night, where she'd been, what she'd been doing for years . . . Imagining the shock and horror on her parents' faces, she shuddered.

"Alexis?" Mary prompted. "Do you think you can make it?"

"I don't know. I've got work that night."

"Alexis Eleanor Rogers, your shift starts at midnight," her mother said, exasperated. "You could be home from church in plenty of time to get ready, even if you and Jimmy go out for coffee afterward."

"I'll see, Mom. Look, I've got to go. If I don't get in my five miles now, I'm not going to get them in at all."

Her mother had been married to a high school coach too long not to understand the importance of working out. "Well, all right, dear. Love you!"

"Love you, too, Mom." Alex swiped her thumb over the screen's end button and slumped back against the pile of pillows, flinging one arm over her eyes.

When she was younger, she'd tried dating the kind of man her mother was always pushing on her. It had ended in disaster every single time. Perfect gentlemen bored the hell out of her.

Or worse.

She'd been seventeen when she'd lost her virginity to Bruce, the first of Mom's matchmaking efforts. Just as it had every single time she'd attempted a relationship with someone Mary fixed her up with in the years since, the sex had sucked, and the relationship had gone down in a bigger ball of flame than the *Hindenburg*.

Alex had expected so much more. In the romances she'd devoured as a teen, sex had been described as an intense, transcendent experience, a union of hearts and souls.

Unfortunately, Bruce had been every bit the virgin she was. His idea of immortal passion had been to suck her nipples just long enough to get her halfway interested, then climb on and start thrusting. Alex hadn't even been wet, and it had hurt. She'd told him to stop, but he'd kept on, apparently determined to come no matter what she said. So she'd punched him in the mouth, tossed his ass on the floor, and stormed out.

Alex wasn't Ken Rogers's little girl for nothing.

That hadn't quite been the end for them. Two days later, Bruce's life had gone Chernobyl in a spectacularly ugly tragedy that left both his parents dead. Alex had comforted him in his loss, and they'd made up. The sex still hadn't gotten any better, though, and her relationship with the grieving young man had been stormy. In the end, he'd been the one to leave. He'd enlisted in the Army and shipped off to Iraq, and that was that.

Alex had made other attempts to find a "gentleman." Had even had sex with one or two of them in college. Both had been a little better than poor Bruce, but she'd always felt something was missing.

Then soon after getting a job with the sheriff's office, she'd discovered BDSM romances. And realized what she wanted. No, what she *needed*, in the sense that no other kind of relationship was going to work.

She needed a Dom.

Google had led Alex to Fetlife, kinkdom's answer to Facebook, where she'd started looking for one of the bondage clubs she'd read about. She'd settled on an Atlanta group without even considering the one in Charlotte, North Carolina. Charlotte was two hours closer, but if she played that close to home, there was too great a chance her family would find out about it.

Her mother had pitched a huge fit when she'd decided to go into law enforcement. To Mary, it was bad enough that Alex's older brother, Tim, had become a cop in nearby Spartanburg. Alex was female, and as far as Mary was concerned, she had no business wearing a badge.

She'd been a deputy for five years now, but Mom had only recently given up on persuading her to quit. If her family found out she was kinky on top of that . . .

God, they'd disown her. She couldn't risk it.

Most of the moral values her parents had taught her formed the bedrock of her character. She believed in God, but she also thought He was a lot more interested in whether you hurt people than in your bedroom activities. Assuming, that is, those activities were consensual and didn't destroy somebody else's life or marriage.

But though God might not blame her for her sexual needs, she knew her parents would. The concept that pain could be a route to pleasure would be totally alien to them. That their precious little girl would think otherwise would horrify them.

Yet Alex needed what she needed. It wasn't just that a good spanking made her hot. For her, it was the way she was wired, and nothing else was going to work for her.

She just had to make damn sure she stayed deeper in the closet than her mother's tie-dyed bell bottoms.

Hell, the whole reason she'd stayed with Gary as long as she had was the mortal fear he'd out her to her parents. She was frankly surprised he hadn't. It had probably been the Fear of Ted that kept him quiet, at least until that fatal encounter with the blunt instrument.

Sickened, Alex thrust that thought out of her mind. She'd hated Gary in the end, but he hadn't deserved such a death.

No longer in the mood for either Thumper or a nap, Alex dressed in sweatpants, a tee, and her cross trainers, then slipped her cell and keys into her pocket. After domesticating her ferocious bedhead with a hairbrush, she gathered the copper length into a ponytail and secured it with a black scrunchie.

Five minutes later Alex stepped out on the house's screened front porch, pushed open the creaking door, and cleared the three cinder-block steps in one long bounce. Breaking into a run down the cracked sidewalk, she headed for the street. It was October, Alex's favorite time of year, with trees burning yellow and red with the shades of fall. Her mother always said the splashes of vivid color made it seem God had been at work with a paintbrush.

Falling into an easy, long-legged lope she could keep up for miles, Alex let her mind float. She'd always found there was no better way to deal with stress than a good hard run. Being more than a little ADHD, she was happiest in motion.

After passing the sprawling four-story redbrick husk of the abandoned mill, Alex paused at a stop sign to scan for traffic, then turned right on Elm and began her usual route. The two-lane road wound past the Whiteside Hospital complex, a number of doctors' offices, and the Myers-Rhodin Funeral Home. A mile farther on lay Elmwood Cemetery, an expanse of green broken by gray headstones, brass markers, and dutiful flower arrangements.

She'd make a stop at the Gas-Up convenience store at the top of the hill for a bottle of water, and then head back along the same route.

Alex had started running five miles a day when she'd made the Harrison High track team as a freshman. After the tragedy with Bruce, running had become a way to deal with her grief and guilt.

Now she had professional reasons for her routine. Being able to run some asshat into the ground was a definite advantage for a cop. She might not be the biggest and baddest deputy on the force, but she was universally considered the fastest. It was the rare drug dealer, convenience store robber, or shoplifter who could outpace her. And once she brought a perp down, three or four other cops could catch up and make sure he stayed there. Assuming she couldn't do the job herself. Most of the time, she could, thanks to Ted's training.

Making the turn, she headed back, breathing harder now, beginning to sweat a little in the brisk fall air. Nothing like the miserable soaking perspiration of July and August, when the South got hotter than hell's armpit.

Her mind slid back to Frank again, but this time she found herself frowning. Was an affair with the big former SEAL really a good idea? What if he turned out to be another Gary? Yeah, Cap liked him, but as Ted had pointed out, Cap wasn't sleeping with him.

Just as well. Alex had no desire to share.

CHAPTER FOUR

Some people preferred watermelons for this purpose, but Bruce liked tomatoes. More of a challenge.

Besides, he needed the practice if he was to put his plans in motion.

He lined the vegetables up on the cardboard boxes he'd stacked at varying heights—approximating the level of someone's head when lying down, standing, or sitting—until he had twelve targets.

Soon enough he'd take out the first of his human targets. But his revenge was intricate, and he had more dominoes to put into place before he could start knocking them down.

He still needed evidence of Ted's perversion. Otherwise the public would see him as nothing more than a cop killer—and that wasn't the point at all. They had to know why this was necessary if they were to understand why he'd had no choice. Ted was a liar, and Gary Ames, Alex's former "master," had said he'd been the one to lead her into deviance. For that, he had to pay.

Unfortunately, Bruce's revenge would have to wait until Ted condemned himself.

It had been a week since he'd replaced the smoke detector in Arlington's bedroom with the dummy containing a camera. Ever since then, the little device had been piggybacking on the house WiFi to send him video files.

The system's password was PASSWORD, for God's sake. *Sloppy, Ted.*

He knew that sooner or later Arlington and his little fruit boyfriend would do something usable. Until then, he'd have to be patient.

Bruce walked back the length of the range, picked up his rifle, and lay down on his belly. Sighting on the first of the tomatoes, he counted his heartbeats and breathed deeply, waiting for his body to calm, to slow, as his father had taught him when he was a boy.

Then, breath held, between one heartbeat and the next, he fired. The first tomato exploded in a rain of red juice and splattering scarlet. Smiling in grim satisfaction, Bruce took aim on the next target.

Soon, Dad.

The Morgan County Sheriff's Office occupied the former corporate offices of Harris Chemical, which had moved to better digs and sold the building to the MCSO for much less than it was worth. It was a surprisingly large complex—it needed to be, since the department had over three hundred sworn officers, along with numerous divisions. Unfortunately, the building was also ugly, a cluster of three-story blocky brick structures in a shade Ted called "baby shit brown." Which may have been the whole reason Harris Chemical moved downtown. Ugly was not a good corporate statement.

Since it was only 5:20 p.m. and Alex was technically off-duty—the sheriff's birthday party being more social gathering than anything else—she'd dressed casually in jeans and a MCSO tee. She found a space near the granite memorial to a deputy murdered in 1978, got out, and started across the parking lot.

The lobby was surprisingly empty; there were usually a few people occupying the uncomfortably utilitarian chairs, waiting to file reports or talk to detectives. The door's metal detector pinged at the off-duty weapon Alex wore in a pancake holster. The desk officer looked up from behind his bulletproof barrier, but relaxed when he recognized Alex. He hit a button, unlocking the department's inner door with a click and a buzz. Alex waved in thanks and sauntered in.

The MCSO was a labyrinth of narrow beige corridors that led to offices for senior officers and civilian admin workers. Divisions like Violent Crimes and Narcotics had big bullpens full of detective cubicles, while Crime Scene Investigation and Forensic Chemistry had multiroom labs. A carefully secured warehouse in the heart of the building was occupied by racks of evidence in boxes and brown paper bags.

Ted often said the judicial system was like a giant python. You put suspects and evidence in at one end and got something, presumably justice, out of the other. *"The trip from point A to point B, however, ain't fun for anybody."*

Alex turned one corner, then another, then a third before she found a door labeled TRAINING. It was crammed ass-to-elbow with cops standing around holding plastic cups of soda. Long gray laminate tables faced a Plexiglas podium decorated with a logo of a gold sheriff's star.

As Alex wound her way inside, she caught snatches of stories about a fishing expedition, somebody's kid's Little League adventures, and an incredibly stupid convenience store robber who'd thought blackface would make a dandy disguise.

Spotting Ted wearing an unusually grim expression, Alex wound her way through the crowd to join him. "Who shot your dog?"

If anything, his expression tightened even more when he saw her. "Just checking out the new deputy." He nodded toward the front of the room.

Alex really should have noticed him the minute she walked in: he was inches taller than every other cop in the room, and looked twice as broad in his black patrol uniform. "Shit," she breathed, astonished. "Frank."

"Frank Murphy, the department's newest deputy. Come on." He jerked his head toward the door, and they ducked out into the hallway, where they could talk a bit more privately. "I am going to kick Cap's ass," Ted said once the door closed behind them. "He damned well knew this and didn't tell us."

Alex felt dazed, blindsided. And maybe a little betrayed. It took an effort to keep her voice low. "Why didn't *we* know this?"

Ted popped his knuckles, glowering. "You know how it works. He'd have spent the last few months either at the Academy in Columbia or working his field training rotation on Able shift." They were on Charlie.

"So neither of us ever ran into him." Which meant he was probably as ignorant about her working for the MCSO as she'd been about him. Alex relaxed, feeling a little less pissed. A memory surfaced, and she threw up her hands in self-disgust. "Oh, hell. I heard something a couple months ago about the department hiring a former SEAL, but I'd forgotten it until just now."

"How are you going to handle it? Could get sticky."

"I don't see why. The sheriff's office doesn't have any rules about deputies dating as long as there's no sexual harassment. And since I'm not in Frank's chain of command, that's not an issue. Besides, I've been working with Bruce for two years now, and I've had no problems. You want to talk potentially sticky . . ."

"Yeah, okay, point." Ted grimaced. He knew more about her sex life than he probably wanted to, self-appointed daddy that he was. "Still, the thing with Bruce was almost a decade ago, and the thing with Frank was *last night*. When it comes to potential stickiness, that's like the difference between a Post-it on your thumb and having your hand superglued to your dick."

"Maybe, but Frank and I aren't even on the same shift. We never even saw him until now. Anyway, you're assuming we're going to get involved in some kind of long-term—"

"Hey, y'all," a familiar voice said. "What's going on?"

Alex looked and thought better of what she'd been about to say. "Oh, hi, Bruce. Just . . . gossiping." You didn't discuss your Rocky Road lifestyle in front of the terminally vanilla. Especially not when this particular vanilla bean was your ex-boyfriend.

Bruce Greer was no longer the seventeen-year-old innocent who'd been her disastrous first love. At twenty-six, he was a tall, powerfully built Iraqi war veteran with handsome features, thick sable hair, and eyes that were Brad Pitt blue. He also had the patrol area adjoining the two Alex and Ted worked, and the three of them often answered the more dangerous calls together. A good man in a fight, Bruce had a cynical sense of humor that made him an entertaining companion.

He also knew nothing about his coworkers' kinky proclivities, and they wanted to keep it that way.

"Hey, what's going on with those break-ins you've been working?" Ted asked.

Bruce, diverted as he'd intended, started grousing about the burglar he'd been trying to catch for the last couple of weeks. Alex used the opportunity to slip back into the training room toward Frank, who stood talking to Sergeant Diane Gaffney and the Able lieutenant, Chris Davis.

The Dom's gray eyes widened when she stepped out of the crowd, his astonishment obvious. He really hadn't known she worked for the MCSO.

Alex gave him a carefully professional smile, aware of the crowd of deputies who surrounded them, eavesdropping shamelessly. Cops were nosy as hell and loved to gossip. Which was why she decided to pretend she'd never seen him in her life.

"I'll . . . definitely give it some thought," Frank was saying.

"Do that," Davis said. He was a short, muscular man,

balding and intense. "I need a good sniper on my team, and I think you've got just the experience we need. It'll mean additional training every week, but you probably won't be called out more than a couple of times a month." Besides heading Able shift, Davis led Special Weapons and Tactics; he was probably trying to talk Frank into volunteering. MCSO didn't have a standing SWAT team. Officers volunteered, and the unit responded to the more dangerous calls whenever necessary. That might mean anything from serving high-risk warrants to the thankfully rare hostage rescue. It could be dangerous duty, and Davis was always looking to recruit experienced military vets.

The lieutenant handed Frank his card. "Think about it and give me a call," he said, and strode off, probably to go do one-armed push-ups or something.

"Frank," Sergeant Gaffney said, "this is Deputy Alexis Rogers. She's with Charlie Platoon."

Frank smiled, cool and professional, as he extended a hand. "Frank Murphy." You'd never have known he fucked her to a screaming orgasm the night before.

Alex let those long, warm fingers engulf hers. A wave of heat rolled over her, but conscious of the interested eyes of the surrounding cops, she restricted her reaction to a distant smile. "Call me Alex. It's nice meeting you."

"The pleasure's mine." But if his smile was professional, his gaze was not.

Oh, God. That hot Dom stare. And that body. He was wearing a bulletproof vest under his uniform, and it made him look even broader than he actually was, no mean feat in itself. His badge gleamed just below her eye level. He'd hooked his thumbs in his duty belt, with its pouches and holstered pistol and Taser. The short sleeves of his uniform revealed a tattoo of the SEAL insignia nicknamed the Budweiser—an eagle gripping a trident, anchor, and a flintlock pistol—decorating the biceps of his right arm. She vaguely remembered noticing it the night before, though frankly, her attention had been on other things.

He thrust his cock into her, his big hands holding her

down with her ass in the air as he ground and ground until she . . .

Alex shut the memory down hard. The last thing she needed was to get wet in front of the entire goddamned department.

God, the way she was looking at him. Her hooded green gaze was enough to give him a hard-on even if her body and his memories hadn't already done the job. He caught his left wrist with his right hand at crotch level, hoping to camouflage his far-too-interested dick.

Alex shouldn't have looked so damned sexy. She wore a department tee neatly tucked into a pair of artfully faded jeans that hugged every inch of those endless, endless legs. Her breasts were full and round and mouthwatering under the tee's soft gray fabric. Remembering the taste of those luscious pink nipples made his breathing go harsh. He started contemplating the state's penal code, trying to get himself under control before his hard-on mortified both of them.

As if realizing she was about to blow their sexual cover in the worst possible place she could do it, Alex turned to the officer with him. Sergeant Diane Gaffney was a stocky deputy who wore her brunette hair in a pixie cut as short as a man's. She'd been his field training officer for the past two months. Gaffney was cheerfully Out to absolutely everyone; she'd told him she was a lesbian within half an hour of meeting him. *"I like to find out if I'm dealing with a bigoted asshole,"* she'd explained. *"That way neither of us gets surprised."*

"How's it going, Sergeant?" Alex asked.

"Fair to middling," Gaffney drawled. She nodded at Frank. "Been training Murph here. He's gonna be a damned good cop."

Alex lifted a brow. "Rare praise, coming from you."

The sergeant smiled a little at that. "Gotta admit, I'm gonna miss his ass. Meanest drunks in the county take one look at him and go right to jail, peaceful as little lambs. My life is gonna get interesting without him looming behind me like a brick wall in a black uniform."

"I can see that." Alex laughed. "Well, it was nice meeting you, Murphy. See you, Sarge."

She walked away. Unable to help himself, Frank dropped his gaze to that round, muscular little ass, remembering the silken feel of it in his hands.

"Yeah, good luck with that, Romeo," Gaffney told him.

He snapped out of his erotic trance and blinked. "What?"

"Rogers. Half the cops in the department have hit on that girl—includin' me. None of us has had any luck."

He barely managed not to grin. He'd had a lot more than luck. "Likes to play hard to get, huh?"

"She don't play at all, son. That's the problem." The sergeant considered him with shrewd brown eyes. "Though if anybody could change her mind, it would be you. Hell, if I didn't bat for the other team—"

"I'd never survive." He gave her an exaggerated suck-up's smile. "Not that I wouldn't die happy."

Gaffney laughed, one of those uninhibited belly laughs that made anybody around laugh with her.

Before Frank could start grilling the sergeant on what she knew about Alex, Major Dominic Jennings raised his voice in a bass boom that silenced everyone in the room. A big, graying cop, Jennings had skin the color of dark chocolate and hands big enough to palm a basketball. "All right, boys and girls, we're gathered here to celebrate the sheriff's birthday, among other things. So y'all try to sing on key for once."

He started belting out "Happy Birthday," his deep voice surprisingly pure. The other cops joined in, most of them considerably less talented.

Standing next to Jennings, the birthday boy listened indulgently. Sheriff Bill Ranger had enough belly to suggest a heart attack lay in his future, thinning white hair, and a round face with a nose like an Irish potato. "Thank you kindly," he said when they finished the serenade. "Major's right, though. Some of y'all wouldn't know the right key if your mama raised it as your brother." He eyed the cake, on which a single candle burned. "I see you can't count to sixty either."

"Fire marshal wouldn't let us put that many candles on the cake," the major told him. "Said it could cause global warming."

Ranger eyed him. "You're a funny guy, Jennings. A funny, funny guy."

The deputies laughed. Ranger blew out the candle to a chorus of cheers and whistles, then straightened. "Now before y'all start stampeding for the cake, we have some business." Turning, he gestured to Frank. "Get over here, Murphy."

Frank, having been told this was coming, worked his way through the crowd to join him.

"In accordance with the department policy of hiring military veterans, I'd like to introduce our newest officer, Frank Murphy . . ."

"Hell, Sheriff, what did you do?" somebody called. "Fill two slots with him?"

"Nah, he was a bargain. The giant, economy-size deputy," Ranger shot back.

Frank, who'd been hearing variations on that joke for years, smiled anyway.

"Frank is a decorated Navy SEAL with two Bronze Stars and a Silver Star—but don't try to get him to tell you what for, 'cause then he'd have to kill you." Ranger slapped him on the shoulder. "Smart guy, too. J.P. Strom Award winner."

Which meant he'd graduated at the top of his South Carolina Criminal Justice Academy class. Becoming a SEAL had taught Frank how to study, something he'd never been particularly motivated to do when he was in high school.

"The Field Training Board cleared him for full duty today,

so he's officially off probation. Not that anyone's surprised." The sheriff turned to him and held out his hand. "Great having you aboard, son."

Frank took it and pumped. "Thank you, Sheriff. I'm honored to be here."

With a last squeeze and back slap, Ranger turned to the cake, picked up the knife provided for the purpose, and started cutting slices as the cops lined up.

Frank, though, was interested in something much sweeter. He bypassed the cake queue and stepped out into the hall beyond. Before he could reach for his personal cell, he heard the door open and close again. "Let's get one thing straight, Frogman."

Turning, he found Alex's faux father glowering up at him. "Hello, Ted."

"That's Master Deputy Arlington," Ted corrected in an icy voice. He smiled, a baring of teeth that would have done Jaws proud. "Like the cemetery."

The man was a foot shorter than Frank was. How the hell could he be so fucking menacing? On second thought, dumb question. Short men were often the meanest. They grew up that way. "What can I do for you, Master Deputy?"

"I won't ask you to stay away from Alex. I can see that'd be a waste of breath. But I will tell you this, Froggy." He took a step closer and upped the menace to eleven. "If you hurt her, I will fucking kill you. I don't care how goddamn big you are."

Looking into those chilly blue eyes, Frank believed him. "I have no intention of hurting Alex."

"Good. Then we've got no problem. Make sure we don't get one."

Enough was enough. Frank leaned down until they were nose to nose, deliberately emphasizing the height difference. "Don't threaten me, Master Deputy. I appreciate the fact that you feel protective of Alex, but I ain't Gary fuckin' Ames." A trace of respect flashed in Arlington's eyes before he pivoted on his heel with a military snap and stalked back into the training room.

Frank sighed and pulled his cell off its belt clip. "Gotta love overprotective Doms."

Alex's personal cell vibrated on her belt, where it hung next to the one the department had issued. She plucked it out of its clip, expecting to see a text from her mother.

But when she swiped open the text app, she saw Frank's number. They'd called each other a time or two, during their D/s . . . courtship, she supposed you could call it. She checked the text.

I'm off duty. Are you?
Yes. I don't go on until midnight.
Do you want to play?

Her fingers didn't hesitate as she typed back, Yes. God yes. Fuck, yes.

Fuck, period.

Heat streamed through her, lighting up her veins until she was surprised she couldn't see them glowing through her skin. She wondered if she was blushing.

He texted an address next. 362 Lighthorse Street. Do you need directions?

That's why God made GPS.
I'll see you there. If you have trouble finding it, call me. Twenty minutes?

It seemed she wasn't the only one who was hungry. And she didn't want to wait either. Yes.

Alex escaped the building after being accosted only a couple of times by various friends and acquaintances. She invented an errand and fled as gracefully as she could.

Ted didn't stop her, though his disapproving gaze did not waver as she headed for the door. Her mentor had always had a Dom's talent for reading minds. Especially when you didn't want him to.

For once, she ignored him.

Alex followed the car's GPS instructions automatically, making the turns it called for with only half her attention. Her body felt like melting caramel below the waist, sweet and hot and creamy. It was damned distracting.

Meanwhile, a voice from the back of her brain was sounding the alarm. It was one thing to carry on an affair on the weekends under Cap's protective aegis. It was another to start something with a guy who lived in the same freaking town and worked the same freaking job. Was she nuts? Hadn't Gary and his Gucci-loafered kicks taught her anything?

The rest of her lust-addled gray matter insisted Frank was nothing like Gary. He obviously believed in a Dom's duty to protect and care for his sub, a principle Ted had always called the bedrock of a BDSM relationship. Just look at the way he'd been so careful not to hurt her during their little wrestling match last night. Another man might have gotten carried away on a wave of blue balls, but Frank had never lost control. He wasn't an abuser, and he sure as hell wasn't stupid. He . . .

Lived out in the middle of fucking *nowhere*.

Which wasn't exactly unusual for Morgan County. Its population of 250,000 lived scattered across eight hundred square miles that included the city of Morganville, one airport, several factories, and a whole bunch of churches, but most of it was as rural as Mayberry.

At last her GPS's mechanical voice directed her to make a left at a sign with flowing script that read *Patriot Commons*. Looked like an older development, she decided as she drove along its narrow main road. The houses had greater variety than you'd see in more modern complexes, where a developer might use the same four or five house plans over and over. Patriot Commons included everything from seventies-era split levels to homes built since the turn of the millennium. Stands of trees bordered each neatly trimmed yard, and the few empty lots were covered in thick woods and brown, frost-killed kudzu.

Headlights flashed in her rearview mirror. Alex looked up to find a patrol car on her tail. She blinked, recognizing the driver as the car pulled even to pace her. At his gesture, she lowered her window.

Frank gave her the kind of cold stare normally reserved for somebody caught doing sixty in a school zone. "Pull over."

"I wasn't speeding."

"I don't care. Pull over."

Alex's heart began to pound. She had a feeling she was in for a rousing game of Bad Cop. "But . . ." she began, playing Hapless Pretty Speeder to the hilt.

"I said, *pull over.*" He stabbed a finger toward a set of tire tracks that led off into the woods between one house and an empty lot.

"Yes, sir." Hoping her beater of a car was up to it, she drove off the street and onto the bumpy, weed-strewn tracks. A tangle of brush blocked the way, but she drove into it, listening to it crackle under the Honda's wheels and hoping Frank knew what he was doing. At least all that brush should hide them from any nosy neighbors who might otherwise wonder why a cop was pulling somebody over *in* the woods.

When she was younger, she'd had her share of Bad Cop fantasies. Not so much anymore—she knew too many deputies, who were a relentlessly straight-arrow bunch unlikely to do anything like this. But she wasn't exactly averse to pretending otherwise.

Especially with Frank in the starring role.

Alex drove down the bumping, rutted track as it curved through the trees, the Dom right on her tailpipe. Finally he flashed his headlights at her again. She stopped and threw her car into Park. They were well into the woods, thoroughly screened from the road.

"Why, Officah," Alex purred aloud in her best Scarlett O'Hara drawl, "whatevah do you have in mind?"

She rolled down her driver's side window as he swaggered up to the car. Big, brawny, and black-clad—her fantasy Bad Cop come to glorious life. He even wore a pair of mirrored aviator sunglasses and a menacing scowl. "Get out of the car, please."

Her panties were already soaked, and he hadn't even started yet.

Alex put on her best *Don't give me a ticket, I'll do anything* expression. "But, sir, I wasn't speeding."

"I didn't say you were," he told her coldly. "Get out of the car."

She gave him big, worried eyes as she obeyed, closing the car door as softly as she could to keep the sound from carrying to his neighbors. "I don't understand. I haven't done anything!"

"Quit trying to play me, lady. There's a warrant out for your arrest." Grabbing her wrist, he dragged her to the trunk of her car, then spun her around so her back was to him. "It says you're armed and dangerous." He pulled her little .38 from the pancake holster on her belt, and displayed it with a threatening flourish. "And look here—you are."

Alex swallowed. Had he been anybody else, she might have broken out into the giggles right about then. But this was Frank. Something about him made this silly fantasy scenario feel a lot more real than it should have. "I can explain."

"I'm sure you can." His voice hardened. "Hands on the trunk, feet apart."

Before she could obey, he planted his palm between her shoulder blades and forced her to bend over as he kicked her feet wide. "I said, hands on the trunk, feet apart!" Automatically, she caught herself on her palms.

God, she was already wet.

He started searching her. Never mind that no male cop ever searched a female suspect if he could avoid it; that was why there were female cops. And this was why they had that rule.

What Frank did wasn't a crude grope—he understood the fantasy too well for that. Instead, he ran his hand down her body in twin slow caresses. Until he reached the curves of her ass.

Pausing, Frank cupped the sensitive flesh through her jeans, squeezing gently, with just enough force to arouse. Breathless, Alex waited for him to circle around between her legs.

He sank to his haunches to continue the search down her legs in that same lazy way. Instead of guns, knives, or drugs, Frank's clever fingers sought bundles of nerves she hadn't even known she had. And made them fire messages of lust and arousal and pleasure until it was all she could do not to writhe.

Regaining his feet, Frank swept his palms around her rib cage to the underside of her breasts. He slid his hands up and around, dragging her bra out of the way, baring the curve of her breasts for his cupping palms, exposing her nipples to plucking fingers. The raw delight of the contact was so intense, it seemed to sting. She moaned, unable to bite the sound back.

"Like that, do you?" he growled, ducking his head down until he could speak in her ear. "Let's find out how much."

CHAPTER FIVE

One hand worked down inside the waistband of her jeans. Alex sucked in her belly, giving him room. Sliding into her panties, he stroked his fingers between the slick, swollen lips of her pussy. "Mmmmmm," he purred in her ear. "You do like that." He chuckled, the sound dark and wicked as two fingers explored her cunt. "You like that a lot." His voice dropped, taking on a note of velvet threat. "Maybe somebody needs to teach you not to be such a slut."

Her belt buckle jangled as he unbuckled it, followed by the hiss of a descending zipper. He jerked down jeans and panties to mid-thigh. With a little moan, she managed to set her feet farther apart, leaning down a little lower, angling her hips up.

"That's right, raise that ass good and high." The first swat bounced her on her toes. She barely remembered to bite back a yelp every neighbor on the block would have heard. "You'll keep that mouth shut if you know what's good for you."

God, he was a good actor. If she hadn't known better, she'd have thought he was every bit the prick he was pretending to be.

Rocking back on his heels, Frank smoothed a wide, warm palm over the bare skin of her ass. "Just look at that butt. So pretty and firm. Just begging for a good spanking."

Another swat, landing with a juicy smack low on her rump, right in the sweet spot—so called because the ripples from a spanking there stimulated the pussy. Some women could even come from that kind of spanking. Frank seemed intent on discovering if Alex was one of them. He heated her rump with slow, stinging swats, pausing in between to tease clit and labia until it was all she could do not to beg.

When he finally stopped, he plunged two fingers into her cunt and pumped, his thumb flicking skillfully at her tight, swollen clit. "Well, you enjoyed that almost as much as I did. Almost. God, I loved turning this pale ass all rosy red."

Jerking her jeans up, he zipped and fastened them, ignoring her moan of disappointment. He spun her around and pushed her down on her knees on the crackling carpet of leaves, doing it a lot more gently than the bastard he was pretending to be.

Clicking open his duty belt, Frank unbuckled the pants belt beneath that. His zipper sang, then he freed his long, thick erection. He dug a condom from his pocket and handed it to her. "Put it on me."

"Yes, sir." Alex took her time rolling it on, enjoying his length and thickness.

When she had the rubber on at last, Frank grabbed a fistful of her hair and dragged her head close. "Suck me," he growled. "Suck me now."

With a low moan of need, Alex opened her mouth for his measured thrust. She suckled, swirling her tongue around the rounded mushroom head, then licking the thick vein running along the bottom of the shaft through the thin latex.

"Deeper." Frank rolled his hips, but carefully, not gagging her as Gary had so often done.

She rose on her knees and angled her head and throat to take more of him in. He was too long to comfortably deep throat, but she compensated by wrapping one hand around the base of his shaft while using the other to stroke his heavy balls.

"That's right. Just like that."

She sucked and licked and pumped her hand, ignoring the burn when her arm started getting tired, too lost in the delight of sucking her new Dominant.

Until he abruptly caught the back of her head and held her still as his cock bucked against her tongue. "Ah, God, Alex!" he groaned. She felt the heat through the latex as he flooded the condom.

Pulling her mouth off him, Alex gave him a couple of last pumps with her hand. Frank sighed, the tension bleeding out of his big body.

For a long moment, neither of them moved. Gradually, Alex grew aware of the cool October breeze and was grateful it wasn't a cold day.

"God, that was good," Frank said, dropping the Bad Cop persona. "You were good. *Are* good."

Delight at his approval warmed her. Gary had always said that if he didn't beat her ass, it was proof enough she'd pleased him. Frank, it seemed, was a more generous Dom. "The pleasure was mine."

He grinned down at her. "Not entirely."

Tenderly, he smoothed her hair back as she zipped his pants for him. After buckling both belts, she straightened from her crouch.

Frank opened his arms and she stepped into them. The kiss was so wet and passionate, it had both of them breathing hard all over again. He broke it at last, smiling down at her. "Let's go on to my place. I want to try something really kinky."

Alex gave him a puckish grin and an eyebrow lift. "What do you have in mind?"

"Sex in a bed."

"Wild man."

F rank lived in an impressive one-story Craftsman-style house that was obviously new construction. Its slate gray cedar siding contrasted with the redwood frames of the windows and the fieldstone porch.

Alex pulled up in the paved driveway and got out, taking in the house and its dark green holly hedges. Fall-bright oaks and maples shaded a yard that would probably be verdant green in the spring. "Wow," she breathed. How the hell could he afford a place like this? A newly-hired deputy damn near qualified for food stamps.

After parking his patrol car in the attached garage, Frank strolled out to join her.

"What a gorgeous place." She turned a slow circle, admiring the orange, yellow, and red fall foliage that clustered around the house like flounces on the skirts of a Victorian debutante.

"Thanks. I own it free and clear." Frank gave her a slight smile. "My grandfather left me some money."

"Enough to buy all this outright?" She closed her mouth, belatedly realizing how incredibly rude that question was.

"Oh, yeah. Granddad was a textile baron in Spartanburg. He had five generations' worth of money he couldn't figure out how to take with him. I was the only other option he seriously considered." He turned back toward the house. "I spent most of my life living in various Upstate shitholes. My mom had trouble paying the rent, a habit landlords tend to reward with eviction. Later the Navy sent me to lots of interesting places where interesting people needed killing." Frank opened the front door. "I wanted a taste of boring suburbia, where I could cut the yard and plant things, with a kitchen where I could maybe learn to cook. Now I've got those things, and it's seriously cool."

Alex hesitated a moment before she decided to go for it. "I know this is rude as hell, but it sounds like you didn't have a lot of money as a kid. Why didn't your granddad help you and your mom, since he obviously could have?"

He stood back to let her enter ahead of him. "I gather your family is tight-knit?"

"So much so a girl could strangle."

"Ah. Well, my mom . . . she had me at sixteen. My father was a guy who wasn't exactly Granddad approved."

"So they were sort of *Romeo and Juliet*?"

"More *Sons of Anarchy*. He got shanked in prison a couple of years ago."

"Oh." Alex blinked. "Sorry."

"Nothing to be sorry about. Dad liked to express his opinions through aggravated assault. I'm lucky he went to jail."

Alex winced. "So your grandfather threw your mom out?"

"So hard she bounced. Which is probably a pretty apt comparison, given the size of her belly. I think she was seven months along."

"Prick. And your grandmother let him get away with it?"

"Apparently he had her pretty thoroughly cowed. And then she died a couple of years later." His gaze iced. "Bastard didn't even tell Mom until it was too late for her to come to the funeral."

"Prick doesn't even do him justice."

"Not really, no." He rested a warm hand at the small of her back. "Come on, I'll show you the house. I'll warn you, I still haven't finished buying furniture. Haven't had a hell of a lot of time to decorate."

He led her through a short foyer into a stunning great room. Floor-to-ceiling windows looked out over a stone back porch to the woods beyond. A massive fireplace built of stone in shades of cream, brown, and beige took up most of one wall, while a seventy-inch flat screen sprawled across another. Lushly upholstered furniture in dark brown—a love seat, a couch, and two recliners—kept the room from echoing under its cathedral ceiling. The floor was a gleaming expanse of dark wood broken up by colorful rugs in red, gold, and orange.

The walls were hung with paintings in the kind of expensive frames that suggested originals. One depicted Frank in his Navy whites, service ribbons in rainbow rows on his chest. "That portrait's nice work. Must have cost you a pretty penny."

"Not considering my mom painted it." He shrugged at her surprise. "Christmas present."

"Damn, you came from talent."

"Which I unfortunately didn't inherit."

"I wouldn't go that far. Making me scream that loud took real ability."

"Flatterer." Laughing, he guided her onward. The open floor plan flowed into an L-shaped kitchen, where stainless steel appliances stood among walnut cabinetry. Brown and cream quartz counters provided generous prep space.

Alex knew a moment of serious kitchen envy. "You cook?"

"Well, I'm learning," Frank said. "Mostly by watching a lot of Food Network and collecting recipes off the Internet. And sometimes by burning stuff."

"I'm impressed."

"You wouldn't be if you tasted the stuff I burn."

"Considering I just nuke something from Lean Cuisine, yeah."

"Well, I like to eat." Some grim memory stirred behind his eyes. "Hunger sucks."

Why did she suddenly want to adopt the man? Bring him home to her folks. Let her mother stuff him full of Southern cooking that would make Paula Deen writhe in envy . . . Maybe even ask Mom to teach her to cook so she could take care of him herself.

And since when did she get an urge to become Susie Homemaker? After Gary, she'd sworn she'd only sub in the bedroom. Despite her ex's attempts to brainwash her, homemaking was not her thing.

Her thing was kink and kicking ass.

A couple of spare bedrooms were next on the tour. One was unfurnished, while the other held a treadmill and a set of free weights beside a weight bench. The barbell was loaded with so many plates, Captain America couldn't have lifted it.

Across the hall, a generous study held a walnut desk so old, massive, and intricately carved, it had probably belonged to one of Frank's textile-baron ancestors. A MacBook Air laptop occupied its gold-scrolled surface, gleefully anachronistic. An oxblood leather desk chair sat behind the desk, big enough to accommodate Frank's warrior frame.

On the back wall hung another of his mother's huge canvases. The sun's blinding gold disk rose over sand dunes like ocean waves—black in the foreground, shading to dark chocolate, milk chocolate, gold. Each rolling silhouette growing paler, dustier as they receded into the distance.

Built-in bookshelves lined the room's other three walls, displaying hardbacks on military tactics and history, along with dog-eared paperback science fiction and fantasy novels. There was still plenty of room on the walnut shelves.

"I read a lot on my phone, but there's just something about holding a book in your hand." Frank gazed around at his collection with the same smile he'd given the landscaping. The boy who'd grown up with nothing finally had something. "I'll fill these shelves up before long."

"I love to read, too." Alex wasn't about to tell him what. Cops didn't soak in bubble baths with romance novels. Not even kinky ones. She gave him a teasing smile. "But I admit, I figured you for more of a *Call of Duty* fan."

"I play that, too. Along with a hell of a lot of *World of Warcraft*."

Why did she find the idea of a SEAL nerd so appealing? "You and Cal should get along, then. He loves him some *WOW*."

"Ted is not going to let me play anything with his sub, not even a video game."

"Ahhh, Ted's not that bad."

"Of course not, he's just protective." Frank headed back down the hall. "And I agree with him. Those we love should be protected."

"Yep, you're a Dom, all right."

"Speaking of which . . ." He opened a hallway door, revealing a set of stairs that led down into the dark.

Alex rose on tiptoe to peer over his broad shoulder. "You have a dungeon?"

"Not yet." He started downward, Alex at his heels. "It's

still unfurnished, though I've got all kinds of wonderfully perverted plans."

The room at the base of the steps would make a dandy place to carry them out. Though not as big as the dungeon beneath Cap's house, it still gave him plenty of space to swing a whip. The floor was polished dark walnut, like the massive ceiling beams that supported the high ceiling, and the four thick square columns that marched across the center of the room. The walls were painted a deep, velvety red. Otherwise, the room was empty.

"Oh, this is nice." Alex turned in a slow circle, her imagination conjuring all sorts of wicked kinkiness. "I really like those beams." She studied them with interest. "Are they real?"

"Meaning could you use one for suspension scenes? Yeah." He nodded at the one directly overhead. "That beam is tied into the house's foundations. You could hang Jabba the Hutt from that thing."

"Jabba as a sub." Alex shuddered elaborately. "Now, there's a mental image I could have done without."

"No, Jabba was definitely a Dom. Or a wannabe anyway, until Leia choked him to death."

"I see I'm not the only nerd in the room."

"Definitely not. I loved those movies when I was a kid. They had them at the dollar theater up the road . . ." The smile faded from his face, as if the association had triggered some darker memory. Then he shook it off. "I've commissioned Cap to make me some furniture."

"Yeah? Cap builds good stuff." You could order BDSM gear online, of course, but there was no way to judge the quality until it arrived. Gary had bought a spanking bench that had collapsed under her once. But then, he'd always been a cheap bastard.

"Unfortunately, it's going to be another week or so before he can deliver the first part of my order, so we're going to have to make do. Come on."

Alex's mouth went dry from pure anticipation.

Once he led her back upstairs, she decided "making do" was a poor choice of words. The master bedroom's California king had a sturdy brass canopy frame that reminded Alex of some of her kinkier fantasies. Sheer cream curtains draped from the frame's supports, setting off a gold comforter piped in chocolate brown. Beside the bed lay an area rug, its wave pattern of chocolate and gold reminding her of the sunrise painting in his study.

His mother had been generous with her work here, too. SEALs patrolled dusty Afghan streets or parachuted out of helicopters or knelt beside robed tribesman. The twenty-first century colliding with the Middle Ages.

A framed photograph of a young dark-haired woman caught Alex's eye. It looked as if it dated from the late seventies, judging from the girl's Farrah Fawcett hairdo. She was lovely, with gunmetal gray eyes and a hint of Frank in the stubborn angle of her jaw and the shape of her mouth. She appeared to be in her late teens or very early twenties. "This is your mom?"

"Yeah."

"Pretty lady."

"Yeah."

Turning, Alex caught sight of his face and froze. There was such stark pain in his eyes, she immediately decided not to ask him anything more about his mother. She managed a smile, intent on hiding any sympathy. She knew he'd see it as pity. "So what now?"

Frank relaxed. "Now I need a shower. Want to join me?"

And run her hands all over his slick, soap-covered body? Oh, hell yeah. "Why not?"

Before she could say another word, he bent and swooped her up into her arms.

"What are you doing?" Alex grabbed for his neck and held on for dear life. She hadn't been carried since she was three. "You'll hurt your back!"

"You've got to be kidding me. I've carried heavier ruck-sacks." He swept her through a doorway into the bathroom beyond with no apparent effort at all.

Alex's inner Scarlett O'Hara swooned. She'd secretly watched the *Gone with the Wind* scene where Rhett carried

Scarlett up the stairs about a million times. Which was probably the birth of her kinky streak, come to think of it.

Frank's bathroom was damn near the size of her bedroom. Gray quartz veined with white surrounded a massive soaking tub before extending into a glassed-in shower. The vanity, its countertop the same quartz, held twin oval sinks. The cabinets below were white and trimmed in gray. The tile floor was patterned with geometric blocks of white, black, and gray. "Have I said 'wow' yet? I'd hate to repeat myself."

He laughed. "You can see why I fell in love with this house. I can actually stand under the shower head."

"You bought this house for the shower head?"

"Well, not just the shower head, but it was definitely a factor. Don't underestimate the importance of not having to duck to wash your hair."

Alex grinned. She'd had to duck a few times herself. "I see your point."

"Speaking of seeing things, I'd like to see a little more of you." Putting her down on her feet, Frank immediately went to work peeling off her clothes. She unbuttoned his shirt and dropped it on the floor before going to work stripping off his Kevlar vest.

Soon they were both naked, clothing and holstered weapons scattered on the tile. Normally Alex would have folded her things instead of just leaving them wherever they fell, but she just didn't have the patience for that right now.

Before she could get to work on seducing him, though, Frank walked into the shower. He gestured her back when she would have joined him, then he turned on the tap, holding one hand under the spray to judge the temperature as he adjusted it. Finally he was satisfied. "Okay, come on in."

"You do take this whole protective Dom thing seriously, don't you?"

Frank shrugged and reached for the soap. "Well, it's a gas water heater. Sometimes the spray gets a little hot."

She joined him, deliberately brushing the tips of her breasts across his wet chest as she moved. Droplets of water glistened on his skin, rolling in glinting trails along the rippled contours of pectorals and abdomen, streaming from his forearms and hands as he worked lather from the soap. Adding to the lush sensations, warm water pounded her head and shoulders, and wisps of steam rolled over her skin. Alex smiled slowly, enjoying the heady eroticism of the moment. "Feels just right to me."

"Let's see if I can't make it even better." Soapy hands began to stroke slow patterns over her skin. Alex let her head roll back. The man definitely knew how to touch a woman.

Instead of heading straight for tits and pussy as another man might, Frank built her anticipation with slick, swirling caresses smelling of mint and lavender.

Finally, Alex reached for the shampoo, poured a handful, and rose on her tiptoes to lather his hair. *God, he's tall.*

Frank paused the erotic torment long enough to duck under the spray and rinse his hair. Water droplets gleamed among the dark hair on his chest. She was glad he didn't shave it as so many men did; she liked her lovers a little furry.

Frank was just perfect.

Exploring his body was an erotic delight. With an effort, she resisted the impulse to head for his erogenous zones, though his cock jutted at her hopefully. Evidently he'd already recovered from the blow job.

Instead she traced the ridged shapes of lean muscle—the pectorals and abdominals, the rise and fall of ribs, the thick curve of biceps and triceps in his upper arms. He was built more like a heavyweight Mixed Martial Arts fighter than a bodybuilder, powerful without being too bulky for speed and agility.

"You must use those weights in the other room every damned day," she murmured. "It's hard for a guy as big as you are to get this built." Being a football coach's daughter, Alex had spent enough time in weight rooms to know all about big men and muscle. The length of those long bones would work against him when it came to building brawn, one reason basketball players tended to look wiry and elongated. It was easier for a short man to get brawny.

Teasing, she asked, "You vain, Murph?"

"Lifting's great stress relief." He gave her a lazy smile. "Besides, the girls seem to like the results."

"It always comes down to pussy. You are so male."

His smile turned into a carnivore's grin. "You bet your ass, baby."

Now he went for her tits. As he sought out her nipples with wicked tenderness, arousal flushed through her, making her pussy go slick and swollen in preparation for that delicious cock.

Frank dropped to his knees in front of her as the spray washed away the soap. His mouth covered her nipple in a breath-stealing rush. Her hands came up to cradle his slick dark head. Teeth nibbled. His tongue swirled, wet and warm even to her shower-heated flesh. He teased and suckled until her knees went weak.

One hand slid between her legs, and a broad forefinger probed as he thumbed her clit. She cursed in helpless delight as her arousal tightened like a coiling spring.

"You're so wet," Frank growled against her breast. "Damn, girl, I think you want me almost as much as I want you."

"Yeah." Her voice was way too close to a whimper. "God, yeah."

He stood and banged a fist against the shower door, throwing it open so he could step out. Alex turned off the shower as he snagged one of the towels hanging on a rack. She stepped out. He started drying her off with slow, thorough strokes, the towel thick and soft against her skin.

Finally he tossed it into the hamper, grabbed another, and dried himself off, storm gray eyes hot on her body. She was about to ask to use his brush and hair dryer when Frank swept her into his arms, wet hair and all, and carried her into the bedroom.

Lowering her to the middle of the bed, he growled, "Don't you move." It was his Dom voice, and she found herself swallowing the protest that her hair was going to dry into a rat's nest.

Rising up on her elbows, Alex watched as he strode to

the walk-in closet and pulled out a duffel. Had to be his toy bag—the crops, floggers, restraints, clamps, vibrators, and other kinky gear that Dominants collected.

Unzipping it, he searched around inside, finally pulling out a neat coil of rope, several condoms, and a pair of paramedic scissors. The scissors, she knew, were to cut her free in case of emergency—anything from a panic attack to a fire.

Alex grinned. "I gather it's bondage time."

He looked up from uncoiling the rope. "You got a problem with that?"

"Hell, no."

Frank's mouth quirked. "Do you even know how a sub is supposed to talk to her Dom?"

"Yes, Master," she said in a tone of saccharine submission before adding, "I just don't do it."

He eyed her thoughtfully. "I may have to change your mind about that, smartass." There was a delicious note of menace in his voice. "What's your safeword?" He'd asked the question before, but she appreciated his making sure of the answer.

"I always use the same safewords. Gary ignored me once when I used the wrong one."

"He really was a prick. You'll remind me which safewords you use no matter how many times I ask."

"Red. Yellow in the unlikely event I want you to slow down."

He grinned, a flash of white teeth. "You just keep pushing it, baby."

The rope was cotton, soft against her skin as he bound her spread-eagle on her back to the bed's four canopy posts. Her heart began to pound with a hot combination of fear and desire.

Picking up the packages of condoms, he tore one open and started to roll it on.

Alex nibbled her lips as the anxiety intensified.

He stopped, staring at her, the desire cooling in his eyes as he frowned. It wasn't an angry Dom frown, but honest concern. "Are you sure you want to do this?"

"You're asking *now*?"

"I mean, are you sure you know me well enough to let me tie you up like this? Ted would kick your ass, and mine, too."

At his sensitivity, the fear drained, leaving only need behind. She realized that, unlike Gary, he really could be trusted not to hurt her once he had her helpless. The thought sent a wave of intoxicating excitement rolling through her, until it seemed her blood foamed like champagne. "You do realize 'cop' is a synonym for 'adrenaline junkie'?" Alex gave him a cheeky smile. "Not that I'm scared of you."

At that reassurance, his gaze turned hot again. "Your alligator mouth just got your hummingbird ass in a great deal of trouble."

"I do hope so. I . . . Hmmph!" The word cut off as Frank swooped down on her, his mouth covering hers in the kind of greedy kiss that stole breath. Bracing on his elbows, he nibbled and licked and ate at her lips. The sensation of that kiss and his powerful body pressing into hers made Alex feel overwhelmed. Taken. Deliciously helpless as he lay between her spread legs, his cock hot on her belly.

Frank began working his way downward, sampling her chin, her throat, pausing to bite gently at her pounding carotid, then continuing lower, nibbling her collarbones, stringing kisses and swirling tongue strokes down to her nipples.

He stopped there, his mouth ravenous on the sensitive jutting flesh, tasting and flicking and sucking hard. Alex pumped her hips, growing desperate. She needed him *in* her. Had since she'd looked across the MCSO training room and seen him standing there like her own personal sex fantasy. Utterly male and dominant.

"Frank," Alex gasped, instinctively pulling her bound wrists, twisting in the ropes. "Frank, please, please fuck me . . ."

"No," he growled in a low, hard Dom voice.

"I need your cock!"

He looked up from her nipple and grinned like a demon. "Good." Then he went back to tormenting her, gathering her heat into a fierce little ball between her legs. It maddened her, that heat, made her writhe.

"Frank!" There was more than a little sob in her voice.

"This is what you get for being such a smartass to your Dom. Address me properly."

"Master!" In her need, she didn't care about old oaths never to use the word again. Didn't care about anything but Frank and the helpless lust he made her feel. Unlike Gary, he actually deserved the title. "Please, Master, please, sir, give me your cock . . ."

"Not. Just. Yet." And he started kissing a trail down her flexing belly toward her pussy.

By the time he spread her lower lips, she thought she was going to catapult right into orbit. But Frank had no intention of letting her come that quickly. He meant to demonstrate who was boss—and it sure as hell wasn't her.

Licking circles around her clit, he swirled his skilled tongue around the opening of her pussy until she almost shot over the narrow edge into climax.

Reading her body language, he drew back, letting the heat drain.

Alex cursed him, Dom or not. Frank chuckled and went back to eating her again. The bastard.

The incredibly hot, skilled, nasty bastard . . . *Oh, God!*

Alex's long, lovely body arched under Frank's hands, writhing like a cat begging for strokes, beautiful breasts bouncing as she fought her bonds. Her panting pleas made him even harder as he delicately sampled her wet, swollen pussy.

"Please, Master!"

"No." He couldn't wait to fuck her. As hot as she was, the trick would be keeping her from going off like a Roman candle the minute he slid inside. It would be better to keep her climbing a little longer; the wait would intensify her orgasm.

Besides, he loved the hell out of making her call him "Master." The fact that she fought him on it was an indicator the word really meant something to her. Most bottoms loved the "M" word because it played into the whole kink of being a sub. Some of them would use it to anyone even remotely dominant, whether they had a D/s relationship with that Top or not.

Alex was different, which was why hearing it gave him such a delicious feeling of erotic power. No wonder just tying the girl up gave him a stronger buzz than flogging the hell out of any other sub he'd ever had.

"Please, Master, please Master, please, pleasepleaseplease, Master!" Alex chanted, rolling her hips against his face.

"No." He clung to his self-control with ripping mental fingernails.

"Please!" She shrieked it as if maddened. "Please, Master!"

Fuck it. His control snapping like a guitar string, Frank reared between her thighs, took his aching, condom-covered cock in hand, and drove to the balls. Her scream made his ears ring.

Teeth bared in furious lust, he braced on his palms and began driving, pounding her hips with his. Each wet, silken thrust blasted fire up the length of his cock. He sucked in a breath and squeezed his eyes closed, straining to keep from going over.

Alex's body bowed, breasts pressing against his chest, almost lifting his considerable weight off the bed with her straining effort to come. "Master! God, Master!"

Fighting to hang on, he kept shafting in and out, despite the pleasure raking golden claws along his spine with every thrust.

"Aiiii! Master!" Delicate inner muscles clamped and rippled along the length of his cock as she writhed in her bonds and began to come. His balls tightened, exploded, coming, coming, *coming.*

Frank roared.

He kept thrusting even after he'd finished, wringing out every last drop of delight.

At last he collapsed over her, sweat slicking his shoulders

and dewing on her heaving breasts. Realizing his weight was probably crushing her, he managed to heave himself onto his back with a groan.

For a long moment, neither of them spoke, too busy panting to manage coherence. Finally Alex spoke. "God, that was incredible, Frank."

Yeah, he'd called it. She'd climaxed, and he was back to being Frank again.

Well, they'd just see about that.

CHAPTER SIX

When Bruce checked his e-mail late Monday, he found a video file waiting. His heart began to beat in hard, eager thumps even as he reminded himself it could once again be nothing more interesting than Ted getting dressed.

Instead, it was everything he'd hoped when he'd broken in. Ted and his little fruit had been busy that morning.

As Bruce watched uncomfortably, the cop's white hands caressed his lover's dark skin as they kissed. He knew what his father would say about that: *disgusting bastard*. Bruce, though, didn't consider himself a racist, despite his father's best efforts to instill a belief in white superiority.

Still, something in him cringed. He shook it off. *I'm not a racist*.

Unfortunately, a mere interracial kiss wouldn't be enough. People were inured to that kind of thing today. He needed a more concrete example of Arlington's lies.

Then Ted gave it to him.

Arlington tied the boy up, got out some kind of whip, and started beating the kid's ass while the little fruit begged for more. In a stroke of luck, they weren't naked, at least in the section he intended to use. Ted was shirtless in jeans, while the kid wore some kind of skin-tight black shorts, which would allow Bruce to get around YouTube's community standards. The video would probably get age-flagged for sexual content even without nudity, but that was fine with him. Kids didn't need to see this kind of perversion anyway.

Bruce grinned. "I've got you now, you sick son of a bitch."

Frank invited Alex to stay for dinner. When she volunteered to help with the meal, he put her to work making the salad while he worked on the spaghetti.

"It occurs to me I may be getting ahead of myself," Frank said while they settled into the homey domestic rituals of chopping vegetables and browning meat.

Alex looked up from the green pepper she was chopping. "How so?"

"I haven't asked you if you want to be my sub." He tasted the sauce, then plucked a bottle of oregano out of the spice rack. "Long term, not just for tonight." He tossed in a pinch of the herb, then looked up. "Because I want to go on topping you."

She stared at him, caught somewhere between elation and terror. "You want to collar me?" In the kink community, wearing a man's collar was almost like wearing his ring. It meant what they were doing was more than just hooking up. A collar signified a long-term relationship.

He hesitated. "Not just . . . yet."

"Oh." *Of course not.* It had barely been twenty-four hours. So why did she feel so damned let down?

Frank must have detected her reaction despite her best efforts to keep it off her face. He shook his head. "You're not the only one with issues from an old lover. I had a sub for a couple of years in San Diego. She did submissive really well—wanted to play the game twenty-four/seven. Called me Lord Frank, for God's sake. I indulged her. But I was a SEAL, and I was gone a lot."

Alex winced, seeing where this was going.

"Yeah, it was the whole clichéd bit. Got home to find her fucking a Marine—in our bed."

"Bitch."

"I didn't kill them, didn't even beat the shit out of the jarhead, though I gave it serious consideration. That was a year and a half ago, and I haven't had a sub since."

"If it's any comfort, you haven't lost your touch." Taking a deep breath, she blew it out again. Damn, but it was hard opening up. Letting him tie her up was nothing next to this. "And yes, I would like to be your sub. I don't know for how long—I want to see how it goes. But you're the only man I've met in a long time I've been this interested in. And for the record, I'm not involved with anyone else, vanilla or kinky. No boyfriends, no lovers, no fuckbuddies." She forced herself to meet his gaze despite her sense of vulnerability. "Nobody but you."

"Good." His voice dropped to that sensual rumble of his. "Because I think you're the hottest woman I've ever met, sub, Domme, or plain vanilla. Hell, Rocky Road. Either way—any way—I want you."

She stared at him. It felt like being on a roller coaster at the top of a hill, seeing that long, long plunge ahead with a blend of elation and terror. Then he pulled her into his arms and kissed her, his lips so demanding and hot, her heart dropped out from under her as she fell into that weightless, dizzying swoop . . .

What the hell am I doing?

I t was just after 1 a.m. when Alex made yet another circuit of her area, 21. Some nights Charlie Shift was so boring she had to alternate Red Bulls and stop-'n'-rob coffee to stay awake. By the end of the night, she'd be vibrating so hard, it would be noon before she could get to sleep.

But on other nights it was like the Chinese curse: *May you live in interesting times.* Midnight-to-eight was when assholes liked doing things they didn't want the neighbors to see.

Sometimes the shift rocked like a Death Metal concert all night long, with wall-to-wall calls. And then sometimes the night started out dull, only to get deadly mean without any fucking warning. You never really knew which kind of shift it was going to be, and you could never make assumptions.

That was why bored, sleepy cops did something they knew better than to do and ended up dead.

So far it was looking like a Red-Bull-and-black-coffee night. No wonder she was having a hell of a time keeping her mind off Frank.

After the kiss, they'd ended up making love again, this time on the kitchen table. Just as things got interesting, the skillet of spaghetti sauce on the stove set off the smoke alarm. Frank had to jump up and throw a lid over the frying pan to smother the leaping flames. He'd then turned off the burners and bent her over the table again for Round Three.

They'd gone out for pizza.

Alex knew perfectly well what her mother would say, even aside from the kink: they were going too damned fast. She'd jumped in with both feet with Gary, too, and what a clusterfuck that had turned out to be.

Yet Alex had no real desire to pull back and let things cool off. A little voice in the back of her head kept insisting Frank was not the kind of guy who came around more than once in a lifetime. If she didn't leap on and ride, she'd regret it.

Trouble was, that little voice was competing with another little voice who swore this was a really, really bad idea.

And she had no clue which schizoid personality to listen to.

Alex answered a shoplifting call at the Gas-N-Go—some asshat had grabbed a six-pack from the beer cooler and raced out the door with it. The store video didn't show anybody she knew from previous shopliftings, so she drove around looking for the next twenty minutes without spotting any little jerk swilling stolen Coors. That was the way it went some shifts.

Ted and Bruce were likewise having slow nights, judging

by the list of calls on Alex's patrol laptop. The computer displayed the calls each car on the shift handled, allowing officers to keep track of what everyone else was doing and where they were at any given time.

At the moment, Bruce had gone 10-7—out of service— to hit the McDonald's drive-through, while Ted was working another debris-in-the-roadway call. Some idiot had been leaving bags of glass bottles on Sanders Drive the last few nights, apparently in hopes of puncturing the tires of unwary drivers. Ted had sworn to catch said moron and toss his ass in jail. Except . . .

Alex paused, staring at the laptop screen with a frown. Ted had gotten out of the car to take care of the trash at 1:40 a.m. It was now 2:04, but he still wasn't listed as back in service. She keyed her car's radio microphone. "Charlie 23—Charlie 21. Are you 10-8?" She let go of the key so he could respond, but there was no answer. She keyed the mic again. "Charlie 23?" Nothing.

Unease slid through her. It should have taken Ted no more than five minutes to take care of that bag of bottles. She keyed the mic. "Dispatch, is Charlie 23 still out with that debris call?"

"Affirmative, Charlie 21," the dispatcher replied, sounding bored.

"I'm going to go see if he needs a hand."

"10-4, Charlie 21." Now she sounded amused. Alex knew exactly what the woman was thinking. *You think he needs a hand with a bag of trash? Do you know Ted Arlington at all?*

Maybe the dispatcher was right. Maybe it was nothing. Maybe Ted had caught his trash-tossing pranksters and was putting the fear of Dom into them. He loved scaring the crap out of idiots, viewing it, as he often said, as a public service to the rest of the planet.

But twenty-four minutes?

Alex hit the gas a little harder than she strictly needed to, though she resisted the impulse to use her siren. She'd feel like a fool if she roared up with blue lights blazing while he was standing there giving some kid a stern talking-to.

She turned onto Sanders Drive and slowed down. Spotting the familiar shape of Crown Vic taillights on the shoulder of the tree-lined curve, she hit her brakes and pulled in behind the idling Ford. She didn't see Ted at all, only a mound of black in the roadway, presumably the trash he'd gotten out to remove.

Frowning, she keyed her mic. "I'm 10-22 at Charlie 23's location on Sanders Drive, but I don't see him."

"Do you want backup?"

"Nah, I've got it." But as she grabbed her Maglite and got out, the hair on the back of her neck rose. She immediately drew her weapon. Ted had taught her that you listened to those little hairs, because they knew things your forebrain hadn't put together yet.

It was only then that she realized the mound beside Ted's car wasn't a black plastic trash bag.

It was a figure in a black uniform.

Her training kicked in, defeating the impulse to break into a reckless run to him that could get her shot. Automatically, she swept her gaze and her weapon over the car, the woods, the tangled brush at the edge of the road. Looking for the faint glint of a muzzle jutting from hiding. *Nothing.* She saw nothing, but it didn't mean the killer wasn't there.

But Ted *was* there, and he was hurt, could be dying. Now she broke into a run, gun in one hand pointed at the ground, keying her mic with the other. "Officer down! I need an ambulance and backup!"

She hit her knees beside him, gun in one hand, flashlight in the other, illuminating a bloodless face staring blankly at the sky. There was a small black hole in the center of Ted's forehead. Blood pooled on the ground beneath his head—the bullet's exit wound had been much larger. It had probably shattered the back of his skull.

Her mind spat out a random factoid: the last time a Morgan County cop had been shot in the line of duty was 1978. Cops had died in the line since then, of course, but always from traffic accidents or being hit by a car while writing some asshole a ticket.

Staring into Ted's empty eyes, Alex felt shock roll slowly over her like a tide of glacial ice. An incoherent mental voice babbled this had to be some kind of test, or maybe a really tasteless prank. Something, anything, other than that somebody had murdered her dearest friend.

Her gaze wandered away from the body, landing on his patrol car. Something wet glistened on it in the moonlight. Mechanically, she aimed her flash at it. Words, scrawled in something red. *Please God, let it not be blood*. Numbly she read what the killer had written.

Filth. Spewed all over the car like crimson vomit. *Queer! Deviant! You suck black cock!* And worse, from the N-word to every homophobic slur she'd ever heard.

This wasn't just a murder. This was a hate crime. That thought banished shock. The reality of Ted's murder slammed home so hard it seemed her skull rocked.

Someone shot him, dumbass, a cold, clear mental voice told her. *And whoever it was could be drawing a bead on you right now.*

B ruce stood in the bend of the road behind the two cars, knowing the glare of her own headlights would blind Alex if she looked in his direction. He raised the rifle and aimed the night vision scope at her glowing green figure, aligning the crosshairs on her head. And waited for her to scream, cry, indulge in some other female emotional display.

He wouldn't kill her. Yet. But he'd enjoy the hell out of her grief. *Now you know how it feels to have someone you love taken away from you, bitch.*

Instead she scuttled the length of Ted's patrol car and around in front of the vehicle. She'd evidently realized where his bullet had to have come from and acted to put the engine blocks of both cars between herself and the shooter. He wouldn't have thought she'd be that cool under fire. Not with her daddy pervert dead anyway. Disappointment blunted his triumph.

Maybe she hadn't really loved Ted either.

The wail of sirens ululated in the distance. Her backup was coming. Slinging the rifle's strap over his shoulder, he ghosted into the trees. He'd need to get his car and show up before she wondered where the hell he was.

B ruce Greer arrived first, grim-faced and cold-eyed, to help Alex string yellow crime scene tape. They looped it around the trees that crowded close to the road until Ted and his car was ringed in yellow.

Neither said anything as they worked. Bruce seemed to sense she'd crack wide open if he offered her any sympathy at all. She felt numbly grateful. Lousy lover or not, he was a good partner.

But then, Bruce's mother had been murdered. He understood the stunned grief she felt, because he'd felt it, too.

The night filled with sirens and blinding blue light as more cops roared onto the scene. Not just deputies, but officers from surrounding municipalities, even a couple of South Carolina Highway Patrol troopers in their pressed gray and black.

Soon the narrow stretch of road was strung with police cars, revolving lights sending waves of white and blue flowing over trees and cops and Ted's corpse. Halogen lights blazed down on the scene to assist the evidence search, the rumbling generator that powered them filling the air with the oily stink of diesel fumes.

Officers milled around like wasps from a smashed nest, shining flashes on the ground as they grimly searched for evidence.

When a cop went down in the line of duty, everybody responded; they'd chase the killer, as the old police saying went, "until the wheels fell off."

But this time there didn't seem to be anybody to chase. The fucker had ghosted. Despite the small army combing the surrounding woods, so far nobody had found so much as a shell casing. He'd obviously cleaned up his brass.

After that, he'd gotten out the spray paint. *Ballsy prick*.

He hadn't just shot Ted and fled, as any other cowardly assassin would have. Simply murdering a good cop hadn't been enough for the son of a bitch. He'd had to try to poison his memory, too.

With dry, burning eyes Alex stared at the homophobic graffiti covering Ted's car. Maybe it was just a coincidence.

Except some of the filth read, *You suck black cock!* And under that were the words *Lev. 20:13*.

Alex knew the Leviticus verse: *"If a man lies with a male as with a woman, both of them have committed an abomination; they shall surely be put to death; their blood is upon them."*

But it was the part about black cock that worried her. That was a little too damned specific to be a coincidence.

Somebody had known Ted's secret. And the bigoted fuck had killed him for it.

But even more disturbing than the graffiti was something she'd realized only after the other cops had started arriving.

Ted's badge was missing. The sniper had taken it. Why? Trophy, maybe? That was serial killer behavior.

Who had done this? That question pounded away in her head again and again like the tolling of a relentless bell. Who had found out Ted's secret?

"What kind of bullshit is this?" Bruce growled, glowering at the car. "Ted wasn't gay. He was as far from a fruit as it's possible to get."

"Some kind of white supremacist crap," Andre Jones spat. He was a big, beefy black cop who'd been a deputy for twenty years. "We need to look for some Klan motherfuckers, maybe those Sovereign Citizen assholes that hate government. Those bastards are not getting away with killing no cop in this town."

"Why did he take Ted's badge?" Alex said, more to herself than the other deputies.

"What?" Bruce blinked at her.

"He took Ted's badge," she said. "It's gone. Why did he take his badge on top of everything else?" *And why the hell couldn't I have shown up twenty minutes sooner and caught the son of a bitch before he murdered my best friend?*

Alex took a blind sip of cold coffee from a Styrofoam cup. One of the deputies had evidently emptied every pot at Burger King into gallon jugs. There were bags of little cheeseburgers, too, but the thought of eating anything made her want to gag.

There was fuck all else to do. She and the other officers had been banished outside the crime scene tape and told to do crowd control. Not that there was a crowd to control; there were no houses on this stretch of Sanders Drive, so none of the usual nosy neighbors dropped by to see what all the blue lights were for.

A couple of media vultures were already circling, though. A live truck idled just up the road, its diesel generator rumbling and reeking. A reporter and her cameraman were working the crowd of cops, trying to get something, anything.

Cassie York was there, too, her blond hair bright under the halogens. The *Morganville Courier* blogger was the only reporter Alex had any respect for, mostly because she cared more for journalistic ethics than her career. Her friend had tried to gesture her over a couple of times, probably not realizing the dead deputy was Ted. Cassie had never been insensitive.

Alex just hoped none of the reporters—even Cassie—had gotten a shot of Ted's car before the shift supervisor ordered it covered with a tarp.

She was distantly aware that Frank had arrived, uniformed and smelling of shampoo. Not like her grubby self, dirt-covered from scrabbling to hide behind the cars from the fucking assassin. Instead of, say, charging out to catch his ass. Never mind that she hadn't known where the fuck the sniper was. Never mind that taking cover was what she'd been trained to do.

She'd let Ted's killer get away.

* * *

Frank stood silently beside Alex, trying to offer whatever comfort he could by his presence. What he really wanted was to put his arms around her, but he knew she wouldn't appreciate being made to look unprofessional. She was hanging on by her ragged fingernails as it was.

Other deputies had tried to approach her, offer their condolences—the whole department apparently knew how close she and Ted had been. Frank had warned them all off with silent headshakes. She wasn't ready to hear it yet.

And if any of them wondered how the hell he was entitled to warn anybody off—well, fuck 'em.

Alex looked pale and frozen in the light of the big halogens, her dry eyes too wide. Frank knew the look better than the cops did. Yeah, they'd all seen plenty of death, plenty of grieving people, but this was different. This was seeing a buddy step on an IED right in front of you, or watching three other SEALs shot down while you watched in impotent horror.

Frank had seen other soldiers struggle with the mortal psychic wounds guilt could inflict. Had felt the weight of midnight regret himself. His fellow cops, on the other hand, had never experienced the sense of black failure that descended when a buddy died.

Besides, she was female. While the male cops around her might blink reddened eyes or wipe away tears, a female cop who did the same thing would automatically be judged too emotional. Which was probably why Alex had herself so tightly locked down. She must be raging somewhere underneath all that self-control.

He wasn't feeling all that steady himself. He'd been listening to the scanner app on his phone before the 10-0 call had gone out. Past midnight or not, he'd been thinking about Alex, wondering whether getting involved in a D/s relationship with her was really a good idea.

Not that "good idea" really mattered. The fact was, he'd wanted to listen to her voice while she worked. Which probably said all that needed saying about how he already felt about her. There was something that fascinated him about the contrast between her cool, clipped radio voice and the honeyed drawl she used when she'd played with him.

Then the shit had hit the fan.

When he'd heard the terror and anguish in her voice as she'd called in the 10-0, his heart had just . . . stopped. *She's out there with a cop killer.*

He'd thrown on his uniform and run for the car. It seemed his heart had only started beating again when he saw her red hair blazing under the halogens.

"I have to tell Cal," she said now in a deadened voice. "The sheriff and the chaplain will tell Ted's mother he's gone, but nobody knows about Cal."

"Do you want me to . . ."

"Shit!" Alex straightened as if somebody had goosed her with a Taser. "I've got to tell the detective!" She jolted forward as if to run.

Frank grabbed her arm, dragging her to a stop before she could race away. "Tell him what?"

Her gaze swung to him, finally seem to register he was there. "What if the fucker has gone after Cal? What if he's already killed him? I didn't even think . . ." Jerking her personal cell phone off its belt clip, she dialed frantically. Frank watched her listen to it ring. No answer. She let it ring.

No answer.

It rang.

No answer. It went to voice mail. "Cal, call me," she snapped. "Call me *now*." She'd gone so pale, he wondered if she was about to pass out. Instead she pulled it together and started for the crime scene tape.

"It's four thirty in the morning," Frank reminded her, following at her heels. "Maybe he turned off his phone."

"Maybe. Or maybe he's dead." She ducked under the tape, forcing Frank to lengthen his stride to keep up with her. She headed for Detective Sergeant Ben Tracy, who stood over the body, scribbling furiously in a pocket notebook.

"Sergeant, I just realized something. I don't know why I didn't think of it sooner, but Ted's lover . . . This bastard could have gone after him, too. He's not answering the phone. He could be dead or—"

"Wait—Ted did have a male lover? That shit on the car is true?" Tracy was a brawny white cop, a hair over six feet, blond and blue-eyed, with the kind of looks that got actors on the cover of *People* with headlines like SEXIEST MAN ALIVE. He was young for his job, in his early thirties, which might explain why, even called out at this hour, he wore a neatly pressed shirt, chinos, and tie.

"Yeah, it's true," Alex said grimly. "Ted was gay."

"And you didn't mention this until now? The boyfriend could be the shooter, Rogers!" Nine times out of ten when somebody was murdered, the killer was the vic's lover or family member.

She made an impatient gesture. "Cal Stephens couldn't hit the broad side of a barn with a flyswatter. He hates guns almost as much as he loves Ted. No way could he have done this. And anyway, he's a bartender. Ted told me earlier he'd be working until three in the morning, which means he's probably got an alibi. But he should be home by now, and the killer could have gone after him. Which means he may be dead or in danger *now*."

"Goddammit. Okay, let's go check on him. One way or the other, I want to talk to this guy." Visibly frustrated, he snarled, "Why didn't you mention this before?"

"She's in shock," Frank snapped back. "Ted was the next best thing to her father."

Tracy stared at him, not placing him for a moment. "Who the hell are . . . Oh, the SEAL. What do you . . . Never mind. Let's go." When Alex started for her car, which she'd moved beyond the tape, he growled, "No, you are not driving. Murphy is right, you're not hitting on all cylinders. You're with me. I want to know what else you haven't told me."

Frank got in his own car and followed, with Bruce right behind him. As he rocketed through the night behind Tracy, he hoped to hell Alex wouldn't end up standing over another friend's body.

"So that wasn't just bullshit on the side of his car?" Tracy demanded over the cycling howl of the sirens. "Why the hell didn't he tell anybody?"

Alex threw him a look. "It wasn't anybody's business."

"Sure as shit is now. Anyway, nobody has a problem with Gaffney." He took a curve with the expert control of a veteran of high-speed chases.

"Straight cops don't find lesbian officers threatening." She curled her hands into fists. "But gay men . . . Some people think they float around on fairy wings. Ted was afraid that he would have been taken less seriously."

"I went hunting with him." Tracy flashed a hard look at her, frowning. "I never had any idea. Was all that some kind of act?"

Alex managed not to snarl; it wasn't a good idea to alienate the detective investigating her friend's murder. "Ted hunted because he liked hunting, not because he was trying to pretend to be something he wasn't. He wasn't like that."

"He pretended to be straight! Everybody thought you two were involved."

Taken off-guard, Alex found herself laughing for the first time since she'd found Ted's body. "We never pretended we were dating. Frank's right—Ted is . . . Ted *was* like a father to me."

"What about Murphy?" Apparently he'd read between the lines of the Dom's protective behavior.

"What about Murphy?" Alex glowered at him, silently telling him to drop it.

Nobody was more immune to social cues than a homicide detective working a murder. "Are you two involved?"

"We're dating." Which was oversimplifying things considerably, but still.

"So you're straight." Tracy added hurriedly, "Not that it's any of my business. I just want to know if you might be a target."

"No, I'm straight. Whether I'm a target . . . Who can tell with a psycho?" Alex almost hoped the killer did come after her. She had a violent need to blow his brains out. "I just pray he hasn't killed Cal. Why the hell didn't I think of this two hours ago, before he got home?"

"Look, we don't know this Cal guy is dead. Don't borrow trouble. And Murphy was right—you didn't think of it because you're holding together with spit and bailing wire." His voice gentled. "I know you, Rogers. You're a good cop."

"Not good enough to catch my partner's killer."

"That's my job, Rogers."

"But I was there, Sarge. I was there, and I—"

"Bruce Greer was Ted's partner, too, y'know. I didn't notice him thinking of this Cal guy either."

"Bruce didn't know about Ted."

He flicked a look at her before returning his attention to his driving. "Why did Ted tell you when he kept the rest of us in the dark?"

Because I went to an Atlanta Munch right after I was hired and ran into him. The local BDSM community was tiny; everybody knew everybody. Alex said simply, "We were close."

The three patrol cars peeled into the complex with its clusters of three-story buildings. A thought flashed through her mind: *The neighbors are going to love this.* But she really didn't give a damn. She just wanted her friend to come to the damned door.

As to how she'd tell Cal the man he loved was dead . . . Well, she just wanted him to be alive to have the conversation. Instead of, say, lying in the living room covered in blood, a vision that had been tormenting her since he'd failed to answer the phone.

Have I failed Ted again? Alex fought a wave of despair. If Cal was dead, she thought she'd finally lose control of the screaming pain inside her.

The car barely had time to roll to a stop before she threw the door open and jumped out, drawing her Glock as she sprinted across the parking lot.

"Rogers!" Tracy snapped as Frank and Bruce roared up.

Swearing mentally, she slowed to wait for the other cops. "This way." Alex took the stairs to Cal's apartment two at a time. She was absently aware that Frank had passed Tracy at a run, obviously intent on keeping up with her.

When she arrived at 2D, she automatically moved to one side of the door, out of the killer's potential line of fire. Frank, Tracy, and Bruce moved to the other side of the door.

It opened before her knuckles hit the wood. "What the hell is . . ." Cal began. He froze as he saw Alex's face.

"You didn't answer the phone," she told him numbly.

"It didn't ring. I probably forgot to charge it again. Alex, what . . ." His eyes went wide with fear as he scanned the cops' faces without seeing the one he was expecting. "Alex, where's Ted?"

CHAPTER SEVEN

A lex tried to speak, found her throat too tight for a long
moment before she finally managed to croak, "Cal, I'm
so sorry . . ."

Every lover, spouse, or parent of a cop knew what it meant
when his coworkers showed up at the door saying something
like that. Horrible comprehension flooded her friend's chocolate eyes. "No. Alex, no." Face going gray, the young man's
knees buckled before he caught himself and straightened
with an obvious, agonizing effort.

"Come on, Cal." She looped an arm around his shoulders and turned him toward the couch. "Let's sit down."

The deputies stepped inside as the pair of them dropped
onto a worn blue love seat.

Tracy gave Alex a look. Her training told her what he
wanted. "Cal, mind if Frank and Bruce take a look around?
Everybody's feeling a little paranoid." She caught his hands
and squeezed them, silently apologizing for the question.

"Yeah, sure," Cal said, though from his stunned tone,

she doubted he was processing well enough to know what she was implying.

The two cops nodded and silently moved off to make sure there was no one else in the apartment. It didn't take long. It was a small place, all Cal could afford on a bartender's salary. Alex knew the apartment as well as her own house: the living room where they sat, separated from the efficiency kitchen by a butcher block countertop bar; a bedroom, and a tiny bathroom.

Being that Cal was a devout nerd, the walls were hung with movie posters from *Star Wars*, *Star Trek*, and assorted superhero movies. Every flat surface held superhero figurines and toys, and a pair of crossed light sabers hung behind the couch.

Frank and Bruce returned a minute later. Greer shook his head at Tracy; they hadn't found anybody hiding in a closet or something. He took up a post beside one of several bookcases, a bust of Darth Vader at his elbow. Frank leaned next to a movie poster depicting Batman in a heroic pose. Tracy crouched down in front of Cal, and all three cops started watching the civilian with the kind of hawkish attention reserved for potential suspects.

Neither Alex nor Cal gave a shit.

The sub stared at her, tears spilling free to run silently down his dark face. "What happened? Did he wreck that damned patrol car of his? I told him he drives too fucking fast . . ."

"It wasn't an accident, Cal. He was . . ." She had to stop and regain control of her voice. "Cal, Ted was murdered. Shot in the head."

He stared at her. His mouth opened and closed several times before he managed speech. "But . . . why? Why would anyone do that? Did he pull the wrong guy over or what?" It was a logical assumption. Usually when a cop was shot, it was because he'd accidentally run into a felon who didn't want to go back to jail.

She was trying to figure out what to say when Tracy

spoke up. "The killer spray-painted racial and sexual slurs on Ted's car about . . . your relationship."

"That's why we all roared up the way we did," Frank put in. "We were afraid the bastard had shot you, too."

Cal froze, looking between Alex and Frank in bewildered pain. "Ted was killed because of me?" He sounded very young.

Alex tightened her grip on his hands. "No, Cal, he was killed because somebody's a bigoted asshole."

Tracy spoke up then, watching Cal's face closely. "Mr. Stephens, I'm Sergeant Tracy . . ."

Cal nodded. "Oh, yeah. You guys went hunting. Ted talks . . ." His expression flattened. "Talked . . . about you. He thought a lot of you."

Tracy looked a little taken aback, as if he'd assumed that because Ted hadn't talked about Cal to him, he'd never talked about him to Cal. "Oh. Uh, thanks. Look, if we're going to catch the killer, we're going to need help. What can you tell us? Had anybody made threats against Ted? Or you?"

"People are always making threats against Ted. He said it didn't mean anything. Just part of being a cop." Which was true.

Tracy scrawled something in his notebook and looked up at Cal again, his gaze intent and analytical. "Where were you between 1:40 and 2:04 a.m. this morning?"

Cal frowned. "Am I a suspect?" Anguish tightened his face, and his eyes shone with welling tears. "I loved Ted. I would never have . . ."

Alex laid a hand on his shoulder and gave it a comforting squeeze. "Of course not, Cal. You're the least violent person I know. And Ted loved you every bit as much as you do him. But the sergeant needs to eliminate you as a suspect so he can find who did do this."

"Oh." Reassured, he met Tracy's gaze. "I'm a bartender at Southern Sports. I was working until we closed up at three a.m."

"Is there somebody who can confirm that? Coworkers, your boss?"

"Yeah, the manager and one of the waitresses." He recited names and cell numbers for the detective, who dutifully wrote everything down.

For the next hour, Tracy questioned Cal exhaustively about Ted, their relationship, and their mutual friends. The submissive managed to answer honestly without mentioning BDSM, even when the detective asked the same question several different ways. Even when tears ran silently down Cal's face until Alex wanted to beat Tracy with his own notebook.

Finally the detective wound down, and Alex saw an opening. "Cal, is there somewhere you can go?" she asked. "Someone you can stay with for a while? We're afraid this guy . . . He might come after you."

"My sister's." He frowned. "Or would that put her in danger, too?"

"Probably not," Tracy said, looking up from his notebook. "Yeah, the sniper may have seen you and Ted together, but I doubt he'd know enough to track down your family. Besides, the stuff on the car didn't mention you by name. For all we know, it was just random racial insults that happened to hit a little too close to home." He grimaced. "People call cops cocksuckers all the time."

"Yeah, Ted says . . ." Cal broke off, and his eyes filled again. He sniffed and swiped a hand over his face. "Look, I'm gonna call my sister. Make sure she won't mind me showing up."

"You okay to drive?" Frank asked. "I can give you a ride."

"Thanks, but I can make it. It's not far, and it's not like there's a lot of traffic this time of night."

"You sure? It's no trouble. I'm not technically on the clock."

Tracy gave him a narrow *Are you gay, too?* look, which Frank proceeded to ignore. Alex could have told him the offer had nothing to do with sexual orientation and everything to do with a Dominant's instinct to protect any submissive, even one he wasn't involved with. Or maybe it was just being a cop, which, at least for someone like Frank, came with a similar set of instincts.

"No, I've got it," Cal said, evidently too upset to notice the byplay.

"Here, use my cell." Alex pulled it off its belt clip. "Yours is dead, remember?"

Cal grimaced. "Yeah, I need to plug the damned thing in."

He stood up and walked off down the apartment's short hallway. "Jaz? I'm sorry to wake you, but . . . Ted's dead." The sob that followed wrung Alex's heart. "Can I . . . Can I come over? Thanks. Thanks, sis. I'll be there in . . . No, I can drive." His voice grew indistinct as he moved into the bedroom.

"That kid wasn't involved," Tracy said softly. "He's too broken up about it. And I don't think he's acting."

"He's not." Alex dug her fingers into her hair in an effort to massage the knots that had taken up residence at the base of her skull. She grimaced, discovering that her French braid had begun to unravel. Apparently this wasn't the first time she'd unconsciously gone looking for knots.

"Hell of a night." Tracy watched her with steady sympathy.

When she snorted, the sound edged a bit too close to a sob. Alex took a deep breath, managed to regain control. "Tell me about it."

Alex walked into the MCSO training room at eight in the morning. Pain stabbed her chest as she remembered the last time she'd been here, Ted had been alive and giving Frank hell.

She fell wearily into a chair, scrubbing both hands over her burning eyes. "I feel like I've been beaten with a two-by-four," she muttered to Frank as he settled down beside her.

For what must have been the tenth time in the past few hours, one of his big hands engulfed her shoulder for a comforting squeeze. It was the kind of thing he might have done to a male deputy, yet somehow it seemed tender. A lover's gesture.

The room filled up around them. Again, she couldn't help but compare this meeting to the one the evening before. The crowd was a hell of a lot quieter, the voices low with grief or growling with anger.

"Can't believe Ted was gay."

"Me either. Hell, he swished less than Richards."

"Fuck you, too, Donaldson."

"You ain't my type, son."

"Damned white supremacist coward. We need to find that bastard and put him *under* the jail." Rather than in it, in other words.

Alex agreed with Richards.

Sheriff Ranger walked in with the department chaplain, a balding elderly minister who had been volunteering his services to the MCSO for years. Ranger stepped up to the podium and said, "Reverend Dave Grayson is going to lead us in prayer."

Alex automatically bowed her head with everybody else.

"Lord, we ask you to be with this department as we remember Master Deputy Ted Arlington. Guide detectives as they seek his killer. Help us remember that we are not to judge our brother, lest we be judged." Evidently somebody had told the reverend that Ted was gay. "And protect these deputies as they serve you and protect those the citizens of this county. In the name of Christ Jesus we pray . . ."

"Amen," the deputies chorused.

"Thank you, Reverend," Ranger told the old man, who nodded and moved heavily to take a seat. His face was set in lines of sadness that suggested he'd known Ted personally. "The chaplain and I just got back from telling the master deputy's mother her son was murdered. Y'all do me a favor— don't make me do that again." He shook his head. "That was brutal. It's one thing to lose one of y'all to a car crash, but to some cowardly slime who set a trap for him and then blew him away?" He swept a hot gaze over the room. "Until this creep is caught, I want you all to be damned careful. Don't take anything for granted. If you've fallen into a routine drivin' your patrols, change it. You don't want anybody knowin' where you'll be and when you'll be there so he can shoot you from ambush. Don't hesitate to call for backup if you get a bad feeling about somethin'. It's better to feel a little stupid and be alive than try to handle a situation on your own and get yourself killed. Arlington had no reason to suspect anybody might be gunning for him. Y'all can't say the same."

Ranger let that sink in a moment before he continued. "I'm sure this doesn't need to be said, but I'm going to say it anyway. If you find out about somebody who might have done this—I don't want anybody trying to go all Rambo on the bastard. You report it to a supervisor, or to Detective Tracy, who's handling the case. I know emotion is running high, but I will not have vigilantism in my department. We're going to play this by the book. I don't want the public thinking we lynched this asshole, no matter how tempted we might be. Y'all got that?"

The deputies chorused, "Yes, sir," but it sounded a little sullen.

"I said," he repeated in a ringing voice, *"Y'all got that?"*

"Yes, Sheriff!" they thundered.

"That's better. Now, I want to address another point. You have probably heard a lot of rumors today about the master deputy's private life. Let me be clear—I do not want to hear any of that repeated to the media. I don't want his mama to have to listen to her son's name getting dragged through the mud. Ted was a damned good cop. Even aside from his military service as a decorated Green Beret, even aside from all the times I know for a fact Ted waded into fights to back up fellow officers over the years . . ." Ranger smiled faintly. "He might have been short, but damn, that man could fight."

The deputies laughed, but the sound held a note that suggested tension relief as much as anything else.

Ranger sobered. "But there was more to Ted than the ability to kick any butt that needed it. About eight years ago—before a lot of you even joined this department—Ted ran into a burning trailer because he was afraid the woman and two little children who lived there hadn't gotten out. It's worth noting he didn't know that for sure. It would have been easy to assume they'd already escaped, or that they were already dead, particularly since we all know how fast a trailer can burn. Ten, fifteen minutes tops, and we're talking fully involved. Ted knew that, but he didn't hesitate. He kicked the door in and charged inside, and somehow he got the woman moving and carried her kids out, one under each arm. Man was strong as a bull." He swept a hard look across the room. "Those three people are alive right now because Ted Arlington was a hero. No matter what you think about the way the master deputy did—or did not—spend his personal time, you need to remember that. As the reverend just reminded us, the Good Book says, 'Judge not lest ye be judged.'"

Alex gave the sheriff a smile. *I knew there was a reason I liked that man.*

She also knew that while his deputies might listen to him, there were plenty of other people who wouldn't.

Frank was about to head on shift when Major Jennings called, "I'd like a word, Murphy."

"Yes, sir." He followed the black cop down the corridor and around the corner to his office.

Jennings dropped behind his desk and nodded at one of the chairs in front of it. "Have a seat, Deputy."

He obeyed. "Yes, sir?"

"We've decided you're going to be assigned to Charlie Shift, Area 23."

Frank blinked in surprise. "Wasn't that Master Deputy Arlington's zone?"

"Yeah. It's not an ideal situation, but we can't leave it unpatrolled."

"I . . . don't suppose so." On the other hand, at least he'd be able to keep an eye on Alex.

Jennings eyed him as if he'd read his mind. "Detective

Tracy tells me you and Rogers are dating. Is that going to be a problem?"

"No, sir."

"See that it's not. In the meantime, Deputy, keep your head down out there—literally."

"I will, sir." And he'd make damned sure Alex did the same.

It was a cold, gray morning, but Alex ignored the temperature, running hard. Ran the way she'd once run track meets, ran the way she chased convenience store robbers and other assorted asshats. Ran until the sweat slid down her face despite the temperature, soaking her tee between her breasts as her arms pumped and feet slapped furiously on the sidewalk. Trying to burn off hours of helpless rage and guilt and grief.

She wished she could cry, but she knew what she'd need for that, and Frank was on duty now. So instead she ran. It was noon, long past the time she should be in bed if she wanted to be able to work tonight without a Red Bull IV drip. So she ran faster, trying to burn off the adrenaline and stress hormones and too much coffee.

And failure. Don't forget the failure.

When she clawed through the tangle of guilt and fury that crowded her brain, Alex knew there was nothing she could have done to save Ted even if she'd come to investigate sooner. He'd died, quite literally, before he hit the ground. A bullet in the brain did that.

She only wished she could find the bastard who had done this and put a bullet in *his* brain. How dare that little shit think he had the right to kill Ted Arlington because of who he loved? How was it the creep's goddamned business?

She ran faster, pushing herself to full speed as she tore through the neighborhood until she bounded up the cement-block steps of her house. Jerking the screen door open with a shriek of rusting hinges, Alex staggered across the porch, breathing so hard it took her two tries to unlock the front door with the key she wore on a coiled plastic bracelet.

"Meow?" SIG looked up as she reeled inside and collapsed on the couch beside him. Panting, she stroked the cat, taking comfort in the Siamese's outboard motor of a purr.

It took her ten minutes before she found the strength to undress for her shower. Half an hour later, she tumbled into bed, more or less clean, her hair still damp. And slid into dreams in which Ted stared at the stars with empty eyes.

B ruce watched red chunks explode from his target and bared his teeth in a rictus of satisfaction. Aiming his rifle at another tomato, he squeezed the trigger again. The weapon boomed, and his target disintegrated in another burst of pulp and juice.

Ranger had dared call him a coward.

The injustice made him boil. The fact that Arlington was a lying bastard didn't seem to matter. Instead, all the sheriff talked about was Ted's heroism.

Yeah, sucking black cock was real heroic.

He took aim again. Fired. A third tomato vanished in a rain of red.

At least one part of his plan was working. Scrawling all that shit all over Ted's car had been brilliant. Tracy was chasing white supremacists instead of looking at Ted's friends—normally the first suspects. No cop would want to believe another cop was the killer, of course, but in case they started entertaining the idea, the graffiti offered a layer of insulation.

Nobody considered Bruce Greer a bigot.

The bit from Leviticus was another layer of icing for the cake. Bruce figured the MCSO's many devout Christians would be turned against Ted by the reminder that the Bible disapproved of perverts.

Instead, Ranger seemed intent on turning Ted into some kind of martyr.

Well, Bruce would just see about that. He still had that video. All he had to do was put it up on YouTube, and

Arlington wouldn't be a hero anymore. All anybody would see was a white man whipping a black man, who evidently liked it. Blacks would be outraged, whites would be disgusted, and everybody would decide Ted had it coming.

As for Cal, that boy would wish he'd never even heard Arlington's name after his fellow African Americans finished taking him apart.

The problem was, once the video was out there, Bruce wouldn't be able to control the fallout. The Feds might get involved, especially when he started the next phase of his revenge.

But he'd do what he had to do, even if he had to pay the price. He owed his daddy that much.

Bruce squeezed the trigger. Another tomato disappeared with a thundering boom, sending faux blood and brains everywhere.

A lex woke to John Fogarty's whiskey voice belting "Put me in, Coach!" Never mind that the song was about baseball rather than football, "Centerfield" had always made her think of her father, mainly because Fogarty, like the Beatles, were among her parents' favorite musicians. Which made "Centerfield" the obvious ringtone for Ken Rogers.

Rolling over, she reached over the side of the bed and groped around until she found her sweats and fished her cell phone out of the pocket. "Morning, Dad." Her mouth tasted like the bottom of a ferret cage.

"Hey, baby girl." His voice rolled over her, dear and deep, a bit rough from decades spent yelling at teenagers from across a football field. Ken Rogers was still as leanly muscular as the quarterback he'd once been, sable hair graying as he settled into a distinguished middle age. He often said educating his players was far more satisfying than the NFL stardom his knee injury had snatched away. "You okay?"

Hell, no. "I'm fine, Daddy."

"I hope I didn't wake you, but I just heard about what happened from one of the boys on the team, and I had to check. You know how your mother is. You sure you weren't hurt?"

"I wasn't even there when Ted was shot."

"The story on the *Morganville Courier* website said another deputy found him. That wasn't you, was it? I know your patrol area is right beside his."

She thought about lying yet again, but he'd find out the truth eventually. It didn't pay to lie to Coach if you didn't have to. "Yes, sir." When she was little, she'd learned everybody on the team called him sir if they knew what was good for them. She'd never gotten out of the habit.

He growled something that was probably a bitten-off curse. Though Alex heard worse every day, her father didn't swear in front of his wife and daughter. "I'm sorry for that, baby girl. Ted was a good man. I know how much he meant to you. Your mother and I always felt better knowing he was on the job with you, because we figured he'd do everything he could to protect you."

He couldn't have said anything that would feel more like a blade ripping into her heart. "Yes, sir," she managed through the knot guilt had tied in her throat. "Ted was a very, very good man."

By the time she hung up, sleeping was out of the question. Alex rolled out of bed, padded into the kitchen to check SIG's water bowl—it was still full—and looked at the time. Four in the afternoon. Late enough that Cal ought to be up, assuming he'd slept at all last night. Which he probably hadn't. She dug the phone out of her pocket and dialed his number.

It rang so many times, she was about to give up when Cal finally answered. His voice sounded deadened and barely audible, as if grief had sucked the life out of him. "Hey, Alex."

"I hope I didn't wake you."

"No. Couldn't sleep."

They talked a few minutes, long enough for Alex to assure herself he was still safely at his sister's, and had taken the night off from his bartending job. That was a relief; she'd been haunted by the thought that the killer might try for him at work. This, at least, gave them a little more time to find the bastard.

Soon afterward, Detective Tracy called to ask her a couple more questions about Ted. The only bright spot about the conversation was when she asked him about Cal.

"At the moment, he's off the suspect list," Tracy said. "When Ted died, Cal was serving mai tais to fifteen members of a bachelorette party. At least six of which were sober enough to remember him. According to his manager, he was at work from seven p.m. to three a.m. Took his breaks in the bar and never left. I doubt seriously he had anything to do with this. Can you think of anyone who might have?"

Alex snorted. "Ted was a cop. We all collect enemies like trick-or-treaters do candy. There is one white supremacist in my zone we butted heads with a time or two, though . . ." She gave him the name, plus a few others, and he hung up.

The call had the effect of submerging Alex in guilt until she longed for a distraction. One immediately leaped to mind: Frank. The big cop should be off today. She, thank God, had several hours free before midnight shift change.

Alex typed a text to his private cell. Do you want to play?

Even as her fingers danced on the keyboard, she knew she didn't necessarily want to scene. But she felt trapped in her own head, unable to say what she really meant: *I need to connect with you because I'm hurting about Ted.* Frank would blunt that bitter ache.

The intensity of her need for him worried her. Alex wasn't sure she wanted to be that nakedly vulnerable with anyone, Dom or not. Particularly a guy she'd known only a couple of days. But regardless of common sense, she craved him.

She only hoped Frank would understand what she couldn't say. Otherwise he'd think she was an insensitive bitch who wanted to get her kink on regardless of her best friend's death.

Alex was just sitting down to a ham sandwich she didn't want when she got his reply. Of course. *My house in twenty.*

Her fingers tightened over the phone as anticipation cut through her grief, bringing with it a wave of guilt. She didn't deserve any pleasure, but maybe the physical pain Frank gave her would blunt her emotional anguish. Good or bad, she needed the release. She went to get dressed.

Frank stared at Alex. "You want me to use *what* on you?"

"Your bullwhip." She frowned, obviously not understanding why he'd refuse. "You're good with it. I saw you use it on Tara."

"That's not the point. I use that whip with experienced submissives who want to fly. I will not use it on a woman who wants to be punished for not being able to save Ted Arlington. I hate to break it to you, Alex, but you ain't Supergirl."

Her pretty, exhausted face took on a mulish expression. "It's not like that."

"The hell it's not. Right now your head is a swamp populated with guilt alligators, all of 'em eating on you. I couldn't trust you to safeword if your life depended on it. And even aside from all that, I'd have to be an idiot to go from spanking straight to using a fucking bullwhip on a sub who's never played that hard before. Sorry, ain't happening."

"But I need it."

"Why?"

Her gaze shifted away. "Because I need to cry."

Of course she did. Hell, during that thing with Cal last night, he'd wiped away tears himself. "So cry."

"I can't." Alex blinked dry, red eyes. "The Coach . . . My dad . . . I was the youngest of four kids. The older ones are all boys." She ran down again.

"You're not a boy." To put it mildly.

"But when I was four or five, I really wanted to be. The boys . . . Dad spent a lot of time with the boys, teaching them to throw a football. And I was always right in there with them, trying to play just as hard as they did." She smiled slightly at the memory. "I wanted to be a better boy than any of them."

He realized where she was going with her story. "So when he told them big boys didn't cry, you didn't." Not the best lesson to teach any kid, regardless of gender. But when it came to parents, what did Frank know? Between his mother and grandfather, he'd never exactly been surrounded by the best parenting examples. Alex was lucky she had Coach, no matter what fucked-up lessons the man had inadvertently instilled.

"I know it doesn't make any sense. Men cry. Coach broke down when his mother died. But me . . . When Nana died, I had to pick a fight with the meanest girl in high school. She dislocated my jaw, and then I was able to cry." She rolled her shoulders in a little shrug. "Of course, I got suspended, and Mom grounded me for a month, but you do what you have to do."

Frank stared at her. He needed to understand her if he was to protect her when she needed it, even when the danger was herself. "So you got involved in BDSM as an alternative to picking fights?"

"No, not really. Or . . . well, kind of. BDSM was the only thing that did it for me. You know? Vanilla men are just . . . vanilla." She brooded for a moment. "But yeah, sometimes when some Top gives me a flogging, it's the only time I can really cut loose and feel what I feel. Otherwise I'm all"—Alex made a fist-clenching gesture—"locked down. I don't know if that makes any sense . . ."

"You know, if you want to cry, I don't need a bullwhip to make you do it." He gave her a deliberately menacing smile.

Alex managed a smile, though he wasn't sure it was genuine. "That sounds like a challenge."

"Oh," he purred, "it is. You're going to find it very challenging."

CHAPTER EIGHT

Once again, Alex found herself chained to the foot of the California king's brass frame. This time she was on her feet facing the bed, the sheer cream curtains of the canopy framing her naked body, the gold comforter's silken surface brushing the front of her legs. Anticipation rolled through her like honey, spiced by a peppery bite of fear. She was at his mercy—again.

And that was just where she wanted to be.

"Is that too tight?" Frank asked, running a finger between the sheepskin-lined cuff and her arm. He was in full-on Dom God mode, deliciously shirtless in black jeans, a thick black belt studded in silver, and the riding boots he'd worn the first time they'd played at Cap's. The shift and slide of muscle in his naked torso was enough to make her cream even without all the leather and steel.

"It's fine." She licked dry lips, acutely aware of the warm air blowing over her skin. Frank had turned the heat up to make sure she didn't get cold standing around naked. Never mind that he was likely to work up a sweat during the flogging; for a Dom, the sub's needs came first.

"Are you sure?" His tone was stern, no nonsense. "Because if you injure all those nerves and veins running there . . ."

"I'm not an idiot," she said, more of a snap in her voice than she'd intended. "I have played before. I have no more interest in suffering a permanent injury than you do in inflicting one."

His palm landed on her ass in a stinging swat that bounced her onto her toes. "Watch your tone."

"Sorry, Master." That last word slipped out by pure reflex. She reminded herself she wasn't using the "M" word anymore, but some little instinct in her hindbrain wasn't convinced.

Neither was her pussy. She was beginning to cream, aroused by that single swat. *God, I'm such a sub.*

For the right man anyway.

Frank lifted her cuffed arm, looping the rope through the D ring, tied it off, and stretched her right arm out to the right post of the canopy. It didn't quite reach, but a taut length of rope made up the difference. He knotted it around the canopy frame, then paused to cup her breast, thumbing the nipple into a tight, eager little erection. Satisfied, he went to work on her other wrist.

When he was finished, her ankles were cuffed and roped shoulder-width apart to the frame. Both feet were planted securely on the floor. She shifted in her bonds, making the chains rattle as her inner flesh grew tighter, wetter. Eager for his cock.

"Can you stand comfortably like that?"

"Yes, Master." Dammit, there was that word again.

"Good. What are your safewords?"

"Red for stop, yellow for slow down. Green for more." She didn't anticipate saying anything but "Green."

Frank picked up a length of black silk from the bureau, where he'd lined up his toys and condoms. He blindfolded her with it, wrapping her head in cool silk that smelled of sandalwood. "That way if you cry," he said in her ear, his voice low, intimate, "nobody needs to know except you."

"Thank you, Master." This time she meant that last word. The man understood her better than she understood herself.

Music began playing softly, some kind of jazz, slow and seductive. Her nipples beaded in anticipation as cream gathered between her spread thighs. Staring into the darkness of the blindfold, Alex licked her lips, waiting for the pain she needed. The pain she deserved for failing her friend.

"You're so beautiful." His voice sounded smokier than the jazz, a delicious male rumble that made her think of sex. But then, where he was concerned, everything made her think of sex. Even when she didn't want it to. "I love this ass." His fingers brushed her rump, a touch so light, she shivered in delicious anticipation. Wondering when those hands would get rougher, more ruthless. "It's the most spankable butt I've ever seen. Almost begs for handprints. Long pink stripes. Paddle prints. I want to hear you yelp. Moan. Beg." He leaned down, spoke directly into her ear again. "Especially beg."

Alex tugged restlessly at the ropes that bound her to the bed frame. The sense of helplessness added to the hot spiral of her desire, driving it higher like smoke rising from a campfire. Never mind that this wasn't about that—wasn't about pleasure. Shouldn't be.

Frank had other ideas.

His warm hands slid up and around her body in teasing butterfly strokes of his fingertips. Until he cupped her breasts. Weighed the soft mounds in his big hands, flicking the erect nipples with his thumbs. "And your breasts. So full and warm. I'm glad you haven't dieted yourself into one of those stick women. There's muscle and strength to this pretty body. I don't feel like you'll break if I'm not careful." His voice dropped another dark, velvet octave. "I don't want to be careful."

His hands slid away. She heard the click of his riding boots as he stepped back, the soft whisper of the deerskin flogger.

The first impact was scarcely harder than the touch of his fingertips as the flogger danced over her skin. Once, then again, as Frank swung the whip in what felt like a slow figure-eight.

The next stroke was a bit harder, the one after that still harder, faster, the impact increasing with each rotation of the flogger, until the soft falls began to sting as they snapped against her ass.

Then he swung up between her spread thighs, and she gasped at the sharp thump against the lips of her pussy. It was hard to remember guilt and loss with her cunt blazing and her body tightening with curls of dark arousal.

"Yeah," he growled, the sound of his voice hot with arousal. "Bounce on those long, long legs. So sweet. So hot." A snap entered his tone. "Call it. Red, yellow, or green?"

"Green," she gasped. *More, oh, God, more.*

The impact on her ass bit this time. Alex threw her head back and gasped into the darkness of her blindfold. Another biting blow. Even as soft as the flogger was, he knew how to get a harder snap out of it.

His bare chest pressed against her back, and his hand slid between her thighs, long fingers testing her pussy, finding it slick and swollen. "Mmmmmm," he purred. "I think you want more out of me than pain, don't you, baby?"

"Yeah. Oh, yeah."

His other hand found her nipple, teased its desperate peak. The heated honey pleasure that rolled through her breast made her writhe in need. "What do you call me?"

"Master," she panted. "You're my master."

"And don't you fuckin' forget it, baby. Not even when you won't use the word. Not even when you can't use the word." He leaned down and lifted his hand to brush her hair away from her ear. His breath heated the tender shell of it. "I'm your master, darlin'. And you're my submissive. I don't need to collar your neck if I can collar your heart."

The words rang through her with that inner reverberation a secret truth carries. And it scared the hell out of her.

But then he stepped away again, and the flogger licked out to taste her ass. The sting made her gasp.

"You're turning a pretty pink now," Frank said, dark satisfaction in his voice. "God, I love that color."

Boot heels clicked. Plastic rattled, as if he tore some

kind of packaging. She sensed the warmth of his powerful body again, and he started wrapping her hips in thin Velcro straps. Cool plastic settled against her clit, and he buckled the thin belts around each thigh, securing something soft and rubbery against her clit and pussy. It began to hum, sending ripples of sensation everywhere it touched.

A butterfly vibrator.

"Now," he growled, "let's quit playing around."

The next swats stung so viciously, she writhed, gasping, even as the butterfly vibrator buzzed against her pussy in waves of sweet pleasure.

He'd switched floggers, she realized. This one had thinner tresses, cowhide or kangaroo, without the doeskin softness of the other toy. Even as he struck again, the vibrations of the butterfly picked up speed. Apparently he had a wireless controller.

"Call it."

"Green." She managed to hold still, though it was tough to do, balanced between the waves of pleasure from the vibrator and the hard, bright stings he flicked over her flexing ass.

"Oh, yeah," he murmured. "God, you look so hot. So tempting, bouncing on those long, sweet legs. Not sure whether to moan or yell." His voice dropped into a vibrating register. "I've got a hard-on up to my navel. I want to fuck you so bad, I can taste it."

Another set of flogger strokes, each tress leaving behind a bright lick of pain. Making her gasp and jerk, unable to hold still. Her eyes stung behind the blindfold. Not crying yet, but close.

Close as the climax she could feel gathering around the vibrations of the butterfly. Sweet, God, it was sweet. The sensations hit her in waves, spinning her helplessly between pain and delight until it became hard to tell one from another. All she knew was that she wanted more.

He was good. God, he was better than any Dom she'd ever had.

I don't need to collar your neck if I can collar your heart . . .

She thrust that frightening thought away before it could act as a brake on her pleasure.

"I think you're ready for something a bit more intense. Here it comes . . ."

The next impact of leather tresses jolted her onto her toes in surprise. The sting was intense, edging into true pain as keen as the pleasure from the vibrator.

"Call it."

"Green!"

I don't need to collar your neck if I can collar your heart . . .

A lex had her fingers wrapped around the ropes that stretched her out for him, unconsciously increasing the tension.

Most subs would have been screeching by now, but she only gasped, panted, writhed in her bonds in steadily increasing arousal. That long, lovely body, those exquisite legs flexing, rolling her ass as if fucking the air. Fucking the strokes of his whip.

Frank could have driven railroad spikes with his dick.

This was why he loved Dominance and submission. Having a woman give herself over to him in utter surrender. The eroticism sizzled in his brain, raw and exhilarating, until he had to clamp down on his need to hit her harder, to force her to give him more. Jesus, she had him halfway to Top space— that Dominant's equivalent to subspace, when you soared like a rocket on a hot blend of testosterone and adrenaline.

He checked her face, though it was harder to read her reactions with her eyes covered. There was a certain twist to her lips he recognized, a blend of pain and arousal and furious pleasure. A storm front of emotion about to break. . .

Spotting his moment, he reached between her legs and plunged two fingers into her wet, deliciously tight pussy.

She screamed, her voice spiraling as she came, shuddering in her bonds. Yet there was a note to her voice, a certain vibrato that suggested pain as much as pleasure.

He couldn't take any more. Tossing the whip aside, Frank

strode to the bedside table and grabbed a condom. He ripped the package open with his teeth, unzipped and pulled his cock out, then sheathed himself without bothering to pull his jeans down.

Returning to his delicious little sub, he jerked the Velcro straps open on her wrist cuffs, leaving them to dangle as he grabbed one shoulder and bent her over the bed. His plunge into her pussy ripped another scream from her lips.

Frank froze. He was a big man, and he had a big cock. Had he hurt her? "Call it!"

"Green!" she shouted. "Green, green, green!"

"Good. Hold on, baby." He started fucking her.

Long and hard and fast, rolling his hips, digging deep and merciless. Fucking as the pressure built until he swore he could feel it right to the eyeballs.

"Master," she gasped, the word becoming a breathless chant of need. "Master, Master, Master! Master, please . . ."

Hearing that word, sensing she used it only when hunger maddened her, turned up the heat on his lust.

"MASTER!" she shrieked, writhing, her pussy clamping down on his sawing dick as she came again in delicious, gripping pulses.

Frank thrust as deep as he could get, right to the mouth of her womb, and filled the fucking condom.

He kept thrusting then, if more slowly, letting them both come down as the pulses died away and his dick softened in her hot grip. God, she felt so good, her pretty ass silken and curving against his hips, her back a long sweep of pale skin against the gold and chocolate of the comforter. Draped over her body, he listened to her heartbeat slow, deliciously wrung out himself. Drained by pleasure. "God," he groaned, "I wish we could stay like this forever."

She laughed. It sounded a little stuffed and unsteady somehow. "We can't. We'd starve."

"Ah. Good point." Yielding to the inevitable, he withdrew, peeled off the condom, wincing a little, and tossed it into the bedside trashcan. Dropping to his knees, he unbuckled the cuffs around her ankles, then picked her up and put her down in the middle of the bed. He sat down to pull off his boots and jeans, then rose to study her for a quiet, delicious moment.

God, she was beautiful. Gloriously naked in nothing but a blindfold, her hair a shining spill of autumn curls, her breasts full and tipped in pink as she lay on her side, her runner's legs long and muscular. Stripes marked the curve of her ass, a sweet reminder of the flogging he'd so thoroughly enjoyed. Her rosy lower lip trembled.

Frank frowned. Probably the guilt again. He lay down facing her and began stroking the rise of one cheekbone under the blindfold. The black silk contrasted starkly against her Celtic-pale skin. "You know, as much as I enjoy a good scene, I love the aftermath just as much. There's just something about feeling a woman go limp . . ."

She sobbed once, then curled her body tight and began to cry in earnest. Deep, tearing sounds of grief and despair that stabbed him right in the heart.

"Alex!" Frank pulled the blindfold off over her head, leaving her brilliant hair to tumble to the comforter in a riot of curls, copper against gold. Tears ran down her reddening cheeks. "Alex, what's—"

He broke off, realizing belatedly why she was crying. And it wasn't from any pain he'd inflicted. She was finally crying for Ted. The sensations he'd created had blasted through the emotional walls she maintained. Just as she'd wanted.

Pulling her close, Frank started murmuring whatever nonsense came into his head. "That's my girl. My good girl . . ."

"It hurts!"

"I know. I know."

She balled her fist and hit his shoulder, but it was a weak blow, rendered powerless by the depth of her grief. "Fucker murdered him, Frank, and there wasn't a damned thing I could do about it. Nothing!"

"No. You'd have saved him if you could have."

"Why? Why did the bastard do it? Ted was a good cop. 'Serve and protect'—it wasn't just a slogan to him. It was everything he was. And that murdering motherfucker killed him because of who he loved!"

Frank stroked her, his heart aching. "I know. They'll catch him."

"*I* want to catch him! I want to go after that Klan son of a bitch and blow his brains all over that sheet he's wearing!"

"Me, too." He combed his fingers through the tangled red silk of her hair. "I want to make him pay for killing a good man. For how you're hurting. For Cal. But Tracy's a good cop. He'll get the bastard."

"But it won't bring Ted back." She lifted her head and met his gaze, her green eyes taking on a gemstone shine behind her tears. "If they catch him, convict him, if they strap him down and pump poison into him until he fucking *dies*, none of it will bring Ted back!"

"No." Frank's heart ached in his chest. "But we can remember him. He's part of you, Alex. You'll always carry a piece of him in you. And so will Cal and his mother, and all the ones who loved him. So will all the people he helped, all the people he served and protected."

"It's not enough!"

"No. But it's all we have."

A lex lay listening to him breathe, limp in the aftermath of the storm of weeping. Long minutes ticked by before she even felt capable of speech again. "Thank you."

He smiled at her, slow and so tender she wanted to cry all over again. "Believe me, the pleasure was mine."

She sniffled, aware suddenly that she probably looked half-drowned. She'd never been pretty when she cried. Frank grabbed a box of tissues from the nightstand and pulled out a fistful, which he handed to her. Alex muttered an incoherent thanks and started wiping everything that ran. "Boy, I'm a buzzkill, aren't I? You gave me the best climax I think I've ever had, and the next thing I know, I'm sobbing like a two-year-old." Balling up the used tissues, she sat up to toss them in the bedside wastebasket, then settled down again with a tear-drugged sigh.

"You needed it, Alex." He gave her hair another slow stroke, his hand so gentle, so kind, it made her eyes well all over again.

"It really was amazing. Hot. Delicious. Just . . . amazing." Which didn't even remotely do it justice, but was still the best she could manage at the moment.

"That it was." Rolling onto his back, he tugged her over to lay her head on his shoulder. She listened to the strong, even thump of his heartbeat, savored the male warmth of him.

"I do have one piece of news." His deep voice rumbled in his chest. "Not sure if you'll think it's good or not."

She made an encouraging hum, stroking one forefinger in circles over the soft fur on his chest, stirring the hair.

"I spoke to the major today. They've assigned me to Ted's area on Charlie shift. I didn't ask for it, but I couldn't really say no either. You think it's going to be a problem, given . . . this?"

Her finger froze before Alex said carefully, "Well, they had to assign somebody to 23. They couldn't leave it unpatrolled." She wasn't sure how she felt about that.

"And I'm the new guy, which means I'm the logical candidate for a third-shift position. Question is, do you mind?"

"No, of course not." The answer was automatic, though she didn't know if it was true. "We may have to keep things professional, especially around Bruce . . ."

"Bruce?"

"Bruce Greer. He's got Charlie 22."

"He's the one who went with us to Cal's last night?"

"Right. We dated in high school, but . . . it didn't end well." Which was a massive understatement if she'd ever made one.

"High school was a long time ago." He paused, lifting a dark brow. "Unless it's not. Does he want to start things up again?" There was a hint of a growl in the question.

She frowned. "I'm not sure. I thought he was starting to get interested again, but then I got involved with Gary and he backed off. Then that ended . . . really, really badly. I wasn't interested in going out with anybody until . . . Well, now, there's you." Alex grinned. "Boy, *is* there you."

"You sure you don't want to keep your options open? He's a good-looking bastard."

"Jealous, Frank?"

"Do I need to be?"

"Considering Bruce is a giant vanilla bean and I'm Rocky Road, hell no."

Frank studied her with narrow eyes. "Are you're concerned he'll get pissed when he realizes we're involved?"

"Probably not. He's about as straitlaced as you can get short of a corset." She frowned. "Sometimes a little too much so, if you know what I mean. I just wanted to make sure you knew the background."

"Yeah, a heads-up is always welcome." Frank stroked a hand down her arm.

Alex closed her eyes, feeling drained after the violent storm of tears. It was like lancing a boil; it hurt, but there was also a sense of relief.

The sound of his heartbeat was so soothing, she felt her eyes drift closed and let herself ride his chest into sleep.

"Alex, wake up," Frank said softly. "We need to get ready for work."

With an effort, she surfaced from a luscious dream of licking her way down his muscled chest. "Oh, God. I do not feel like working. What time is it?"

"Ten o'clock." He grimaced, giving her disordered hair a last stroke before she scrambled off him. He sighed. "My fault for letting us sleep so long. Guess it's dinner from the drive-through. Again."

"Life of a cop, Murphy. We've got two food groups: burgers and Red Bull."

He grinned. "And donuts. Don't forget the donuts."

"Stereotype much?"

"Just because it's a stereotype, that doesn't mean it's not true."

Alex smiled at him. Despite the horror of the murder, it felt good to connect, to joke, to feel like life would go on when the terrible grief abated.

Ted would like that.

A lex made her first patrol of Area 21 that night, absently listening to the voices of her fellow cops over the radio. Especially Frank's, deep and crisp, as he reported pulling over a speeder. Just the sound of him made heat gather in her belly. *Work,* she reminded herself. *Work now, sex later.*

Really, really good sex.

Ted will never have good sex again. She cringed as guilt ambushed her with its sharp fangs of memory and pain. *Do the job. For God's sake, do the job. Concentrate on that, not how much it hurts.* That's *what Ted would want.*

She followed her patrol route until it took her into the Happy Valley Trailer Park. Where she immediately went on the alert. A smart cop did not patrol the collection of aging double-wides with anything less than her full attention.

As Ted had said once, *"You know any place called Happy Valley just has to be a shithole."* And as usual, her mentor had been right. The trailer park was home to gang bangers, drug dealers, hookers, drunks, thieves, and about six different flavors of addicts. And poor elderly people and folks who worked three jobs.

Then there were the children. Way too many children, growing up under the weight of poverty and despair and too-frequent violence.

Alex slowed her black-and-white down to five miles an hour and cruised the rutted gravel road that snaked through the park, sweeping her gaze through the shadows, looking for anyone creeping along where he had no business being.

Huh. Lights were on at 30A Jasmine Drive. Donny

Royce must be up drinking again. Which meant chances were good she'd be answering a call to peel him off Polly before the night was over.

God, she hated domestics. Of course, every cop she knew hated domestics.

Stopping the car, Alex hit the button to roll down the windows and listened. Crickets, frogs, canned television laughter from one of the neighboring trailers, but no yelling or screams. Which meant either that Donny was just having a beer before bed, or he wasn't yet drunk enough to start using his fists on his wife. That might change as the night wore on, but there wasn't anything she could do until and unless he got pissy.

Alex drove slowly away, making a mental note to keep an eye on 30A as the night wore on.

She stopped off at the Gas-N-Go, ostensibly to grab a coffee, but mostly to check on the third-shift clerk, a comfortably plump black woman named Betty who had survived three convenience store robberies. Alex liked to swing by periodically in hopes of discouraging anybody else who might want to target the fifty-year-old.

She paid for her coffee while Betty recounted the latest adventures of the grandson she was raising. He'd made the honor roll, thanks mostly to his grandmother's relentless badgering.

"Don't want the boy to end his days workin' somewhere like this," Betty said, handing Alex her change. "I want him to go to college and make something of himself."

"He's a good kid," Alex assured her, taking a sip of her coffee, "I don't think you've got anything to worry about."

Leaving the store, she headed off on the next leg of the patrol, cruising through another couple of neighborhoods, then checking the rear doors at a local strip mall to make sure none of the shops had been burglarized.

It was then she realized she'd been unconsciously listening for Ted's voice on the radio. Her eyes began to sting as she turned into Happy Valley again.

Alex was headed past 30A when she heard the screaming.

With a soft curse, she braked, threw the car into park, and radioed dispatch for backup. Judging from the drunken curses, she was going to need a hand with Donny Royce.

"No, Donny!" Polly shrieked over the screams of her three young children.

"Fuck." From the sound of it, she couldn't wait for Bruce and Frank to arrive. Flinging the door open, Alex drew her gun and hauled ass for the wooden steps. They rang under her boots as she took them two at a time. "Police!" She hammered a fist on the door hard enough to make it rattle on its hinges. "Open the door, Donny!"

"Get lost, bitch!" Royce roared back. "This ain't none of your business!"

"Help!" a childish voice screamed. "Help my momma! Daddy's hurtin—" A sharp slap, and the girl broke off with a yelp.

Alex tried the door. Dammit, locked. She hated breaking down doors. Using your own leg as a battering ram was never a good idea. Rearing back, she slammed her foot into the wood beside the door handle. It was a cheap lock, but it was harder to kick down a door than cop shows would have you believe. It took her four more kicks to get the door open, accompanied by a rising chorus of screams, curses, and threats from inside the trailer.

At last the door burst wide and Alex ducked inside. She was vaguely conscious of sirens wailing closer, but she was more interested in keeping Donny from beating his relatives to death. None of whom was in sight.

"You keep your fuckin' mouth shut, Polly!" a slurred male voice roared from somewhere farther back in the trailer. Probably a bedroom.

"Police! Mr. Royce, get away from your wife!" Glock pointed at the ceiling, Alex strode through the trailer, past a sagging couch and duct-taped vinyl recliner, stepping over dolls and plastic dinosaurs, Legos grinding underfoot. Her instinct was to run, but that was an invitation to a bullet, and she wasn't in the mood to get shot.

Particularly after what happened to Ted.

Good thing Donny had been too busy beating Polly to blast her while she was kicking in the door. She'd known she was taking a risk while she'd done it, but she hadn't had much choice. Not with the children screaming.

As she'd thought, they were in the back bedroom. Alex found Royce kneeling astride his wife, who was curled in a fetal ball, trying to protect her head with both arms as the big bruiser plowed his fists into any part of her he could reach. A wiry ten-year-old boy hauled fruitlessly on his arm, trying to get him off. The couple's two girls, four and six, huddled crying in the corner. To Alex's fury, one of them cradled a badly bruised face as she sobbed.

Cursing mentally, Alex holstered her gun. No matter how much the son of a bitch deserved a bullet, she couldn't shoot him. She might hit his wife or one of the kids. She could Taser him, but again, there was too much chance of hitting somebody else. She was going to have to do this the really hard way, which meant she was probably going to get a punch in the teeth. Or two. Or four.

In the words of Ted Arlington, *"So you get punched. You're a cop. It's the job."*

Alex grabbed her handcuffs from their belt pouch, jumped on the bed, and snapped at the boy, "Get out of the way!"

The child had seen her coming and was already tumbling clear. She clicked one bracelet of the cuffs on the arm Donny had drawn back to hit his wife.

But before she could apply torque to the captured wrist, he whipped around, snarling at her through the tangled growth of his graying beard, his eyes beady and black with rage. "Bitch! I told you to stay out of this!" His fist slammed into her head before she could block, and she saw stars as she fell on her back, half off the mattress. The taste of blood filled her mouth as she fought to shake off the impact. The bastard could hit like the bull he resembled.

"Where's your little blond fruit friend?" Royce landed astride her and slammed his fist into her jaw. Her teeth cracked together, pain radiating through her skull. "Oh, that's right—he got his brains blown out, didn't he? Couldn't have happened to a nicer homo. Where did either of you hypo-crites get off charging me with shit, after the way he beat on that black boyfriend of his?"

A wave of fury made the pain recede. "You shut your foul, bigoted mouth!" Alex drove a fist into the balls his kneeling position had placed in easy reach. He howled and tumbled off the bed, gagging and clutching himself. She leaped on him, teeth bared, the need for revenge filling her mouth, mixing with the copper taste of her own blood.

Hitting him felt damned good.

CHAPTER NINE

Frank skidded to a halt behind Alex's patrol car, blue lights sweeping over the scene to the banshee wail of the siren. Shrill screams and male bellows rang through the double-wide's thin walls, along with what sounded like Alex's voice shouting orders. Some of his tension eased. If she was yelling, she was okay. Probably.

Another Crown Vic pulled up behind him in a rattling spray of gravel. He wasn't surprised to see Bruce Greer get out of the unit. They exchanged tense glances, and Greer fell in behind Frank as he charged up the wooden stairs with his weapon drawn.

The door was standing open, its jamb splintered. Kicked in. "Dammit, Rogers," he snarled, "why the hell didn't you wait for us?"

"She wouldn't have if she heard a woman or kids yelling," Greer observed.

Frank snarled under his breath. Glock leading the way, he moved through the trailer with the cold skill of more than a decade spent clearing houses and hunting terrorists in Iraq and Afghanistan.

A memory ambushed him: pressing down on Randy Carson's wounded abdomen as blood gushed. Watching his best friend die . . . *Dammit, Alex, I'm going to kick your luscious little ass for this.*

He found her struggling to handcuff a barrel-chested bull of a man, who cursed her viciously as they rolled on the floor. To Frank's utter fury, blood streamed from her cut and swelling lower lip. He holstered his Glock, stepped in, and rammed a fist into the side of the asshole's jaw. The man fell off Alex into a stunned heap. Frank dropped a knee on his back while Bruce knelt on his ass.

As the man spat drunken curses, Alex jerked both his beefy wrists together and snapped the cuffs on. She stood, wiping the blood off her cut lip. Hot rage burned in her green eyes. "You should have hit him harder, Frank. This is the asshole who killed Ted."

Polly scraped her gray-shot chestnut hair back to allow Alex to shoot a cell phone picture of her round, bruised face. She was a short woman who weighed about thirty pounds more than she should, and looked ten years older than Alex knew she was. Evidently marriage to Royce had aged her. "I'd be the first to say Donny's a mean drunk, but he didn't murder that deputy."

"He knew things that haven't been released to the public," Alex told her, looking at the phone's screen. She cursed; the photo was blurry, probably because the adrenaline crash was making her hands shake. Pulling her elbows in close to her ribs to steady her hands, she tried again. Checked the screen. Better.

"Didn't you see the eleven o'clock news?"

Oh, hell, what did the local media get hold of? "I've been at work."

"They had video of that deputy beating on this black man

they said was his lover. That was what set Donny off. He started ranting about y'all bein' hypocrites for arrestin' him for hitting me when the deputy did the same thing."

Alex's stomach dropped into her toes. "Video? Where did they get a video?"

Polly shrugged. "The news said somebody sent them a link. It's on YouTube."

"YouTube?" Conscious of the three shell-shocked little Royce children watching her, Alex managed to bite back her curses. Who the hell had put a video of Ted and Cal sceneing on the Internet? She knew Ted wouldn't have done it, and Cal wasn't that stupid. She supposed it was possible someone had shot it at the party, though the Millers strictly forbade cameras. If that was the case, Cap was going to kill whoever had done it.

Which did Cal, Ted, and the MCSO no damned good whatsoever. The fallout was going to suck. Being gay was bad enough—but being kinky? The scandal was virtually guaranteed to blow up into a shitstorm that could cost the sheriff the next election. Alex and Frank could end up fired if the same asshole had somehow gotten video of them, too.

No, that wasn't likely, she told herself, struggling to control her paranoid panic. Their scenes had been conducted in private.

At least with Frank. The ones with Gary . . . *Oh God, Mom and Dad. If they saw some of the things I did with Gary* . . . She was going to be sick.

Calm the fuck down, Alex told herself, dragging herself back under control. *Don't freak until you have a reason to. Nobody shot any video of me. I would have noticed.*

But who the hell had made the one of Cal and Ted?

Frank and Bruce wrestled the handcuffed Donny Royce through the trailer, planning to stuff him in the backseat of one of patrol cars for his ride to jail. "I'm going to have your badge, bitch!" the man shouted back at Alex, who was talking to his wife. "This is police brutality! You broke my goddamn tooth!"

"Police brutality? Seriously?" Frank growled. "You outweigh Rogers by fifty fucking pounds. The judge will laugh your ass out of court."

Yet Alex had gone up against the beefy bastard by herself. Frank was going to give her a spanking she wouldn't forget. And not the fun kind either.

"I'll take him to jail and get him booked in," Bruce volunteered. "I figure Alex is going to have her hands full with the family."

At that, Royce started blustering again. "You don't tell that bitch anything, Polly, you hear me? You or the kids! Or you'll answer to me!"

"Shut your mouth, asshole," Bruce snapped. "Or I'll show you what real police brutality looks like."

Donny paled and shut up. Like most bullies, he was only tough with somebody he outweighed. He didn't give them any trouble when they stuffed him into the back of Bruce's car.

As Bruce slammed the door, Frank growled, "She's lucky he didn't kill her before we got there. She should have waited for backup."

"Lone Ranger's got nothing on Rogers. Any woman needs rescuing, she's gonna hat up and ride." Something bitter flashed in Bruce's eyes. "She's like her daddy that way."

"That's all well and good, but if you get yourself killed, nobody gets rescued." *Randy Carson's blood gushed over his hands as he tried to hold pressure on the gut wound* . . . It could have been Alex. He didn't want to go through that again.

"You gotta remember, Rogers is compensating for a handicap."

Frank stared. He had examined Alex's pretty body thoroughly, and he hadn't seen a damn thing that needed compensation. "What handicap?"

The deputy grinned. "Tits."

Frank snorted and spoke before he thought. "Believe me, Alex's tits do not constitute a handicap."

Greer lifted a brow as he opened the driver's door. "I never thought so." He drove off, Donny sitting hunched and sullen in the back.

An ambulance rolled in, red lights flashing. Frank led the two paramedics inside, where the Royce kids huddled on the couch, bruised and crying silently. He knew what that felt like—afraid to sob lest it draw the erratic attention of a parent who might take offense.

He found Alex in the trailer's short hallway, talking in low-voiced tones to the children's mother.

"No, you're right," the woman was saying, to Alex's obvious satisfaction. "I'm leaving the son of a bitch. It's one thing for him to take his shit out on me, but this time he hurt the kids. I'm done."

"That's definitely the smartest thing you could do. If you don't get out now, it will only get worse. I can take you to the women's shelter tonight, but there are other county programs that can help you find a job, get an apartment . . ."

"Actually, I think I'm going to leave town." Determination filled the eye that hadn't swollen shut. "My brother lives in California—works for a Silicon Valley startup. He's told me a bunch of times he'd take me and the kids in when I decided to get the hell away from Donny."

"That might be wise. Sometimes a clean start somewhere else is safest in situations like this."

"Yeah," Polly said grimly. "It's when you leave that men like Donny try to kill you."

Alex winced. Frank wondered why; it was true, though he hadn't wanted to say so in front of the children. He started to offer to help gather the family's things, but Alex turned to him. "Fr—" She broke off and corrected herself, "Deputy Murphy, would you mind covering our areas while I take Mrs. Royce and her children to the shelter?"

"Of course." He gave her a cool look. "I do have something to discuss with you when you get time."

A trace of wariness lit her green gaze. "Ah. Sure."

Turning, he stalked out.

* * *

B radfield Auto Seating was a small firm that specialized in manufacturing leather seat and wheel covers. Since the facility didn't operate a third shift, that left its loading dock unoccupied from midnight to 7 a.m. For the past couple of years, Ted, Bruce, and Alex had been in the habit of parking there between calls, since it was located on the border where the three patrol areas met. The garage was a good place to write the reports policing always generated. There was room in the loading dock for the deputies to park the cars three abreast and work. Tonight, of course, the third car sitting in the darkened garage wasn't Ted's, but Frank's.

That realization gave Alex a pang when she arrived at Bradfield after delivering Polly Royce and her children to the Sharon Mayhew Crisis Shelter. Polly's brother had already gone online to buy plane tickets for her and the kids. They'd be out of Donny's reach before he knew what hit him. Polly would go to court to seek a divorce and custody. She had ample documentation to show he was an abusive prick, so she should have no trouble getting it. Especially since Alex had made sure to take cell phone photos documenting the children's injuries.

Alex was writing the incident report on her unit's laptop when she heard Bruce drive off on a patrol of his area. No sooner had he left than Frank rapped on the passenger window. Rolling it down, Alex gave him a grin. "Well, hello, handsome . . ."

"Unlock the door," he growled.

Her brows lifting, she obeyed, watching as he dropped into the passenger seat and slammed the door before giving her a hot look. "What. The. Fuck?" he snarled. He wasn't just irritated, she realized. He looked downright furious, his sexy mouth tight, his gray eyes stormy.

"What? What are you talking about?"

"You couldn't wait five minutes for me to get there before charging into the goddamn trailer? What if that bastard had a gun?"

"Donny? He does have a gun. More than one, in fact."

"That does not make it better! Did it not occur to you he could have shot you?"

"I was more worried he'd shoot his wife and children. They were screaming their lungs out when I drove up. I wasn't sure how far away you were or how quickly you'd arrive. I didn't think—"

"No, you *didn't* think. What good does it do to go riding to the rescue like the frickin' Lone Ranger if you get your ass blown out of the saddle?"

She was starting to get as pissed off as he obviously was. "Frank, I'm not going to sit in the damned car with my thumb up my butt while innocent people are in danger. That is not what the sheriff pays me to do."

"He doesn't pay you to get shot either."

"Would we be having this conversation if I had a dick?"

"I wouldn't be sleeping with you if you had a dick!"

"What the hell does that have to do with anything?"

"What do you think Ted would have to say about this little stunt?"

"That it's my damned job!" She took a deep breath. "Look, I usually do wait for backup—I'm not stupid. But if I think somebody may end up getting badly hurt before my backup can arrive, I'm not going to wait. And somehow, I don't think you would either."

"I can handle a guy like Royce a lot more easily than you can."

"Maybe, but you're no more bulletproof than I am." She glowered at him. "I'm a cop. One way or another, I'm going to do the job. If that means taking a calculated risk to keep innocent people safe, I'll take the fucking risk. I know you're not used to working with women, but you're going to have to deal. I will not quit doing whatever my judgment tells me is necessary because you don't like me taking a chance. Especially not because I happen to be female!"

"Look, it's not just because you're female, okay?" He muttered a frustrated curse and looked away. For a moment he stared out the windshield, visibly wrestling with his temper. "Right before I left the Navy, my team was hunting an ISIS terrorist. Bastard named Asad Abd al Jabbar, who had the charming habit of sending truck bombs into girls' schools."

Alex frowned, taken off-guard by the sudden topic change. "Sounds like he needed killing."

"Actually, we were trying to capture him, and we did. But his buddies wanted him back bad, and we found ourselves having to fight our way out. My friend Randy Carson took a round in the abdomen—tore him all to hell. I put pressure on it, but he bled out before the helo got to us. I watched him die, and there wasn't a single fucking thing I could do about it."

Pain rang in his voice, the echo of old grief. Alex felt her eyes sting in sympathy. "He sounded like a good friend." *Like Ted.*

"Yeah. The best. A hell of a man. We went to BUD/S together—we got each other through Hell Week." BUD/S was the legendary Basic Underwater Demolition/SEAL training course that graduated only a fraction of its recruits. Hell Week was a big reason why, as recruits were forced to endure the worst their SEAL instructors could throw at them. "Randy saved my life twice, once in Iraq, again in Pakistan, but I couldn't save his." He looked at her. "One minute he was kicking ass, the next he was dying. I don't want to watch you die, Alex. After what happened to Ted, I'm sure you understand. Yeah, we're cops. Risk is part of the job. But you shouldn't make the risk greater by taking chances."

She sighed, feeling her anger drain away. This wasn't the kind of infuriating sexism she'd fought her whole life; he was expressing genuine concern. And after what she'd gone through finding Ted's body, she didn't want him dealing with the same futile guilt if she screwed up and got herself killed. "I'll keep that in mind."

Frank nodded. "Do that." He straightened his broad shoulders. "I'd better go patrol."

She watched as he got out of the car, slid into his own, and drove away.

* * *

"Trouble in paradise," Bruce murmured. "Bet that stung, huh, Alex? Now you know how it feels."

He had bugged Alex's car after Gary had told him what she and Ted had done to him. He'd hoped the son of a bitch was lying. Instead, Arlington and Alex had condemned themselves.

Alex was every bit as perverted as her idol. She, Ted, and Cal went to disgusting sex parties every time they got the chance.

God, he ached to take a whip to Alex's tight little ass. Fantasized about making her scream—and not with pleasure. He ached to make her pay. Make her parents pay.

One day soon he'd get his chance.

As for Arlington, he'd been a blot on the badge. Which was why Bruce had taken it away. Now that same badge leaned against his father's photo. Dad would have been delighted. He'd hated cops almost as much as he did Blacks, Mexicans, and Jews.

Bruce would take Alex out next. That would really stick it to the Coach, wouldn't it? Fit revenge.

Her badge would join Ted's, and her parents would suffer as they deserved.

Alex returned to the plant garage after the last patrol of the night. The bruises from her fight with Donny were making themselves felt. She was trying to decide whether she'd rather have a couple of Advil or a glass of wine after she got home when Frank knocked on her window again.

Given their last conversation, she felt more than a little wary as she unlocked the door and watched him slide into the passenger seat.

He stared out across the car's hood at the darkened loading dock. "I've been thinking about our little discussion . . ."

Alex snorted. "Don't you mean knock-down-drag-out fight?"

Frank smiled slightly. "Yeah, okay. Fight. I was out of line. I wasn't there when you rolled up—I don't know what you heard. If I'd thought a woman and children were being hurt, I wouldn't have waited for backup either. And you're right—if Bruce had done the same thing, I wouldn't have chewed him out for it. For one thing, I'm the junior partner on this team. You've got five years' more experience being a cop than I do, regardless of the decade I spent hunting Taliban tangos."

"But you're also my Dom, and you've got a protective streak wider than your killer shoulders."

He grinned at that, suddenly boyish. "Yeah, I am your Dom, and I am protective. Maybe even overprotective. Goes with the territory." Cool gray eyes took on a dark male glitter. "And I reserve the right to punish you suitably for scaring the shit out of me."

Heat rushed through Alex like a sudden spring flood. "What have you got in mind?"

He smiled, a slow revelation of white teeth. "You like to hunt?"

Not precisely. She'd never enjoyed shooting animals. But hunting was a sort of male bonding ritual. For her fellow deputies, it was an excuse to get together somewhere other than work, drink beer, and participate in an activity where you didn't have to talk—involving guns. In other words, the perfect cop sport.

So Alex hunted, though she did so these days more for the chance to hone her skill at hitting a moving target. Judging by that grin, though, she suspected Frank had something else in mind. "Yeah, I hunt, but it's not deer season."

"Actually, I didn't plan on you being the one doing the hunting."

"I have no desire to play Bambi's mother."

"There'll be no weapons involved, of course. Just you, me, and the woods in back of my house. And possibly a whip or two."

That's what she'd thought—which was why heat had gathered in a tight ball between her thighs. "In that case," she drawled, unable to resist the shameless deer pun, "I am feeling a little horny."

When Alex got off shift, she went home to take a shower and dress. Remembering Polly Royce's comment about the video, she gave Cal a call.

"Did you see the news?" her friend asked before she even had time to say hello. He sounded tense.

"Uh, no, but I did hear they ran some kind of YouTube thing of you and Ted sceneing." She frowned. "And how the hell did they put a sex tape on the evening news?"

"We were actually dressed, thank God. It cut out before we got around to the sex part." He sighed. "But what they did run was bad enough. I had to delete my Facebook and Twitter accounts. The shit people were saying about Ted . . ." His voice broke. "God, Alex . . . None of those fuckers knew him, but they were all saying he had it coming. Even the people who aren't bigots keep asking how I could let a white man beat me like that. My sister thinks I'm going to hell."

Alarmed, Alex demanded, "Is that the sister you're staying with? Do you need to come stay with me for a while?"

"No, Jaz doesn't really get the BDSM thing, but she's okay with whatever makes me happy. At least, that's what she said after I convinced her Ted never hurt me." He made a low sound of pain in his throat. "No, the one who's freaking is my older sister, Laticia. She said she's not sure she wants me coming around my nephews anymore."

Rage tightened Alex's hands into fists. "That . . . *bitch!*"

"Well, vanilla people just don't understand kink, Alex. And anything they don't understand . . ."

"But implying you might be some kind of fucking pedophile . . ."

"Yeah." His voice dropped, went soft. "That hurt."

"Look, you want to go have lunch later, or . . ."

"No. Not today. Maybe . . . maybe later. I've got an interview scheduled with Cassie York. You know, the *Courier* blogger? I want to tell my side of it."

"Are you sure that's a good idea? I like Cassie, but she is a reporter . . ."

"And Ted hated reporters. I know." His chuckle sounded like there were tears in it. "But she's fair, and she swears she's not going to use me as her ticket to her fifteen minutes of fame." His voice dropped and went bitter. "Or in my case, infamy."

If anyone could understand Ted and Cal's relationship, it would be Cassie. Her friend had mentioned attending the bondage club in Charlotte a couple of times. Even so, Alex had kept her mouth shut about her own kinky streak. She and Cassie might be friends, but with media types, you never knew what bombs they might throw. "Tell her if she's not good to you, I'll beat her up."

Cal laughed. "And you would, too. Are you going to the visitation on Friday?" It would be an opportunity for friends and family to view Ted's body at the funeral home and pay their respects to his family.

"I'm going to the funeral, but I was planning to attend the visitation, too. Will you be there?"

"Yeah. Ted's mother asked me to sit with her. I'm still trying to make up my mind." Ted had been Out to his widowed mother, who'd often invited Cal and Alex to Sunday dinner. That, however, was very different from sitting in the midst of Ted's family as though Cal were his spouse. His young, *black* spouse.

Alex winced. "Yeah, that would be a lot like waving the proverbial red flag in front of the bull."

"More like a rainbow flag." She could hear the ghost of humor in his voice. "What do you think I should do?"

She hesitated. "That kind of depends. You think you're up to dealing with the blowback?"

"To be honest, I don't know. On the one hand, I feel as if not sitting with her implies I'm ashamed of loving him— which I'm damned well not. On the other hand, people can get really fucking vicious to folks who don't follow the script of what they consider normal. And I'm feeling more than a little fragile just now." His voice cracked, as if he was about to cry again.

"Of course you are. You need to do what's best for you, Cal. I know if Ted were here, that's what he'd tell you to do."

"That does sound like him." He was definitely crying now, his voice hoarse and breaking.

"Whatever you decide, I'll be there for you. You won't be alone. People really thought a lot of Ted . . ."

"They did before last night. Maybe not so much if they saw that damned YouTube thing."

"I swear to God, if I ever found out who shot that, I'm going to knock their teeth in."

There was a pause before Cal spoke again. "Alex, something's bothering me about that."

"Yeah?"

"It was shot in Ted's bedroom, but neither of us had anything to do with it. Another thing—the angle's from really high, like around the ceiling over by the door. Almost like surveillance video, but Ted didn't have a surveillance system."

A chill stole over Alex's skin. "So who shot it, and who the hell posted it?"

Cal asked the question she was thinking. "Could it have been the killer?"

"I don't know, but I think I'll have a long talk with Detective Tracy."

"He called last night after the segment ran. Asked if we shot it."

"Did he believe you when you said you hadn't?"

"I don't know. He's pretty hard to read."

"Well, he's a violent crimes detective. They have to have pretty good poker faces. I think I'll ask him if he searched Ted's house for that camera. Don't know if he'll tell me anything, but I'll ask."

"Thanks, Alex. The idea that his killer might have planted some kind of hidden camera in Ted's bedroom . . . That's just . . ."

"Terrifying."

"Yeah." His voice sounded thick with tears.

"Cal, if there's anything I can do . . . If you need anything, need a place to stay, anything . . . All you have to do is ask."

"I don't think that'll be necessary, doll, but I appreciate it."

"I mean it, don't hesitate. There's nothing I can do for Ted now—except help you. I want to be able to do something." She felt her eyes sting with a sudden burst of frustration and rage. "I didn't catch that bastard, Cal. I can't catch him now—I'm not a detective. I can't access the evidence, I can't talk to witnesses, I can't do shit. If I can help you in any way, at least I won't feel so fuckin' useless."

"You're not useless, Alex. Ted loves . . . loved you. He thought you were one hell of a cop. And from everything I've heard, everything I've seen, he had good reason to think so."

"Thank you, Cal." She dashed tears off her face. "That means a lot."

"And listen, I will call you if there's anything you can do." He sighed. "Just knowing I've got one good friend in this town helps more than I can say."

"Not just one, babe. But stay the hell off the Internet, would you? It doesn't do you any good to read that crap. Who cares what those idiots think anyway?"

"Good point." But there was pain in his voice, and she knew that whatever ignorant comments he'd read had hurt.

"Love you, babe."

Now she heard the shadow of a smile in his voice. "Love you, too, PoPo."

They said good-bye and hung up.

Alex sat there a moment, feeling battered by grief—both her own and Cal's. She needed to see that damned video.

But . . . She thought of Frank and his dark, seductive smile. She found herself craving the distraction he offered. She knew the video would only exacerbate her grief and rage, making it impossible to enjoy the escape she'd find in Frank's arms. There would be time enough later to wallow in that helpless, futile pain.

For now, she wanted Frank. Needed Frank.

*   *   *

Alex arrived at Frank's house an hour later, showered and dressed in pants and tee in hunting camouflage.

Good thing it was still relatively warm in the Upstate this time of year, or naked fun time would be right out.

When she knocked, she heard his deep voice from inside the house. "Come on in."

Entering, she stopped dead and blinked. He leaned against the foyer wall, six and a half feet of muscle in combat boots, jungle cami pants, and a T-shirt in the same pattern. But what drew her up short was the green, black, and brown paint that covered his face in irregular, asymmetrical splotches, giving him the savage look of some kind of twenty-first-century barbarian. His gray eyes gleamed in the midst of that paint, lupine and hungry.

"Hi," he purred, the Big Bad Wolf to Little Red Riding Hood.

Something about the look on his face made everything below her waist clench in primitive need. "Hi." Her voice sounded embarrassingly throaty. "Interesting"—she had to stop and swallow—"costume."

"I thought you'd like it." He took a long, lazy pace toward her. Something about the way he looked at her made her feel stalked. "What're your safewords?"

"Red for stop, yellow for slow down, green for 'Oh God, harder.'"

"Heh. Cute. You can defend yourself this time—if you can. Blows at half strength, like in combat practice. Once I get you pinned, you're mine. Any objections?"

She licked dry lips. "No."

"Any injuries I need to know about?"

"A couple of bruises from playing rodeo clown to Donny Royce's bull, but nothing that would keep us from sceneing."

"You sure about that?" He looked her over, gray eyes flicking over her in their mask of war paint. "If I hurt you because you're lying about a strained muscle, I'm going to be one pissed-off Dom."

"Nothing like that."

Frank paused a long moment, eyeing her before he finally nodded. "All right." Turning, he led the way through the cool dimness of the house and out the glass French doors into the bright morning sunlight. "You've got a ten-minute head start." He showed her his teeth, flashing against the jungle paint. "I'm going to be seriously disappointed if you don't give me a good chase."

She gave him a deliberately cheeky grin in return. "Oh, I'll give you a chase, Frank. Hell, you could find yourself the one hog-tied."

He laughed, the sound of it more than a little sinister. "Better run now, little girl. Before I get pissed off."

She ran.

CHAPTER TEN

Frank watched her bound off like a startled deer, all flashing legs and lithe grace. Her ass was a thing of beauty working behind the fabric of her pants. He was hard as a hammer, his cock bulging rebelliously against the tyranny of his fly.

Damn, she got to him. Common sense and caution didn't stand a chance against his desire. Never mind that he'd had her just yesterday—and explored some of his favorite fantasies in the process. He craved her just as recklessly now.

Some of it was the kind of games they played, so different from the usual tie-her-up-and-beat-her-ass scenarios he'd done with previous subs. Not that he didn't love watching Alex's lovely rump turn pink under his flogger, but somehow the mock fights were so much kinkier.

Frank bided his time with considerable difficulty, forcing himself to give her the head start he'd promised. He'd always been the master of his body, despite its sometimes violent clamor for rest, or water, or food. Or sex. He ruled it, not the other way around. Kept his focus on his mission, ignoring any animal demands like the growl currently coming from his balls.

When he judged the promised time had passed, Frank moved after her, giving her plenty of time to build the lead he'd permitted her.

He wanted to work for this.

Frank trailed Alex for as long as he could tolerate the delay, until he decided they'd both had enough. Listening with a warrior's keen attention, he heard her moving ahead, a faint rustling in the underbrush, her booted step crunching the autumn leaves. Pines filled the air with the smell of resin and green needles. He imagined that scent overlaid by the musk of woman and sex, and his cock jerked.

Lengthening his stride, he bit into her lead, hungry to put his hands on her. Hungry to take her here in the woods as birds chirped and the wind sighed in the bright trees, sending maple leaves swirling down around them. Hungry to taste her skin, to feel it silken soft under his hands, to feel that surprisingly strong, athletic body of hers straining against his. She'd fight him, green eyes bright and a little bloodthirsty, red hair flying. Everything he wanted, everything his body craved, female to his male.

Alex wasn't far ahead now, moving just short of a run as if sensing he was right behind her, would have her in minutes. He could almost feel her blend of eagerness and that delicious feminine wariness. Not true fear—she had to know he'd cut his arm off before he'd actually hurt her. But the thought of her erotic dread stoked his lust to a crackling blaze.

She wouldn't make it easy for him. He couldn't wait.

Alex could almost feel Frank on her heels, those pale eyes savage in their mask of paint. She thought she heard the tread of a combat boot, the passage of a big body through the brush, but she wasn't sure. She'd known plenty of hunters, but never anyone who moved with such deadly stealth.

A man who'd done his killing in a desert had no business

being so fucking quiet in an environment where every tree, bush, and dead leaf could give him away. Yet Frank might as well have been a panther. His silence had the effect of winding her up like a watch spring, tighter and tighter with the anticipation of his sudden male rush.

There. The crunch of dried leaves under a man's weight. She pivoted toward the sound, tensing, waiting to see him come for her. Waiting. Annnnnd . . .

Nothing.

Swallowing a sigh of disappointment, she turned.

He towered over her, broad as a wall, his gray eyes patient and primal, staring from asymmetrical slashes of black and green.

Alex froze, staring up at him, her heart vaulting into her throat. One tick of her mental stopwatch. Two.

She turned to sprint away—one tick too late. He hit her, twisting as he took her down so she fell on him rather than the other way around. Alex attacked as they landed, ramming an elbow into the underside of his jaw. His teeth snapped together with the force of the impact as she jerked free, rolled upright. She was faster than he was, more agile. If she could get any lead at all . . .

A hand fisted in her waistband and jerked her right off her feet. She slammed into his body on her back, and his arms and legs snapped around her like a bear trap, unyielding as steel.

He chuckled in her ear. "Now what are you going to do?"

"Well, I'm sure as fuck not giving up." Though she wanted to. She really, really wanted to, especially with that tempting erection nudging her ass. Digging an elbow into his gut, she threw herself to the side, levering herself out of his grip and popping to her feet. Almost escaping.

Almost.

Dead leaves crunched and crackled in an explosion of moment. An arm swept around Alex from behind, hooking her shoulder as a leg curled between her thighs, jerking one of them out from under her. Frank's weight came down on her like the wrath of God, crushing her facedown on the leafy ground. Inhaling, she got a breath of mold and loam and hungry male. And heard him chuckle, deliciously menacing.

"Dammit!" She clawed at the ground but failed to get any purchase at all. He immobilized both her legs by coiling his own around them. Long fingers encircled her wrist, jerked it behind her back and up toward her shoulder blade, sending pain blasting up the bone like a lightning strike. She turned her head and went for his biceps with her teeth, only to have him drag the wrist higher. A yelp tore from her lips despite her best intentions.

"Now," he rumbled in her ear, "don't you think you'd better give up?"

Oh, God, yes. Especially considering his hard, intoxicating masculinity. And that cock . . . She went limp. "All right, all right—you win!"

Frank laughed. "Do I look like that big a sucker?" His tone hardened. "Give me your other hand."

Dammit. Alex writhed—rubbing herself against that maddening dick while she was at it. He still didn't release the white-hot pressure on her captured arm. She knew he wouldn't actually break it, but he obviously wasn't in the mood for mercy either. "Give it up, Alex," he growled. "I want that hand."

She spat a curse and twisted her free arm back to let him capture it. Sheepskin encircled her wrists, accompanied a moment later by the ring of the buckle and sharp tugs as he bound them, the chain between the two cuffs rattling. He stood and helped her to her feet. Before she could thank him for his chivalry, he spun her to face him, then reached for the snap of her pants. Gray eyes narrowed in a mask of cami paint, he stared down into her face as he unzipped her and caught her waistband. She couldn't seem to tear her gaze away as he bent to pull the pants down to her mid-thighs. Cool morning air caressed her bare ass; she hadn't worn underwear.

Alex licked her lips. Was he going to fuck her now? Here, in the leaves, where anybody could happen by . . .

Frank straightened and picked her up as easily as she'd

have lifted her cat, then swung her across one shoulder in a fireman's carry. Frustrated hunger drove her to try to knee him in the jaw despite the encumbering pants that bound her thighs.

"Alex," Frank growled, low and rumbling. Her nipples tightened. "I've caught you. Now, what are you?"

Stubbornly, she refused to answer. A broad palm came down on her naked rump in a swat hard enough to make her yelp. "Answer me, sub!"

"Yours! I'm yours, you son of a bitch."

"Is that what you call me?" Another swat, even harder.

"Master! I'm yours, Master!" God, she loved his snarls.

"And don't you fucking forget it." He started through the woods, carrying her like Tarzan making off with Jane. If anybody came along, they'd see her bare ass, the plump swell of her pussy lips . . . Oh, God, the thought made her even hotter.

To distract herself from the clawing need rising in her belly, she asked, "Where are we going?"

Another swat. "You'll find out—eventually."

Dangling head down over Frank's broad shoulder, Alex felt her arousal grow, thickening like sugar water coming to a boil. "How the hell do you do this to me?"

"Do what?"

There was that growl again. "Make me so damned hot, even when you're beating my ass and generally being a dominant asshole."

He laughed, low and rough. "We want what we want. Pussies aren't politically correct." His palm hit her ass again. "God knows dicks aren't."

She kicked at the sting, but couldn't get any force with her pants down around her thighs, binding her as effectively as the leather cuffs around her wrists. "What the hell was that for?"

"My amusement. Just like this." His palm slid over her burning ass, a finger sliding between the petals of her pussy. With a growl in satisfaction at the cream he found there, he sent a second finger to join the first. His hand pumped in a delicious sliding friction that made her groan in raw need. "Jesus, you make me hot. I can't wait to fuck you."

She closed her eyes as the rough words, tongue flicking out to lick dry lips. "Do it now. Right now."

"You making demands, sub?"

She couldn't resist. "Oh, hell yeah."

Frank gave her precisely what she was angling for. The next swat was followed by five more, all of them so hard she had to grit her teeth against the need to squall like a two-year-old. His voice was low and dark when he finally finished. "Any demands, sub, come from me." Another stinging slap, even harder. "Got that?"

"Yeah. Oh, yeah." Panting, Alex went limp over his hard shoulder, trying to distract herself from her clawing hunger by listening to the sound of his even breathing and the sigh of the cool wind through the pines. Birds sang as her ass stung. He was moving faster now, as if spurred by hunger, his boots crunching through dry leaves. No longer taking the slow care that silence required. "God, Frank," she sighed, savoring the burn in her butt.

Damn, she was kinky. And fuck if she cared. Frank was right; she had a politically incorrect pussy.

He turned his head and gave her bared hip a promising lick and the slow glide of two fingers into her sex. She groaned.

By the time he finally stopped, she was so wet she wouldn't have been surprised if she dripped. He swung her down to stand on a sleeping bag spread over some kind of padding, her pants still at half-mast around her thighs. "On your knees." The savage heat in Frank's eyes was enough to weaken her legs; kneeling was the only way to avoid falling on her face, so she obeyed. "Don't you move," he growled, and reached over her head. Looking up, she saw some kind of complicated arrangement of straps hanging from a pulley, in turn attached to a thick tree limb by another wide leather strap. A rope ran from the harness to thread through the pulley, then down to a second, lower limb. He untied it and lowered the strap arrangement, which she realized must be some kind of harness. "Arms up."

When Alex obeyed, Frank attached the leather belt of the harness to her waist. A thick strap led upward to another set of bands, which he buckled around her upper arms. He clipped the cuffs around her wrists to the belt with a carabiner.

"Suspension?" She'd never enjoyed that particular kink, mostly because her previous Dom had never been all that good with knots. Gary's idea of Shibari—Japanese rope bondage— had mostly been an exercise in frustration while he struggled to straighten tangled ropes, cursing the whole time. Then there was the very real fear that the hook he'd screwed into the ceiling would tear free as she hung helplessly from it, resulting in broken bones. Or worse.

Frowning, Frank stared into her face and broke character. "You need to use your safeword?"

Alex hesitated. He was a hell of a lot more competent than Gary; even after such a brief acquaintance, she knew he'd make damn sure anything he did posed no threat to her. She relaxed. "No, I'm good."

"You sure? Because I'm not going to be pissed if you've got a problem."

She glanced at the leather cuffs around her waist, arms, and the tree overhead. They all looked thick and well cared for, as did the rope that ran through the pulley to the tree. "Everything looks good."

He eyed her. "That dumb son of a bitch dropped you, didn't he?"

She knew he'd be seriously pissed if she lied and he found out about it. And he probably would; she'd told Joanna, Cap's wife, about the accident. "Yeah. Hook came out of the ceiling. Luckily I didn't break anything." Had suffered one hell of a sprain, though, not that she intended to tell Frank that.

"Okay—red." He reached for the harness belt around her waist and started unbuckling it.

"Wait," Alex said. "What are you doing?"

"Using my safeword, since you're evidently too proud to do it yourself." He straightened and looked down at her. There was absolutely no anger in his eyes. "You don't know me well enough to trust me to do something that injured you with a previous Dom."

"No, don't safeword." Ignoring her instinctive protest, he went back to unbuckling the harness. "I don't want to ruin the scene. Look, if I really had a problem with suspension, I would have included it on my hard-limits list." During their e-mail "courtship," they'd sent each other the lists of things they wouldn't even consider doing—at Cap's suggestion—before they'd even formally met at his house. Like safewords, exchanging hard-limits lists let kinksters avoid misunderstandings and outright injury.

Having freed her arms, he folded the harness and turned to put it in his toy bag. "Alex, whenever we play, I want you driven half out of your mind with lust, not worrying if I'm going to hurt you by being as careless as that stupid motherfucker Gary." Reaching up, he unbuckled the pulley from the tree limb, wound the chain around it, and stuffed the whole thing back in his bag. Straightening, he gave her a wicked grin. "And you haven't ruined the scene. I'm still going to bang your brains out."

"But . . ."

"You know the rules, Alex. Once somebody safewords, that's it. You don't argue. Everything stops."

"But that's subs!"

"Applies just as well for Doms. Yeah, it's rarer that we do it, but if a Dom thinks his sub is endangering herself—physically or psychologically—he's got a duty to call a halt. Which I just did." He cupped her cheek in a big, warm hand. "I take care of my subs, Alex. Whether it's making sure a hook is properly embedded in a ceiling joist, or using my safeword. That's what good Doms do."

"Yeah, I know—but you put a lot of thought into this scene, and I—"

"Alex, shut the fuck up," he growled in his Big Bad Dom voice. His mouth crashed down on hers in a kiss that had her grabbing his brawny shoulders to keep from falling on her ass.

Which was basically a waste of time, because his boot hooked around her ankle and jerked left. She toppled, but he caught her, carrying her down on the padded sleeping bag. An instant later, she found herself pinned by well over two hundred pounds of horny Dom. Judging by the bulge she could feel against her belly, safewording hadn't done a damn thing to kill his libido.

His tongue slid between her gasping lips in a thrusting demand that reignited her own need. When she yielded, he eased up to lick and swirl along lips and teeth and tongue, suckling and playing until she went limp under him. One hand promptly swept up under her tee to discover her breasts. "No bra," he groaned against her mouth in obvious approval. His fingers pinched and tugged, sending delicious little sparks through her system.

"God, Frank . . ." she moaned. "You drive me insane!"

"Good." Straightening away from her mouth, he used his free hand to jerk the tee up over the curve of her breasts, baring her nipples to his flaming gaze. "You fuck up my head, too."

With a satisfied growl, he engulfed her nipple, suckling so hard, the pleasure damn near blinded her. He gave her pull after delicious pull even as his tongue circled and danced over the tight little peak. *Christ, he's good.*

By the time Frank pulled away, Alex was panting. Cool air blew over her wet, liberated nipple as he went to work on her boots, untying them with hands that weren't quite steady, then pulling them off and pitching them over her head. They hit the leaves with a rustle and thump. As soon as they were gone, he grabbed her pants and stripped them off, then sent them sailing after the boots. Bracing on her elbows, she sat up to watch as he shoved her thighs apart and dove between her spread thighs. His mouth covered her pussy with delicious gluttony.

Alex threw back her head with a gasp at the sensation of his hot tongue working between her vaginal lips. Its agile wet tip circled her clit skillfully, not quite touching it, then swept down to swirl around the opening of her cunt before trailing down over her perineum. Then up again for another maddening circuit.

As if that wasn't enough to drive her out of her mind, two fingers slid into her pussy and went straight to the hidden bundle of nerves that was her G-spot. She panted, tossing her head, teeth gritted as she fought a scream that would have the neighbors calling 911.

"Jesus, Frank!" Gasping, she hunched against his face, all control blasted to eggshell fragments.

His eyes flicked up at her, possessive and pale in their demonic mask of cami paint, now smudged by contact with her body. She was probably wearing most of it by now, not that she cared.

All she cared about were those wicked fingers, that clever tongue. And the lust that blazed in his eyes like a torch in the dark. He went on licking, alternating his tongue work with gentle, arousing nibbles and deep finger-thrusts. Until he pulled his hand free and slid a slick forefinger up her ass.

"Frank!" Alex cried, writhing at the ferociously intense sensation.

Lifting his head from her pussy, he watched his finger glide in and out. Added a second one, scissoring the two apart to make her stretch and sting. She tossed her head on the sleeping bag.

"You've got a nice tight ass, baby." He dropped his voice to a growl. "I want it." His gaze flicked up to hers, took in her stunned, anxious expression. He grinned. "But I think I'll save it for later. I want pussy now."

With that, he sat up, pulled his hand away from her body, and unzipped his pants to pull out his cock. She stared at it like a hypnotized rabbit as he found a condom in his toy bag and sheathed himself. Grabbing her thighs, Frank hauled them over his shoulders—she assumed so he could get at all sorts of pink territory down there. Instead he grabbed her ass and slid onto his knees, lifting her butt well off the sleeping bag. An instant later, he fed the endless length of his thick cock into her slick, swollen opening, and thrust hard and deep. Alex sucked in a breath at being so mercilessly stuffed.

"Give me your hands," he snapped, once he was in to the root.

She obeyed. He caught them and pinned them beside her head. Teeth bared, Frank shifted his bodyweight, rolling her up onto her shoulders. Sliding his thighs up behind her back, he braced her into position and began to fuck, grinding his cock even deeper. Alex was completely pinned now, unable to move. Impaled on Frank's thick shaft.

"God, this is hot," she moaned.

Frank's only response was a flash of white teeth in the mask of paint—and a deeper thrust that seemed to send his dick past her bellybutton. She could only writhe in blind pleasure, loving the way he used her so ruthlessly.

Frank fucked her hard, making her breasts dance and waves of dark pleasure/pain ripple up her spine. "You know," he gritted through his teeth, "I think I'll fuck your ass like this. Good and deep."

Her eyes widened. She'd done anal sex a couple of times with Gary—he'd demanded it—but she'd never really enjoyed the act. Yet the thought of Frank taking her like that . . .

He bared those teeth at her again. "Yeah, I knew you'd like that idea."

Deliberately, he circled his hips as he entered again, raking his dick over her G-spot in the process even as his pelvis pressed hard at just the right spot to stimulate her plump clit.

She came, bucking at the savage delight of it, screaming like her car's siren. Somebody was definitely going to call 911.

And Alex did not give a damn. All she cared about was Frank's cock. So deep. So good . . .

Frank watched Alex come, crying out, her beautiful face wearing an expression of blind pleasure he found every bit as arousing as the tight grip of her cunt. Which was saying a lot, because her pussy felt so good, he was hanging on to his self-control by his ragged fingernails. He'd managed to roll her into a ball that made her feel even tighter than she normally was. And delicious little sub that she was, she loved being so thoroughly helpless—held down and fucked.

God knew he loved doing it to her. Watching those pretty breasts bounce with his deep thrusts, red hair flying around her face as she tossed her head in helpless reaction. The way she pulled the hand that pinned both her wrists to the sleeping bag, as if trying to escape.

And failing.

Oh, Jesus God, it was hot.

Screaming, she used her strong thighs to lift her contorted body and grind against him. That kicked him right over. Fire streamed out of his tormented balls and up the length of his cock in hot pulses. That snug little pussy clamped around his cock, her silken body grinding against his with such surprising strength . . .

Lust and pleasure beating at his brain, he came and came and came.

When the storm was finally over, they were both sweat-slick and shaking. His heart banged furiously in his chest as he hung his head, gasping as he tried to gather enough strength to pull away. Managing it at last, Frank groaned as he drew his cock carefully out of her pussy so as not to lose the condom. "You'll be the death of me yet, woman." He sat back on his heels and pulled his toy bag closer, so he could slide the used condom into a Ziploc bag he carried for that purpose. Grinning up at her, he added, "But it'll take the mortuary three days to get the grin off my face."

Alex wrinkled her nose at him. "Eeeew."

"Yeah, deal with it. You okay?" He studied her as he remembered the merciless way he'd fucked her. "I didn't hurt you, did I?"

"God, no." She sat up on the blanket, using one hand to sweep her hair out of her face. "Though I didn't see that many stars the last time I got hit in the head with a beer bottle." Noticing his lifted brows, she added, "Typical haul-the-drunks-to-jail Saturday night."

"Ah," he said, though the idea of somebody slamming a bottle upside that pretty face made him want to kick some ass. "Hope you Tasered the son of a bitch."

"I didn't, but Ted did. God, he was pissed." Pain at the memory flashed in her lovely eyes. Her grief made something hot twist in Frank's chest.

They got dressed, though they had to search for one of her boots—he'd thrown it harder than he'd thought. Finally, decently attired in boots and camies, and still feeling deliciously wrung out, they started back toward the house.

CHAPTER ELEVEN

Bruce lay in his sniper's nest, utterly still as Daddy had taught him. His face pressed against the cool stock of the rifle, gazing through the scope with all the patience of a lion at a water hole. He'd wanted to get close enough to watch Alex and her lover fuck, but he didn't trust his ability to move silently in all those dead leaves. Murphy was a big bastard; if things went sideways, Bruce wasn't confident he could take him out. Too many things could go wrong. He had no interest in the humiliation of an arrest.

He frowned, reminded just how close he'd come to getting caught a couple of hours ago. He'd broken in to Ted's house to get his camera. He'd just pulled it off the wall when he heard a car pull up. He'd had to leap out the bedroom window and run like hell. Luckily he'd parked his personal car a couple of streets over, or Tracy would have spotted it and had him then.

But he hadn't been caught. He was safe, which meant he still had a chance to kill Alex. She was the one who'd betrayed him, had lied and laughed at him. She was as guilty of tarnishing her badge as Arlington.

But more important, her death would kill the Coach and his wife. Bruce vividly remembered sitting with the Rogers family in the Harrison High stands nine years ago, watching Alex run in a track meet. When she'd won, Ken's face had glowed with pride. He hadn't looked that delighted when Tim, his eldest son, made the winning touchdown in the state championship.

When Bruce killed her, his father would finally be avenged.

L eaves crunched underfoot as Alex and Frank walked through the woods, headed toward his house. A pleasant breeze hissed through the trees, cooling their sweating skin. Alex used the wipe he'd handed her to scrub off the camouflage paint he left on her skin in fingerprints and smears, a dappled trail of their erotic play. "That was a really good scene." She shot him a smile. "I can't remember the last time I got so turned on." She paused, and let her smile grow sly. "With the possible exception of the last time we played."

He grinned down at her, scrubbing at his own face with the wipe he held. "We do have pretty good chemistry. There's something about these little wrestling matches that gets me turned on every time."

"I noticed." She flicked a glance below his belt and leered playfully.

As they stepped onto the house's broad lawn, Frank grinned down at her. "What do you want to do for our next—" His head snapped around, shooting a glance over his shoulder before he grabbed her and dove behind a massive oak that shaded the backyard. The bruising impact knocked the breath out of her. Frank wrapped himself around her like a human blanket, his arms encircling her head, his own head tucked against her neck. Before she could demand what the hell he thought he was doing, a shot cracked over their heads. Alex yelped as he cursed, curling tighter around her.

Someone's shooting at us, Alex realized with a blood-chilling rush of fear. *Frank's shielding me.* "Is it the same asshole who killed Ted?"

"Don't know. I think I'll shoot the fucker and ask his corpse." He reached into the toy bag he still had hooked over an arm and pulled out his Glock as another shot whined past.

Who carries a weapon in his toy bag? She grimaced. *Somebody a hell of a lot better prepared than me.*

Frank ducked around the tree to fire. The gun boomed over her head once, twice, three times. In the distance, a man cursed, and brush and leaves rustled, limbs crackling and snapping as someone raced away. Frank's weight vanished from atop her as he catapulted himself after the shooter, legs eating up ground. His gun thundered again.

"Dammit, Frank!" Alex lunged to her feet, but before she could sprint after him, she remembered she didn't have her gun. Whirling, she sprinted toward her car and the Glock in the Honda's glove compartment. It was a damned good thing she never went anywhere without her weapon. It just hadn't occurred to her she'd need it when she was actually *sceneing*.

Goddammit.

Now if only Frank doesn't get himself shot before I can back him up. As she ran for the car, Alex thrust a hand into her pants pocket and dragged out her smartphone to dial 911. "Dispatch, Charlie 21! Officers under fire! Requesting backup at 362 Lighthorse Street." She juggled the phone into her left hand and used the right to dig her keys out of her pants pocket. The Honda chirped at her as she thumbed the key fob. Jerking the car door open, Alex dove inside, popped open the glove compartment, and grabbed her gun. "We're pursuing an armed suspect into the woods behind the house." She slammed the door and whirled to pound in the direction Frank had taken into the trees.

"Description?" dispatch demanded.

"Haven't gotten a look at him yet," she panted as she flew across the lawn. "Fired at us twice . . . as we walked . . . out of the woods. Didn't see the . . . weapon . . . sounded like a deer rifle." She'd gone hunting often enough to recognize the weapon's distinctive sound.

"Nearest unit is ten minutes out."

"10-4, dispatch." Alex stuffed the phone into a pocket without turning it off, which would allow dispatch to make an audio recording of whatever was happening. She poured on the speed until she was bounding over the ground faster than she ever had during those long-ago track meets, leaping bramble bushes and shoving through tree branches as she went.

There were no more shots. *God, what if Frank's been hurt?* Sick fear iced her veins as she increased her speed even more, sucking air desperately as she flung herself through the trees without even noticing the lash of branches and or the brush tearing at her hair and clothes.

Somewhere ahead of her she heard the roar of a car accelerating away, followed by Frank's vicious cursing. Her heart lifted in sheer relief. He wasn't dead.

But he might still be hurt.

Alex leaped out of the woods to find Frank standing in the middle of a narrow road, his weapon pointed skyward, staring in impotent fury up the road as a car's engine roared away. He did not appear to be injured. He was, however, really, really pissed. "I'm going to get you, motherfucker," Frank yelled. "I swear to God, I'm going to skullfuck you to death!"

"Did you get the tag number?" Alex asked, hoping desperately there was something, anything, that might let them catch Ted's killer.

"No, goddammit. The fucking tag was so covered with mud I couldn't see shit." He thumbed the safety on and jammed his Glock into his waistband at the small of his back.

Alex did the same and fished her cell phone out of her

pants pocket. She hadn't hung up. "I have 911 on the line. Do you have a description?"

"He was wearing camo pants and a long-sleeve shirt, plus a baklava and gloves. I couldn't get hair or skin color. I know one thing, bastard runs like a jackrabbit. Drove a late-model sedan, dark blue or black, so mud-splattered he must off-road in it."

Alex relayed the description to dispatch, then broke off to ask, "What street is this?"

"Francis Marion Drive. He was headed east." Frank turned and stalked back into the woods. Alex could almost see the fury boiling off him like heat on summer pavement.

Again she relayed the information. Satisfied that they were no longer in immediate danger, she ended the call and followed him.

"You and Ted pissed anybody off lately?" He caught a branch and held it aside it so it wouldn't smack her in the face.

"I'll tell you what I've told Ben Tracy every time he asked that question. We're the PoPo, Frank. We piss people off all the time." She shot him a searching look. "So you think the same guy who killed Ted just shot at us? I'd thought it might be, but . . ."

"It's possible. We won't know for sure unless we can find that bullet for comparison to the one that killed Ted." He lengthened his stride until she had to hurry to keep up.

Failed.

He'd failed utterly. His father would have put him through a wall.

Angrily, Bruce swiped away tears of anguish, shame, and rage as he drove. He'd had Alex in his sights. All he'd had to do was squeeze the trigger. But he'd pussied out.

He'd looked at her bright head in the crosshairs, and he'd remembered the taste of her mouth, the feel of her young body moving under his as they'd made love. Even though she'd said he hurt her that first time, it had been magic to him. She'd been so fucking tight, so perfect. He'd never felt so close to another human being. And then he'd seen the tears and realized the expression on her face was pain. Hurt, he'd said something stupid, and she'd bloodied his nose for him.

Their entire fucking relationship in a nutshell.

Maybe he could have shot her if that had been the only thing he'd remembered. But then there'd been the warm strength of her arms around him, holding him as she'd cried for his mother—and for him. He had hated everyone else's expressions of sympathy, but not Alex's. Alex hadn't made him feel ashamed. No other woman in almost a decade had been able to touch him the way she had.

Remembering that moment, he hadn't been able to bring himself to pull the trigger. His head had dropped forward in frustration and self-disgust. Not much. Maybe an inch. Her fucking SEAL had still spotted the motion. The bastard had knocked her flat and covered her with his body. He hadn't even hesitated.

They'll call him a hero, Bruce had thought. *She'll see him as her hero. Him, not me.*

The idea had pissed him off so much, he'd fired twice. Unfortunately, he'd been so shaken, he'd missed both times. By then, Murphy was up and running, and he'd realized he'd better haul ass or Frank would put a bullet in him. Not that he didn't deserve it after the day's multiple fuckups.

The next time he had Alex in his sights, he'd by God fire. He wouldn't pussy out again.

Alex is dead. She just doesn't know it yet.

Frank found the sniper nest at the edge of the woods bordering the house, more or less where he expected to. The signs were faint, but he knew what he was looking for, and he found it: broken plant stems and crushed leaves where the shooter had lain. The area was screened from the yard by ferns, beech redbay, and great rhododendron.

He pointed them out to Alex. "He moved and the plants here rustled. Otherwise I'd have had no warning."

Alex stared at the nest, her expression grim. "You saved my ass, Frank. I didn't hear a damn thing." Visibly shaking off the fear, she gave him a narrow, searching look. "You must have ears like a bat."

He shrugged. "This isn't the first time a sniper's shot at me."

"The thing that bothers me is, if it's the same guy who shot Ted, how did he know we were going to be here?" Alex looked at him, her green gaze fierce. "I didn't even know until we . . ." Her eyes widened. "The car. He bugged the car! That's where we talked about this." She turned and started toward the house.

Frank frowned and followed. "You mean your patrol car?"

"Yeah. I'm going to have to go back home and search it."

He caught her arm before she could take another step. "Not without backup, you don't. Besides, that's the crime scene investigator's job. You don't mess with a potential crime scene."

She threw him a look over her shoulder, a hint of rebellion in her gaze. Her mouth tightened, but she didn't argue. "Yeah, all right. Good point."

He glanced back at the sniper's nest, eyes narrowing. "In the meantime, we need to locate the bullet he fired at me."

"Isn't that CSI's job?" She smirked.

"I'm not going to dig the bullet out, Alex. I'm just going to locate it."

"Because the CSI, clearly, can't."

He gave her a narrow look. "Because the CSI is not the one who got shot at, and therefore isn't as aware of shot angles as the guy with the bull's-eye on his ass."

"Yet another good point."

"I have a lot of those—at least one of 'em on the end of my dick."

"I am fond of that one."

But Frank was staring along the path the bullet must have followed, based on the sniper's nest and where they'd been standing when the bastard fired at them. Sure enough, he thought he could see a tiny dark something on the outer wall of the house. He started in that direction warily, sweeping his gaze over the lawn and surrounding woods, acutely aware that Alex followed him.

There was no guarantee the sniper wouldn't return and take another shot at one or both of them. Even if he didn't come back today, Frank thought it was likely they'd get targeted sooner or later; they'd humiliated the bastard. Not only had they survived, they'd driven him off. The prick who'd murdered Ted and painted bigoted slurs all over his car wasn't the type to take that kind of thing lying down.

The first patrol vehicles rolled up just as he located the first bullet hole. Other units followed, deputies spilling out wearing grim expressions, eyes wary. The idea someone might be actively hunting cops had obviously put everybody on high alert.

Sergeant Diane Gaffney arrived and organized the mob of cops to search for evidence and interview the neighbors. After the teams dispersed, she joined Frank and Alex as he pointed out the bullet holes for the CSI.

"Damn, Rogers, you just can't stay out of trouble, can you?" she asked Alex.

"It's my sunny personality," Alex said dryly. "Inspires love from all who know me."

"Nah, that's the tits," Frank said. The CSI snickered.

Gaffney shot him a menacing look. "What was that, Murphy?"

He blinked in exaggerated innocence. "What was what, Sergeant?"

"The blatant sexual harassment, noob."

He turned to Alex. "Was that sexual harassment, Rogers?"

"Nope," she said serenely, "just a statement of fact."

The CSI, cackling, almost lost his balance and fell against the wall he was trying to dig the bullet from.

Gaffney glared him into silence before turning back to Frank and Alex. "So what the hell happened?"

They filled her in—except for the sex—finishing with Alex's suspicion that her car had been bugged.

"So go get the car and let's find out," Gaffney told her.

"I could follow her over there," the CSI volunteered. Jerry Mathews was a round little man just short of forty, with sandy blond hair and intelligent hazel eyes. He wore green fatigues with CRIME SCENE INVESTIGATOR in white block letters across the back.

"No, I want you here to bag any evidence we manage to find. Besides, she'll be back with the car before you finish the scene anyway."

"I'd like to go with her in case she needs backup," Frank said. "He might decide to take another shot at her."

"God, I hope not." Grimacing, Gaffney waved a hand. "Okay, go on. Faster you get back, faster we can get the hell out of here. My shoulder blades are starting to itch." When Frank raised an eyebrow, she added sourly, "Ted wasn't the only Morgan County deputy flying the rainbow flag. I'd just as soon not hang around until somebody tries to force-feed me a bullet."

Frank, Alex, and Mathews all winced.

Alex and Frank drove to her house and picked up the patrol car without incident, though her shoulder blades were itching as hard as the sergeant's by the time they headed back.

No sooner had she braked at a stoplight than Paul McCartney began crooning "Let it Be" from her pants pocket. She sighed and dug the iPhone out under Frank's amused gaze. "Hi, Mom."

"Hi, baby. How are you this fine morning?"

I just got shot at by a cop killer. And you? Nope, not the kind of thing to say to a mother who'd never liked her choice of career to begin with. "Doing great, Mom. How are you?"

"Well, your father decided he wanted to have y'all over for a hamburger cookout at five. Can you make it?"

Alex frowned and accelerated as the light turned green. She wasn't sure she liked the sound of that. It was, after all, Wednesday. "Aren't you going to prayer meeting tonight?"

Her mother paused a beat too long. "Not tonight, dear. We haven't seen you kids in what it seems like forever . . ."

Oh, she definitely didn't like this. "We were all at the last home game a couple of weeks ago."

"Yes, dear, but your dad has something he wants to say to you."

"'You' as in all of us, or 'you' as in me?"

Another long, worrying pause. "You as in you." As if sensing Alex's reaction, she added hastily, "Your brothers are coming, too. It'll be just the six of us, like it was before all my chicks grew up and left the nest."

Shit. "Oh."

"So can you make it? I'm fixin' your favorite peach pie."

Oh, hell, Mom's Southern accent was thickening. Whenever the magnolia quotient increased in Mary Rogers's voice, she was setting somebody up. Thing was, ducking the invitation would just piss her off and make the inevitable explosion worse. "Yeah, I'll be there."

"Great! I'll see you then." She hung up.

"Fuck." Alex tossed the iPhone into the center console in disgust. "I am in so much trouble."

"What's the problem?" Frank asked.

"Mom asked me over to a cookout tonight."

He grinned. "Is she that bad a cook?"

"No, she's a great cook. The trouble is, it's Wednesday. Mom always goes to prayer meeting on Wednesdays unless there's a dire emergency."

"Could she have heard about the sniper taking a shot at us?"

Alex frowned. "I don't think so. She was way too calm, and anyway, she'd have asked about something like that first thing. No, I think this is an intervention, because my brothers aren't bringing their wives. We haven't had one of those since Harry was dating that stripper."

"Should I be worried?"

"Not unless you've been moonlighting as a stripper. No, I've got a feeling this is about Ted and that damned YouTube video of him whipping Cal."

"Which is an issue why?"

"Because I brought Ted to dinner at the house damn near every time I went myself. And I never warned them about his sexuality."

"And they think it was their business why?"

"My brother Andy's got a four-year-old son."

"And they're indignant because Ted could have sneezed on the kid and given him the gay?"

"No, but I'll bet you fifty bucks everybody's pissed because they think I put Bryson in danger of being molested."

"By Ted?" He stared at her, outraged. "Tell me you're kidding."

She shook her head. "Cal's sister accused Cal of the same thing after the local news ran the YouTube thing. She won't even let him see his nephews anymore."

"Your family and Cal's sister both sound like fucking . . ." He shut his mouth firmly.

Alex sighed. "I see I've given you the wrong impression. Yeah, Mom's very religious, but she's loving about it. My dad couldn't care less; his defensive coach is gay. But Andy is really protective when it comes to his kid. Harry and Tim are still single, so they're less paranoid on the subject."

"Yeah, but pedophiles are a lot more likely to identify as straight than gay. After all, it's women who have all the kids. If you're a pedophile, even if you're not straight, you're going to want to pretend to be straight so you can get at kids through their mother."

"You know that, and I know that, but Andy Junior's pissed-off daddy does not give a shit."

As they turned into his development, he gave her a long

look. "Want me to go with you? Sounds like you could use backup."

Alex hesitated. The thought of telling her mother she was dating the tall, handsome Navy SEAL hero was tempting; it would distract Mary nicely, and Andy would be less likely to tear into her in front of company. "No, better not," she said reluctantly. "This is likely to get really ugly."

Frank shot her an *Oh, please* look. "Alex, I spent ten years getting shot at by terrorists. I think I can handle your brother acting pissy."

She gave in. "Let me ask Mom if she'd mind another guest."

As it turned out, her mother was more than pleased to have Alex bring a date, despite the night's supposed objective. Which was something of a surprise; the family didn't often wave its dirty laundry in front of strangers. Then again, maybe Alex wasn't the only one who hoped Frank's presence would spike Andy's guns.

Considering the way my luck's gone lately, she thought grimly, *exposure to the entire Rogers clan in a raging snit will drive Frank off for good.*

CSI Jerry Mathews backed out of Alex's patrol car. She and Frank watched, along with Detective Tracy, who'd arrived while they'd gone off to pick up the car. Mathews held two objects in his blue-gloved hands, one a tiny black cylinder, the other a flat device the size of an iPhone. "Well, you were right. I found this attached to the underside of the passenger seat."

"What is it?" Alex eyed the two devices warily.

Mathews gestured with the tiny cylinder. "Mic." He held up the flat rectangle. "Can't say for sure what this is until I send it off to the FBI for analysis, but I suspect it's some kind of radio."

Frank cursed in disgust.

"That about sums it up," Mathews agreed.

"Will we be able to backtrack the sniper with this?"

demanded Tracy, blue eyes narrow as he studied the devices, a grim set to his jaw. Today he wore pressed navy pants and a pink dress shirt and tie striped in pink and blue. The color did absolutely nothing to blunt his over-whelming masculinity.

Mathews shrugged as he slid the mic and recorder into an evidence bag. "Ask the FBI. I don't have the expertise to take this thing apart."

Alex glowered in simmering frustration. "What I want to know is how that thing got in my car."

Tracy hesitated a moment, his mouth tight. "Same way the camera got in that dummy smoke detector at Ted's apart-ment."

"So Cal was right," Alex said.

"Looks that way," Mathews said.

"What are you talking about?" Frank demanded.

Tracy told them about Cal's suspicions that someone had planted a camera in Ted's bedroom to shoot the You-Tube video. "We'd searched the apartment before, but we didn't find anything. After I talked to Cal, Mathews and I went back to take a look again. This time we noticed a pale circle over the door where the paint was a different color, as if something had covered it in that location."

"Like you get when a picture frame's been moved," said Alex.

"Right. Except I knew for a fact it hadn't been there before. I compared it to the photos Mathews took when we went in the day before, and sure enough, there'd been one of those battery-operated smoke detectors in that location. Got on the Internet, and come to find out, they sell cameras that fit inside phony smoke detectors, supposedly to hide nanny cams."

"So the killer must have gone back to get the smoke detec-tor," Frank said.

"Exactly. But apparently there really had been a smoke detector there in the past, long enough for the paint to be dis-colored. What I can't figure out is why he didn't put the origi-nal detector back up."

"Maybe he's a dumbass," Mathews suggested.

"Or maybe something scared him off before he could finish the job." He gestured at the bag, his handsome face grimly satisfied. "But this time we beat him to the evidence. We'll send this off to the FBI. They'll use the serial number to determine the manufacturer, who'll be able to tell us what website they sold it through. Feds'll get a warrant for the website, who'll be able to give us the credit card or whatever used to buy it." He grimaced. "Assuming it wasn't one of those prepaid debit cards the killer paid cash for."

Alex stared at him. "That's going to take weeks."

Tracy looked grim. "At least."

Frank said what they all were thinking. "And in the meantime, the bastard's going to keep shooting at cops."

"Maybe not," Mathews argued. "Maybe this is some-body who targeted Alex and Ted in particular. Could be a case they worked that's going to come to trial, and some-body doesn't want them to testify."

"Yeah, we're working that angle. The rest of Violent Crimes is checking the court docket and going over every ticket they wrote and drunk they've arrested." Reading their expressions, Tracy shrugged. "Cop killer. We take care of our own."

Alex voiced the ugly little suspicion that had been nig-gling at the back of her mind. "Do you think it could *be* a cop?"

Tracy, Frank, and Mathews stiffened and stared. "You suggesting a *cop* killed Ted?"

"I don't like the idea either, Frank, but between getting the thing into my car and planting that camera at Ted's . . ."

"You don't have a garage, Alex. You park your car in the front yard. Anybody could get at it."

"I lock the damned car. How would he have gotten inside to plant the bug?"

"There are ways to jimmy a locked car door."

"And cops know most of them." Though car manufac-turers had made that a lot harder than it used to be.

"So do car thieves and everybody who knows how to do a Google search," Tracy put in.

Frank's mouth pulled into a grim line. "Not that I'm real thrilled with the idea of somebody just coming into your yard and breaking into your car."

"Another thing: he was able to get our addresses in order to plant shit and snipe at us. The department doesn't exactly give that information out, given that none of us have listed phone numbers. I could buy learning where one of us live, but all three?"

"Could be a hacker," Mathews suggested. "Maybe he figured out a way to get into the department's computers."

Alex stared at him. "That's an ugly thought."

"Not as ugly as the idea of a cop-killing deputy stalking other officers," Tracy said.

"Granted, but is it really a good idea to completely dismiss the possibility?"

"I'm going to have to see a lot more evidence that can't be explained by some racist with a hard-on for cops." His eyes narrowed. "In the meantime, I'm going to have tech support see if somebody's hacked the department's computer system."

Alex opened her mouth, but before she could speak, Sergeant Gaffney walked up. "Hey, Murphy and Rogers— what're y'all doing, padding your overtime? Get lost. Go get some sleep."

"I'm not done going over her car yet, Sarge," Mathews protested.

"So quit running your mouth and get to work. In the meantime, Murph, give Rogers a ride home."

"Sure, Sarge," Frank said.

"Yes, ma'am," Alex added, suddenly aware of the pull of exhaustion on her body like the weight of an anchor. Gaffney was right; she desperately needed some sack time. Besides, by now SIG was probably plotting to claw her to shreds for aggravated cat neglect.

As she and Frank turned to go, Gaffney spoke again, her

voice deliberately lower. "Keep an eye on each other, you two. Some bastard out there wants to hate y'all to death."

"Yes ma'am," Frank said, and damn near saluted before he arrested the gesture. It seemed old SEAL habits die hard. "Come on, Rogers."

"Want to crash over at my house?" she asked him softly, following him to his garage. "The boys are going to be swarming around yours for a while yet. Doubt you'd be able to get any sleep."

He gave her a grateful look. "That'd be wonderful . . . Though I doubt I can manage anything more taxing than falling facedown onto the nearest flat surface."

"You saved my life today. Literally. The least I can do is provide you with the flat surface in question." She grimaced, remembering her mother's invitation to tonight's intervention-slash-lynching. "Besides, considering you promised to help me fend off my relatives tonight, it's in my best interest to make sure you're well rested."

"Hey, Afghanistan, Iraq, or your mama's dinner table, we SEALs are up to the job."

Alex snorted. "You haven't met my relatives yet." She paused and lowered her voice. "The sniper heard us plan our thing today. He must have, to know where we'd be. If he recorded it . . ."

"You're afraid he'll release it to the media the way he did the video of Cal and Ted." He sighed and looped an arm around her neck. "Maybe we'll get him before he gets a chance."

"But the odds are, we won't. Sending that bug off to the Feds, waiting for it to come back, then backtracking it . . . that's going to take weeks. If we're lucky. And that's assuming he was dumb enough to use his own credit card." She gnawed her lower lip, imagining her family's reaction to learning the kind of relationship she and Frank had.

Then there was the sort of public shitstorm that would descend on the department . . . People would demand they be fired. And in a right-to-fire state like South Carolina, there wasn't a damn thing they could do about it. Yeah, they could sue, but they'd probably lose. Her eyes filled. "I love being a cop. I don't want to lose my job because of a bunch of self-righteous assholes sticking their noses in my bedroom."

"Look." Frank moved around in front of her and took her by both shoulders. "We'll deal with it, whatever happens. That bastard *shot* at us. With real bullets, not innuendo and gossip. We survived, Alex."

"This time. But what happens next time?"

"Next time we'll keep surviving." He rubbed her shoulders. "Look, I've been in combat. I've seen what happens to men who let themselves get distracted by worry and fear. They get shot, Alex."

"But—"

"But nothing. You have to concentrate on now, on staying alive this minute. You have to believe that whatever you face in the future, you'll be able to handle. And you will. The woman who didn't hesitate to take on that asshole Donny Royce without any backup at all is more than a match for a bunch of gossips."

"It's not the gossips I'm worried about. It's the Coach." Her hands curled into helpless fists. "And my mother."

"We'll handle it, Alex."

She subsided, hoping to hell he was right.

CHAPTER TWELVE

As they pulled into the house's gravel driveway, Alex felt a sudden uncomfortable awareness of the contrast between Frank's near mansion and the little mill-village place she'd inherited from her grandmother. "I'll warn you," she said as she turned off the engine, "it's not what you're used to."

"What?" Frank asked absently as he drew his weapon and got out of the car in a wary glide. He scanned the yard and surrounding houses as he straightened, obviously searching for threats.

Prodded, Alex did the same. The Glock was a cool and comforting weight in her hand. She didn't see any sign of gun-brandishing killers. "My house. I'm afraid it's going to suffer by comparison to yours."

Frank snorted, scanning the yard as he following her to the short sidewalk and up the stairs onto the screened porch. "Baby, I once slept sitting up in the Pacific Ocean, in water so cold I had to piss myself to fend off hypothermia. I guarantee your house is a fuck of a lot more comfortable than that."

Alex laughed as she unlocked the front door and led the way inside. "Well, yeah, I'd hope my bed would beat Hell Week in terms of physical comfort."

"The Bataan Death March beat Hell Week in terms of comfort . . . Whoa." Frank rocked back on his heels as a small furry blur headed toward them, growling feline obscenities. "Incoming."

The cat leaped into Alex's arms, still grumbling. She gave him an apologetic ear scratch. "Yes, SIG, I starved you horribly." She headed toward the kitchen carrying her bitterly complaining burden. Curious, Frank followed. "I know, I know—if you had opposable thumbs, you'd have called the SPCA and reported my ass. But I have a good excuse: this asshole shot at me."

Judging by his raucous complaints, SIG didn't think a near-death experience was a good enough excuse for not running a can opener. "Okay, okay!" She put the cat down and opened a cabinet to grab a can. When the can opener began its familiar grinding hum, SIG's complaints took on a near-hysterical volume.

"Boy, that beast is a cat video waiting to happen." Frank picked up SIG's water bowl and filled it at the sink. "You need to get him his own YouTube channel. You'd have a million people subscribing, just to watch him cuss you."

Alex laughed as she filled SIG's food bowl. The cat plunged her head into it with an ecstatic growl. "SIG already has seven thousand three hundred and sixty Facebook friends."

He stared at her. "You're shitting me."

"Nope." She ran a hand down SIG's sleek back. The cat was too busy eating to lift his head. "The neighbor's Pekingese is bitterly jealous. She's only got three thousand."

Frank blinked at her in wordless astonishment.

"What?"

"You got your cat his own Facebook page—and you named him after a gun? And how does he post?"

"He kind of paws the keys," Alex told him, deadpan. "I considered naming him SIG P-239, because he's small, but he's really loud. But it was too much a mouthful. As it is, I call him by his full name, he knows I'm pissed. Isn't that right, SIG Sauer?"

The cat looked up at his name, then went back to eating when Alex gave him a comforting ear scratch. "It's kind of like when my mother calls me by my full name. I hear Alexis Eleanor Rogers, I instantly become six years old again, and my mama ain't happy." She grimaced and straightened. "Speaking of which, we'd better hit the sack if we're going to get some sleep before reporting to Casa Coach for my ass-chewing."

Frank ran a hand down the length of her back in a stroke not unlike the one he'd given SIG. "Look on the bright side—at least none of them will be armed. Day's looking up."

"My family doesn't need guns," she told him glumly, heading for her bedroom with Frank ghosting at her heels. "They prefer fangs and claws."

With Frank curled warm and hard around her, Alex slept dreamlessly for the next three hours.

Frank, unfortunately, could not say the same. He woke her with a low, desperate moan. "Alex, Alex, no, don't . . . Don't go. Don't." His voice dropped into a deadly snarl. "You fuckin' bastard, I'll kill every last fucking . . ."

"Frank . . ." She tried to turn in his arms, but they tightened painfully around her. "Frank, wake up."

"Fuckers, I'll blow your fucking heads . . ." His fingers dug into her skin. She suspected she'd have bruises.

"Frank!" Her voice spiraled toward a shout as she tried to pull free of his painful grip.

"Alex?" He jolted against her. She knew he was completely awake when he let go of her as if her skin burned his. "Oh, Christ, Alex, did I hurt you?" He turned her in his arms. "Are you all right?"

"Fine, babe." Her gaze searched his. "You okay?"

"Fine." The word was so clipped, she knew it for a lie. He rolled out of bed and straightened to his full height. Big, muscled, and gloriously naked, he raked his hands through his hair. It was so short, he barely managed to muss it. "Just a dream. I have those." Frank gave her a probing stare. "You sure you're okay?"

"You've got a hell of a grip, but you didn't hurt me." She gave him an exaggerated leer. "And if you had, the view right now would be worth it. Man candy. Yum."

He grinned at her, taking his cock in hand. "I've got your man candy right here, baby."

"Slut."

His eyes glinted dangerously, and his voice dropped to a growling register that made her cunt go slick and tight. "Is that any way to talk to your Dom?"

"You gonna put me in my place, big man?"

"I'd love to." His eyes flicked to the alarm clock sitting on her vanity. "Unfortunately, we have to be at Casa Coach in half an hour."

"Oh, shit!" She shot from the bed. "Dammit, I knew I should have set that alarm!"

As the shower pounded them five minutes later, she remembered the moments before he woke up. "Who did you dream was killing me, Frank?"

He stilled in the act of soaping her breasts. "Couple of Taliban assholes." His hands went back to work teasing her hard nipples. "You know how dreams are. Made no damn sense at all. We were back in Afghanistan. You remember my BUD/S buddy Randy Carson?"

She nodded. "The one who got shot, right?"

"Right. That was Randy. Anyway, we were hunting Asad Abd al Jabbar, and they shot him in the gut. Then somehow he was you, and you were dying in my arms . . ." He broke off, shaking his head before giving her a sharp look. "And no, one nightmare does not add up to PTSD."

"I didn't think it did. The close call with the cop killer must have triggered it. Actually, I'm surprised I didn't dream about it myself." She grimaced. "Probably too worried about dinner and my Alex-ivore relatives."

He gave her a slap on the ass that made her jump. "The

only one who's going to be eating you tonight is me. I am really possessive that way. Now quit stalling; get out and get ready."

Alex swept the shower curtain open. "Easy for you to say. You're not on tonight's menu."

Casa Coach, as all and sundry had called the Rogers home for a couple of decades now, was a quirky brick two-story with high ceilings and a wide balcony that featured a wrought-iron railing worthy of the New Orleans French Quarter.

The house's overstuffed furniture, sturdy enough to accommodate a family of large, football-playing men, leaned toward earth tones. Afghans that Mary Rogers had crocheted were draped over anything that seemed to need one, lending splashes of turquoise, sandstone, and peach.

The dining room featured a Shaker-style blond pine table and chairs, while the knotty pine floor there was darker, warmed by rugs in Southeastern shades.

At the moment, Frank and the Rogers men were outside on the brick patio drinking beer in the shadow of the balcony and kibitzing as the Coach cooked burgers. The gas grill he presided over was stainless steel and enormous; he swore it cost more than his first car.

Judging by the cheerful rumble of deep male laughter, Frank seemed to be getting along pretty well with the Rogers men. *Or maybe that's wishful thinking*, Alex thought with a sigh. *My luck's not been the best today.*

If, that is, you ignored the fact that neither she nor Frank had been shot. Definitely something to be thankful for, though Alex was carefully keeping the sniper's attack secret from her mother. Mary had only recently quit trying to get her out of law enforcement. This would only set her off again.

Which was why, badge and gun notwithstanding, Alex was currently doing her best imitation of a proper Southern girl. She and her mother were at work on the meal's side dishes: baked beans, deviled eggs, and green beans seasoned with fatback—all those luscious Southern staples that weren't even remotely healthy. Mary was normally more conscious of fat and calories in the meals she prepared—otherwise she and the Coach would be the size of sumo wrestlers. But when it came to special occasions, she'd never met a dish that couldn't be improved by the addition of a stick of butter. Alex secretly agreed, though she usually kept her butter addiction in careful check. As it was, she'd be paying for tonight's meal the rest of the week by adding an extra mile to her daily five-mile run.

"I really like your new young man, Alex," Mary said as she stirred the green beans. "He's very handsome, and he's seems like such a nice boy."

At the thought of whip-wielding Frank Murphy being described as a "nice boy"—hell, as a "boy" period—Alex almost did a spit take with her mouthful of sweet tea. Regaining breath control, she wheezed, "Oh, he is."

Her mother eyed her over the strip of fatback she was about to add to the green beans. "You like him a lot, don't you?"

"I've only known him a few days, Mom."

"Sometimes it doesn't take long. Answer the question."

Resisting the urge to roll her eyes like a teenager, Alex gave up. "All right, yeah." She added brown sugar, mustard, and ketchup to the baked beans and began stirring. "He's been a good friend." Her throat suddenly thickened with grief. "Especially after what happened to Ted."

"I'm sorry, honey," Mary said softly. "It must have been tough finding him like that."

Alex looked up from the beans to find her mother watching her with sympathetic moss green eyes. Fifty-plus or not, Mary was a lovely woman who looked a good ten years younger than her driver's license would have you believe. She'd been trying to lose twenty pounds since the eighties, but as far as Alex was concerned, the extra weight only made her hugs warmer and more comforting. Tonight she wore a flowing maxi dress in a green and blue paisley cotton that swirled around her tall body when she moved. She'd gathered her silver-streaked red hair in a messy knot on the top of her head. Alex only hoped she looked as good at her mother's age.

"Yeah, finding Ted was . . . It was really tough, Mom."
The words started pouring out of her without permission
from her brain. "I don't care what those jerks on television
said—he was a good guy, a good friend. He never abused
Cal. He wouldn't. Anything they did . . ." She swallowed
the rest, knowing it would only upset her mother.

But to her surprise, Mary stepped away from the stove
and moved to hug her. "I know he was a good man, sweet-
heart. Maybe I don't agree with his personal choices, but I
do believe he loved you. Loved you so much I wasn't sure I
approved of him because I thought he was too old for you . . ."

"It was never like that, Mom." Alex hugged her back,
taking comfort in the soft warmth of her mother's arms.

"I realize that now. Actually, I realized that even before
all this . . . business. Ted loved you more like a father than
anything else." A smile flickered around her mouth as the
two women drew reluctantly apart. "Not like your new
friend outside. *He's* not fatherly at all."

"God, I hope not," Alex said with involuntary honesty.

Her mother only laughed.

Since Mary had held her fire during food preparations—
a perfect opportunity for maternal mayhem—Alex had
relaxed by the time the family and Frank sat down to eat.

They were discussing the playoff chances of Harrison
High's basketball team when Alex became aware of her
brother Andy's brooding glower. Not that there was anything unusual about that. Alex had grown up getting glowered at by Andy.

Some accident of genetics had left the ginger-haired
thirty-year-old shorter than his two older brothers—and a
half-inch shorter than Alex herself, for that matter—resulting
in a serious a case of short man's disease. Like Ted, he was
aggressive as hell; he'd never met anyone he'd back down
from, with the possible exception of the Coach. Unlike Ted,
he didn't have a sense of humor about his height—or much
else, come to think of it. He taught history and Western civ

at Clancy High, Harrison's crosstown rival; his brothers ragged on him endlessly as a result.

Yet beneath that prickly exterior was a sensitive man who loved his family with a fierce, devoted loyalty. Alex, knowing that about him, had always given him a pass when it came to his occasional hissy fits.

Today, though, he seemed intent on glaring a hole in her skull while working his way through a six-pack of Budweiser Light. He was making her twitchy as painful childhood experience yammered warnings that her brother was getting ready to unload in her general direction.

Her instincts were right.

"So, sis," Andy finally drawled, "I got a text-alert from WJIT this afternoon. Seems they had a story that a couple of deputies got shot at from ambush this morning. A source inside the department identified the officers as Alexis Rogers and Franklin Murphy." His eyes narrowed to pissed-off hazel slits. "You got something you want to tell us? Like maybe why a guy who shot your partner because he was a pervert is targeting *you* now?"

Alex stared at him, stunned. It had never occurred to her the department would out them. *Who, and why, for God's sake? The sheriff wouldn't have done it . . . He's been busting his ass to stress Ted's heroism.* She longed to defend herself, but her vocal chords seemed paralyzed.

Frank lowered his cheeseburger to his plate, and leaned back in his chair, a muscle flexing in his jaw. He smiled, but it wasn't even remotely friendly. "What exactly are you implying, Andy?"

Alex's mother stared at her in horrified shock. "Somebody shot at you today? And you didn't even mention it?"

"I didn't want to upset you," Alex said absently, glaring at her brother. "Besides, neither of us got hurt."

"It sounds like that was only by the grace of God!" Mary cried.

"I'm saying," Andy said, ignoring both sister and mother, "that since the guy who shot Ted apparently did it because he was gay, that kind of begs the question, *Frank*."

"And what question is that, Andy?"

"Are you a f—" He shot a glance at his mother and obviously thought better of using a homophobic slur in front of her. "Gay, too?"

"What do you care?" Frank's upper lip curled in a snarl that would have done a werewolf proud. "Gotta say, just in case the thought has crossed your mind, you ain't my type."

Andy's redhead-fair complexion flushed an ugly shade of red. "You saying you aren't gay?"

"No, not that it's any of your business, he is not!" Alex exploded, unable to take any more. "He—"

"So what kinda pervert are you, then? You must be some kind of perv, if the sniper shot at you. 'Cause that's why he shot Ted . . ."

"Did it ever occur to you he shot at us because he's an assh—" Like her brother, Alex thought better of her vocabulary. "Jerk? I mean, we are talking about a cop killer."

"Was it really the cop killer who shot at you?" If anything, Mary's soft moss green eyes widened even more like a woman whose worst nightmare had just missed coming true.

Alex met her mother's gaze and discovered, not for the first time, that she couldn't lie to her worth a damn. "We don't know for sure. It could be a copycat inspired by all the media attention."

Glaring, Andy rose and stalked around the table toward Alex, radiating drunken menace. He jerked his chin at Frank. "So is this guy like the other pervert you brought around my child, you—"

Frank rose and stepped into his path, towering over the much shorter man. "I wouldn't finish that sentence if I were you." His tone was utterly calm. The look in his eyes was not.

"I'm not talking to you, 'hero,'" Andy spat. "Now get the hell out of my way."

Alex had heard just about enough. She boiled out of her chair. "He is a hero, goddammit!"

"Alexis Eleanor Rogers!"

Ignoring her mother for once, Alex spat, "He saved my life today! When that bastard shot at us, he knocked me down and covered me with his own body! And you have the unmitigated gall to—"

"You brought a fucking fruit around my little boy! What if he'd—"

"That is *enough*!"

Everyone in the room froze at Ken Rogers's impressive roar, even Frank. Alex hadn't heard the Coach shout at one of his kids like that since her rebellious teenage years.

"I thought I taught you how to be a gentleman." Ken, too, was on his feet now, giving Andy his best frigid glare. He was several inches shorter than Frank, yet somehow he seemed to take up a lot more room than someone his size should be able to.

"But Ted—"

"Being gay doesn't make you a pedophile, boy. Otherwise I can assure you Matt Greggory wouldn't be my defensive coach."

"It's not the fact that he was gay," Andy spat. "It's the fact that he liked to beat that poor little bastard he slept with. Who knows what else he liked to do!"

"It wasn't like that!" Alex spat. "Cal's a friend of mine, and he told me anything that happened was something he—"

"How can you defend that, Alex? He *beat* the man!"

"I said *that's enough*, boy," Ken said in a low, furious growl. "Frank is a guest in our home. I don't need to tell you what to do now, do I?"

Andy stared at him, high, hot flags of color in his cheeks. "I'm not a boy," he gritted. "And I'm damned if I'll apologize to either one of them." He wheeled to stomp toward the door.

"Drive him home, Tim," the coach snapped. "He's had too much to drink. I don't want the idiot to wrap that minivan of his around a tree."

"Sure, Dad." Tim got to his feet, a broad-shouldered, blue-eyed blond who looked like a bigger version of his father. He also looked grateful to escape as he hurried after his brother. "Andy, wait up, you damned fool."

After the door banged closed behind them, Ken turned

to contemplate Frank, his gaze assessing. "My little girl seems to think you saved her life."

"He did," Alex insisted stubbornly.

"Maybe not," Frank pointed out. He still sounded like the calmest person in the room. Better yet, his eyes no longer belied the tone. "We don't really know who he was aiming at. Could have just as easily been me."

"You still covered my body with yours."

Ken paused to give her a long, thoughtful look before turning back to Frank. "That's good enough for me." He extended his hand. "Sorry my son acted like an ass."

Frank took the offered hand and gave it a squeeze. "Man is entitled to be protective of his child, even if his assumptions are flawed."

"I agree." Ken leaned in a little too close, deliberately invading Frank's personal space. "And have no doubt, I will protect *my* child," he said softly. "Don't give me a reason."

Frank lifted a black brow, but there was respect in his gaze. "Believe me, sir, I don't intend to."

"Then we don't have a problem." The Coach squeezed Frank's hand. Alex noticed both men's knuckles turning white.

"Men." Mary shot her daughter a look. "I don't know about you, but I think I'm getting testosterone poisoning."

"I am mortified." Alex slid into the front seat of Frank's personal car, a candy apple–red 1964 Mustang. "I'm so sorry I dragged you into that."

"Alex, you didn't drag me into a damned thing," he said, starting the car. He smiled in pleasure as the vehicle rumbled into life. He'd told her he'd restored the car himself and kept it running by a combination of babying and prayer to the ghost of Henry Ford. "And I know this is probably going to piss you off, but Andy seemed genuinely motivated by what he perceived as a danger to his son."

"Ted Arlington was the last man who'd ever be a threat to kids! Hell, he used to work sex crimes. He had nothing but contempt for anybody who'd abuse a child."

"I know that, and you know that, but Andy didn't know Ted."

"But he knows me! I would never put Andy Jr. in danger!" Alex had adored her four-year-old nephew from the moment she'd first seen his wrinkled little newborn's face. "How could my own brother think I'd bring somebody around who'd be dangerous to that child?"

Frank shot her a glance before returning his gaze to the road in order to pass an SUV. "People don't always know somebody's dangerous."

Alex had heard about enough. She lifted her voice in an outraged shout. "Ted wasn't—"

"That's enough." His tone was icy enough to freeze steam.

Obeying out of sheer startled subbie instinct, Alex shut her mouth.

More evenly, Frank continued, "I know Ted was a good man. So's your brother. I didn't much like some of the things he said to me either, but as I told your dad, a man has a right to be protective of those he loves."

Alex deflated. He was right, as much as it pissed her off. Letting her head fall back on the headrest, she closed her eyes. "Annnnnd, we have to work a shift tonight. God, I feel like somebody beat me with a shovel. No matter how tough any given situation is, you can trust my family to find a way to make it worse."

"You really have no idea how lucky you are. When I was a kid, I'd have given my left nut to have somebody love me that much. You've got five somebodies."

Startled, Alex lifted her head and stared at him. "Say what?"

"Your family loves you. Your daddy is proud of you. All he could talk about while we were out on the deck was how smart you are, and how much ass you kick. Your brothers love you, too—including Andy."

"Yeah, I could tell when he accused me of introducing Chester the Molester to his four-year-old."

"Yeah, okay, he's overprotective and willfully blind, but he's also worried about you. He's afraid I beat you the way Ted beat Cal in that video. You know how BDSM looks to vanilla types. They do not understand. He's afraid I've somehow brainwashed you into thinking abuse is sex."

"You haven't brainwashed me into a damned thing."

"Again, you know that and I know that, but if your brothers knew . . ." He shook his head. "They'd kick my ass if they had to get the Coach's entire defensive line to help them do the job."

"Let's hope that asshole sniper doesn't figure out a way to tell them," Alex muttered.

CHAPTER THIRTEEN

It started out as a quiet night. Alex should have known that wasn't going to last.

She was at the other end of 21 trying to settle a dispute between a drunk and his exasperated neighbors when the call came in. A woman had walked into the Gas-N-Go and threatened the clerk with a gun.

"Dispatch, Twenty-Three responding," Frank said, his radio voice utterly calm. "I'm about two minutes away."

"Dispatch, Twenty-One en route. I'm at the other end of my area. ETA in"—she did a quick estimation— "five minutes."

Alex shot a look at the drunk, who stood swaying on his neighbor's front porch. She knew George Sharpe well from previous encounters. He was harmless, despite an affection for running off at the mouth whenever he got too much Bud onboard. Not unlike a certain dumbass brother. "You've got two options, Mr. Sharpe. Go home or go to jail when I get back. Your choice."

Clearing the porch steps in one bound, Alex sprinted across the neatly trimmed yard.

Three minutes. Frank was going to be dealing with the armed woman for three minutes before she could reasonably get there to back him up. A lot of very nasty shit could happen in three minutes. Suddenly she understood why he'd been so pissed she hadn't waited for backup.

She also knew he wouldn't wait for her either.

Alex slid into her still-running patrol car, flicked on her blue lights and siren, and peeled out of the Larkins' driveway headed for the Gas-N-Go. The patrol car's rotating blue and white lights lit up houses and trees on either side of the road as the siren's cycling wail scraped at Alex's nerves.

Adrenaline streaked through her, urging her to go even faster, but the car was already flying; much faster and she'd outrun her headlights and risk a crash. The words of her academy driving instructor echoed in her head: *You can't save anyone if you get killed on the way.*

But Frank's there alone. He might need me. Alex fought down the panic that thought inspired, forcing herself to do the combat breathing Ted had taught her. The slow, deep breathing would decrease the rabbiting heartbeat that might otherwise make her hands shake too badly to do Frank a damned bit of good.

Fear was a cop's worst enemy. It could turn the best sharpshooter into a hapless schmo who couldn't hit the broad side of a barn. Alex was damned well not going to be that schmo. Not when Frank's life might be at stake.

Alex roared into the Gas-N-Go's parking lot and bolted from the car as if her seat were full of tacks. *And where the hell's Bruce?* She hadn't heard him respond. Fuck it, she didn't have the time to wait for his late ass. She started to charge the door, then pulled up short.

No, a mental voice said. It sounded a lot like Ted. *You can't bull in there like an idiot. You could scare the bitch into opening fire on everybody in the shop.* Drawing in another deep breath—which was doing less to calm her down than it should have—she stared through the store's plate glass window.

Oh, shit. Her heart sped up again.

Frank was faced off with a white woman dressed in a rumpled pink track suit and Day-Glo green running shoes. Her dark hair stood around her head in disordered tufts, as if she'd been clawing her hands through it. She had a gun in her hand.

He did not have his weapon drawn.

What the hell? Alex thought furiously. *I don't care how fast you are, you're not going to get that gun out of its holster and aimed before she can shoot you.*

Chew him out later, dammit. Save his ass now.

Forcing herself to move slowly, quietly, she drew her weapon, crouched, and slipped into the store behind the armed woman, who was ranting something at Frank. Ghosting to the candy display aisle, Alex paused, weapon aimed at subject while she tried to figure out what the hell was going on, and what to do about it.

The woman didn't even appear to notice Alex was there, being completely focused on Frank.

"... don't know what it's like. The snake ... the snake never goes away." Though Alex could see nothing more than her profile, the glint of tears rolling down the woman's pale, drawn face was obvious. "It's eating me alive. Every day, a little bit more of me is gone, down the snake's throat, disappearing, swallowed, dying a tiny bit at a time ... Help me, please, please, I can't let it eat any more of me, please ..."

Alex's mouth tightened as she understood why Frank hadn't drawn his gun. The idiot's chivalric streak wouldn't let him shoot a woman begging for help. Not even one who was obviously batshit crazy and armed with a deadly.

The woman swiped at the tears on her face. Alex tensed, considering firing, but Frank caught her eye and gave his head a hard shake, then jerked his chin toward the door. Telling her to get out.

Fuck that, Frank. Alex shook her head in return.

His gaze went steely in what she recognized as his Alpha Dom glare.

Alex glared right back. *I'm not leaving you to get shot, dumbass.*

The woman frowned and started to turn toward Alex, but Frank spoke in that hypnotic croon he did so well. "I can help, Charlotte. *I can handle this.*"

That last bit sounded as if it was intended for Alex's benefit. She tuned him out, mind working furiously as she tried to see a way out of this.

This looked like a situation that was about to go catastrophically off the rails. Charlotte—who was either mentally ill or had smoked some seriously bad meth—could easily decide to shoot everyone in the store.

Wait, where's Betty Mason? Alex dragged her eyes away from Frank and his psycho damsel in distress for a quick scan of the Gas-N-Go. At first she didn't see the third-shift clerk, and started to relax fractionally, thinking Betty had fled the scene.

Then she spotted a pink cell phone in a woman's hand, sticking out just above the store checkout counter. *Oh, for God's sake. She's shooting a damned video.*

Well, at least Betty had taken cover. As long as she didn't go in for a close-up, she should be safe.

Charlotte was begging again, rocking back and forth from foot to foot as words spilled out of her in a torrent. "The doctors, the meds, they're not helping. You're the only one who can save me. I can't . . . I can't take this anymore. You can do it . . ."

"Wait, darlin', just listen," Frank told her, pouring on the seductive Dom, whether the poor bitch realized that was what he was doing or not. "I want to help you, but not that way. If the meds aren't working, there are others that can blunt the pain until you—"

"No, no!" She waved the gun, her voice spiraling higher, taking on an even more frantic note. "Don't you understand, I can't take any more. No more snake . . . Shoot me, goddammit!" She rocked forward on the balls of her feet, her free hand curling into a fist as if she wanted to hit him.

Shit. Alex's Glock felt slick and clammy in her sweating palms. *We are so fucked. Frank's not going to shoot her. I'm going to have to do it.*

The woman glared at him so murderously Alex instinctively ducked lower. Frank didn't even flinch. "Do it, you fucking bastard!" she shrieked. "You can! Cops shoot people all the time!"

And pay for it for the rest of their lives, Alex thought.

"I'm not going to shoot you, Charlotte," Frank said in a low, calm voice. Alex wanted to hit him. "Think of your little boy. Do you want him to grow up without you? A mother's love is something nobody else can ever give him, because nobody else is his mother. Just you. Only you. Don't deprive him of that. Hang on for him."

The frantic way Charlotte was rocking back and forth would make her hard to hit.

Alex wanted to throw up. She'd never killed anyone, had never even fired at another human. Most cops never did.

Maybe a nonlethal weapon? Not the pepper spray—if Charlotte was under the influence of something, she might be too high to feel the effect.

The Taser, too, was out of the question, since Charlotte was armed. Both the barbs the device fired had to sink into flesh for the charge to work, just as both jumper cables have to be attached to jump-start a car. If one of the barbs missed or got caught in clothing, there'd be no circuit and Frank was as good as dead.

Alex could jump the woman, of course, but there was too good a chance she'd end up shot herself, in which case Frank might well be next. Any way you sliced it, she didn't like the odds.

And the damned video Betty was shooting was guaranteed to end up online. Even if Frank, Alex, and Betty survived, the media would go berserk with people saying she should have shot the poor mentally ill lady in the leg.

Never mind that the bitch could then turn around and put a bullet in Alex's brain. The only thing that wouldn't result in dead cops was shooting Charlotte center mass, bleeding her out so fast she wouldn't have time to kill anybody.

Yeah, I'm fucked.

Frank saw Alex settle herself, her gaze going flat. Preparing to fire.

Time seemed to lengthen, heartbeats stretching into slow thuds. Charlotte's too-wide brown eyes were wild with the agonized need for something, anyone, to take the pain away.

Even a bullet.

But he was damned if Alex would be the one to fire it. She'd carry the weight of Charlotte's ghost the rest of her life. Frank couldn't let that happen.

Dammit, if you'd given me one more lousy minute, I could have convinced her to give up the gun.

Fuck it, we'll do it the hard way.

He caught Charlotte's gaze with his in that *You will do what I demand because I will make it better* stare he'd learned before he could shave. Her dark, mad eyes grew uncertain, as if wondering if he really could take away the delusions and voices that tormented her. Holding her stare, he eased forward, gathering himself even as he purred low-voiced reassuring bullshit. From the corner of one eye, he saw Alex ease off her shooting stance as she realized he was making his move.

Charlotte noticed what he was doing. Alarm stirred belatedly in her pain-glazed eyes, and she started to bring the gun to bear. He pounced, his left hand thrusting her weapon to the side so any bullet would hit the beer display case instead of one of them. Seizing the gun barrel in the same motion, he used it as a lever and twisted it out of her grip. She started to grab for it, but he raised it over her head, well out of reach as he seized her wrist with his free hand.

Alex came boiling out from behind the candy shelf and

grabbed the other flailing arm, simultaneously whipping out her handcuffs as she hit Charlotte from behind. Over-balanced, all three of them went right over, Charlotte on the bottom of the pile. She cried out as the two cops landed on her, a howl of frenzy.

Wincing, Frank tucked Charlotte's weapon in the back of his pants.

"Nooooo!" Charlotte howled. Then he had his hands full, because the woman went wild, screaming and bucking as she realized she wasn't getting the death-by-cop she'd sought.

"Charlotte, you're under arrest!" Frank bellowed, but she didn't seem to hear, too busy clawing, kicking, and biting in a psychotic frenzy.

Even with his size advantage, a hell of a lot of U.S. government training, and Alex's help, it was all Frank could do to get the woman handcuffed. He counted himself lucky he managed it at all. As it was, she sank her teeth into his right arm. He had to stick a thumb into the hinge of her jaw to force her to let go. The bite stung like a bastard, but he didn't let it stop him. Ignoring the pain from a woman's teeth, nails, and fists was a skill he'd mastered when his idea of great TV was *Teenage Mutant Ninja Turtles*.

Getting her out of the store and safely into the back of his patrol car proved to be a fight of epic proportions. For such a little thing, she was impossibly strong. Frank couldn't even get a hand free for his shoulder mic to call for backup.

Charlotte fought him and Alex every inch of the way until he was afraid she'd dislocate her own arms as she howled demands that they *fucking shoot her!*

At long last, they wrestled her into the car and buckled her in. She promptly threw herself down on the bench seat and began slamming kicks at the windows and the metal grate that protected the driver's compartment from the back. Frank got in, cursing under his breath and hoping the glass would survive as he started the car. "Calm down, Charlotte!" he bellowed over her howls, but she only screeched louder.

The poor bitch was in desperate need of mental health care and some serious psychotropic drugs. Unfortunately, she'd pointed a gun at the store clerk, so her next stop was the county jail. Frank had no choice except to charge her with assault with a deadly weapon. If he was lucky, she'd have concerned family he could contact who could work with the judge to get an emergency detention order to hospitalize her for observation. From there, they could hopefully get her into treatment.

Unfortunately, Frank knew even after he had Charlotte taken care of, he'd have another angry woman to deal with. Judging by Alex's frozen expression when she'd yelled she'd meet him at the jail, she was just as pissed as Charlotte.

She might be his submissive, but this wasn't the bedroom. No amount of Dom was going to save him from her wrath.

The Morgan County Jail was a two-story redbrick complex with what looked like a mile of glass fronting its lobby. Inside it was all-gray industrial carpeting and rows of chairs with thin, ratty upholstery. Beyond the front desk, the metal detector, and the locked steel doors lay clusters of jail cells built for two that now housed four. The place had been overcrowded the day it was opened in 1993. Things had not improved in the decades since.

It was not, in short, the kind of place Frank would have chosen to leave anyone who was suicidal. Unfortunately, state law, miserly funding, and a resulting lack of mental health facilities meant there was nowhere else.

It took the better part of an hour to get Charlotte booked and into a set of restraints that would hopefully keep her from battering herself against the cinder-block walls of her cell.

Frank then went to work trying to contact her next of kin. Charlotte had no purse or identification with her—no surprise—but fortunately she was no stranger to the county jail either. Three months before, she'd been briefly held on assault and battery charges for attacking a clerk at a Verizon store. Evidently she'd thought the company was using her cell phone to beam things into her head she didn't want to hear.

Frank used the information on file to contact the woman's long-suffering parents. Forty-five minutes later, he left Victor and Raeline Shepherd talking to the judge about their options, and escaped the jail with a sensation of vast relief.

Outside, the night air was cool, the tree-shrouded horizon beginning to brighten toward dawn. He leaned a hip against one of four bullet-shaped concrete car barriers that were supposed to deter would-be jail-breakers from ramming the building. Or truck-bombing it, depending on whether the driver wanted to free an inmate or kill the whole lot of them.

In the parking lot, Alex got out of her patrol car, where she'd been using the unit's laptop to write the report on the incident. He supposed he owed her one for that. Since Frank was the first officer on-scene, the report was technically his job.

"Talked to Sergeant Henson and found out why we couldn't get backup," she told him, her voice a little too professionally courteous. Yeah, she was still pissed. "Apparently our friend the sniper took a shot at Bruce right after I walked into the store. While we were fighting Big Ball O'Crazy, every other cop in the county was out hunting the sniper."

Frank stiffened. "Did Bruce get hit?"

"No, thank the good Lord." Wearily, she ran a hand over her French braid, looking tired and defeated. "Apparently Bruce suddenly stopped to look at a scratch where somebody had keyed his patrol car, and the shooter missed. Bruce took off after him. Must have almost got him, too, because this time the fucker left his rifle behind."

"Let me guess, it was unregistered."

"In this state? You bet your big Dom dick. Had no papers at all, in fact, not even for the original purchaser." By South Carolina law, weapons were usually registered only if they were sold through federally licensed gun dealers like pawn shops. More often, people bought and traded firearms privately, without leaving a paper trail.

"Why can't we catch a break with that son of a bitch?" Frank growled.

"We did," Alex told him. "We're alive. Being alive constitutes a break."

"I'd like to break something. Like that bastard's skull with a bullet." He sighed. "We'd better get back." They still had two hours left in their shift. "Let's hope that fucking sniper doesn't have a spare rifle and a yen to try for us again."

Sergeant Rob Henson was a thin, angular man who wore his dark hair buzzed so close it looked like peach fuzz on the smooth curve of his skull. He had a beaky nose, a mouth that seemed perpetually thinned, and the cold blue stare of a Siberian husky in a snowbank. He was also waiting impatiently at the Bradfield Auto Seating garage.

Bruce fidgeted by his side, visibly tense. But then, given that he'd been shot at, that was understandable.

"What the hell took you so long?" Henson growled as they got out of their cars, the doors slamming with a heavy double thunk. He stalked over to them with long, aggressive strides, as though claiming the ground he walked on. "You should have been back here half an hour ago."

"I had to book Charlotte Shepherd in and get in touch with her family," Frank said calmly, despite the waves of Pissed Bastard the shorter man was beaming at him. "She's suicidal; she needed to be hospitalized for observation as soon as possible."

Henson's lips thinned even more, going almost invisible in the shadows cast by the garage driveway's security lighting. "You ain't a social worker, Murphy. You're a damned cop. You should have let the jail personnel handle the family. Your job is to be here, patrolling your area and serving the people who ain't crazy. Especially with some son of a bitch shooting at fellow deputies."

A muscle worked in Frank's jaw as he said stiffly, "Yes, sir."

Henson turned to Alex. She'd never liked the sergeant, for whom "asshole" was evidently the preferred leadership style. But he knew the job, and he'd never hesitated to roar to the rescue whenever she, Ted, and Bruce had their hands full. He waded into fights with the vicious intensity of a honey badger on a snake; if you fucked with cops, Henson would fuck with you right back. That counted more than a sunny personality in her book, a viewpoint she shared with every cop she knew.

But now, as that cold stare raked her, Alex had to work not to squirm. There was a hostility in his eyes she hadn't noticed before. She wondered if it was her imagination, or if he was just pissed in general. "What's your excuse, Rogers?"

She met his glare, fighting her submissive's instinct to drop her gaze before that Alpha Male eyefuck. "I was backing up my partner. The woman fought us pretty hard, Sarge."

He grunted, flicked a look at Frank. "Thought you were supposed to be some kind of badass SEAL. You couldn't handle some little female?"

"You know how crazy people are," Alex said, knowing better than to stick her oar in, but doing it anyway. The bastard hadn't been there; he had no right to judge Frank, supervisor or not. "It was like stuffing a bobcat in a bag." She gestured at the bruise she could feel swelling on her cheekbone. "My bruises have bruises."

"Wasn't talking to you, Rogers." Henson hadn't shifted his gaze from Frank's. "Your partner's got a nice little mouse coming up on that cheek. You don't seem to have any."

"The subject couldn't reach my face," Frank said, his expression utterly neutral. He didn't seem to give a shit whether Henson believed him or not. "She did take a chunk out of my arm with her teeth, and she kicked like a Clydesdale. It's lucky she didn't break every window in the back of my vehicle. She sure gave it her best shot."

Henson grunted sourly. "Yeah, well, get used to it. The good, the bad, and the batshit are all part of the job. You're with me, Murphy. I want to see how you do on the road, find out if you're really as good as Gaffney says you are." He turned to Alex. "You and Greer are together. With some fucker using y'all for target practice, you three will not be riding alone until further notice. I don't want any more dead cops on my shift. Is that clear?"

"Yes, sir," they chorused.

Henson started for his car, then broke step to glower at Frank. "Why're you still standing there, Frankencop? Let's go."

"Glad you're okay," Frank told Bruce before turning to follow Henson.

"Let's take my car. I want to drive," Bruce told Alex, a snap in his voice.

Alex eyed his flexing jaw on the way to his Crown Vic. "You sure you're okay?"

He shrugged and got in. "It was a clean miss. CSI was still looking for the bullet when Henson and I left to go back on patrol."

"Scary as hell, though. And they couldn't give you the rest of the night off?" Pushing his laptop aside on its swinging arm, Alex got in the passenger side and buckled up.

"Henson offered, but I turned him down. I'll do better if I've got something else to think about besides getting shot at."

As Bruce started the car, Alex watched Henson slide into the driver's side of his own vehicle. Frank took shotgun, stone-faced. Pissed though she was at him, Alex winced on his behalf, knowing the rest of the shift wouldn't exactly be Happiness and Glee.

Bruce grunted, watching the other car pull out and take off up the street with a screech of burning rubber that spoke of Henson's temper. "I do not envy Murphy having to spend the rest of the shift with Sarge in that mood."

"When is Henson ever in a good mood?" Alex asked as he pulled out and headed in the opposite direction the sergeant had taken.

"That would be—oh, let me think—never." Bruce drove well, his big hands sure on the wheel. The lights of passing cars painted sliding patterns of illumination along his handsome profile, with its strong nose and rounded chin. He looked a hell of a lot less battered than Frank, between the SEAL's scars and broken nose. Bruce's hair was just as thick and shining as Frank's, too, the color of roasted coffee beans. His smile was quick and frequent, an expression of his warped cop sense of humor.

Dammit, why couldn't she be attracted to him? Life would be a hell of a lot simpler. Unfortunately, he didn't he do a damned thing for her. Anymore, that is. Back in high school, she'd been head over heels for him. But that was before she knew she was kinky.

Fact was, Alex just didn't go for nice, normal guys like Bruce. She wanted a Dom. Worse, she wanted a Dom who played knight errant for every female wingnut who tried to commit suicide in his presence.

"What's got you stewing?" Bruce asked.

Alex shook off her irritation. Her old lover had a finely honed intuition that served him well on the street. Unfortunately, those same instincts could make him a pain in the ass when there was something she didn't want to talk about. "Nothing."

He shot her a longer look before returning his attention to the road. "Now that sounds like a nothing that's definitely a something. What's going on?"

"I meant 'nothing' compared to that murdering bigot taking a shot at you. I'm glad you're okay, Bruce."

He threw her a glancing smile. "Right back at you. We have definitely pissed somebody off. But I have no idea who, and I just spent the last three hours getting grilled about it by Tracy and Henson. I'd rather talk about why you look so damned unhappy."

Oh, what the hell. Maybe if she got some of the pissed off her chest, she could be a little bit more rational when she finally did have it out with Frank.

Alex sketched the encounter with Charlotte Shepherd in a few sentences that emerged as a hot snarl. "It's not that I wanted to shoot that poor woman—I'm damned grateful Frank got the gun away from her so I didn't have to—"

"But the fact that he had his weapon holstered under those circumstances makes you mad enough to chew through Kevlar," Bruce finished for her. "And I don't blame you. It was boneheaded. Especially for a guy who spent most of the last decade exchanging fire with jihadis. He knows better than that."

"The thing that gets me is . . ." She broke off as Bruce pulled up in front of a strip mall and killed the engine.

Picking up the car's mic, he keyed it with a click. "Dispatch, Charlie 22 out at Southern Shops."

"10-4, Charlie 22," dispatch replied.

"I've got to check doors," Bruce told Alex, pulling his Maglite out of its magnetic clip on the side of the radio. "Make sure no enterprising burglar has broken in and had himself a good ransack."

Alex nodded, pushed his laptop out of the way, and got out. "I'll take the other end and meet you—"

"We're supposed to stay together, remember?"

"Oh, hell, right. Okay." She trailed after him. But as she scanned the surrounding area for snipers, she saw nothing but parking lots, streets, gas stations, and shops. "I don't think he's going to try anything here. It's too open. Bastard likes trees."

"Maybe, but I still feel better with you on the lookout." His smile this time was definitely a little tight. "I'm a bit tense."

That was a plea Alex couldn't resist. *Damn, he knows me entirely too well.* She followed him, one hand on her weapon, alert for motion, for any pattern of shadow and light that could suggest a face, a hand, a rifle.

A watching killer.

Bruce moved quickly and efficiently along the length of the mall, pulling at doors to make sure they were locked, shining his flash into each store and scanning for burglars.

Alex followed him around the strip mall's corner. There in the deep shadow of the building, he paused to rattle a doorknob. Moving closer, she kept an eye on the stretch of empty ground that lay between it and the gas station beyond. If somebody was out there, her money was on the long, dead grass.

"Alex?"

She turned her head to glance at him. "What?"

To her utter shock, he caught the back of her neck and leaned in. His lips settled against hers, wet and shocking. She tried to jerk back, but the hand on her nape held her where she was. His mouth slipped and tasted, his tongue investigated hers with delicate skill.

And she felt nothing at all. *Damn, Frank's really done a number on me.* Finally she wrestled loose. "What the fuck, Greer?"

"I just wanted you to know that when you grow tired of Murphy, I'm here." His lips curled. "And I'm not an arrogant asshole."

Shocked, she stared at him. Bruce turned and walked away. "But he's not an asshole," she said. The other deputy didn't turn.

Which was when she realized she hadn't denied that Frank was arrogant. But then, he was a Dominant; arrogance was part of his job description.

And so, at least sometimes, was "asshole."

*I*nto every life, Frank reminded himself, *a little asshole must fall.*

And all too often, that asshole somehow became his supervisor. This was a problem, because assholes found fucking with him irresistible. Maybe it was his size that set them off, or maybe it was because of the alpha male streak he could never quite disguise. Whatever the case, they just had to put him in what they fondly imagined was his place.

This wouldn't have been a problem, except military organizations frowned on bitch-slapping superior officers. So Frank was always forced to suck it up. Fortunately, he'd learned how to ignore irrational, infuriating, and even outright terrifying behavior when he was still playing with Legos.

"So," Henson drawled. "We've all been wondering how Rogers managed to piss this prick off enough to make him want to kill her. Given that he went after Arlington for being a fruit, the gossip says she must have a taste for pussy. But since I hear you two are dating, maybe it's something else."

His mouth stretched in something more leer than grin. "Unless she's using you as a beard. How about it, Murphy? You ever tasted catfish on her breath?"

Gay, lesbian, or bisexual had never mattered to Frank. Bullies, though . . . He fucking hated bullies. "Are you really willing to say that kind of stuff on the job, or are you just testing me to see if I'll explode?" Which was outright insubordination, but he was too pissed to care.

"So that's a yes on the fish tacos."

Frank stared at the man, narrow-eyed and unspeaking.

Henson turned back to his driving. "Hope you're gettin' something out of it, because you could've taken a bullet for that girl. And you still could."

"I've been shot at before. I'm still here. The shooters aren't."

The sergeant raised an eyebrow at him. "Let's hope you're as good as you think you are, or you could be the one getting a skull full of lead."

Frank showed his teeth. "We'll see, won't we?"

CHAPTER FOURTEEN

Frank got through the rest of the shift without decking the little bastard, despite Henson's efforts to goad him. Even so, he was simmering with frustrated anger as he followed Alex home.

It was, he thought, a nice little place. There was a warmth and coziness about it, as if the ghost of old love still clung to its well-worn furniture and chipping paint. Stepping into the tiny living room, he took a deep breath of air that still bore the scents of mothballs and cedar, looking around at three generations of family photos that decorated damned near every flat surface.

Some of the anger bled out of him, soothed and . . .

Something furry exploded out from under the couch and attacked his feet, sinking claws into his boots and yowling like a demon out of hell. He didn't shoot it. Quite. Mostly because he looked down and realized his attacker was Alex's cat just before his weapon had cleared the holster. SIG, unfazed by his brush with death, chewed the toe of Frank's boot, growling maniacally. "For the love of God, cat! I almost shot you."

Instead of rescuing him from the cat, Alex rocked back and lifted an eyebrow at him. "Big guy like you, afraid of a little pussy?"

"Jesus, not you, too." He bent and gingerly reached for the cat, only to jerk back as the psychotic little beast went for his hand with a rumbling growl. He straightened, glowering down at it. "Henson spent half the shift talking about pussy. Either yours, your girlfriend's, or mine."

"Yours?" Taking pity on him, she crouched and started peeling her pet off his right leg. SIG cussed, but allowed himself to be detached with a minimum of bloodshed. Straightening, Alex cradled the cat and lifted red brows. "I've checked you really thoroughly. I don't remember a pussy."

"No, only a pair of balls that wanted me to clock him."

Stroking the cat, she eyed him. "And what's this about my girlfriends?"

"Not your friends who are girls," Frank clarified, dropping down on the armchair beside the door and scraping his hands through his hair. "The lesbian girlfriends who inhabit his fetid imagination."

"Henson actually said that?" She carried SIG off into the kitchen. The grind of a can opener and greedy feline yowls sounded a moment later. "Doesn't he realize the sheriff could fire him for that kind of crap?" She returned, pausing at the refrigerator to pull out a Coke for herself and a Mountain Dew for Frank.

"He assumes I won't rat him out because he's my sergeant."

"And male, and therefore share his Jurassic opinions."

"Which I don't. On the other hand, I'm not sure I like the idea of tattling either."

"There's that." Alex strolled over to hand him his drink. Dropping onto the couch next to his chair, she popped the top on hers. They both took long swallows and sighed, almost in unison. At last she said, "Though to be fair, he's never behaved like a sexist or bigot with me."

"How can you tell through the waves of asshole he emits?"

"Takes effort. But he's doesn't discriminate. He's a dickfritter with everybody."

Frank paused, considering it. "Point." They drank again, the silence companionable. "You know, I've been thinking," he said at last. "I wonder if our sniper buddy has planted any surprises in this house like the one in Ted's."

"That's . . . crossed my mind, too. You want to search, see if he's left us a present?"

"Actually, what I'd rather do is adjourn to my house. I've got a pretty good security system I'm willing to bet he won't be able to bypass. You can stay with me until the bastard's caught."

"Frank, that could take months."

"All the more reason for you to be somewhere he can't get to you. Especially since he's demonstrated his skills at breaking and entering."

Alex gnawed her lower lip, then sighed. "I'll pack my bags and get the cat carrier."

"Don't forget the litter box."

An hour later, Alex was busy stashing her clothes in the two drawers he'd cleaned out for the purpose. SIG was off exploring the house.

Probably making sure there was a can opener.

"Henson wasn't the only one to do stupid shit tonight," Alex told Frank, who was clearing space in his closet for her uniforms. She launched into an account of Bruce's kiss.

"He did what?" Gray eyes narrowed and went hot as he stared at her.

"Kissed me."

Now his frown was pure Dom, forbidding and dark and deliciously sexy. "And you let him?"

"He grabbed my neck and planted one on me. There wasn't much 'let' about it."

"Oh, bullshit. I've seen you fight." A muscle rolled in his jaw.

Alex eyed its restless flex with a certain wicked amusement. "Are you *jealous*?"

"Of *Bruce*?"

"Hey, he's a good-looking guy."

"And if he was any more vanilla, his ass would be ice cream."

"Good one."

"I thought so." They worked in silence for a minute or two before he asked, "What the hell happened with you two? I know you have a history."

Alex pulled a stack of athletic bras from her bag and tucked them into the drawer. "Ancient history."

"History has a way of thrusting its nose into the present. Next thing you know, you've got the whole camel in your tent." He gave her a gimmee finger wiggle. "Confess, wench."

"Pushy Dom."

"Yeah, we do that. I'm listening."

She hesitated, then gave in with a sigh. "Bruce and me, we've known each other since elementary school. He was always a cute kid, but when we were in high school, he was boy-band cute. I had it bad for him."

"Did you?" Frank definitely did not approve, judging by the way he watched her with his fists on his hips.

Alex started hanging her clean uniforms on the section of rack he'd cleared for her. "Yeah. His mom, Amy, was best friends with mine, so we spent a lot of time together. Maybe a little too much. Amy and Bruce would come over, and there'd be these bruises on her arms and face she always had lame explanations for."

"Walked into a lot of doors, did she?" Despite the arch words, his tone was sympathetic.

"Yeah. My mom was always after her to leave Steve, Bruce's dad . . ."

"The abusive prick in question."

"Right. And what a prick he was. Bruce told me he was even a member of the local Klan."

Frank's eyes widened.

"What?"

He shook it off. "Nothing. So why didn't his mother pack up Bruce and go?"

Clothes put away, she walked over and dropped down next to him on the bed. "Amy had been raised strict Catholic, and she didn't believe in divorce. But the beatings kept getting worse. When Bruce and I were dating, she went to the ER damn near as often as my mom went to church."

"Did he ever beat the kid?"

"Early on, but by the time we were in high school, Bruce was playing football for the Coach and had thirty pounds on Steve."

"And daddy's self-control miraculously improved." He moved a little closer, picked up her hand where it lay in her lap, began toying absently with her fingers. His hand felt big and warm as he cupped hers, rough with calluses. "But what about you and Bruce?"

Alex leaned one elbow on a knee, watching his strong fingers stroke hers. "It was one of those wild teenage things. We'd fight like ferrets in a sack one minute, then we were necking the next. Mostly we fought about sex. He wanted it, but I was afraid the Coach would find out and kill both of us. I finally gave in—I think it was his birthday, and he didn't want to be Harrison High's only seventeen-year-old male virgin."

"I seriously doubt he would have been. Boys that age lie about sex every time they open their mouths."

"Probably. Anyway, I gave in. I was expecting fireworks and little pink cherubs. What I got was a baseball bat covered in sandpaper shoved up my girl parts."

Frank winced in sympathy. "He had no fucking idea what he was doing."

"Nope. I didn't much enjoy being on-the-job training either. I asked him to stop, he kept going, it hurt more, and I punched him in the teeth."

"Yeah, you're Coach Rogers's kid." Smiling slightly, he brushed a lock of hair back from her face.

"Yup." She traced an absent pattern on his knee. "So we broke up. That probably would have been that, if it hadn't been what happened to his parents."

"What *did* happen to his parents?" Frank turned on the bed, pulled her between his spread thighs, and gathered her against his chest. "He got a look on his face when we backed you up on that domestic the other night. Kind of haunted."

"Because he probably is." She relaxed back into his arms. They felt comforting, particularly when she was dwelling on such dark memories. "About a month after we broke up, Bruce brought Amy to Casa Coach, begging Dad to hide 'em. She had finger marks around her throat."

"Bad sign."

"Very bad sign." Any time an abuser started choking his partner, nine times out of ten he was going to kill her. "So Bruce, my folks, and I took her to the cops to swear out a warrant. But they had to find him before they could arrest him . . ."

"And he was nowhere to be found."

"Exactly. Back then, Coach was buying houses to flip—the housing bubble was just starting to inflate—so we took them to his latest project, which he'd just completed. Unfortunately, they hadn't even unpacked when Andy narrowly avoided a head-on with a drunk driver. Rolled his brand-new Jeep. My brothers were with him."

Frank gathered her closer. "How badly were they hurt?"

"Andy broke three ribs and his leg." She shivered, taking comfort from his hold. "Tim was concussed, and Harry had a bruised kidney. Mom tried to get Amy to go with them to the hospital, but she felt so rough from the beating, she just wanted to sleep. Coach figured she'd be okay with Bruce there, and the three of us headed to the hospital."

"And Steve came after her while you were gone."

She nodded, remembering the horror of that night. "Mom and I stayed at the hospital while Coach went to check on them. Found Bruce tied to a chair with a head injury, and Amy beaten to death. Steve had eaten his own gun."

"How the hell did the bastard find out where they'd gone?"

"He called Bruce's cell and bullshitted him that he just wanted to make up." Alex slumped. "Bruce bought it."

"Fucking moron."

"Classic abused kid behavior." She shrugged against Frank's warm strength. "Bruce never got over the guilt."

Tilting his head, he studied her face. "You made up with him out of pity."

"Yeah. Our second wind didn't last, though. He was so moody and tormented. Nothing I did made it any better."

"PTSD is like that." He dropped his chin on top of her head again.

"I know that now, but then—no clue what was happening. We struggled along until the night he told me his parents would still be alive if my folks hadn't convinced his mother to leave. I was afraid he'd say that to them; they already thought it was their fault as it was. That was it for us."

"They realize that's bullshit now, right? If Steve choked Amy, he was working up to killing her. Only thing that could have saved her was leaving town."

"As Coach tried to get her to do. But Amy didn't want to pull Bruce out of school because he'd miss his last year playing football. Didn't want to do that because Coach thought he could win a scholarship to Clemson. There'd be no way they could have afforded it otherwise. Amy thought if they could hide until the cops found Steve . . ."

"He'd have bonded out of jail and come after her then." Which was pretty much the pattern in cases of domestic murder.

"Yeah. Steve was determined to kill her, and he didn't stop until he did." The memory chilled her, and she snuggled into Frank's arms. "So Bruce ended up enlisting in the Army, and that was the last I saw of him until he came back a couple of years ago to become a cop."

Frank tilted his head to look at her. "You went into law enforcement because of him and his mother, didn't you?"

"Yeah, I guess I did. It was my first experience with violence, and when I saw the wreckage one bastard left behind . . ." She shrugged. "I wanted to save the victims I couldn't save then. I guess Bruce must feel the same."

Frank frowned. "Wait, you think Bruce had PTSD *before* he went to war? What the hell is it like now?"

Alex considered the question, frowning. "I haven't noticed any problem, even when things have gotten hairy. And they have. Hell, Bruce's control when people push him is better than mine. He never loses it, even when the situation is over and he can safely blow off steam."

"So what you're saying is maybe he's a little too controlled."

"No, what I'm saying is that Bruce is a good cop." She eyed him, and the penny suddenly dropped. "You're wondering if he's the sniper. I thought you didn't believe the killer was a cop."

"I didn't—until just now." Frank started ticking off points on his fingers. "White supremacist father—do the words 'you suck black cock' ring a bell?—who murdered his mother while he watched, resulting in PTSD . . ."

Alex shook her head, impatient. Frank didn't really know Bruce, not the way she did. "Bruce doesn't have a racist bone in his body. And he thought as much of Ted as I did. He sure as hell wouldn't have murdered him. Besides, PTSD doesn't make you a psychotic killer. *You* probably have it, and you haven't killed anybody. Hell, you holstered your weapon when you confronted Charlotte, when damn near any other cop would have shot her. Including me."

"Alex, think about it." Frank shifted around from behind her until he could more comfortably meet her gaze. "I know he's gone through a lot, but—"

"He got shot at too, Frank." She rose from between his thighs and turned to face him. "He recovered the sniper's rifle. You think he'd have handed the murder weapon over if he was the killer?"

Frank considered the point, then grimaced, conceding. "Okay, okay. It was just a thought. God knows Tracy doesn't have any other decent suspects."

"Well, no." Alex sighed. God knew she shared the desire to do something, anything, to catch Ted's killer. She started to bend down for a makeup kiss. And stopped, realizing she wanted a lot more than a kiss.

After all the painful memories, the guilt and grief, she wanted to do something fun. And she couldn't think of anything more fun than screwing Frank's brains out in one of the delicious little games they so loved to play.

But this time, she didn't want to lose. It was time Frank ended up in the handcuffs. Thing was, how was she going to get him there? If she started a fight, he'd win. He was too big, too strong, and too damned skilled.

Unless she cheated.

Wicked inspiration struck. Suddenly she knew the perfect game to both arouse Frank and teach him a badly needed lesson about underestimating women. "Let's get this straight, you thought you'd play Sherlock Holmes?" Her grin was deliberately taunting. Which, knowing Frank's hatred for brats, was like waving a red flag in front of a bull.

Sure enough, those cool gray eyes narrowed and sparked, and the corners of his mouth kicked up in a grin that was downright evil. "Sounds like somebody needs a spanking . . ." He came off the bed and reached for her wrist.

Sailing right into her trap.

Moving with the smooth speed Ted had worked years to teach her, Alex grabbed his hand and jerked, throwing him off balance. As he instinctively reared back, trying to regain his footing, she slipped behind him. Expecting her to try to sweep his leg, he turned to counter. But the move had been a feint: she sidestepped into his pivot as he straightened his arm, trying to pull it from her grip. Wrapping her fingers around his hand, she braced her thumb against the end of his pinkie and cranked his wrist toward his biceps. As the fierce pain on the end of his pinkie distracted him, she grabbed her handcuffs and snapped them on his captured wrist.

Frank growled like an enraged grizzly.

She knew the tiny window surprise and pain had given her had just slammed closed: he wouldn't yield now even if she broke the finger. Given his strength and size, he'd be free in a heartbeat. So she started talking. Fast. "Uh-uh, Murphy. I caught you fair and square." Stepping behind him, she took the chance of illustrating the point with a little more pressure on his pinkie, while using her grip on the cuffs to twist the bracelet painfully on his wrist. A forward nudge got him headed for the straight-backed chair that stood to one side of the bed.

"Yeah? Know what I'm going to do when I catch *you*?" The menace in his voice made her sex clench and heat.

"I've got a pretty good idea," she said dryly. "But since I like living dangerously, I'm going to sit you down right here."

"You know, you may be a switch," he said, his tone deceptively mild. "But I can assure you, I'm not."

A switch was a BDSM term for someone who could play either submissive or dominant. "That's the God's honest truth. There's not a submissive bone in your entire towering body." She dropped her voice into a seductive croon. "But why don't you sit in this chair and pretend there is?"

Pain lanced up Frank's arm from the abused wrist, blending with the sharp protests from the finger Alex was torturing with such expert delicacy. He considered whether to buck anyway, just to teach his little sub he was the wrong person to try to Dom.

But if she broke that finger, even accidentally, it would be a giant pain in the ass.

"You do realize I'm going to take my revenge out on your pretty little butt." His cock bucked a little at the thought.

"That's a risk I'm willing to take," she told him, with

a teasing note in her voice that told him she wasn't nearly as worried about the thought as she should have been.

But truth was, his dick was equally interested in just what she did have in mind. So when she cranked the handcuff on his wrist, he decided to sit down after all. He didn't even refuse when she told him to put his free arm back. Listening to the click of the bracelets locking, he plotted his revenge.

This was the kind of thing that would normally freak him the hell out. Being bound and helpless was a nightmare he'd had more than once. His SEAL training had included having his hands tied behind his back while being thrown into the deep end of the pool. And that was nothing next to the training to re-create what it was like to be handcuffed and waterboarded by terrorists.

Yet now he wasn't nearly as furious and panicked as he should have been, given all that ugly trauma. There was probably no stronger evidence of just how much he trusted Alex. It went right down to the bone, even after such a short time knowing her.

So, wrists chained behind the chair, he sprawled and gave her an insolent smile that matched the hard-on behind his fly. "You got me. Now what?"

"Just illustrating a point," Alex purred, smiling at him as she rotated her hips in a slow figure eight. The baton holstered at her hip swayed on her belt, emphasizing the motion. Humming a bluesy melody—he thought it was something by Adele—she reached up and went to work on the French braids that crowned her head, freeing bobby pins and rubber bands, dropping them on the floor one by one. Finally her hair collapsed around her shoulders, bright copper gleaming. And all the while, her hips rotated to that throaty female croon.

By all rights, he shouldn't have found the seductive grind so erotic, considering all the weapons she wore. His cock gave another ravenous buck anyway. He cleared his throat, tried to bludgeon his lust-drunk brain into remembering what they were talking about. "What point was that?"

She reached up to the top button of her uniform shirt. Began sliding it out of the button hole, taking her time, her lids partially veiling her vivid eyes. "Well, women have much less upper body strength than men."

Frank gave her a toothy grin. "A point I'm looking forward to illustrating on that pale, lovely ass."

"Mmm." Another button popped free, and then another. There was something hypnotic about the movement of those long, tapered fingers on her buttons. "The point I'm trying to make is that women have to be creative when it comes to our weaknesses."

All that showed in the gap of her open shirt was a wedge of familiar coarse fabric. "This is the first time I've ever seen a striptease involving Kevlar."

"Another weakness I've got to compensate for with creativity." She spun on the toe of a booted foot, leaving him to contemplate the curves of her ass under black fabric and the ugly belt with all its clunky pouches and weaponry. A twitch of her slim, muscled shoulders, and the shirt slid down to hit the wooden floor. Something clinked—her badge and nameplate probably.

There was the tearing sound of Velcro releasing like the rip of silk. The bulletproof vest thumped to the ground on top of the shirt.

Frank's eyes widened. She wore a white tee under the vest, just as he did himself—the thing would rub your skin raw otherwise. She'd sweated under the vest, just as he had, so the tee was plastered to her skin, almost transparent in places.

"You're not wearing a bra," he said hoarsely.

"Under a vest? That damn thing's like a sports bra. It mashes you flat." She braced her feet apart and swayed as she hummed that low, slow melody.

God, he wanted her to turn around.

Hypnotized, he stared at the line of her spine rolling sinuously under the soaked white fabric down to that clunky black belt. She reached down, and he heard the hiss of a zipper. Breaking off that soft, yearning hum, she wiggled a little as she fought to pull the tee free of her pants.

His lips parted as she peeled the tight fabric upward, leaving pale, damp skin gleaming softly in the lamplight. Then she hitched up her duty belt onto the bare inward nip of her waist. The buckle of the pants belt she wore under it jangled, followed by tiny clicks as she unsnapped the small straps that held the belts together. His cock jerked against his fly.

Alex skimmed the thick, tough polyester fabric down over her hips and the curving length of her endless, beautiful thighs.

She was wearing a pair of red lace panties underneath.

His eyes locked helplessly on that scrap of candy-apple crimson curving up the sweet mounds of her ass cheeks. His mouth began to water. When she bent double to deal with the boots, her lovely body curled with the effortless ease of somebody who did a lot of yoga. He heard a groan, and realized it was his own.

The boots must have given her some trouble, because she remained deliciously bent, her lovely ass waving back and forth in its luscious red veil. The plump lips of her pussy parted as if waiting for the kiss Frank was dying to give her.

He really wished he had his hands free, because at the moment his rock-hard cock was mashed painfully by the fabric of his pants. He ached to free it—and then plunge the whole thing right into that luscious cunt.

Inhaling, Frank swore he could smell her arousal, a faint musk blending with the scent of clean female sweat and a hint of some perfume that smelled like cinnamon and tart apples. "You smell like pie." His voice sounded deep, roughened by hunger even to his own ears.

She tightened the bend until her hair brushed her feet and looked around her bare calf at him. "What kind of pie?" Straightening, she stepped out of the boots and murmured, "Cherry?"

"No." He croaked it. "Apple." Frank swallowed. "I love apple pie." For once during a sexual encounter, he hadn't calculated his words for maximum seductive effect. There was no Dom artistry to them. Nothing but raw male need.

She bent and ran her lovely hands up the backs of her thighs to her ass, where those pretty fingers edged under the red lace. Just brushing the bright copper tuft covering her pussy. Once. Twice.

Straightening to her full height, she caught the waistband of her panties, and pulled them down those legs. Slowly. So slowly, lace whispering over smooth skin. Until she was bent double again.

His hands were sweating. He started to dry them off on his pant legs, only to hear the clink of the handcuff chain, the tight rake of the bracelets around his wrists. She had him fucking helpless . . .

God, her ass. The full, round curves of it. The bulge of her pussy lips between her thighs. Those legs, long and curving with feminine muscle. She could probably run him into the ground with those legs.

Pulling upright again, Alex turned to face him, settling her duty belt over her lush hips. Leather creaked and the baton rang against the ring that held it.

He swallowed. "Why did you keep the belt?"

"This?" She ran her right hand over her Taser, the pepper spray canister, the collapsible baton. Cupping the grip of the pistol protruding above its leather holster even as the tapering fingertips of her left hand traced the extra magazines for the weapon. "It has something I need." She unsnapped one of the smell leather pouches and pulled out a familiar square of plastic packaging.

"You keep condoms in your duty belt?" he managed, his voice a little choked.

"Not always," she informed him. "Just since I met you." She tucked the condom between the belt and her bare belly.

"Jesus God, what you do to me." It was all he could do to talk, staring at the contrast between her pale skin and the black leather of the belt.

"It's so fucking male, isn't it?" Alex asked softly, both hands weighing the belt. "It's designed to be worn by men, with their narrow hips and broad shoulders. Makes women just look chunky."

"You don't look chunky." His voice rasped.

"Thank you." Her soft lips curved. Any lipstick she'd put on at the start of the day was long gone, leaving her mouth lusciously bare and softly pink. Only a shade lighter than the nipples that rode so proudly on those full, pretty breasts. Hard nipples, jutting as if eager for his mouth.

She walked toward him, the swing of her naked hips emphasized by her duty belt. The delta of her neatly trimmed pubic hair gleamed like threads of copper in the soft light. He stared at the swaying triangle, entranced. She stopped right at the barrier of his knees. He spread his thighs, and she stepped between them. Leaned in.

It was a delicious promise of a kiss, all tease and warmth, her pointed tongue sliding between his lips, tracing the edge of his teeth as his own tongue chased hers. Sliding together in a sinuous erotic dance, wet flesh brushing wet flesh, caressing and stroking.

Until she drew back a fraction so she could look into his eyes as she sat down astride his lap and began to unbutton his shirt.

He panted with need. And didn't care what power he was surrendering to his sub. Didn't give a shit about their respective roles. About anything other than the hunger to touch those perfect breasts, tight nipples, creamy skin. "Uncuff me."

She bit her lip, a gentle press of teeth on flesh as she considered. Then, deciding, "No."

"I want to touch you."

"I don't care." Her clever fingers made short work of his buttons. Flick, flick, flick. One after another, sliding free of their buttonholes. "I haven't made my point."

"Oh, believe me . . ." He rolled his hips against her weight and suppressed the need to groan. "You've made your point so well my balls have turned blue."

"Blue balls? Really? Are you a sophisticated Dom or a sixteen-year-old boy?"

"You seem to have convinced my dick I'm a sixteen-year-old boy." He contemplated the eager intensity of his lust. "Maybe thirteen."

She pulled his shirt out of his belt, moving, it seemed to him, with all the speed of honey in January. How the hell was he supposed to survive the removal of his vest, tee, and pants without embarrassing the hell out of himself like some overeager teen at the prom?

Unfastening the plastic buckle of his duty belt, Alex dropped the whole thing on the floor with a ringing thump. She went after his pants belt next, unbuckling it, letting it hang with a jangle. Slim hands unfastened his pants and unzipped him.

Dragging his aching, desperate erection free, she hooked his boxers under his balls. She reached into her belt, pulled out the condom, tore the package open with her teeth. Slid it down over his throbbing length, making him gasp at the wicked promise of the friction. "Oh, Jesus, hurry up," he managed between set teeth.

"Well, if you insist." Alex grinned wickedly. Before he could even draw a deep breath, she'd impaled herself on his rubber-sheathed cock, her pussy tight and just slick enough.

"Oh, Christ!" he groaned, throwing his head back at the blaze of sensation burning its way up his spine.

Alex inhaled sharply, loving the feel of Frank's thick cock filling her so completely. Somewhat to her surprise, teasing him had aroused her every bit as much as it had him. Now each slow stroke teased her sex with delicious friction that drove her to grind down even harder, stimulating her clit as he rolled up to meet her. She watched as he threw his head back, panting in delight, the cords of his strong throat rigid with the effort of controlling his pleasure. "God," he gritted. "What you do to me! You feel so fucking good, so tight, so . . ."

Incredible.

He filled her as if God had designed his dick for the job—its meaty length spearing to her slick, tight depths, its thickness pressing deeper and deeper as she slid down over him until her ass met his hips. She paused, loving the pure intensity of the moment, the silken sensation of being linked to him. Then he lifted his head and met her eyes, and the psychic snap of that instant rocked her. She'd never connected so perfectly with a man in her life.

Alex rose upward, and still he stared into her, making her feel like a Caribbean tidal pool, clear all the way to the bottom, every thought swimming through her brain visible. Staring into those gray eyes, she watched them darken as his pupils expanded, to the near-black of hurricane clouds. Hungry eyes, desperate not just for sex—that was easy enough—but for something more. Something she couldn't quite see, could only sense in his shadowed depths. Something that swam through his darkness like sea monsters in the Mariana Trench.

Hungry, lonely monsters.

She sank again, chasing the liquid silver burn of her orgasm. His cock reached deep, and her pubic bone ground on his pelvis with a delicious buzz of pleasure. Circling her hips, Alex moaned as the delight intensified into a hot electric spark. Frank made a needy sound, hunching up at her, each thrust burning her senses like an arc welder's flame, until . . .

The bright detonation ripped a scream from her mouth that became a drawn-out yowl as she paused, her thighs shaking as she held herself in place, and he lunged up and pulled out and . . .

Roared, a deep male cry of climax as he bucked, Alex riding his heaving thrusts, her orgasm intensifying with the savagery of his.

Until he finally collapsed under her, panting, as she let herself fall against his chest. One side of his open shirt was caught beneath her body, and his badge scraped her cheek as he recovered his breath. She curled her arms around him, listening to his heart thumping hard.

God, she loved this moment of sated connection. Loved it so much she was tempted to keep her mouth shut just to preserve it. Unfortunately she had to say what had to be said, or her stubborn Dom would keep making the same mistake. Until it got him killed.

And that was an unacceptable outcome no matter how much she wanted to preserve the moment.

"I trust," she said when she was capable of speaking a sentence without panting it, "I've made my point."

"Any number of them," he agreed. His breathing, she was gratified to notice, was no steadier than hers. "But I gather you mean one in particular."

She drew back and straightened to meet his gaze with as much cool confidence as she could muster wearing only a duty belt. "I just kicked your ass."

At that his head rocked back, and he frowned slightly, as if a little jolted from the delicious aftermath. "What?"

"You heard me." She gave him a deliberately taunting smile. "You might be able to bench-press my body weight, but I still won."

"Won what?"

"You're in that chair, despite the fact that you didn't want to be there."

Frank grinned toothily. "Well, it was a damned good floor show."

"Yep. But you're still right where I want you." She ground her hips a little, and he sucked in a breath, despite his softening cock.

He swallowed at the tight, slick friction. Hard. "Okay."

"Even though in any direct hand-to-hand contest, you'd kick my ass."

"Honey, kicking your ass is the last thing I want to do to it."

"Exactly. I know your weaknesses and I exploited them. I goaded you into reaching for me, giving me the opening I needed to put you in a pain-compliance hold, exploiting another weakness. I handcuffed you, used more pain compliance to put you in that chair, and seduced you into staying there."

"And made me come so hard I saw stars. I consider that a win."

She reached down and pulled the tube of pepper spray off her belt, and raised it right in front of his eyes.

Patrol cops had to submit to being shot with pepper spray in order to carry it, so he knew exactly how unpleasant it would be to get a direct blast in the eyes from two inches away. He reared back instinctively. "Alex!"

"SSSSSSSSSssssss," she hissed, pretending to fire. "And you have a face full of pepper spray, just as you could have had a face full of bullet earlier tonight. And in both cases, it would have been because you underestimated a woman who used your weaknesses to kick your ass."

Angry heat replaced his lazy pleasure. "I knew what I was doing. I had it under control."

Alex lifted a red brow. "Like you have me under control?" She slid the slender spray can back into its holster on her belt.

His voice lowered to that deep Dom thrum that made her pussy heat, even after everything they'd just done. "I'll show you control."

"And I'll probably enjoy every minute of it," she said, ignoring the blend of arousal and delicious anxiety that rolled through her. "But having your gun holstered while you tried to talk Charlotte down was stupid."

"Yeah, if she'd wanted to shoot me. But she didn't want to shoot me. She wanted me to shoot *her*. And if I'd had my weapon out and cocked, it would have been too easy to do just that, even if only by accident."

"She's mentally ill, Frank! Which means, by definition, that her actions are not rational. Anything you said could have triggered her into shooting you, me, and that poor bitch Betty, who was armed only with a cell phone. Video from which, by the way, is probably already on the Internet."

"I was watching her eyes, Alex. I'd have known if she was about to fire."

"It's not the eyes you have to worry about. It's the damned gun!"

"Look, if she hadn't been crazy, you can bet your ass I'd have had my weapon drawn. Hell, if she'd just been a run-of-the-mill robber, I'd probably have already shot her. But I know crazy." He paused, swallowing. "My mother is bipolar."

Alex stared at him in dismay. Bipolar disorder was a major mental illness in which victims alternated between periods of frenzied, manic joy and depressions that could drive the victim to suicide. Victims were also prone toward delusions when their brain chemistry got particularly bad. "Oh. Oh, shit, Frank, I'm . . . I'm sorry."

"Yeah, it didn't make for the most stable childhood. When she was manic, Mom would stay up for days at a time, drawing all over the walls, talking a mile a minute, so damned happy she'd break into dancing in the middle of the mall. When she was in a depressive phase, I had to practically drag her out of bed to get her to go to work. When she was healthy—and most of the time, she was— she was a good mother. When she was bad . . . sometimes she'd go psychotic."

"Violent?"

"And delusional." He nodded grimly. "I learned how to predict when she was about to explode. Good thing, too. When I was sixteen, she had a really bad episode. She cut my throat." He turned his head and gestured at a short scar on his neck not far from his left ear. It was only a couple of inches long, but it was thick with knotted scar tissue. It must have been a hell of a wound.

Alex gaped at him. "Your *mother* did *that*?"

"Yeah. I always hid the knives when she got bad, but somehow she'd gotten her hands on a half-rusted box cutter. I got into the bathroom and locked the door. Luckily she'd left her cell in there and I was able to call 911. Damn near bled to death before the cops arrived. They saved my ass." He smiled faintly. "That's why I became a cop after I got out of the Navy. Wanted to pay it forward."

"If she was that bad, why were you with her at all?" Alex

demanded, outrage stirring behind her astonishment. He'd spent years at the mercy of a woman slowly losing herself to mental illness. "Why didn't DSS take you?"

"Because I went to considerable lengths to make sure they didn't." Rolling those delicious shoulders, he added, "Could you take off the cuffs? My arms are beginning to cramp."

"Oh. Yeah, sure." Mechanically, she rose from his lap, taking the key off her belt and unlocking the cuffs, then pulling them off his powerful wrists and stashing them in the cuff-shaped pouch on her belt. "You *wanted* to stay with her?"

"She was my mother," Frank said, as if that went without saying. "I took care of her, just like she'd taken care of me when I was small." He stood, rubbing his reddened wrists. "You know, as bondage gear goes, handcuffs kinda suck."

"Sorry." Alex shook her head. More for something to do with her hands, she took off her duty belt, then looked around and started collecting her uniform from the floor. "I just don't understand how you managed to stay with her, unless a whole lot of people really dropped the ball. Didn't you go to school?"

"Of course. She wanted me to go to school. Hell, she wanted me to go to college. She wasn't always sick, Alex. Mom had a lot of good days." He shrugged his broad shoulders as he zipped his fly and buckled his belt.

"But what about your grandfather? The one who left you the money. Why didn't he do something?"

"He didn't know. She didn't get sick until I was ten or so. After she tried to kill me, I realized she needed serious help. I got Granddad on the phone and told him if he didn't start taking care of my mother, I was going to the media. I'd tell everybody all about how he'd abandoned his grandson to the psychotic mercies of his mentally ill daughter."

"And it worked."

"It worked. He finally stepped up to the plate, and Mom got the care she needed to recover. Since I was only sixteen, I had to move in with him. That was no party—Granddad really was a prick. When I finally decided I couldn't take it any longer, I enlisted in the Navy. After I warned him that if Mom didn't keep getting the care she needed, I'd make him pay."

"Ballsy. Not that I'm surprised." She studied him. "When you said you knew what you were doing with Charlotte, you meant it."

"Yeah. There's this look they get. At first there's all the usual pain and fear as they fight whatever the disease is trying to make them do. And then . . . their eyes just go flat. Dead. They give up. That's what I learned to look for, dealing with Mom."

"That's what you were watching for with Charlotte," Alex said softly.

"Right. That's why I holstered my gun. I was trying to show her that I hadn't given up on her, so she shouldn't give up on herself. She still had a chance."

"And then I forced your hand because you knew I was about to shoot her."

"Right." He shrugged. "But you never had to develop your instincts the way I have."

"You obviously have good instincts—otherwise the sniper would have gotten us both yesterday." She searched his eyes. "But, Frank, what if you trust them, and they're wrong?"

He just shrugged. "Then I guess I'm fucked."

CHAPTER FIFTEEN

There weren't nearly as many cars in the Myers-Rhodin Funeral Home as there should have been. Normally the visitation for a cop—particularly one who'd died in the line of duty—would draw every officer in the department, plus representatives from departments all over the state. Alex knew that, because she'd attended a visitation for a cop in Greenville, fifty miles away.

"Where the fuck is everybody?" Frank growled as he parked the patrol car.

"At home," Alex said, getting out. They'd ridden in together; Frank had insisted, knowing how torn up she'd be. She'd decided not to fight him on it, suspecting she'd need the energy to get through the event, never mind the shift to follow. "They saw the fucking video."

"Speaking of video . . ." He glowered at the street, where two news trucks from rival stations were parked. Four or five people with iPads and television cameras loitered on the sidewalk, watching for anybody moving slowly enough to accost. "The vultures are here."

"Walk fast." They headed across the parking lot toward the funeral home's columned entry. It was a long, one-story redbrick building that looked like a cross between a church and an old Southern plantation house.

A female reporter strode toward them, moving with surprising speed on her high heels. A man with a camera balanced on his shoulder hurried in her wake. "Deputies, what do you think—"

"No comment," Frank snapped, shooting both of them a Dom glare that sent them quickly into retreat.

"Nice work," Alex murmured when they were out of earshot.

"I hate the fucking press," Frank muttered back.

She shrugged. "Like you said—vultures."

"Hey, vultures need love, too." A woman stepped out from around one of the funeral home's white columns to intercept them, a wicked little smile on her face. She was just over five feet, delicately boned in a way that had always made Alex feel like a horse by comparison. Short blond hair exposed her ears, and her bangs were long enough to hang in front of her guileless blue eyes. For once, she wore a dress and heels, both navy blue, instead of the jeans and tee that were her habitual reporting wear. "And we perform a useful service. Otherwise the bodies would pile up. Hey, Alex."

Alex gave the blonde a sincere smile. Despite her dubious career choices, Cassie York had been a friend for years now. "Hi, Cassie. Circling again?"

"Flap, flap." The humor drained from her lively face. "I'm sorry about Ted. He was a good guy."

"Yeah. I really appreciate the story you did on him." The piece on the *Morganville Courier* website was the sole bright spot in the coverage. Cassie had not only interviewed the sheriff and Ted's mother, but also tracked down Terry Peterson and her children, Darius and Katilia. The three had talked about their memories of the night Ted saved them eight years before. Terry's heartfelt defense of the man who'd rescued her kids had made Alex's eyes sting.

"Thanks." Cassie's eyes flashed. "I hate seeing a good

man get shredded by morons who don't know what the hell they're talking about."

Frank eyed her dubiously. "And you do?"

"Yup." Cassie looked up. And up some more, until she could finally meet his eyes. "Boy, the sheriff likes 'em big."

Frank opened the funeral home door for Alex before turning to Cassie. "You going in?"

"Yes, thanks." Cassie strolled past him, Alex in her wake.

Alex winced, remembering her manners. "My mother would smack me. Cassie, this is Frank Murphy, who's the new deputy. Frank, this is Cassie York. She's a reporter for the *Morganville Courier*, but don't hold it against her. She's an actual person and everything."

"Just ignore the feathers."

"So are you trolling for quotes, or what?" Frank asked suspiciously as they walked up the funeral home's carpeted foyer.

Her expression cooled. "Actually, I'm here to pay my respects. Ted was a friend."

Inside, the building was cool, its walls painted a pale sea foam green, with thick brown carpet underfoot in the foyer that led to the main hall. Rooms lay off to either side with small signs standing in front of each listing the names of the deceased on view there.

A line snaked along the corridor that led toward the room where Ted's family and casket waited. Most of those in line were uniformed deputies. There were civilians, too, some with the logos of local businesses embroidered on their shirts; they'd apparently stopped by on the way home from work. That was the whole point of a visitation, after all—to give people who couldn't attend the funeral an opportunity to pay their respects.

"At least there's a line," Alex murmured. "I was afraid nobody would show."

"Yeah, WJIT didn't do Ted any favors, the assholes," Cassie growled. "You know, I have my faults, but at least I don't use a cop killer as one of my sources."

Bruce Greer turned toward them from his space farther

up the line, then walked back to join them. "Hey, Alex, Frank." His eyes flicked to Cassie and went cold. "York."

"Hi, Bruce. Sorry it couldn't be under nicer circumstances."

"With you, it never is."

Cassie blinked, looking a little hurt.

"So, Cassie," Alex said softly, meaning to distract her friend from Bruce's uncharacteristic slap, "what do you think the chances are that County Council will give us a raise?"

"It's an election year for three of them," Cassie murmured back. "You've got a better chance playing the lottery."

They spent the next few minutes chatting as the line wound through the corridor, only to fall silent when they reached the room where Ted waited.

He lay in his black dress uniform in a dark walnut open casket draped with a flag. Nearby a shadow box display of his Army medals stood on a small table, along with a portrait of a younger Ted in his Green Beret uniform, looking every inch the stern warrior.

Alex's eyes stung fiercely. Cassie give her shoulder a comforting squeeze as she blinked hard, clenching her teeth against yet another wave of the grief and rage that had caught her off-guard so many times over the past week.

The idea that Ted had been shot from ambush by a coward . . . That the entire fucking country felt entitled to sneer and joke about a hero because of something that was none of their goddamned business . . .

Even liberals who might have supported a gay cop shot down in a hate crime sneered at him for the YouTube video. Some said it was just another example of a white cop getting off on beating a black man, and mocked Cal for allowing it. Alex had stopped watching TV or reading e-mail altogether over the past week, unable to tolerate another ignorant word from any of them.

Fuckers. Stupid, ignorant fuckers.

She shut the rage down hard, afraid she'd start screaming curses, particularly at the so-called friends who not only had avoided the visitation, but had not even sent flowers.

There were a number of arrangements, but not as many as there should have been. Beside the casket stood a huge circle of roses and lilies on a wire stand from the MCSO. Alex had contributed when they'd taken up money for it, though she'd also sent a peace lily personally.

As the receiving line snaked around the room past more floral displays, Alex read the cards protruding from each arrangement. Cap and his wife had sent an enormous philodendron so Ted's mother would have something more permanent than flowers. The couple hadn't been able to attend the visitation, though Cap had texted to say they were going to the funeral tomorrow. There were arrangements from other members of the Atlanta BDSM group, including Roy and Tara, the pair Frank had done the whipping demo with, plus a number of others. At least they—

Suddenly a large, warm hand closed around hers, and she started, jolted out of her daze of pain.

Frank watched her with concern in his gray eyes. "Are you all right?"

Swallowing hard against the knot in her throat, she shrugged. He squeezed her hand, his grip comforting, a silent message of *I'm here*. Alex blinked, realizing they'd reached the couch where Cal sat beside Ted's mother.

Karen Arlington was a tiny white-haired woman whose face retained a seamed, elegant beauty despite her age. Alex had helped Ted organize her sixty-sixth birthday party a few months before. She'd looked barely older than Alex's mother then.

Now she looked as if she'd aged two decades, grief weighing at her face like gravity, deepening fine lines into deep creases. Her reddened eyes were so swollen, it was a wonder the poor woman could see out of them. She sat rigidly in her simple black dress, a strand of pearls gleaming around her neck, a tissue in one hand, the other clasped tightly in Cal's.

He wore a black pinstriped suit and a gray tie, his shoulders rigid, his jaw jutting like a proud man grimly determined to get through an agonizing ordeal without shaming himself.

"Cal," Alex choked. "Mrs. Arlington . . ." She bent to clasp the older woman's hand, fighting the tears. One of them escaped anyway, rolling down her cheek. "I'm so, so sorry." *Sorry I couldn't have gotten there in time to save him. Sorry I couldn't have at least killed the bastard who killed him. Just sorry.*

"Alex." The old woman's thin shoulders shook once before she straightened them. "Thank you so much for coming."

"He was a hero. He didn't deserve this." She had to swallow around the knot in her throat. "None of this."

Mrs. Arlington nodded, her effort not to sob so obvious it was painful. Cassie stepped in to speak softly to her as Alex turned toward Cal. Her friend was on his feet, shaking Frank's hand as the big deputy murmured something low-voiced and comforting.

"Cal . . ." Alex said. He turned to her and extended a hand, as if to shake hers. "Oh, hell with that." She pulled him into her arms, hugging him hard. "Don't listen to any of those bastards," she whispered to him fiercely. "It's all bullshit. Every bit of it. Ted would be the first to tell them to fuck off."

It took him a moment, but he hugged her back. She thought she heard a sob, ruthlessly bitten off. "This sucks, Alex. It sucks so bad."

"I know, baby. I know. But I'm here for you, no matter what."

He chuckled, though it sounded watery. "I know you are, PoPo. People like you are all that's getting me through this nightmare."

She hugged her friend a little longer, exchanging murmurs about Ted, about the unfairness of it all, aware of Frank's low, deep voice speaking to Ted's mother.

Finally, unable to put it off any longer, she pulled away from Cal and turned toward the casket.

Ted lay in his dress uniform, resplendent in the black jacket with its high collar and row of silver buttons. They'd produced another badge for him, polished lovingly until it shone against the dark fabric. Next to it lay the rows of ribbons he'd received, along with the Medal of Bravery for saving Terry Peterson and her children from the burning trailer.

Mortuary makeup hid the wound in his forehead. His features looked sharper, more drawn than she'd ever seen them, and his mouth appeared abnormally thin, as those of funeral home corpses always did.

In a hard dark flash, she saw him lying on his back in the road with a bullet in his head. Pain stormed through her in a molten lava rush.

Alex had thought she'd known anger before, whether as a teenager pissed at her parents, or a cop outraged at an abuser. None of it could touch this murderous fury.

She squeezed her eyes shut, fighting the need to scream her rage. Remembering all the times Ted had waded into fights to keep her from getting her ass kicked by someone bigger, stronger, more vicious. He had never been a big man, yet he'd loomed large in her life, casting a shadow almost as long as the Coach's.

He'd taught her how to fight so patiently, with flashes of sarcasm that made her want to both swat him and earn his approval. Every time she mastered a throw, a grapple, a takedown, he had flashed that rare, proud grin of his that made her glow for days.

He'd loved her. Oh, they had never said the "L" word— their relationship had been almost masculine that way.

God, this hurts. Cal's right, this hurts so fucking bad.

And she had no business showing her pain.

Suddenly Alex remembered a fragment from one of the homicide books she'd read so obsessively when she decided to become a cop. The writer had said serial murderers often came to funerals to drink in the suffering of their victim's family and friends. It wasn't just the killing they craved. It was the power that came from watching people grieve for those they'd murdered.

Every corpse was surrounded by a web of suffering victims. Killers loved that.

Alex gritted her teeth, fighting to get herself under control. Fighting to hide her pain in case his killer watched.

Suddenly a big hand appeared below her chin holding a Kleenex. Frank. She accepted it, swiped at her eyes and running nose. "Thank you."

Cassie rubbed a hand down her back. "Tracy's a good cop—though if you tell him I said so, I'll call you a liar." A trace of humor entered her voice. "He'll chase the sniper until the bastard gives up just to get rid of him."

"Yeah." *He'll chase the sniper.* Not Alex. Tracy was the detective, the one whose job it was to nail the cop killer. Unless the murderer took another shot at Alex herself, she wouldn't get a chance to bring him down.

A television cop would swear revenge and start looking for clues, nailing him in an hour with frequent breaks to sell expensive cars. Real life didn't work that way.

It was Tracy's case. He was the one with access to the evidence. If she tried to get her hands on any of it, the officers in the evidence room wouldn't let her have it. It didn't matter if she'd been the female embodiment of Sherlock Holmes. They had to protect the chain of custody. Otherwise some defense attorney could use her sleuthing as evidence of a police conspiracy to frame his client. That kind of thing could get a case thrown out of court and let Ted's killer walk free to kill somebody else.

But God, she wanted to do something.

Actually, what she really wanted to do was press the barrel of her gun against the killer's head and blow his brains out. Fuck the law. Fuck the system. What she wanted was the bloody justice of the heart.

"Hey, are you okay?" Bruce asked suddenly, shouldering past Cassie, who stepped back reluctantly.

"I'm fine," Alex lied, swiping at her eyes. Resisting the temptation to snap, *"Does it look like I'm okay?"*

He gave her shoulder a comforting squeeze. "Cassie's right. Tracy's a good cop. He'll do what it takes."

"Yeah," she said. But it wasn't enough.

* * *

That night's shift was one of those thoroughly boring ones that demanded an IV drip of Red Bull and black coffee. Since it was her turn to ride with Henson, Alex actually counted herself lucky on that score. Frank had told her about some of the shit the sergeant had said to him during their ride together the night before. Given how frayed her temper was from grief and outrage, she'd feared one sexist, homophobic comment from the jackass would have set her off like a human IED.

Fortunately Henson had just enough sense to fear she'd report him if he said anything out of line. He didn't poke at her, and in return, she didn't shoot him.

Nobody took a shot at her either, though her shoulder blades itched every time she got out of her patrol car. Apparently the sniper had taken the night off. Maybe he'd decided to go looking for easier targets in some other town.

Maybe. But she doubted it.

For once, Alex and Frank didn't make love when they got home from work. Like most Doms, he had a keen ability to sense his submissive's moods. She was grateful for his perception; the visitation had brought the pain of Ted's loss back to the surface like an oil spill boiling up in the ocean. Her soul felt scraped raw, and her eyes burned with the tears she'd fought all night to suppress.

She realized suddenly she'd been keeping so furiously busy concentrating on Frank, the job, and her parents in order to avoid the aching pain of losing Ted. And the guilt of being unable to do anything about it.

Oh, she could have. There'd been a perfect opportunity when the killer had tried for them at Frank's house, and she'd missed it.

Epic fail.

Eyes burning, Alex curled on her side in the bed. Silent,

respecting her need to grieve, Frank wrapped himself around her, his big, naked body feeling warm and comforting against her bare back. SIG, as if sensing her pain—or maybe just wanting to be petted—curled up next to her belly. She stroked the cat, taking comfort in his soft fur and motorboat purr as Frank stroked her in turn. Back. Shoulder. Arm, carefully avoiding her bare breast, obviously realizing pain had blunted her usually healthy sex drive.

"Let it go," Frank murmured in his ear. "You don't have to act with me, Alex. Let it go."

And she, who normally found crying so difficult, choked out a sob as the tears started running down her face, unstoppable as rain.

Alex and Frank got only a few hours' sleep before they had to get ready for the funeral, which would be held that afternoon. Luckily, this was their weekend off, so they'd be able to make up for lost sleep later.

While Frank showered and dressed, Alex made sure her badge and every silver button on her dress uniform gleamed, working over each with a soft cloth and a can of silver polish. Inhaling the astringent reek of the polish, she'd found something oddly soothing in the mindless repetition of rubbing slow circles over the metal.

Alex pointedly did not let herself think about the badge the killer had taken. That would only trigger another fit of useless rage and guilt. She'd indulged in enough of that as it was.

She'd never cared for the MCSO dress uniform. Its high collar felt as if it was slowly strangling her, and its wide, gleaming belt made the skinniest female look broad across the ass. Worst of all was the black campaign hat that always reminded Alex of Smokey the Bear. The hat was traditional wear for county deputies, but Sheriff Ranger rarely required them to actually wear it.

"Only you can prevent sexual contact," she intoned to her reflection, then added in her normal voice, "Because it's for damned sure I'm not getting laid in this getup."

When Alex emerged from the bedroom, she found Frank waiting. "Oh, that's just not fair."

The same uniform that made her look dumpy enhanced his drop-dead sexiness. The boxy tailoring emphasized his height and the breadth of his shoulders, as did the strap that cut diagonally across his broad chest. Silver buttons engraved with sheriff stars marched down the front of the jacket, and a blue stripe piped the outside of each pant leg.

"Somebody needs to take a picture and put you on a recruiting poster," Alex told him.

"Thank you." He gave her one of those hot, hooded looks he did so well. "You, on the other hand, make me want to unbutton all those buttons and . . . muss you. Thoroughly."

She grinned, cheered that he thought she looked sexy. Hat notwithstanding.

They arrived at the Prince of Peace Lutheran Church to find its parking lot packed, in contrast to the visitation the night before. No surprise; the sheriff had sent out an e-mail Thursday saying he expected everyone who was not on duty to attend the funeral.

Inside the sanctuary, the windows bled colored light into the room from their stained glass. The pews were filled with cops in pressed black uniforms, badges looped with black ribbons to show the department's collective grief. In among all the cops and civilians were a surprising number of men in Army olive green dress uniforms. Men Ted's age, for the most part, wearing the green berets that gave them their names.

And every one of them wore expressions of stubborn defiance.

Never mind that most Special Forces warriors were every bit as conservative as the sheriff's office's deputies. Never mind the media coverage of the scandal that branded Ted a pervert who beat his lover. They didn't even care that it had been more than a decade since he'd retired from the Army.

All that did matter was that he'd fought beside them in

Afghanistan or Iraq or the first Gulf War, or whatever shit hole the Army had sent them to. That kind of bond, sealed in blood and bravery, couldn't be broken by YouTube or talking-head snark.

There were also a number of black faces among the whites, though Cal was one of the few not in uniform. He sat next to Ted's mother. Ted's brothers sat on her other side, studiously ignoring him.

Alex and Frank found Captain Kyle Miller and his wife, Joanna, in the back row. Cap, wearing dress whites, looked even more sternly handsome than usual. Joanna was a trim woman who wore her hair in a silver pixie cut that made the most of her elegant cheekbones. Her large, dark eyes were surrounded by a filigree of fine wrinkles. She wore a pretty jersey dress in navy blue that swirled around trim calves.

Joanna couldn't resist playing mother to every sub she knew—and many of the Doms, for that matter. What's more, even the prickliest Dominants allowed it. "So here we sit, in the back," she murmured.

Alex dredged up a smile and the rest of the old Southern joke. "Like good Baptists."

"I'm sorry about Ted, baby," the woman added softly, giving her a swift hug smelling of Chanel No. 5.

Cap stood as they eased into the pew and shook first Alex's hand, then Frank's. "He was a good man. I hope they catch the bastard."

"So do we," Frank growled. "Preferably before he takes another shot at Alex."

Joanna looked alarmed. "He shot at Alex?"

Before either of them could explain, the organist started playing to signal the beginning of the service.

The service hit all the traditional notes of a cop funeral. There was the requisite kilted piper playing "Amazing Grace" on the bagpipes, followed by a couple of soloist friends of Ted's mother. Next came the hymns Alex knew by heart thanks to her mother's habit of dragging her to church whenever the doors opened. One of Ted's commanding officers from the Army detailed his military history—at least the parts that weren't classified.

The surprise came with Sheriff Ranger's eulogy. Apparently Ted had been buddies with Ranger's eldest son growing up, so the sheriff followed his military career with interest. When Ted had retired after twenty years with the Army, Ranger had convinced him that, at forty-two, he was far too young for a rocking chair.

"Though lately," the sheriff added grimly, "I've thought I should have let him rock."

After a couple of years on the street—during which he'd been recognized for saving Terry Peterson and her children from the trailer fire—Ted became a sex crimes investigator, a bit of history Alex had known. What Ted hadn't mentioned was that he'd cleared more cases than anyone in the unit.

"I can't tell you how many times I listened to Ted rage about some pedophile he'd just caught," Ranger said, hands braced on the massive oak podium beside the altar. "He had a talent for wringing a confession from even the most soulless predator. But it took a toll on him, because he was haunted by the women and children we as a society hadn't been able to protect. That he, personally, hadn't been able to protect.

"Ted felt driven to protect those who couldn't protect themselves. He worked sex crimes as long as he could, and then he went back to patrol. He told me it was cleaner, a little less like wading through raw sewage.

"I know what Leviticus says, but I also know how many women and children Ted helped, and how many monsters Ted caught. I don't know whether he's in heaven, but I can't believe he's in hell. I do know that one way or another, Ted is with God, because I believe we're never without God, no matter where we are or what we do. God is infinite, and that infinity includes the heart of each of us."

After that, the minister's sermon on tolerance and forgiveness came as something of an anticlimax.

* * *

Alex, Frank, Joanna, and Cap joined the funeral procession to the cemetery. The uniformed pallbearers lifted the flag-draped coffin from the hearse and carried it to the tent that sheltered the grave. After the minister performed a short graveside service, the deputies came to attention.

Ranger used his car's bullhorn to announce, "Charlie 23 is 10-7." His voice cracked on the ten-code for "off duty."

As a bugler from Fort Jackson played "Taps," the honor guard fired their rifles with deliberate precision. One volley, then two, then three rolled across the gray headstones surrounded by the reds and yellows and oranges of fall.

Her shoulders held painfully erect, Alex joined the assembled officers in saluting as Ted's casket was lowered into the ground.

Fury rolled through Bruce as he stared around at the crowd that surrounded Ted's grave. He wanted to just open up on every fucker there.

Yes, he'd succeeded in turning a lot of people away from Arlington thanks to the video. The recording had worked just the way he'd intended, sending talking heads into a frenzy of condemnation from both ends of the political spectrum. Liberals and conservatives had been, for once, in complete agreement: Ted Arlington deserved it. Maybe not in those exact words, but that was the gist.

Which was why it so infuriated Bruce that somebody had the gall to put a badge back on him. As if Bruce hadn't had a right and a duty to take it away.

People had spouted sanctimonious bullshit about the little fruit until he wanted to throw up. The sheriff had put the cherry on the B.S. sundae by taking about Ted's heroism and honor. Bruce was tempted to put the fat bastard on the kill list. Too bad he didn't have time to kill everybody who needed killing.

Take all those Green Berets. He'd been Army, dammit.

He knew how conservative Special Forces types were. They had to have seen the video. Hell, Fox, CNN, and all the networks had played it until even Bruce was sick of it.

So why had all those Green Berets shown up like Arlington was some kind of hero?

But the thing that really, really pissed him off was the cops who'd started speculating about the targets he'd missed: Frank, Alex, and supposedly Bruce himself.

Some of the bastards had actually suggested he'd gotten lucky when he killed Ted, that he couldn't really hit the broad side of a barn. They couldn't know he'd done tours in Iraq, but it was still insulting as hell.

Well, he was going to show them all. He would, by God, take out every one of his targets, including Alex and her strutting Navy SEAL.

But first, a little practice. Something that would shut up the skeptics and throw a little fear into them all. A killing that would hurt Frank as much as Alex had been hurt by Ted's death.

A nice little warm-up for the main event.

CHAPTER SIXTEEN

The Millers had invited Cal to stay with them at their home in Atlanta while he looked for a new job and a new place to live. Between Ted's murder and the scandal, life in Morgan County had become too damned painful for the young submissive. He had no reason to stay. His boss had fired him a couple of days before in a fit of morality. He'd claimed to be sorry, that Cal was attracting too much of the wrong kind of attention. Business at the bar was down as the usual customers found somewhere else to get drunk.

"I'm going to be notorious for a while," Cal told Alex, Frank, and the Millers as they helped him pack his things into boxes Saturday afternoon. "But in a city the size of Atlanta, people will find something else to run their mouths about a hell of a lot sooner."

In the meantime, he was going back to school to study computer graphics. He meant to own his own business. Frank and Cap said they intended to invest in it.

So the Millers, Frank, and Alex helped Cal load everything into a U-Haul for the trip before driving over to Frank's house.

He'd invited the three to spend the night rather than make the three-hour trip back home after such an exhausting day.

Two takeout pizzas later, the subs ended up in the kitchen making strawberry daiquiris. Their laughter and teasing rose and fell over the periodic grind of the blender. Frank and Cap, meanwhile, drank beer and pretended to watch a football game in the den.

"So." Cap paused to dip a tortilla chip into Frank's nuclear-meltdown-hot salsa. "How's it going with you and Alex?"

Frank took a swig of his Coors, running his free hand down SIG's honey-brown spine. The cat lashed his chocolate tail and purred like an electric drill.

"And that, ladies and gentlemen, is what we in the business call a 'pregnant pause,'" Cap said dryly. "Come on, boy. Cough it up."

"I'm not sure it's going to work." Honesty forced him to add, "The sex has been great, but . . ." Frank broke off, absently scratching SIG under the chin.

Kyle lifted a silver brow. "It's only been a week. You may want to give it a little more time."

"Yeah, but . . . sometimes she seems more switch than submissive." The cat rolled over into his lap, offering his belly for a scratch. Frank obliged him.

"Alex and every other woman on the planet. Including the ones in burqas. They may act submissive as hell when it suits them, but there's a reason Mom rhymes with Dom."

Frank toasted him with the beer. "Ain't it the truth."

"So, other than having been a cop for the past five years, what has she done to make you consider her insufficiently submissive?"

"Insufficiently?" Frank snorted. "She's not submissive at all, especially when you get her pissed." He described the encounter with Charlotte and the chewing out Alex had given him afterward.

Cap frowned, dunked a chip in salsa, and ate it, munching as he considered. Finally he swallowed. "Hate to say it, boy, but I agree with Alex. That was a truly boneheaded way to get yourself shot."

"Not you, too." Frank settled back in his seat and propped a foot on the coffee table. SIG folded his paws under his body and shuttered his blue eyes, rumbling. "Look, I know—"

"Your mother. And she still damn near cut your throat. You didn't know this Shepherd woman at all. I realize you've got a chivalrous streak—most Doms do—"

"Except for the assholes."

"Except for them. But chivalrous or not, you can't be stupid about it."

"That woman wasn't really a danger to anyone but herself. Most mentally ill people aren't violent. And as long as they take their medication, they—"

"Yeah, but when they go off their meds, some folks are fucking dangerous, Frank. And you've got the scars to prove it."

Frank looked away, grinding his teeth a moment before admitting, "Yeah. Okay, you're right. I was convinced I could handle her, and I took a chance I shouldn't have. But that doesn't mean Alex gets to jump me, handcuff my ass, and fuck my . . ." Belatedly realizing what he was admitting, he snapped his mouth shut, feeling his cheeks go hot.

Cap roared with laughter. "Did she? Good for her! And you loved it, didn't you? Maybe you're as much a switch as she is."

"Oh, bite me. And no, I'm definitely not a switch. I'm just male." Frank bared his teeth in a wolf smile. "As for Alex, believe me, old man—I'm plotting my revenge."

"And I may have something in the truck that will help you with that."

Frank grinned in genuine delight. "You finished the bench."

Cap nodded. "Yep. Come take a look." A burst of laughter rolled from the kitchen, barely audible over the whir of a blender. "If we're quick, we can get it down into the dungeon before the subs finish getting plowed on daiquiris."

"Then let's get a move on." He exchanged a feral Dom grin with his friend as he scooped the cat off his lap and dumped him on the floor. "Be a shame to spoil Alex's surprise."

* * *

The next morning, Frank treated his guests to Belgian waffles, scrambled eggs, and bacon. Once again, he and his collection of Food Network recipes produced something delicious.

"It's a good thing we packed the truck yesterday," Cal groaned. "Moving furniture while waddling sounds impractical."

Frank laughed. "Glad you enjoyed it."

"That's putting it mildly."

Cal pulled Alex into his arms for a ferocious hug as Frank and the Millers said their good-byes. "Be good, PoPo. I'm going to miss you."

"Don't worry, you'll see me every weekend I have off." She hesitated. "You will be going to Cap's parties, right?"

"Maybe the munches. I don't really want to scene for a while." His dark, handsome face tightened with grief. "No Dom alive would be able to replace Ted."

"Of course not. You'll never forget him—I doubt you'll ever want to. But Ted would be the first to tell you you'll eventually heal. You'll need someone in your life, and it'll probably be another Dominant, because that's a part of who you are and what you need. He wouldn't consider that a betrayal, Cal."

"No." But Cal's closed expression told her he wasn't ready to hear it, and wouldn't be for some time. "Look, you be careful, you hear? I couldn't take it if something happened to you, too . . ."

"Hey, don't worry about me." Alex jerked a thumb at Frank. His handsome head was thrown back as he laughed at something one of the Millers had said. "I've got Super-Dom over there to protect me."

"Uh-huh." He hesitated. "I'm a little worried about that bug they found in your car. If the sniper made a recording and releases it to the media . . ."

She shrugged, though the muscles between her shoulders

tightened. "He hasn't yet, and it's been almost a week. Maybe the audio was lousy."

"Well, don't let him make any better ones, then." Cal grimaced. "Believe me, you don't want your sex life on You-Tube."

"Frank's house has an excellent security system. He says the sniper would have a hell of a time getting in to plant anything. Which is why I've decided to move in with him, at least for the time being."

The pain in Cal's dark eyes lifted. "Really? Already? That's great, PoPo!"

"It's not permanent. I'll just be staying here until we catch the dickhead." Alex grimaced. "I doubt I'd be able to sleep back home anyway."

"I hope you catch the fucker soon." Cal's lips peeled off his teeth. "Or even better, that you blow his fucking brains out with Ted's name scratched on the bullet."

Alex slid her arms around him and gave him a fierce squeeze. "I'll do that, subbie."

His arms tightened at her use of Ted's favorite nickname for him. When he spoke, his voice sounded a little choked. "See that you do."

They stepped apart, and Alex exchanged hugs with Cap and Joanna.

As the three got into their vehicles, Frank pulled Alex against his side. They watched as Cap's truck, the U-Haul, and Cal's car—with Joanna driving—pulled out of the drive and rumbled for Atlanta.

When all three vehicles were gone, Frank looked down at her. "Hey, doll, would you mind cleaning up the kitchen for me? I need to take care of something."

"Sure . . ." She gave him a sly smile. "Master."

"You bet your ass."

The kitchen didn't take long; Joanna had insisted on helping her clear off the table before she left, so all Alex really needed to do was load the dishwasher and wash down the countertops and stove. She spent more time dodging SIG's attempts to wind around her ankles than actually cleaning up.

Unfortunately, the waffle iron had a cord. She was contemplating the best way to clean it when she heard the click of boot heels on slate flooring. She turned, meaning to ask him how to remove the waffle iron plates from the device for cleaning.

Instead, she damned near swallowed her tongue.

Frank stood watching her, a dark grin on his face, gloriously bare-chested, in black jeans tucked into black riding boots. "I wanted to have a . . . word with you about your little performance yesterday."

"Um . . ." She took an instinctive step back. "Which performance was that?"

"The one right before your striptease." He took a step toward her. "Which, of course, I thoroughly enjoyed." His voice dropped into a deep male growl. "The part I have a problem with is the bit where you *attacked* your master and *handcuffed me to a chair.*"

"Ah. Yes. That probably wasn't wise." She backed away, a delicious kind of dread sliding over her.

"No," he crooned, following her with slow, relentless steps. "It wasn't wise at all."

God, he looked hot. So damned big. His bare chest flexed under the cloud of soft, dark hair that covered it, thick pectorals shifting as his powerful arms tensed, ready to grab the minute she gave him an opening. Which she was tempted to do right now, except that wasn't the way they played the game. She had to make him work for his conquest, or it wouldn't be as much fun for either of them.

So she bounced on her sneakered toes as she retreated, leaping back every time he tensed as if to pounce.

Alex knew perfectly well she was being herded, of course. He was getting her out of the kitchen—which was designed for cooking, not combat—into the great room, where there'd be a bit more room to roll around.

So she spun on her heel and took off, darting through the

doorway into the room beyond. His booted heels thudded on the floor as he lunged after her. She zipped around the corner, then whirled and jumped him with a gleeful lack of consideration for tactics, their relative sizes, or basic common sense.

Frank being Frank, she didn't manage to take him off guard. He knocked aside her strike, pivoted away from her attempt to trip him, and launched his own attack—a cat-quick grab she barely managed to block.

They circled and dodged, punching, blocking, kicking. She was faster than he was, but he had the advantage of long arms, not to mention the power of that big body. Alex felt a grin of reckless pleasure stretch across her face.

Until she stepped closer when she should have danced back. A big hand fisted in the fabric of her shirt as he hooked her ankle with his. Then she was falling—sort of. Frank wrapped his arms around her as she went down, his free hand cradling the back of her head. They hit with a meaty thump as he landed on top of her, pinning her thoroughly under his muscled weight. He felt deliciously heavy, thoroughly solid. Very male.

"I do enjoy dancing with you," he purred. "Almost as much as I enjoy fucking your brains out."

Alex bared her teeth at him as he grabbed one wrist and pinned it to the floor beside her head. "Same to you, Frank." She strained to break his grip, more for the pleasure of failing than anything else.

He lifted a dark brow, his grin dangerous. "Is that how you're supposed to talk to your master?"

"Top," she corrected, then pretended to consider the question. Knowing all the while, of course, that she was asking to be punished. "Maybe Dom. But Master?" She grinned, snotty as a thirteen-year-old in a snit. "I don't think so."

"And yet, I seem to remember you calling me 'Master' any number of times," Frank observed, his tone silken. "Mostly when you were trying to talk me into letting you come."

"Did I?" Alex blinked, pretending doubt. "Are you sure?"

"You know I don't approve of bratting."

"I'm bratting?"

"Definitely. And as I said, I don't like it." He tightened his grip on the material of her tee. A quick, hard jerk shredded it like Christmas wrapping paper in a ten-year-old's grip. "In fact, you could say I strongly disapprove."

Excitement tightened low in her belly, but she faked an outraged yelp. "Hey, I liked that shirt!"

Frank grinned, feral and very male. "I like it better off." Reaching a free hand beneath her body, he unfastened her bra with a skilled twist of his fingers, then peeled it off her. "And at the moment, it's what I want that counts." One black brow rose. "Unless you'd like to use your safeword, of course."

Alex pretended to sneer. Her heart was hammering in delighted lust. "I wouldn't give you the satisfaction."

"Oh, believe me, you're going to give me all kinds of satisfaction, baby." Releasing her hand for the moment, he went to work on her jeans, unbuttoning, unzipping, dragging them down her thighs and off. She briefly considered fighting, but decided she wanted to be naked for him as much as he wanted to strip her.

Sitting back on his heels, Frank contemplated her nudity. The fierce glitter in his eyes made her cunt grow slick. Apparently he agreed with her about nudity as her preferred state. His cock hardened as she watched, stretching thick and ready along the line of his jeans zipper.

Until he dropped on top of her, a warm and welcome weight. He contemplated her bare breasts with wolfish interest, then lowered his head and flicked his tongue over the tight peak of one nipple. Alex caught her breath at the sweet, hot sensation of his mouth on her breast, so incredibly lush. Tilting his head, he admired the curves topped by their eager pink peaks. His free hand stroked over her skin, making her want to moan as she imagined other places he might touch her. His eyes flicked up to meet hers. "Ready to call me 'Master' yet?"

She tried to twist her captured wrist from his hold. "Hardly."

Frank smirked. "Give me time. I'm only getting started."

Then he dropped his head again and went to work on her right nipple, suckling and licking by turns. At the same time, he teased her left with thumb and forefinger in delicious little tugs and squeezes.

She twisted under him, writhing, Her free hand slid up, tried to tangle in his hair, though it was too short for her to get a good grip.

His head snapped up, pulling free of her attempted hold as he glared fiercely into her eyes. "Did I give you permission to touch me?"

The arousal tightening her belly gripped tighter, making her gasp.

His free hand snapped up, fisted in the long hair that spilled around her head. *"I asked you a question!"*

"No!" His eyes narrowed, and she corrected herself. "No, sir."

The fist tightened, though the pull wasn't quite savage. "That should be, 'No, *Master.*'"

Alex panted, keenly aware of his hot strength mantling her body. Her instinct was to give him the honorific he wanted, but she didn't want to spoil his fun with a too-quick surrender. "No, Top."

"Oh, you're pushing it." If she hadn't known he'd cut his own arm off rather than hurt her, the deadly snarl in his voice would have scared the hell out of her.

Frank released her hair and reached into a pocket of his jeans. Before she could cringe, he caught her left nipple, rosy and erect, in the jaws of a clamp.

The sting was fierce enough to make her gasp. "Dammit, Frank, that hurts!"

He grinned. "Good." Ducking his head, he sucked the right nipple until it ached almost as much as the left, then clamped it, too.

Gunmetal eyes flicked to her face with a Dom's focused intensity. "What's your safeword?"

"Red. Yellow for slow down, green for okay."

"Good." He rose, sitting back on his haunches. Despite

the bite of the clamps, she found herself admiring the flex and work of smooth muscle beneath sleek chest hair. One hand still gripping her captured wrist, he rose, pulling her to her feet. For a moment he paused, looking down at her, reading her expression as he dropped the role of Big Bad Dom. "Are you okay?"

She gave him a reassuring grin. "I'm considerably better than okay."

"That's for damned sure." Leaning in, careful not to dislodge the clamps, he kissed her. It was a surprisingly sweet kiss, considering the bright sting in her nipples. He tasted her lips, suckling the lower lip, then tracing his tongue over the contours of the upper before stealing inside to explore. Slow, thorough, it was the kind of kiss that made a girl's knees go weak—even one with Alex's taste for kink.

She'd always thought of kink as just fun and games. But that kiss suggested emotions that went deeper than fun and games. Heart deep.

Soul deep.

Finally he pulled away and reassumed his big, bad Dom face. "Come along, slave. I'm going to give you exactly what you've been begging for."

Oh, God, I hope so. She let him drag her toward the stairs she knew led to the house's bonus room.

Aka, the dungeon.

It still looked a bit bare, though there was a table against one wall, his toy bag open on top of it. In the center of the room stood a complicated wooden bench positioned where the light was brightest. Thick red padding covered the seat and armrests.

"Why, Mistah Top," she purred in an exaggerated Scarlett O'Hara drawl, "I think you have evil intentions."

"Actually, that kind of depends on what *you* want," he told her, dropping out of Big Bad Dom character, at least for the moment. "You said when we started these games that you wanted me to use my bullwhip on you. I was thinking tonight might be a good time to try it."

She looked up at him, startled. "I thought you said we didn't know one another well enough."

"There are people who've been together thirty years without going through as much shit as we have in the past week. I trust you as a partner." Frank hesitated, then added, "But considering that you'd be on the other end of the whip, you might not feel the same. If you'd rather wait . . ."

She licked her lips, feeling her heart begin to pound. "No, I'd like to try it."

"I don't intend to play hard enough to make you fly, though if all goes well, I'd be open to trying it next time. Don't get me wrong—it'll definitely sting, but not all that much more than the session I gave you a couple of days ago."

"That . . . sounds about right." Excitement flashed through her, a hot and eager craving. She wanted it. The lush climb to arousal as she tested herself against Frank's whip, the delicious roller-coaster fear that always intensified her desire during a scene instead of blunting it. There was something about balancing on the razor edge of risk that made her feel deliciously alive. Yet somehow he made her feel safe, despite the danger posed by the whip popper breaking the sound barrier. He'd make damn sure she was never in any danger.

At least physically. When it came to her heart . . . *It's too soon for that*, she told herself. *Shake it off.*

She'd fallen for Gary fast, too. Or at least, she thought she had. Compared to what she felt for Frank, that relationship hadn't even been a crush.

"I'm glad you approve." He reached out, caught one of the clamps, and opened its jaws. Alex caught her breath as blood flooded the tormented point with a fierce, bright sting. "Or do you?"

Her eyes drifted closed as she let the sharp sensation spread through her, triggering the sensual rise of need. When she opened them again, she found Frank watching her, his expression hooded, a glitter heating the cool gray of his eyes. One corner of his handsome mouth kicked up. "Yeah, you want it."

"Yeah." Her voice sounded so hoarse, she paused to clear it. "I want it. Want *you*."

"'Master,'" Frank corrected. "'I want you, *Master*.' You *will* call me by my title, sub."

Alex bared her teeth. "Make me."

"Oh, I will." He sobered. "But if you need to use your safeword, you will damned well use it. When it comes to scenes involving bullwhips, you don't fuck around. I've never injured a sub, and I'm not going to start with you. Got me?"

"Believe me, I'm no more interested in getting seriously hurt than you are in doing the damage. If I need to safeword, I will."

"Good." He walked over to the table and picked up a coil of braided black. She watched it spill to the floor as he shook it free. Spinning, he sent the whip snapping well clear of her. The crack sounded as loud as a pistol shot in the enclosed space.

Alex managed not to jump—just. And wondered if her mouth had gotten her in trouble.

His cock hard and throbbing, Frank guided Alex over to the bench and helped her arrange herself along it.

Cap's creation was constructed from solid oak, so it wouldn't collapse or pull apart no matter how the sub struggled. It was designed to support her comfortably on all fours, with padded rests for the arms and shins. There was more padding along the bench's top for the sub's belly and hips, and a padded face rest with a hole in the center, something like a massage table headrest. Straps and neoprene cuffs were designed to secure her in place so firmly she'd be unable to move. A wide belt served double duty in keeping her motionless while simultaneously protecting her vulnerable kidneys and spine from any errant whip blows.

Frank normally wouldn't strap Alex down so completely. However, he knew a sub's first time under a bullwhip could provoke involuntary jerks that might land a lash in unintended places. That was how people got hurt.

Which was why he fastened every strap the bench had, including the one designed to hold her head in the ring-shaped rest. With her head held down, he didn't have to worry about hitting those delicate facial bones—or worse, her eyes.

At last he stood back to admire the contrast between the black straps and her redhead's Celtic-pale skin. "You good? Any claustrophobia?"

"Green," Alex said.

Frank nodded. "If you need to safeword, I expect you to sing out good and loud. The whip makes a lot of noise."

"Understood, Top." He thought he heard her swallow.

"Top my ass." Frank smiled a bit wolfishly and walked over to the table, coiling his whip as he went.

He had no intention of starting with the bullwhip, of course. Alex needed time to warm up, to relax into the sensuality and pleasure of this demanding form of submission. With that in mind, the first whip he chose was the light doeskin flogger he'd used on her before.

Flogger in hand, Frank paced over to her, pausing a moment to admire the lush curves of her ass, the cheeks spread by her position. At the base of that shadowed cleft, her pussy parted as if begging for his touch, for the cock that jerked in lust at the sight of her.

Running his index finger in a slow, teasing stroke between those plump lips, he was delighted to find her as deliciously wet as he was hard.

"Do you have any idea how beautiful you are?" His index finger found the opening of her sex, slid deep. Pumped in and out. Her hips jerked—or at least tried to. She was too tightly bound to do much.

Helpless. She was completely helpless. At that thought, his cock pressed hard into his zipper, demanding to be freed. He ignored it. This encounter wasn't about his dick or his need to spill the contents of his balls into her tight little pussy.

Or at least, it wasn't just about that.

It was about Alex, her fantasies, her need to submit even as she tested him—and herself.

It was about pushing her to the limits, to that edge where desire and dread met, where fear stoked need into raw lust and the human mind yielded to the animal body. But she needed a little bit more preparation first.

Frank dropped to his knees, dropped the flogger on the floor, and parted her vaginal lips with his fingers. Leaning in, he paused, breathing in the luscious musk of a woman losing herself to heat. Then he licked a slow stroke from clit to perineum. Not thrusting his tongue inside, but drawing a wet promise the length of her sex.

A promise of pleasure he fully intended to keep.

CHAPTER SEVENTEEN

When it came to sending a woman into subspace, Frank didn't need a bullwhip. He could do it with his mouth. And he definitely knew what he was doing. His tongue danced teasing circles around her clit, then lapped upward in a figure eight around her inner lips, making her jolt in delight.

He teased her slowly, working every nerve she had until an orgasm hovered just out of reach. Her hips pumped helplessly at the air, aching for the friction she needed to climax.

Now his fingers got into the act, index and middle finger slipping into her slick pussy, pumping in and out, in and . . .

Suddenly he was gone, leaving her sex frustratingly empty. Demanding that long, gorgeous cock of his.

She heard the *swish* of the flogger the instant before her ass lit up with a scarlet flare of pain. Not that he'd hit her all that hard, but the contrast between the pleasure of a moment before and the pain of the blow intensified the sensation. Both sensations.

"Call it," he growled.

"Green," she gasped. "Green."

"Good," Frank growled, and proceeded to lay three stinging blows right after that, hard and bright, leaning into them so that even the doeskin lashes carried a bite.

"Call it!"

"Green!" Never mind that her voice shook with the need to yowl.

Frank moved to the table, laid the flogger aside, and unzipped his pants. Biting back a groan at the pleasure of freeing his aching cock, he picked up one of the condoms he'd left there and sheathed himself.

He moved back to the bench and Alex's delightful ass, now as pink-striped as peppermint candy. She tensed, probably assuming he'd returned with the bullwhip. "Call it," he ordered.

"Green!"

"I think it's time to reward you for your bravery." He thrust his sheathed cock deep, enjoying Alex's gasp at the unexpected pleasure when she'd been anticipating the crack of the whip.

She was so fucking slick. He drew out, his eyes narrowing at the rich sensation of snug, wet flesh sliding the length of his shaft. And God, the sight of Alex's pretty pussy wrapped around his slowly pumping cock. Reaching down, he strummed her clit, savoring her delighted moan.

But if he kept that up, he'd never be able to finish the scene as he'd promised. And he owed her that. He withdrew, despite the vehement disappointment of his dick.

"Are you ready?" Stripping off the condom, he zipped his fly. He had no desire to leave his dick sticking out to get hit by an errant swing of the whip.

She didn't hesitate. "Yes. I'm ready, Master."

Frank grinned, wondering if she'd intended to call him that, or if it had been instinctive. "Then brace yourself, slave." He turned back to the table, tossed the condom in the trash, and picked up the bullwhip, shaking out the lash for the second time.

He'd spent uncounted hours practicing the use of the bullwhip. This one had an eight-foot tail, and he'd worked with it until he could put the popper at its tip exactly where he intended.

Now he gave the whip a hard throw—sending the lash licking out to crack beside Alex's bare ass, in part to check the distance. The crack echoed in the dungeon's space. She jerked, but only slightly, obviously controlling her reaction. He smiled in approval of her discipline.

Then Frank proceeded to test it.

The lash snapped out, cracking on the curve of the ass already red from his efforts with the flogger. She gasped, and her head jerked, but the strap around it held it still.

Frank smiled, enjoying this strong woman's willingness to offer her submission. It was the ultimate gesture of trust—and the ultimate rush.

Or maybe she really was just testing herself, pursuing the high. He was never sure if Alex wanted him or just how he could make her feel. His smile faded. "Call it."

"Green." Her voice sounded surprisingly steady.

He nodded, pivoted so his body was at an angle to hers, and went to work, sending the lash to kiss high on the curve of her right cheek. Then her left. Again. And again. The muscles in her thighs, her glutes, flexed as her body instinctively fought the restraints. Despite his doubts about whether she was his submissive or just his fuck buddy, lust flooded him, fierce and sweet. He chose another target on that lovely backside and threw the whip into another perfectly executed snap.

Another burning point blazed up on her ass to the sound of the whip's sharp crack. Alex clenched her teeth, suppressing her yowl of pain into a strangled grunt.

Adrenaline flooded her, a reaction to the pain, the fear inherent in being the target of a whip breaking the sound barrier. *Why in the hell did I think this was a good idea?*

Silence. The click of boot heels as he moved around. She strained her ears, trying to figure out what he was doing. The boots came closer. Something about that measured sound, about the memory of Frank in jeans and those glorious boots—and nothing else— made arousal bloom through Alex like a rose. That chest, all that sculpted power . . . *Oh, yeah, that's why I thought this was a good idea.*

Alex desperately wanted to lift her head and look at him, but the straps held her head still in the face cradle. She tensed, wondering what he intended to do . . .

Fingers stroked the length of her pussy in seductive promise. Spreading her vaginal lips, Frank dropped to her knees and began to feast on her again. Arousal that had begun to simmer at his approach went to a full boil.

This time Frank gave her clit his full attention, first lapping, then suckling, then lapping again, shooting her up the sweet climb to orgasm like a rocket. Licking swirls met the hot sting of the stripes, the pain making the pleasure more intense, the climb tighter, sharper. She gathered her breath to scream out her climax . . .

"Not yet." The order came in that rich, dark velvet voice of his. "You don't come until I say you can come."

Alex wanted to yowl like SIG out of sheer frustration. She also knew he was right. Denying orgasm made it even sharper when it came—assuming you didn't squelch it altogether.

Frank gave her another set of maddening licks before wrapping something around her hips and thighs. Cool plastic touched wet flesh, nestled between vaginal lips. *What the. . .*

The thing began to hum, accompanied by deliciously intense vibrations that ran from her clit to her anus. She cried out at the sweet thrumming against her erogenous zones. *How the hell does he expect me* not *to come?*

Boots headed for the other side of the room. Paused. She tensed, waiting for another of those searing cracks . . .

The boots came back. Something blunt and cool and slick touched her anal pucker, then pushed inside, stretching sensitive inner flesh. She worked on relaxing those muscles, letting him seat the plug in her ass.

He stepped back. Alex groaned as the thing in her butt began to hum, sending a second wave of vibrations to compete with the ones from the butterfly vibrator he'd placed against her pussy.

The climax she could feel brewing gathered tight, intensifying.

"Ahhh! Frank, let me—"

"No." A cool, growled command.

"But—"

"Are you my sub, or aren't you?"

"I—" She had to stop, panting as she fought the sensation. "Yes, I'm your sub!" The next word slipped out. "Master!"

"You don't sound sure about that." Click. Click. Boots moving away. Click. Click.

CRACK!

"Ahhhhh!"

CRACK! But now the sharp pain seemed an ally in her quest to prove her obedience, helping her keep the orgasm at bay.

CRACK! The pleasure from the vibrators and the pain from the whip met, battled for control of her battered nervous system.

"Call it!"

"Green!"

CRACK! "God, you're so fucking hot, lying there like that, all spread and wet and shivering. Submissive." CRACK! "My hot little slave." CRACK!

The praise added tinder to the blaze of pleasure, now burning so fiercely even the pain of the whip only stoked it higher. But it was getting hard to remember why she shouldn't give herself over to it, in the face of that flood of blinding sensation.

CRACK!

* * *

"Call it!" Frank paused, trying to retain some shred of control over himself in the face of her lush, straining nudity, her effort to keep the climax at bay in obedience to what he wanted.

She didn't answer.

He stopped. "Call it!" This time he put some drill sergeant bark into his voice. Maybe she was just flying, he told himself.

Silence.

Or maybe he needed to cut her the hell out of her restraints and make sure she was . . .

"Gr-green . . ." Her voice sounded slurred, dreamlike.

Relief loosened his muscles. She wasn't hurt, just deep in subspace. He hadn't intended to fly her, but evidently she was a lot easier to put in an altered state than he'd expected. He tossed the whip on the table with a mental note to clean it later, then unzipped himself and grabbed a condom. Sheathing took too long to suit his eager cock, but finally he strode over to her, shoved aside the thin vibrator that he'd snugged between her lips, and thrust to the balls.

She groaned in pleasure, a woozy, barely aware sound, and he began to fuck her, riding hard, thrusting deep.

Her cry as she tipped into orgasm seemed to light the fuse on his own climax. Stiffening, he came with a roar as his pulsing cock filled the condom. The pleasure was blinding, a flood of burning delight that lit up every nerve in his body.

All Frank really wanted in the aftermath of that draining orgasm was to find a bed and go to sleep. But he prided himself on being a good Dom, and good Doms took care of their subs first.

Straightening, he peeled off the condom and stuffed it into a trash bag before taking off the belts that held the vibrators on and in Alex's body. He piled them on the table with the whip and the flogger, making a mental note to clean everything.

"Ooooh," Alex groaned, sounding delightfully sated.

"Yeah, you can say that again." He unbuckled her from the bench, lifted her in his arms, and carried her up the stairs to the great room. It was a mark of just how stoned she was that her only reaction to this was to loop her arms around his neck with a happy purr.

Frank was damned near purring himself. Usually, he carried her as part of a scene as a means to reinforce his strength and dominance. This time he did it simply because she needed to be carried. He was surprised at how good it felt, the sweet and simple pleasure of Alex in his arms.

After depositing her on the great room couch, he wrapped her in a crocheted throw his mother had made him for Christmas. "Are you going to be okay while I get you something to eat?"

She mumbled something that might have been a woozy "green." Deciding she'd be okay for the moment, Frank headed for the kitchen for a bottle of water and a granola bar. Alex needed calories, and all the panting during a scene tended to dry you out.

Come to think of it, he was feeling a little thirsty himself.

So he got a bottle of water for each of them, along with a couple of energy bars, the ones with fruit, honey, and cashews that should take care of any low blood sugar. Returning to the couch, he opened one of the bottles and pulled her into his lap. "You think you can manage to drink this?"

"Yes," she said and accepted it. Or at least tried to; she promptly spilled some, so he took it back and tilted it up for her. Evidently discovering she was thirsty, Alex gulped down several swallows.

"Slower. I don't want you to get sick to your stomach."

She obeyed the command in his voice and sipped the

rest, then curled against him, still happily flying through subspace. Frank put the bottle aside, then broke the trail bar into pieces and fed it to her a bite at a time.

By the time she finished it, Alex looked a lot more alert. "My ass hurts."

Frank laughed. "I'm not surprised. Your butt's probably got more spots than a leopard's from all the little round whip bruises." He'd been careful to hit her with only the popper, avoiding cutting lash blows, so the marks didn't look too bad.

She fell silent for a moment, probably enjoying the buzz. "I've never done that before."

"What, a bullwhip scene?"

"No, I've never flown before. Gary tried, but no matter how hard he beat my ass, he could never get me into subspace."

Probably because it took trust to fly. Which, judging from what Frank had heard about Gary, was an indicator of good sense on her part.

Though he supposed true good sense would have been to avoid the bastard to begin with . . .

"I guess that's because I never trusted him."

He looked down at her and gave her a half smile. She was definitely looking more alert. "I was just thinking that." Frank paused to stroke a hand over the copper silk of her hair. "I'm honored that you do trust me."

"You know what you're doing. Gary never put in the kind of time to become as skilled as you are. Not just with the bullwhip, but with anything. Dominance is about more than being able to swing a whip or a crop." She grimaced. "It's sure as hell about more than swinging your fist."

"I'm glad you kicked his ass."

"Yeah. Should have done it sooner, though. I guess I was no different than most abused women. I wanted somebody to love me a little too much. And I believed all the bullshit he fed me about asking for what I got." She fell silent and just lay against him. Stroking her hair, he elected to respect her need for silence.

Frank knew what she meant. He'd held on to his relationship with Sherry long after he should have kicked the cheating little bitch to the curb.

He'd wanted to be needed. The galling truth was that all he'd been was used. Sherry had never really loved him—and he'd never loved her either. When he'd caught her with that Marine, Frank had been angrier at himself than he'd been at her, because he'd let it happen. Sherry had enjoyed being the lover of a Navy SEAL, both for the bragging rights and the access to base housing. But no matter how many times she called him "Lord Frank," and "Master," no matter how many times she'd sucked him off, it had never really meant anything. When he'd finally thrown her out, she'd been more pissed off about the loss of that check than the loss of their relationship.

Alex was nothing like that. She never called him "Master" to flatter or manipulate—hell, she actively fought using the word at all. As for faking submission, she didn't. Ever.

Frank grinned, remembering how she'd given him hell over his handling of Charlotte Shepherd. "Servile" was definitely not the word that came to mind where Alex was concerned. She might submit, but she always made him work for it.

Which was probably why he enjoyed her submission so much when she did give it.

The question is, am I enjoying it too much? His grin faded. *Does it mean too much to me? And what, exactly, does it mean to her?*

Alex sat, curled up in the great room armchair with SIG in her lap. The cat was purring furiously, having been fed and watered. SIG was a creature of simple needs.

So, it seemed, was Alex. She'd had a shower with Frank, which of course had led to shower sex, surely one of the true pleasures of being in a relationship.

So she was surprised when Frank emerged from the

bedroom, his expression surprisingly grim for a man who had just enjoyed not one, but two thoroughly delicious orgasms. At least, judging by his full-throated roars.

"I have something to attend to," he told her, looking tall and deliciously broad in jeans, running shoes, and a vivid blue tee that brought out the blue in his gray eyes. Both the tee and the jeans bore smears of paint, oddly enough. "I need to go see my mother. I usually visit her before work three or four times a week, but I haven't managed to get by at all this week." He met her gaze, his eyes steady. "And I'd like you to come with me."

This is the same mother who tried to cut your throat? But she didn't say it. Looking into his eyes, she realized this was a test. *Love me, love my mother?* Well, perhaps not literally *love* . . .

Alex considered making a joke about him being a mama's boy, but she had a feeling that his mother was not a topic Frank would find funny. At all. But then she wasn't exactly an awesome ball o' laughs when it came to her parents either.

Besides, she supposed she owed him for that disastrous dinner at Casa Coach. "I'd be happy to go with you," she lied. "I'd love to meet your mother."

He smiled at her, but there was a stinging degree of skepticism in his eyes.

On some level, Alex had no idea what she'd expected of a residence for Frank's bipolar mother. Perhaps some grim and foreboding institution. Instead Barbara Murphy lived in a neat two-story house with white siding and black shutters. Brick steps led up to a porch with white wooden columns and a door inset with leaded glass etched with daffodils.

At Frank's knock, a round motherly person came to the door, opened it a crack, then flung it wide, beaming a smile. "Frank!" The woman sounded just as delighted as she looked. She was dressed in cherry red slacks and a yellow top that looked almost fluorescent against her dark skin. "Your mother'll be pleased. I realize you've called every night, but she's still been worried, what with that sniper taking shots at cops." She didn't appear to know Frank was one of those who'd been targeted; he probably hadn't told his mother.

"Hi, Lena. Lena Larkin, this is my shift partner, Alex Rogers." Turning to Alex, he explained, "Lena's Mom's nurse and therapist. Plus cook and whatever else needs doing."

"Hi, Alex. Speaking of cooking, I've got a pot of spaghetti sauce on the stove I'd better get back to. You'll be staying for dinner, I hope?"

He looked down at Alex and lifted a dark brow. At Alex's nod, he smiled, approval in his eyes. "Of course. Where's Mom?"

"In the garden, painting."

"So we're having a good day?"

"Oh yes. Barbara never gives me any trouble." Lena stopped and sniffed. "I have got to stir that sauce, or it's going to be tomato-flavored glue!" She hurried off.

"Live-in caregiver? That must be expensive."

"Not live-in—Mom doesn't need that, at least not now. Lena's usually here through lunch and dinner. I could probably dispense with a caregiver altogether, but Lena needs the money and Mom enjoys the company. Besides, I like making sure she takes her meds."

Sometimes the mentally ill stopped taking their medication out of a refusal to believe they really needed it. That could lead to their brain chemistry going dangerously awry, which in turn could lead to incidents like the one Charlotte Shepherd had been involved in.

"I floated the idea of moving her in with me, but she won't hear of it." He pitched his voice high in evident imitation of his mother. "'We tried that, and it didn't end well.' Yeah, when I was sixteen. Things are, thank God, different now. She's a lot healthier, and I'm . . . well, not sixteen."

Alex gave him a leer designed to break the gathered tension. "That's for damned sure."

Laughing, Frank led the way down a short hall into the den.

"Nice house," she commented, looking around with interest. Redolent with the scent of garlic and tomatoes from Lena's sauce, it was a cozy place. The den was furnished in comfortable overstuffed furniture, its cream upholstery dotted with a fine pattern of roses and daffodils.

Paintings hung on every wall, originals by the look of them—here a woman in a burqa led her child along a dune against the vivid blaze of a desert sunset. There, a close-up of a camel, longed necked and a little goofy, its bridle festooned in colorful tassels. In another piece, an American soldier and his bomb-sniffing dog walked along surrounded by a dancing bevy of young children.

And over the couch hung a portrait of Frank in full SEAL body armor, the set of his mouth grim as he held his rifle propped on one braced thigh.

"Gorgeous work." Alex stepped closer to check out the brush strokes. Definitely originals. "Your mom again?"

Frank beamed like a proud son. "Yep. She sells her paintings in galleries around the country."

"The paintings of the SEALs are based on your photos?" Including, she remembered, the one of him and his best friend, Randy Carson, the SEAL who'd died in the line of duty.

"Yeah." His expression grew distant. Neither of them spoke, remembering dead comrades. Finally Frank shook off the memories and said, "Well, let's go see Mom."

They found her standing beside a lovely water feature, studying the dance of water falling from the head-high rocks into a pool surrounded by brown and cream stone. The bright orange shapes of koi slid lazily through the water.

Barbara, clad in jeans and a Led Zeppelin tee, both liberally smeared with paint, plied her brush delicately as she worked to capture the colors of the fish, a pair of gold-framed glasses perched on the end of her nose.

"Hi, Mom."

"Frank!" A delighted grin spread across her face as she dropped her brush into a mason jar of turpentine and gave her son a smacking kiss on the cheek. "No, don't hug me—you'll get paint all over your clothes."

"This is the same shirt you got paint on the last time." He pulled her into his arms for a warm squeeze. Drawing back, he put a hand on Alex's shoulder and steered her close. "And this is my shift partner, Alex Rogers."

Barbara's gunmetal gray eyes lit. "It's a pleasure to meet you, Alex. I've heard so much about you. I'd offer to shake hands, but . . ." She spread her long fingers, displaying yellow, orange, and green paint, blended in places until it looked like thick brown mud. Her resemblance to Frank was obvious in the shape of her generous mouth, angle of the brows, and the eyes, though her facial bones were more delicate than his broad-jawed masculinity. She wore her gray-shot dark hair in a ponytail, probably to keep it out of the paint that smeared one high cheekbone with streaks of umber and orange.

"Mrs. Murphy, I'm delighted. I love your work!" Alex smiled. "Particularly the gorgeous son you raised."

Sadness ghosted through the smile Barbara shot him. "I'm afraid the raising was more his doing than mine. But thank you."

They exchanged pleasantries for a moment before Frank snapped his fingers. "Dammit. Just remembered something I need to talk to Lena about. I'll be right back."

He strode off. Alex stared after him, caught flat-footed.

Barbara laughed. "My, he must be serious about you if you're getting the Mom Test."

"Mom Test?"

"Yes. I hope you won't mind if I work on my painting while we talk. I'm about to lose the light." Picking up her brush, she wiped it off on a rag, then picked up her palette and dipped it delicately in one of the shades of orange paint smeared there.

"Ah, sure."

"At eighteen, he got very serious about a pretty young cheerleader. But when he brought her over to meet me, the girl basically ran screaming, Of course, that was before we found the right medication, so that might have had something to do with it." Barbara stepped back a pace to consider the painting, then moved closer to delicately place a tiny bead of paint. "Ever since then, he's made a point of introducing me to whatever female he's involved with to see what she'll do." She turned from the canvas to consider Alex. "Though you got the introduction sooner than most." Her mouth curled in a dry smile. "Now that you've met the crazy lady, do you intend to run screaming?"

"Nope." Knowing a challenge when she heard one, Alex folded her arms and rocked back on one heel. "I'm a little harder to terrify than his other girls."

"Well, you're a cop. You would be." Barbara glanced toward the waterfall, head tilted as she considered it. "I hope you stick. He could use a little happiness. Sure as hell didn't have much when he was growing up—not once I started getting sick. By the time he was nine, he was doing more taking care of me than the other way around. Made sure I got up to go to work, made sure I ate. Lied like a rug to every teacher, cop, or social worker who asked too many questions, trying to make sure they didn't take him away from me." She fell silent, adding another bright highlight to a koi scale. "Though in retrospect, he'd have been better off if they had."

"I wouldn't be too sure about that." There'd been cases where the South Carolina Department of Social Services had placed children with foster families who turned out to be worse abusers than their birth parents. Some of those kids had died.

"Oh, I'm sure. When he was sixteen, I almost slit his throat with a box cutter because I thought demons were going to possess him."

Yep, Barbara was testing her. "You don't seem too worried about demons at the moment."

The woman grinned wickedly, looking so much like her son, Alex had to grin back. "By the grace of God and the pharmaceutical industry." She sobered. "The meds I take can have some ugly side effects, but I never skip a dose. I'd do anything for that boy."

"I hear that."

The painter's gaze met Alex's, suddenly fierce. "Don't hurt my son, Alex Rogers. He's been hurt enough."

CHAPTER EIGHTEEN

It was a chilly, bright afternoon. Bruce lay in his sniper nest in hunter's camouflage, almost invisible among the weeds, brown stalks bobbing under the playful touch of an October breeze.

He wasn't expecting his target for another hour or so—she hadn't even radioed dispatch she was going 10-7 for lunch yet. But it was better to arrive early and settle in than cut it too close and risk movement that would spook his prey.

That damned well wasn't happening again.

Adrenaline hummed seductively in his veins as he imagined the shot he'd take—the sight of blood and brain exploding from the dyke's head. The heady power, the grim satisfaction of getting revenge on Murphy for poaching on Bruce's territory. He'd known from the way the SEAL talked about Gaffney that the bastard considered her a friend. Maybe losing her would hurt Murphy enough to throw him off his stride.

He could handle Alex. Frank worried him.

Obtaining Gaffney's badge might be problematic, though. Bruce badly wanted it for his father's shrine, but it was broad daylight. He wasn't sure he'd have a chance to retrieve it without being observed by some nosy bystander. And painting the patrol car was definitely out.

He frowned, brooding. Since he'd gotten rid of Ted, nothing had gone right. He hadn't had a chance to plant a camera at Murphy's house, for instance. Getting one in place at Rogers's mill village shack had been no problem, but all it had recorded was her packing a suitcase and stuffing her cat in a carrier.

Alex had only been seeing Frank for a week, and she was already moving in. That said everything you needed to know about the little whore, didn't it?

Murphy's house was probably where all the really good action was happening. Unfortunately, the SEAL had a hell of a security system, and Bruce had yet to determine how to get past it without attracting every cop for miles.

So the audio recording of Frank and Alex making their little date in the patrol car would have to do. Unfortunately, he doubted it had the pop to go viral the way Arlington's video had. Might still be enough to get them fired . . . but he doubted it.

Which was why he'd sent the recording directly to the Coach's wife. That would hurt them all where it really counted. Bruce was willing to bet her parents had no idea of what kind of disgusting things Alex did.

They knew now, though. Or they would.

Imagining their pain and distress, Bruce smiled. Another bit of revenge for Dad. Next he'd send it to the television stations, see what would happen.

Hell, by the time he killed her, her parents, and her fucking SEAL, she might welcome the bullet.

Smiling, he lay in his nest of weeds like a copperhead. Waiting.

Diane Gaffney had known she was a target since the night Ted was shot. That had been made painfully obvious by the bigoted slurs painted all over his patrol car.

Somebody definitely did not like gay people—and Diane had been out of the closet for years.

So she'd evaluated her daily schedule, looking for the moment when she'd be most vulnerable. The good news was, she didn't make a particularly easy target. As the sergeant for Able platoon, she drove around Morgan County, acting as backup or providing management to whatever cop needed her. Even she never knew where she'd be at any given time, which would make her a seriously hard target as far as the sniper was concerned.

The only point of vulnerability was her lunch hour. Diane had a favorite restaurant she'd hit anytime she wasn't at the opposite end of the county. Rose's Home Cooking lay off I-85, one of those places that served a meat and three—some kind of entrée and three vegetables. The fried chicken was damned near as good as her mother's, the corn bread had a wonderful, buttery crunch, and the iced tea was so sweet, you could stand a spoon in it. All of which was why Rose's was usually packed.

What's more, there was a hill overlooking the parking lot where she'd set up if she were the sniper. Brush and weeds would provide cover beside an access road, which would make a perfect escape route.

It stood to reason that the sniper was using some kind of scanner to keep track of police activity. Either an old-fashioned radio-type unit, or one of the cell phone apps. Diane's money was on the app. If the killer was monitoring police communications, he'd know when she went to lunch.

So every day since Ted died, Diane had played bait.

Ben Tracy and a couple of deputies from the SWAT team had spent every afternoon staking out the section of road overlooking the restaurant. And every day, she'd radioed in that she was going 10-7 at Rose's for lunch.

Not that she'd actually pranced out where she could be shot. Diane had better sense than that. But she had left her vehicle parked in the parking lot, hoping the killer would take the bait so she, Tracy, and the SWAT volunteers could grab his psychotic ass.

Unfortunately, he hadn't, much to the frustration of the hunters. Instead, he'd gone after Frank, Alex, and Bruce. It was only by the grace of God that he'd missed his targets.

Unlike certain idiots she could name, she tended to assign the deputies' survival to luck more than any lack of skill on the killer's part.

Diane had had hopes that today their trap would net the killer, but unfortunately, she'd received a call from Tracy twenty minutes ago telling her he wouldn't be available. Evidently somebody had managed to get himself killed, and the detective had been called in to assist on the case. Which wouldn't be a problem, except the two SWAT team members were also working the same murder, leaving her without any backup at all.

Diane had dropped by to see if she was needed, but so many deputies had already responded she decided there was really no point. She'd be more useful making sure all hell didn't break loose elsewhere in the county.

So they'd just have to try to trap the sniper tomorrow.

But . . . She was only about ten minutes from Rose's, and she was in the mood for some chicken. She'd go 10-7, make sure the sniper hadn't shown up, then go have lunch. Odds were slim the asshole would have picked today to try for her, but she was feeling paranoid enough to want to check.

It'd be a damned shame to get her head blown off over a chicken breast. Even one of Rose's.

So Diane parked her patrol unit at the base of the hill, beyond a stand of trees that should conceal it from the sniper—assuming he was even there. According to the SWAT guys, the bastard would have gotten into position long before he was expecting her to arrive.

Diane got out of her car and left the door open a little way so the sound of it closing wouldn't betray her. Then she drew her weapon and padded silently along the road, keeping alert for any sign of the shooter as she went.

This was probably going to end up being another complete waste of time—but she didn't care to take the chance that the killer was waiting to cap her.

Rounding the bend, she spotted a shape lying in the long weeds. Diane froze. A man in hunting camouflage with a rifle braced against his cheek, sighting on the parking lot below.

Diane's heart leapt into a thundering roll as she aimed the gun at the back of his head. "Hey, asshole! You're under arrest! Drop your rifle and lace your fingers behind your neck!"

He moved so fast, he caught her by surprise, flipping over on his back and jerking his rifle around. For a split second, she saw his face—and recognized him. The surprise of it froze her finger on the trigger for a deadly split second. "Greer, you son of a bitch!"

She fired a heartbeat before he did.

Alex sat in Frank's lap in his favorite chair in the great room as he fed her lunch—taking a bite himself, then giving her one as the television murmured something mindless in the background. The meal was one of those stir-fry creations from a recipe he'd gotten off the Internet—chopped steak, peppers, squash, and snap peas all simmered together in teriyaki sauce. In between bites, he caressed her nipples through the MCSO tee.

Feeding a sub was one of those minor acts of dominance and care that Doms in general—and Frank in particular— seemed to enjoy, particularly when building up to some sort of scene. He'd told her this one wouldn't be all that demanding, mostly because she was still sore from last night's adventure in the dungeon. But any form of sex with Frank had a way of getting her stirred up. And she wasn't the only one, judging by the erection she could feel growing under her deliciously sore ass.

A manic purring sounded at their feet, where SIG was demolishing his own bowl of Frank's creation. The cat, like Alex, had happily settled in at his temporary home. The Dom was always doling out strokes, which were all it took to win SIG's love.

Alex's, too, come to think of it.

Frank presented her with another bite of teriyaki. She closed her mouth over it, making the bite sensual: sucking on the tines of the fork, then licking away every trace of sauce. "Delicious," she murmured. "But then, everything you do is delicious."

He grinned. "Suck-up."

The comment sounded like the kind of banter Ted and Cal used to exchange. The memory hurt worse than Frank's whip.

Something of what she felt must have shown on her face, because his expression darkened to sorrow. He wrapped a big hand around the back of her head and pulled it down for a kiss, slow and sweet and lingering. *I know how you feel*, the kiss said, *because I feel it, too.*

In gratitude, Alex deepened it, licking at his teeth and dueling with his tongue until the pain fell away in the slow rise of desire.

Blam blam blam!

She jolted against Frank as a fist pounded the front door again. SIG yowled and darted under the couch to hide. *Blam blam BLAM!* "Alex! Alex, you get out here!"

"Coach! That's the Coach!" Springing off Frank's lap, she raced for the bedroom to search for the bra she'd removed the night before. "Oh, God, oh God, what's he doing here? How'd he find out where I am?"

"Calm down, babe." Frank strode after her, both of them ignoring her father's continued pounding as she snatched off her T-shirt, grabbed the bra off the floor, and thrust her arms into the straps. He pushed her fumbling hands out of the way and fastened it for her. "It's none of his business where you're staying."

"Tell him that!"

BLAM BLAM BLAM! The blows seemed to be getting louder as the Coach's patience eroded. "Alexis!"

"You're not a teenager he caught in the back of some-body's car." Irritation dropped Frank's voice to a growl.

"You're a grown woman. You have a right to be any damn where you want."

"I don't think he got the memo!" Alex dragged the tee back on.

"Alexis Eleanor Rogers!" Oh, God, he was using her full name. She had to get that door open, but first she swept a frantic glance over Frank.

He looked presentable, a towering, barefooted man, broad shouldered in his black jeans and tee. A disapproving glower darkened his handsome face. He obviously didn't think she should be running around in a panic, but he didn't know her father. Unlike the popular stereotype of ranting high school coaches, Ken rarely got mad, being more inclined to cool displeasure than flamboyant rage. But when he did get pissed, you'd better duck. The lightning bolts were on the way.

BLAMBLAMBLAM! "Alexis, open this door!

She skidded to a stop in front of it, started to jerk it open . . .

"Security system," Frank reminded her. He punched the code in on the foyer keypad. It disengaged with a birdlike chirp. Alex unlocked the door and jerked it open. "Coach!" And instantly felt a fool, knowing her bright tone didn't fool anybody.

"It's about time!" Her father glared at her from the front porch. "What were you, naked?"

"Mr. Rogers," Frank said coldly over her head. "What brings you here?"

The Coach ignored him. "Get your things, Alex. I'm taking you home. "

Alex's inner Daddy's Girl wanted badly to obey. Her outer cop, on the other hand, started to get pissed. Frank's looming presence behind her gave her the courage to voice what she was thinking. "In case you haven't noticed, Daddy, I'm an adult now. I don't have to—"

"Your mother got a recording in her e-mail this afternoon." The Coach directed his next icy glare at Frank. "Are you my daughter's"—his lip curled—"Dominant?"

Cold flooded her body, a wave of ice rolling from her chin to the top of her head. It seemed the shooter had indeed recorded them, and he'd done exactly what she'd most feared he would: sent it to her parents.

That fucker. That vicious fucker. She'd rather he'd shot her.

The Coach looked like he wanted to do the job. "That's the right term, isn't it? Dominant." He glared up at Frank as he stepped forward, forcing Alex to retreat. She bumped into her lover, who still hovered protectively behind her. When he didn't move back, she instinctively pushed her shoulders against his chest. He retreated a step, allowing Alex to move aside. The Coach stomped in, radiating enough testosterone to choke a bull elk.

"I looked it up on the Internet," her father spat. "Found out all about that sick BDSM . . . stuff the e-mail said you've been doing to my daughter."

Frank raised a thick dark eyebrow. "I fail to see how your daughter's love life is any of your business."

"*Love* life? What you're doing to her has nothing to do with *love*!" He turned to Alex, and scanned her body, apparently checking for bruises. "Has he hurt you?"

Alex's bruised ass checks instinctively tensed. "No, but *you're* hurting me right now. Not to mention embarrassing the heck out of me. Frank is right—what we do in bed is none of your business."

"If he's abusing you, I'm making it my business. I stayed out of it with that jerk Gary. Told your mother you were grown, and you could make your own choices whether we approved or not. I'm not going to stand by this time. *You're coming home!*"

"Alex is safer here," Frank said, his tone emotionless. "This house has a good security system. Unlike the lock on her house, which a two-year-old could jimmy with a credit card. Or have you forgotten she's been targeted by the sniper? The same one, by the way, who apparently sent you that recording. Probably hoping you'd make her leave this house, so he could get at her more easily."

"She wouldn't be a target if it wasn't for you!" Ken gave Frank a hard, calculating stare. "What if I forward that recording to the sheriff? What's he going to think?"

"Go ahead." The Dom's expression was stony as sculpted marble. "You *should* forward it. It's evidence in a murder investigation."

"Don't dare me, boy. If you're convicted of domestic abuse, you'll lose your badge."

Alex stiffened, realizing he was right. If you were convicted of domestic abuse in South Carolina, you couldn't carry a gun. If you couldn't carry a gun, you couldn't be a cop.

Frank would lose the job he loved because the Coach was outraged he'd banged his precious little girl in a way he didn't like. She'd already lost her parents; now she'd lose him, too.

No. *Don't panic, Alex.* "I'll say this one time: *I have not been abused.*"

"Yeah, that's what Amy said. Look what happened to her."

"BDSM play is just that, play. Abusers don't ask their victim's permission, they don't set limits, and they don't give a damn if somebody gets hurt!"

"So you admit he is beating you?" Ken stared at Frank as if considering jumping the bigger man and pummeling him black and blue.

Alex flung her arms wide. "You see any marks, Coach?" Forget the stripes on her ass; they didn't show. "If there are no visible marks, there are no grounds for arrest if the abused person doesn't press charges. Don't try to bluff us with law we know better than you do."

"Send the file to the sheriff," Frank said, coldly expressionless. "Or better yet, to Ben Tracy. He's the detective investigating the case. I'll give you his e-mail." Pivoting with a military snap, he stalked to the end table, where a pen and pad lay, and started writing down the address.

"I'm not sending that file to anybody, including Tracy. You think I want the whole damned world to know about this? Assuming the bastard doesn't put it up on the damned

Internet." He turned to glower at Alex. "You've broken your mother's heart. She's at home sobbing her heart out."

Alex blanked her expression with the skill of five years as a cop. "She's got no reason to cry. I'm fine. *Coach and Mom hate me now. They think I'm some kind of pervert bound for hell.*

"No, you're not fine. I can see that just by looking at you. Come home with us, Alex," the Coach said, his voice softening as he sensed the anguish she fought to hide. "Break this off before it's too late. We're afraid for you, honey. After what happened to Amy . . ."

"I'll say this one time: I'm not Amy Greer. And Frank sure as hell isn't Steve." At least she still had Frank. He'd help her get through this. While she didn't know if he cared about her the way she cared about him, she did know he'd take care of her.

That was what a Dominant did.

The Coach moved closer. She stepped back, though pain flared in his eyes. "Alex, baby, please don't do this."

"I'm not a baby anymore, Dad. And my sex life isn't your business."

He squared his shoulders. "Alexis Eleanor, you won't be welcome in my home as long as you're with him."

Alex bit off the words despite the bitter, metallic taste they left in her mouth. *"I. Am not. Going anywhere."*

"Fine." Ken stalked to the door with regal dignity. "When you come to your senses, call. We'll be there for you." He closed it behind him with a carefully controlled snap.

Ken Rogers controlled the impulse to peel rubber out of Murphy's driveway. He was fifty years old, dammit. He wasn't a teenager to indulge his temper.

Or his hurt.

He didn't understand how the daughter he'd raised would voluntarily do some of the things he'd seen women do on those websites. Asking a man to spank her, even flog her with a riding crop? Put clamps . . . *there*?

Before today, he'd have broken the nose of any man who suggested his little girl could get off on something like that. He and Mary had taught Alex to stick up for herself. He'd seen her do it repeatedly in high school. Once she'd beaten the snot out of a boy who'd bullied a younger kid she'd befriended.

Then there was her outrage over the treatment Bruce Greer's mother had suffered at the hands of his sadistic father. Ken vividly remembered comforting her after Amy Greer's death.

Beaten to death at the hands of the man she loved. Was there any greater betrayal?

The tragedy had hit them all hard; Amy had been Mary's best friend, and Alex had dated Bruce for months before the murder.

How could she ask that big deputy to beat her after all that? It defied understanding.

What was going on couldn't have been as bad as the e-mail made it sound. Maybe Alex and Frank had done nothing worse than a little spanking.

He and Mary had been friends with a couple who were into spanking. They'd claimed it spiced up their marriage. It had made no sense to Ken. He couldn't conceive of hurting Mary even if she'd asked him to. He had no use for a man who'd raise his hand to a woman.

Mary had been so crushed by the idea Alex could be into kink. So disappointed that the daughter she'd raised to be a good Christian had been playing sex games. Alex had wounded his wife to the heart. How could he ever forgive that, even from the daughter he loved?

Another thing: look at the size of that bastard, Frank. Did Alex have any idea of the kind of damage a man like that could do? No amount of *Krav Maga* training could even those scales. She wouldn't have a prayer against Frank Murphy in a fight. No matter what tricks Ted had taught her.

Ted. According to the e-mail, it all came back to Ted, who'd evidently taught Alex more than *Krav Maga*. He was the one who'd gotten her into kink.

Oh God, did Alex sleep with Ted? The man was supposed to be gay, but what if he were bi? For God's sake, he'd been Ken's age.

Alex had worshiped the son of a bitch to such an extent, Ken had been a little jealous. She'd have done anything for Arlington.

Ted beat his own lover. Had he beaten Alex, too? Was that how she'd become addicted to kink?

What was Ken supposed to tell Mary? What was he going to tell the boys? Hell, he owed Andy an apology for the asschewing he'd given him after that disastrous dinner.

Abruptly, Ken realized he was almost home. He'd been so lost in thought, he didn't even remember the trip.

Feeling battered, he pulled into the driveway and parked in the garage. He switched off the SUV's engine and sat listening to the cooling metal tick as he tried to decide what to say to his wife. How he could tell her Alex had refused to come home?

How could he tell her Alex had chosen kink over her family?

Ken got out of the SUV feeling like someone had beaten him with a crowbar. Mary's Mercedes sat in the other space.

The good news was she was still at home. The bad news was there'd be no putting the conversation off.

When he walked into the house, everything was quiet. No sounds of his wife indulging her *Real Housewives* addiction. No sounds of crying either, thank God.

"Mary?"

No answer.

He walked into to the kitchen, but it was empty. The house was still. A chill began to creep along his spine.

Upstairs, something thumped. There was a muffled sound. A female voice groaning in pain?

Shit. He whirled and headed for the stairs. "Mary!" Ken was running by the time he hit the top step. He sprinted down the hall to the master bedroom he shared with his wife.

And stopped in the doorway, staring.

Mary lay on the bed on her side, her hands behind her back. A wash cloth was stuffed in her mouth. She made a sound behind the gag, a kind of high squeal of warning. The same sound he'd heard downstairs. "Mary, what the heck are you—"

Her desperate eyes flared wide, staring at something over his shoulder.

Ken whirled. Bruce Greer stepped out of the bedroom across the hall, some kind of weapon pointed at his chest. "Hi, Coach." He fired.

The Taser's leads punched through his shirt and into his chest. Fifty thousand volts sizzled through the twin barbed hooks in his skin. Every muscle in Ken's body instantly coiled in agonizing knots, like a giant full-body Charley horse. White fire exploded in his skull, but he couldn't even scream. He toppled like a felled tree, his head bouncing on the carpeted floor.

"You had that coming, you fucker." The deputy holstered his Taser and pounced, rolling him over onto his stomach. Ken groaned, trying to jerk away, but his cramping muscles refused to respond. Metal clicked, and something cold closed around his wrists.

Handcuffs.

What the hell is he . . .

"Now," Bruce said, "we're going to call your daughter."

For a long, stunned moment, Alex stared at the door her father had just closed behind him. Frank's chest ached with physical pain that intensified as she bent and began to sob.

"Alex!" He pulled her into his arms. "Oh, baby, don't cry like that. It's going to be okay."

He only hoped he wasn't lying.

Despite his stinging eyes, Frank guided her over to the couch and sat down, pulling her into his lap. "Shhhh," he said into her bright hair, encircling her in his arms. "Shhhhh."

"They . . . they think I'm a . . . pervert."

"I seriously doubt that." Frank propped his chin on the crown of her head and stroked her back. "They may not understand, but they know you. You're decent all the way to the bone. Nobody who knows you could ever think anything different."

"Mama . . . Mama b-believes I'm . . . g-going to hell . . ."

"Alex, they love you. No damned audio file is going to change twenty-six years of love, no matter how pissed they may be now. Hell, Mom tried to cut my throat, and I still love her . . ." *Okay, maybe not the smartest thing I could have said*, he thought, about ten seconds too late.

Her only answer was another of those heartbreaking sobs. Periodically she tried to talk, but she was crying so hard, he had no idea what she was saying.

There was no point in trying to reason with her. It was probably best to let her cry herself out, then attempt logic again once she'd calmed down.

Frank stroked her shaking back as her tears gradually soaked her shirt to the sound of her broken sobs. And did some thinking. There was no doubt her pain was genuine and wrenching—and she was suffering because of him.

The question was, what was he going to do about it?

God, she felt so painfully precious curled in his arms, even sobbing as though her heart had cracked like a cheap Christmas ornament. When had she grown so important to him? He hadn't felt this intensely about Sherry, 24/7 submissive or not.

He'd known Alex only a week, while he and Sherry had been together two years. It made no sense, yet there was no doubt that what he felt for Alex was far stronger. That was why her every sob felt like a knife driving home in his chest. If he didn't know better, he'd think he was in love.

Frank didn't believe in love at first sight. Only the very young and impulsive tried to rationalize lust by giving it a pretty name. Unlike your average seventeen-year-old, he was no stranger to lust. Alex wasn't the only pretty woman to stoke his desire by submitting to his need to dominate. By the time he finished swinging his single-tail, he usually had a hard-on up to his navel.

This wasn't like that. His feelings for Alex weren't born in his balls. He admired her fierce need to protect the vulnerable, especially given that she was so vulnerable herself.

Sometimes she scared the hell out of him with her willingness to fight abusive pricks like Donny Royce in order to rescue the man's abused wife and kids.

Sherry wouldn't have put herself on the line for anyone, even children. But Alex—his beautiful, intelligent, courageous Alex—didn't even hesitate.

The question isn't how could I love Alex, but how could I do anything else?

The thought burst in his skull like a psychic IED. The shattering impact set off blinding lights behind his eyes and made the world spin around him.

Frank stilled, holding her. By the time she finally stopped crying and pulled away, he knew what he had to do.

"I'm sorry," she croaked. "I just don't know how to fix this . . ."

"I do."

Alex looked up at him, wiping her tears away with the back of her hand. "What . . . what do you think I should do?"

Frank looked away from her and made himself say the words. "Go back to your folks. I'll ask for a transfer on Monday."

She looked at him like he'd slapped her. "What?"

He lifted her off his lap and put her down on the couch beside him. He grabbed a handful of tissues from the box on the end table and handed them over. She accepted them mechanically. "Your relationship to your parents is too important to you. You shouldn't throw that away over a man you've known a week."

Alex wiped her face and blew her nose, then stuffed the wad of tissues in a pocket. "I'll tell you what I told the

Coach—my folks don't have the right to dictate my love life. I'm an adult. I want to be with you . . ."

"Are you sure?"

Green eyes narrowed. "Yeah. Yeah, I'm sure."

"Alex, the sex was good—but was it that good?"

"What we have is more than sex, Frank, and you know it."

Of course he did. And that was why he had to protect her, even from himself. "They're not going to accept me, Alex. But if you apologize . . ."

"And do what? Go back to lying to them? Go back to pretending to be something I'm not?" She sprang off the couch and began to pace. "If there's anything good about this nightmare, it's that I don't have to pretend anymore. They know what I am . . ."

"You're not a 'what,' Alex. You're . . ." *The woman I love.* But he couldn't say that, or she'd cut herself off from the family she loved.

"I'm not a child, Frank! How many times do I have to say it? Women are supposed to leave their mother and father . . ."

"And cleave only unto me? Are you sure that's what you want?" Even if it was what he wanted. Desperately. But if he loved her, he had to do what was best for her.

That was how it was with D/s. The top might control what went on in the scene, but the choice of whether to submit at all was the bottom's. She could end it whenever she chose just by using her safeword.

For all the talk of masters in BDSM, slavery was nothing more than a forbidden bedroom fantasy. That's why people treated dominance and submission like a play, with scenes and certain definite roles.

It wasn't real.

When the sub chose to end it, a responsible Dominant walked away. To do anything else was to take the first step down the slippery slope to abuse.

No matter what her parents thought, Frank Murphy was not an abuser.

* * *

Alex stared at him, her chest aching with disbelieving pain. Now he wanted to end their relationship? Really? Now, when her parents had rejected her? When she was most vulnerable, most in pain?

When I need him?

"Alex . . ."

"Whatever, Frank." More for something to do with her hands than anything else, she scooped up the remote and started flipping channels absently.

A scarlet banner splashed with the words "Special Bulletin" caught her attention.

". . . spokesman says a second Morgan County sheriff's deputy has been shot and killed in the line of duty today. Major Dominic Jennings said the deputy was found dead near Rose's Home Cooking at 348 Deersprings Road of I-85."

"What?" Stiffening, Alex stared at the television. "Not again. Goddammit, not again."

"It appears that the deputy and the sniper exchanged fire," Jennings said in a taped segment, his dark face set. "We believe the killer was wounded in the encounter, judging from the amount of blood on the scene."

"Jennings did not identify the deputy," the local anchor continued, her tone sober. "Master Deputy Ted Arlington was shot and killed by a sniper in what is believed to have been a hate crime . . ."

"Oh, fuck." Alex scrubbed her hands over her face.

"Diane Gaffney." Frank stared at the huge flat screen, a muscle rolling in his jaw as his teeth clenched. "That's her favorite restaurant. We ate there every time we were anywhere in the area."

"And she was homosexual. Like Ted."

"She was afraid he'd get her." Frank met Alex's gaze. "And he did. The son of a bitch did. We need to get dressed and get over there."

* * *

Bruce's leg hurt like a son of a bitch. No surprise, given that Gaffney's bullet was still lodged in his thigh.

Ideally, he needed to get it removed, but going to the emergency room was out of the question. They'd have to report it. And when the injured man turned out to be a deputy with a murdered cop's bullet in him, they'd know exactly what he'd done. The only way he'd ever leave that ER was in shackles.

Not an option.

He'd bandaged the wound, but he was still losing blood. Like it or not, he was done. It looked like he'd be following the old man's playbook after all.

But first he had to settle accounts with the Coach, Mary, and Alex, all of whom had contributed to his father's destruction—and his own. Before he ate his gun, there had to be an accounting.

First, though, he had to get Alex to Casa Coach without bringing the SWAT team down on his head. He wasn't going to be the victim of a sniper. That'd be just a little too much irony.

Settling into the rocking chair beside the bed where his hostages lay, he ran his hand along his aching thigh. His uniform pants were wet through where the wound had bled. Luckily, the scarlet didn't show against the black fabric. Reaching into his pocket, he closed his fingers around a hard, metallic shape. Ted's badge. He took comfort in the reminder that he'd succeeded in killing two deviants already. Now he just needed to eliminate Alex and her parents, and he'd be able to rest.

Mission accomplished, Dad.

A muffled growl drew his attention. Boy, the Coach was seriously pissed. Ken and his wife lay on the bed back to back, arms linked, wrists cuffed. Getting them there was the main reason Bruce's wound was bleeding again.

After the first shock of the Taser, Ken had fought like a grizzly, kicking, writhing, trying to head butt. The coach had even attempted to bite him, for God's sake.

In the end, Bruce had been forced to choke him out in order to get him secured. Mary had screamed into her gag the whole time, even managing to plant a kick on his chin. Damn, he wished he'd thought to bring the shackles he kept in the trunk of his car. Too late now; God knew what the Coach and his wife would get up to if he left.

But now the stage was set. All he had to do was play it right, and he'd get what he wanted.

Dad would finally be able to rest in peace.

CHAPTER NINETEEN

Alex's private cell rang as she was buckling on her duty belt. She plucked it out of a pocket and glanced at the screen. It was Bruce's number. She swiped the Answer button. "Bruce, did you see the news about Sergeant Gaffney?"

"Yeah, because I killed her."

She froze, eyes widening as her belly went into free fall. *Oh shit, Frank was right.* It had been Bruce.

Bruce had murdered Ted and Diane Gaffney and wrecked Alex's life. "You son of a bitch."

Frank froze in the act of lacing up his uniform boots.

"Shut up." She'd never heard Bruce sound so cold, so savage. It was like listening to his father. "You're going to do exactly what I say."

"Fuck off!" God, she wanted to throw up. Frank moved to stand over her, his gaze locked on her face. "You're a dead man, Greer. We're going to—"

"I have the Coach and your mother."

It was like being dropped into a frozen lake, feeling the

ice crack under her, plunging in the airless cold, water closing over her head as she sank into darkness. "That isn't funny, Bruce."

"I'm not joking, bitch."

A muffled voice cried out in shock and protest. "Tell her!" Bruce snapped. It sounded like he was shaking someone. "Tell her I have you and the Coach. Tell her I've got a gun to your head."

"Alex, stay away!" her mother screamed. A slap, the sound meaty and unmistakable. Mary yelped, echoed by an enraged bellow that could only be the Coach. "Go to hell, Bruce!" her mom cried. "Alex, you—"

"Quiet, bitch!" Another slap, followed by a short, vicious struggle before Greer came back on the line, panting. "Alex, I have them, and I have a gun. You do the math."

Oh, my God! What the hell am I going to do?

Stall. Think. "What do you want?"

"Come to Casa Coach. Come alone. And you'd better be here in twenty-four minutes. I know exactly how long it takes to get here from your pervert lover's house. I timed it. But if you tell Murphy I've taken them, if you breathe a word to the cops, they die."

She felt strange, as if the earth had fallen away. Replying by rote, she regurgitated her training. "Cops don't give themselves up to hostage takers, Bruce."

"If you don't, they're dead."

"And if I do, you'll kill me and them. I'm not that stupid."

"Nobody has to die, Alex. All I want is to make a little cell phone recording. You, admitting what a slut you are. Admitting how you betrayed me and my father. Obey me, and I let everyone go. If you don't . . ."

He really did think she was stupid. Frank stared at her, shaking his head, mouthing, *"No, Alex."*

"Why should I believe you're telling the truth?"

"You'd better hope I am, hadn't you?" Contempt dripped in his voice. "Besides, submitting's your thing, isn't it? You like obeying Murphy in those deviant games, right? Well, this time you're going to obey *me*. If you do, I won't kill anyone. If you don't, well, you and your brothers are going to be scrubbing Daddy's brains off the walls."

"Don't hurt them!" *He's going to kill them, and then he's going to kill me.*

"Do what I say, and I won't."

Fury came to her rescue. *No. No, I'm not going to just give up.* Ken Rogers's little girl didn't roll over for some asshole with a gun. *I've got to stall for time. Figure out a way out of this.*

Alex knew one thing about Greer: he loved the sound of his own voice. If she could get him talking . . . "Just let them go, Bruce. They never did—"

"Yes. They. *Did.*" It sounded like he snarled it from between clenched teeth. "And so did you. The only question is, how am I going to punish you for it? I could just humiliate you by making you tell everybody what a little whore you are. Or I could kill them—and make sure it takes them a long time to die. It's up to you, whore. Twenty-four minutes. That's how long you have before I start doing damage."

Stall. For God's sake, Alex, stall! "Don't hurt them! I'll come!"

"Don't try anything and nobody dies. Get cute—"

"Fine! Fine, look, I won't tell—"

"You really do think I'm stupid." She heard the thud of something hard hitting something meaty, heard a muffled male grunt.

BOOM!

At first she thought he'd set off a bomb, the gunshot was so loud. Her mother cried out, the sound echoed by her father's hoarse cry.

Bruce said something, but half deafened, Alex couldn't tell what. Her knees buckled, but Frank was there, bracing her upright. She fumbled the phone to the other ear. "What—what did you just *do*? If you hurt them, you fucker, I'm going to blow your fucking head off!"

"Daddy's fine, whore. There's a nasty hole in the dry-wall, that's all. But maybe next time I'll put a bullet in something that bleeds. Choose, Alex. One little five-minute recording, or do I shoot them?"

"All right! All right, I'm coming, you son of a bitch!"

"You better watch what you call me. In fact, I think you better call me Master."

Fury steamed through her, but she made herself lie. "Whatever you want. I'll call you whatever name you want." *Until I can blow your brains out.*

"'Master.' 'I'll do whatever you want, *Master.*'"

She wanted to tell him where he could shove his gun. And then she wanted to pull the trigger. But she didn't dare say any of that, not with her parents' lives on the line. "Master."

"Oh," he purred as if trying to copy Frank's delicious rumble. "I like the sound of that." His next words emerged in a vicious snap. "'I'm coming, Master.' Say it! My gun is pointed at your mother's hip. You know how fragile old women are. A broken hip really hurts for a long, long time."

"I'm coming, Master!" *And then I'm going to gut you.*

"I've got friends on the force, whore—and you don't know who. If you try to call for help, I'll know it. And then you'll find a hell of a mess."

Shit. He might be lying, but she couldn't take the risk. "I won't call anybody . . ." Alex paused and added through her teeth, "Master."

"Twenty-four minutes, Alex." He sounded smug, as if he held all the cards. And he did. "Don't be late."

Her phone beeped, signaling that he'd hung up. She sagged, sick horror running through her. *What the hell do I do?*

"It's Bruce." Frank picked up his Glock, checked the safety, and holstered it. "He's the sniper."

"And he's got my parents at Casa Coach." She strode out of the bedroom, making for the garage, where her patrol unit was parked. "He's going to kill them, unless I do exactly what he says."

"Wait. We need weapons." Frank veered for the gun cabinet, produced a key ring, and unlocked it.

"We?" But if he had additional firepower, she wanted it.

He pulled out a rifle and handed it to her, then started buckling knives in leather around his forearms.

"He told me not to bring anybody, Frank. Look, I've only got twenty-four minutes. I don't have time to argue!"

"Then don't. Come on." He stood, took the rifle she'd leaned against the wall, and headed for the garage.

"Y ou drive," Frank said to Alex's surprise, striding around to the passenger side of her patrol car.

"Frank, he told me not to bring help or he'd shoot them."

He shot her a look over the roof of the car. "Which is why you're letting me out around the block, where he won't be able to see me. I'll cut through the woods and go in from behind the house." He sounded utterly matter-of-fact, as if he were talking about dropping by the Gas-N-Go for a donut.

"But what if —"

"Alex, I'm not going to fail you. We're going to get your parents away from that fucker alive. Period." Frank opened the passenger door and slid inside. "Drive. Drive fast."

Swearing, she got in, started the car, and threw it into reverse, waiting impatiently for the painfully slow garage door to rise.

Slapping the car into drive, Alex flicked on her lights and siren. She'd turn them off once she got close. At the moment, though, she needed to avoid a crash while she hauled ass.

"I'll call the SWAT lieutenant, tell him what's happening." Frank took his department-issue cell off its belt clip. "He can get the SWAT team into place around the house."

"Bruce said he's got a partner among the deputies." The tires squealed as she hit the gas, made a three-point-turn, and shot toward the road.

"And you believe him?"

"I don't think I can afford not to believe him." Her hammering heart was making it hard to think, and the siren's cycling wail only made it worse. *Dammit, I've been in touchy situations before!* But never with her folks' lives on the line. "He'll be monitoring scanner traffic. If he finds out we've called in the cavalry—"

"Then I'll tell the lieutenant to contact his men individually and caution them not to use the radio. They'll go in quiet, keep him from finding out they're there until it's too late."

"Until SWAT surrounds the house, and he kills everybody."

"Think like that, and everybody will die—starting with you." Frank began to dial. "Instead, you're going to distract him while I go in there and put a bullet in his brain. Do you know combat breathing?"

"Yeah. Ted taught me." The technique used a pattern of deep, slow breathing similar to what she'd learned in yoga class. It had the effect of slowing down the heart rate and forcing the body to calm so you could retain frontal cortex function. Otherwise the rapid heartbeat of an adrenaline dump was likely to erode fine motor control and make it impossible to think. Sometimes fight or flight wasn't the best choice.

"Good. Use it."

She obeyed, drawing in deep breaths as she drove, holding them, and exhaling slowly. Her heartbeat began to slow.

As panic receded, Alex listened as Frank briefed Lieutenant Chris Davis, the SWAT commander.

The lieutenant didn't like their plans. Strenuously.

"We don't have time to wait for you to assemble the team, Lieutenant." He still sounded calm, despite the white-knuckled grip he had on his phone. "Rogers will go in and distract him while I—" He paused as Davis interrupted. "I know, but he's obsessed with her, sir. This whole thing has been about hurting Alex from the start. Killing Ted. Shooting at us . . . They dated in high school and . . .

Nine years ago. She and her parents were involved with his parents' death. Bruce's father was abusive, and Alex's father sheltered Bruce and his mother . . . Yeah, *that* case. His father beat his mother to death and committed suicide. I'd bet my next paycheck this has been brewing ever since."

He told the lieutenant about Bruce's threats. "Obviously I'm not about to let her go in there without backup, so . . . Yeah. Alex and I will keep a lid on the situation until you and the team can move in." Frank paused again, his expression going grim. "We're aware of that, sir, but if we wait, he's going to kill them . . . No, I doubt the hostage negotiator will be able to talk him into surrendering. Greer's already killed two cops—he knows the state'll execute him. Going in hot and taking him by surprise is the only way the hostages have any chance at all . . . Fine, we'll be there."

Frank ended the call and sighed. "Well, Davis is mad enough to chew bullets and spit BBs. He's probably going to write me up for insubordination."

Alex glanced at him. "He insisted I stay the hell out of there, didn't he?"

"His exact words were, 'Does she think this is some kinda fuckin' TV show?'"

"I wish. TV heroes always get away with this kind of stupid shit." She wove the car around an SUV that had slowed down at her approach, probably trying to avoid a ticket. "I would have thought there's no way in hell you'd let me go in there, if you had to sit on me to keep me out of it."

A muscle rolled in his jaw. "Yeah, well, I'm not exactly thrilled. Davis is right—we're effectively handing Greer another hostage." Which you were *never* supposed to do.

"I'm not going to sit on my thumbs while that bastard kills my parents."

He glanced at her and said mildly, "And I don't expect you to. We'll save them, Alex."

"Yeah." She glowered at the road ahead, praying silently that he was as good as he thought he was.

* * *

Letting her do this went against every instinct Frank had. Subs by their very nature tended to be less aggressive, and anything less than a brutal willingness to kill would get you seriously dead in a situation like this.

But if he'd learned anything in the last week, it was that Alex wasn't your typical sub. Letting him tie her up in the bedroom didn't mean she wasn't capable of kicking his ass outside it. She was a cop. The words she'd said about Ted were just as true for her: the phrase "Serve and protect" wasn't just a slogan on the side of a patrol car to Alex. It was etched on her soul.

Frank knew that, because he had that same deep drive to protect those weaker than he was, to serve those who found themselves in dangerous situations they weren't equipped to deal with. Alex was equipped to deal with this; Ted and her parents had spent years turning her into a warrior.

You couldn't deny a warrior the opportunity to fight, even if you were stronger. You had to let her use the weapon she'd made of herself, or she'd always be less than she should be.

Besides, Frank needed a distraction. He needed that crucial ten seconds when Bruce's gun wasn't pointed at his captives' heads. Alex could give him those seconds—and keep herself alive in the process.

Like it or not, he had to trust her to do just that, or Mary and the Coach were dead. Even if Alex survived, she'd never get over the loss. True, parents eventually died, but having them die because of what you saw as your own failure could gut you.

Look at what it had done to Bruce.

Frank didn't know for certain the Greers' murder-suicide had warped their son into a killer, but the idea had the sharp, solid weight of truth.

And I'm sending Alex up against that? A military vet

who was three inches taller, with somewhere around three times her upper body strength. And who was batshit crazy on top of that.

He'll kill her.

A memory flashed through Frank's mind: clamping his hands over the wound in Randy Carson's belly, listening to his best friend's last sighing breath. The thought of Alex's eyes staring empty and fixed made him want to howl like a grieving wolf.

He thrust the emotion away hard, stuffed it down deep. He couldn't afford the lethal distraction.

Frank breathed in deep, let it out slowly, calming himself, reaching for that glacial chill that had made him so effective in battlefields halfway around the world. He'd gut through this with the same ruthless stubbornness that had gotten him through Iraq, BUD/S Hell Week, and his childhood. When it was over and everyone was alive, he'd have Alex.

And by God, he'd keep her.

"Stop here," Frank said, his voice emotionless in a way that reminded Alex of a skim of barely cooled stone over lava. Instant incineration lurked beneath that thin control.

She pulled the patrol car over to let him out in a lot wooded with hickory, maple, and oaks blazing with all the colors of fall. Automatically, she looked toward him, wanting to see those cool gray eyes, fiercely handsome face, sensualist's mouth.

In case it was the last time.

A big hand encircled the back of her head, pulling her in. He took her mouth like a brushfire attacking a forest in the grip of August drought. She made a tiny, helpless noise, and his tongue stroked and swirled around hers. Alex sank into the kiss, tasting desperation and mint toothpaste. For a precious moment the kiss unspooled like a glowing ribbon, binding them both in need.

Finally he ripped away from her. His gaze stabbed her. "You fucking stay alive."

"You too, Frank." Her chest ached, the pressure thick and relentless.

And then he was out of the car and gone, out into the tree line to find his way to Casa Coach. He didn't look back at her.

She swept a cautious look over the woods, but there was no sign of the SWAT team. How long would it take them to gear up and find their way here? Would they be in time to back Frank up?

Would she be in time to save her parents?

Alex checked the dash clock. Three minutes left. She really had driven like a bat out of hell. Heart pounding, suddenly afraid the clock was wrong, she hit the gas and raced down the familiar stretch of road to God knew what.

A lex walked into her parents' house with her gun drawn, wondering if she would leave it alive. Wondering if any of them would leave alive.

"Up here." Bruce's voice, sounding bizarrely cheerful, rang from somewhere upstairs.

"I'm coming. You'd better not hurt my parents, you son of a bitch."

"That depends on you."

That's what I'm afraid of. She thought of Ted, sprawled on his back, a bullet hole gaping above empty eyes.

Bruce had killed him. Bruce, her friend, her former lover, the boy they'd invited to Thanksgiving and Christmas after the death of his parents.

Now he was threatening to kill hers.

Raging terror kicked her heart into her throat, and her hands began to shake. She sucked in a deep breath and went back to combat breathing. She was definitely in combat.

Ted had taught her to breathe like that. There were a lot of things Ted had taught her over the past five years. Hopefully some of them would save her life today. Save her parents, save Frank.

Bruce, she really didn't give a shit about.

"Go into a fight knowing that you're going to get hurt," Ted had told her. *"If it's fists, you're going to get hit. If it's a knife, you're going to get cut. If it's a gun—well, try like hell not to get shot. But accept whatever pain you suffer and don't let it stop you. The thing is to win, and get the innocents out alive. That's all that matters. You're a cop. That's the job."*

"Are you trying to get cute?" Bruce snapped from upstairs, no longer amused. "Because I'm standing here with a gun pointed at your parents' heads. At this range, a bullet would go through both of them."

I've got to keep him talking. Talking was a hell of a lot better than shooting. "I'm coming, dammit." Alex bolted up the stairs two at a time, then slowed down, moving more cautiously toward the master bedroom. Judging by the sounds, that's where they were.

Alex ducked to come through the doorway in a low crouch, hoping that if he fired, he'd aim where her head should be, rather than where it was.

The first thing she saw was Bruce standing over her parents with his gun aimed at their heads. "Throw it down, Alex."

Neither of the hostages moved. Something about their stillness iced her blood.

"Fuck off." Instead she brought her weapon to bear on him. She swept a quick glance over her parents. They lay back to back on the bed, arms linked, wrists handcuffed with two sets of cuffs. Getting them off the bed would be awkward and slow. Then she looked closer, and anger iced her blood. "What have you done?"

But she could see the answer, and it fill her with rage. He'd used his fists on them.

One of her mother's eyes was swollen shut, and blood had dried on the Coach's nose and swollen lip. She'd shoot the fucker if she hadn't been afraid his gun would go off and hit one of her parents.

"Put the gun down, Alex. I'd hate to have to blow someone's brains out by accident."

She didn't move, her weapon still pointed squarely at his skull. "Fuck off."

"Alex. Put. The gun. Down."

She really, really didn't want to give up her weapon. All her training insisted it was the worst possible thing she could do. She also didn't have one damn bit of choice. It was time for the best acting job she'd ever given in her life.

Alex began to cry, letting the tears come slowly at first, until she was heaving in sobbing breaths. Drawing on all the pain and terror she felt, she let it all boil up and stream down her face in hot tears.

And judging by the contempt on Bruce's face, he was buying it.

Despite how well he knew her, he was still his father's son. And his father had had nothing but contempt for women.

Steve Greer expressed that contempt throughout her childhood on his wife's vulnerable body. Now, her only hope was to use that emotion to make his son forget everything he'd learned about Alex on the street. Make him forget she was the Coach's daughter.

And Ted's, too, in every way that counted.

Tears streaming down her face, Alex reeled toward the bed. Dropping the gun at Bruce's feet, she bent over her parents' handcuffed bodies, letting weak tears fall in fat droplets. "Oh, God! Dad, Mom, I'm so sorry about all this! I'm so sorry this bastard involved you in this. I love you, I—"

"Shut the fuck up!" Bruce's voice rang with all the disdain and male superiority she'd hoped for. "Get the hell away from them, you stupid cunt!"

Alex lifted her head and glared through her tears. "You get away from them!" Under the cover of her body, she grabbed the Coach's hand, sliding her thumb under the handcuff key she'd taped to her palm. Flicking the key into his hand, she raged at Bruce, "You cocksucking bastard! You killed Ted! Why? How many times did he back you up when you were getting your *ass* kicked?" Her hand tightened on the Coach's, gave it an encouraging squeeze. Even with the key, it wouldn't be easy for him to free them. Not trying to unlock an unfamiliar mechanism with his hands bound behind his back.

From the corner of one eye, she saw the Coach's startled expression become comprehension. His lips twitched in something that was almost a smile, and his eyes narrowed in determination. She hid her own satisfied smile. If anybody could free him and her mother, it would be the Coach.

A male fist hit the side of her head in an explosion of light and pain. Alex reeled, fell sideways, and turned to glare at Bruce. "Asshole!"

"When I give you an order, slut, I expect you to obey it!" Bruce glared at her with what he probably thought was a Dominant's icy stare.

Alex had known a real Dominant, and she wasn't impressed. Now she had to distract him while the Coach and Frank played their parts. Her job was to be sufficiently distracting to let them get away with it.

Channeling her inner Angelina Jolie, she snarled, "Why? Why kill Ted and Sergeant Gaffney?" She gestured at her parents. "Why do this?"

Not that she gave a shit about his reasons. He was a murderer and a psychopath just like his father. His upbringing didn't matter. Frank had had one every bit as bad, but he'd overcome it.

Frank was a hero. Bruce was just an asshole.

The asshole's eyes narrowed in rage. "Your dad is getting exactly what he has coming to him! He set my parents up. If he hadn't stuck his nose in, convinced my mother to leave Dad, none of it would've happened! My father—"

"Your father would have murdered her anyway. Probably the same day, the same way. That's what murdering pricks do."

Bruce's gaze slid away from the certainty in hers. "He'd only knocked her around a little. He wouldn't have—"

"*He choked her.* He'd put his hands around her throat and started squeezing. You told me yourself that if you hadn't hit him in the head with one of his own whiskey bottles, he'd have choked her to death that afternoon!"

"And maybe she had it coming!" His voice went shrill. "She was always setting him off, never doing things the way he wanted them done. When he blew up and hit her a few times, she'd do better for a few days. If—"

"Are you listening to yourself? What utter bullshit! Amy was a *victim*. I always thought you were a victim, too, but I guess the asshole really didn't fall that far from the tree after all."

On the bed, her mother made a muffled cry of protest behind her gag that sounded like *"Shut up!"*

Alex found herself staring down the barrel of a gun a fraction of an inch from her face. "Yeah, Alex," Bruce snarled. "Shut up." He took a step closer.

"Don't!" Alex raised her hands in a *Don't shoot* gesture as she let the fear she felt fill her eyes.

"This is your fault, Alex! I wouldn't have done any of this if that prick you were fucking hadn't run off at the mouth!"

"Who, Frank?"

"Not Frank! That other prick. Gary. The one who beat you!" He was breathing hard, his gaze wild. "I couldn't let him just get away with that, could I? All I planned to do was hit him a couple of times, show him what it felt like . . ."

"It was you." Alex stared at him in astonishment. "You were the one who beat Gary to death."

"He gave you a black eye, Alex! I only meant to punch him a couple of times, only enough to teach him not to do that to another woman." His eyes narrowed to deadly slits. "Then he told me I'd never have a prayer with you. That you all laughed at me, you and Ted and Gary. You said I was a vanilla bean! I couldn't ignore that, could I?"

"You beat him to death because he said I said you were a vanilla bean?"

"I was defending you! I couldn't let him get away with saying that kind of sick shit about you! I had hit him with my fist, but then when he started mocking me, I grabbed my flash—" For an instant, anguish flashed through his furious gaze. "Then it was just too fucking late."

Alex became conscious of her mother's green huge eyes over the gag, flashing from her to Bruce and back again. She knew what Mary was thinking—that Bruce had lost control and beaten Gary to death. And Alex was goading him just as hard, risking the same kind of deadly explosion. She had to avoid driving him into that kind of frenzy.

"I didn't intend to kill him. Not like that. But he kept laughing at me, talking about how you and Ted played kinky sex games . . ."

"I didn't play anything with Ted."

"Of course not, because Ted was a homo! He was a fruit, and he lied to me, fooled me into thinking he was normal . . ."

"He was normal! Just because he—"

"He wasn't normal!" Reaching into a pocket with his free hand, he jerked out something metallic and gleaming. Ted's badge. "He didn't deserve this! That's why I took it away!" His mouth twisted. "Just like I'm going to take yours when you're dead. You're a blot on the badge."

"You're the blot, you murdering psychopath!"

"And you're a perverted freak. You like gettin' your ass beat during sex!' His eyes narrowed, taking on a rabid wolf gleam. "Maybe I should give you what you like right in front of your folks. Show them what kind of freak you are . . ." Throwing Ted's badge aside, he lunged for her, reaching with one hand as he kept the gun trained on her with the other.

Alex surged forward in a move she'd drilled with Ted over and over and *over* again. Ducking under the gun's line of fire, she drove her joined hands upward, thumbs catching under the weapon's muzzle and shoving it toward the ceiling. It went off with a thundering boom.

Bruce reacted just as Ted had taught her an attacker would, instinctively recoiling from the blast he hadn't expected.

Alex wrapped her fingers around the gun, jerked it down, and rammed it into his belly, breaking his grip. Simultaneously, she drove a knee toward his groin. He twisted, and her knee hit his thigh instead. But now she had the gun in her hands, and she danced back, bringing it up.

Something hit her back hard, rattling her teeth. She staggered, knocked off balance. *Fuck, hit the wall . . .*

Bruce attacked, backhanding the gun aside even as she fired at him. The weapon went flying at the side wall and bounced to the floor. He lunged at her, his hands wrapping around her throat as he slammed her into the back wall. His big hands tightened, choking off her air.

Seconds. She only had seconds before he crushed her trachea . . .

Frank's instincts howled that he'd gotten Alex killed by letting her go in alone. He roundly ignored the thought, knowing it would instill panic he couldn't afford. He needed to be as cool and emotionless as dry ice.

The sun was going down and the house's interior lights were on, so Frank could see Bruce and his hostages through the sniper scope. They occupied the second floor, at a bad angle for a shot from ground level.

He needed to be at a better angle to shoot through the sliding glass doors and take the fucker out. Frank had taken his share of sniper shots in Afghanistan. He . . .

The first shot was clearly audible, even through the closed glass door. Frank slung the rifle over his shoulder, and ran like hell for the house. If bullets were flying, he was going to have to be a hell of a lot more up close and personal if he wanted to save Alex and her parents.

Bang! Another pistol shot, the sound thinned by glass.

He didn't break step, throwing himself upward and grabbing for the balcony, with its wrought-iron railing. His hands slapped the balcony ledge, and he grabbed hold of the railing support, using his momentum to swing upward until he got a knee on the ledge.

Staring between the rails through the glass door beyond, he saw Alex and Bruce struggling for the Glock. With a roar of fury, the big bastard slapped the gun out of her hand and lunged, slamming Alex against the wall with both hands clamped around her throat.

Snarling, Frank swung his body upward with a wrench of effort, swarming up and over the balcony railing without quite noticing how he managed it. Dropping to one knee, he tossed the rifle off his shoulder and brought it around to sight on Bruce's skull. They only had seconds before the bastard crushed her trachea and she suffocated.

Alex ducked, rolling against the wall, the quick jerking leverage of the move loosening Bruce's grip and taking him by surprise. Simultaneously, she threw one arm up over her head and brought her elbow smashing downward into the killer's arms. The maneuver levered his hands free from her throat. Twisting, Alex rammed her elbow toward his chin. He blocked it, but she exploded off the wall in a flurry of blows so fast Frank didn't dare take a shot.

Instead, he leaped to his feet, ran forward, and drove the butt of his rifle into the glass door. The glass spider-webbed, but didn't break. He hit it again, and glass showering into the room, raining down on the carpet and leaving jagged fragments behind.

The killer glanced around, saw him, and his eyes widened with panic. Before Frank could bring his weapon up again, Bruce hit Alex so hard, her knees buckled. She would have fallen, but the killer grabbed her by her uniform shirt and duty belt and dumped her on top of her parents.

Frank crashed through the glass, ignoring the icy sensation of shards raking across his skin. All he cared about was getting to her.

Bruce dropped to his knees, using the bodies of Alex and her parents as cover as he snatched up a gun that had fallen to the floor. He shoved it against Alex's face. "Drop the weapon, Murphy! Drop it now!"

"Fuck off, you murderous coward." But he couldn't get a shot. All he needed was one good shot. He strode forward, trying to angle the rifle downward over Bruce's human shields.

Bruce ducked lower behind them, fisted a hand in Alex's hair, and dug the gun into her cheekbone. "Drop it, or I'll—"

Mary Rogers, caught under her daughter's unconscious body, jerked the pepper spray canister off Alex's duty belt and shot Bruce in the face. The killer recoiled with a roar of pain as the capsicum spray began swelling his eyes shut.

Frank exhaled, his finger tightened on the trigger, and fired.

The sound of the rifle was deafening in the confined space of the bedroom. Bruce fell, a hole gaping red in his forehead.

He was dead before his body bounced on the carpeted floor.

CHAPTER TWENTY

"Is he dead?" Mary demanded.

Frank crabbed his way cautiously around the bed, his rifle still raised.

Bruce lay sprawled on his side. Frank planted his boot on the man's shoulder and flipped him over.

Greer's eyes were fixed, a hole just above his brows. The back of his head was more of a mess, judging by the spray of gore across the bureau behind him. Frank didn't even have to check his pulse. "He's dead."

"Good riddance," Mary snapped, raising her head to study her daughter, who lay across her hips. "Is Alex all right?"

"Mom?" Alex lifted her head and began to stir, frowning in confusion. "'M all . . . I'm all right. What . . . what happened? Where's Bruce?"

"Down, thank God." The Coach rolled off the bed and moved around to reach for her. Frank slung his rifle back over his shoulder, bent, and lifted Alex off her mother. Cradling her in his arms, he savored her warm weight.

Ken helped his wife slide off the bed on the other, avoiding Bruce's body. Frank scanned them. They were battered and bloodied, but both of them seemed all right. "You've still got a handcuff on," he pointed out.

The Coach grimaced and pulled off the cuff that dangled from one chafed, reddened wrist. There was a reason you didn't use real handcuffs in BDSM. "I thought I'd never get these damn things unlocked." He studied Alex as Frank cuddled her. "She all right?"

"She's fine. I think she just got her bell rung. He hit her pretty hard."

"Frank?" Alex slurred. She lifted her head and looked woozily around. "Where's—" Her gaze landed on the body, and she stiffened, seeming to jolt instantly to full consciousness. "Oh. Ah, yeah. Frank, put me down. We need to get off the evidence."

"God, you are such a cop." Mary didn't sound as if she minded; there was a note of admiring affection in her tone.

Frank stepped clear of the body before he put her on her feet, supporting her when she stumbled. "You sure you're okay?" He frowned, suspecting she had a concussion, considering how long she'd been out. Catching her chin between his fingers, he lifted her face. "You've already got a good little shiner coming up there." Along with a bruise on her cheek and a fat lip.

The good news was that her pupils were the same size as they shrank in reaction to the ceiling light. He was tempted to kiss her, but with her father standing right there, he decided against pushing his luck.

"I'm fine," she told him, not convincingly. Then she frowned, looking up into his face. "But you look like shit. You're pale. You're really pale . . ."

"You're bleeding." Mary swept a gaze down his body. "Your pants are wet."

Frank looked down and cursed. She was right. There were slashes and tears in his uniform pants and across his shirt, revealing the bulletproof vest underneath. "Shit." He glanced at Mary with a Southern boy's automatic courtesy.

"Excuse me, ma'am." Frowning, he looked around for the source of the cuts and spotted the glass door. A chilly October wind blew though the huge hole he'd made bulling through it. Jagged blades of glass jutted around the opening, several of them red and wet. More glass littered the floor and crunched underfoot. Spotting a glint of silver among the glass, he walked over and picked it up. The room spun around him as he rose, and he steadied himself on the bedpost. "It's a badge."

"It's Ted's." Alex's eyes narrowed and her lip curled in a snarl. "Bastard taunted me with it."

"You should give it to his mother." He walked over and fumbled it into her hand. Flecks of gray danced at the edge of his vision, and he realized dimly that was a bad sign. He staggered.

The Coach was suddenly there, grabbing his arm and steadying him. "Cut yourself up coming through the glass door, Frank. Did a pretty good job of it, too. You were pumping so much adrenaline, you never even felt it." To his wife he added, "Watch it, Mary. Don't cut yourself."

"Let's get out of all this glass and bandage you up," Alex said, sliding an arm around Frank's waist and helping her father guide him toward the door. "Mom, can you call 911? Tell them to send an ambulance and the cops."

"Cops should already be here." Frank frowned, realizing they were probably right about him being cut up. His thighs and calves stung from multiple wounds and something wet rolled down his legs. Quite a lot of something wet.

"Come on, big guy." The Coach tightened his grip on his waist. Frank started to tell him he was fine and could damned well walk on his own, but the room decided to roll sideways. He shut his mouth as his lover and her father helped him across the hall to a pretty little bedroom decorated in bows and floral prints. He resisted their efforts to push him inside. "I'll bleed all over everything." He glanced down, concerned for the pale gold carpet. "I'm probably leaving a blood trail."

"That's why there are carpet cleaning companies, boy."

His knees gave, and the Coach pivoted, half carrying him as Alex stepped out of the way. "Bathroom might be better, at that. Need to clean him up, see how deep the cuts are."

Frank frowned, belatedly recognizing the symptoms of a really nasty injury from past battlefield experience. He stopped resisting the Coach's efforts to help him walk.

Ken was pretty strong for a guy over fifty.

He sat down on the toilet in the surprisingly spacious bathroom with a sigh of relief. "I'm usually not this much a fuck-up, sir."

"Last I checked, we're all still alive, except for the ass-hole I wanted dead anyway." There was weight in the coach's gaze that said his words weren't just polite social bullshit. He meant them. "You saved our lives, Frank. You saved my wife and daughter, and you could have died doing it."

"I had to." Something told Frank he needed to shut up, but his mouth kept running anyway. "Gonna ask her to marry me."

Ken stared. "I thought you'd only known one another a week."

Frank smiled at the man he hoped would be his future father-in-law. "If the Archangel Michael had personally taken my order for the perfect woman, she wouldn't be as perfect as Alex." *Pretty good speech*, he thought smugly, *considering the blood loss.*

They were all staring at him now.

Then he blew it. "Sorry. Gotta . . ." Putting his head between his legs, he fought not to topple off the toilet.

"Oh, hell." There was an unfamiliar note of panic in Alex's voice. "Call for that ambulance!"

"Already on the way," an unfamiliar male voice said.

Frank jerked his head up and scrabbled for his weapon, only to realize belatedly that someone had taken it. Just as well, because a man he belatedly recognized as Lieutenant Chris Davis was standing in the bathroom doorway, eyeing them all with a mix of relief and irritation.

"I've got half the cops in Morgan County surrounding this

house, and you've already got the bad guy dead in the bedroom. Is there something you want to tell me, Murphy? Rogers?"

Which was when the darkness closed in, and he passed the hell out.

Frank's most serious injury was a four-inch cut down his thigh that just missed the femoral artery. If he'd hit that, he would have died about the time he killed Bruce. There were also a couple of shallow cuts on his face—those should heal up without scarring—and one across his right shoulder and down one arm. Though Kevlar was generally little protection against being stabbed, his thick bulletproof vest had saved him from any life-threatening torso wounds. As it was, he ended up with dozens of stitches, a blood transfusion, and an hour or so having a physician's assistant pick glass out of his skin.

Alex, for her part, got a CT scan and a diagnosis of a concussion from exchanging punches with Bruce.

Her parents were similarly bruised and battered, and Alex suspected they'd have nightmares for years. Other than that, though, their injuries weren't serious.

There was a certain grim satisfaction in the knowledge that it had been Ted's training that had let her hold her own with the bastard. Just as it had been Diane Gaffney's bullet that had ultimately forced the final confrontation. Otherwise, who knows how many people he'd have killed? Alex had no doubt she and Frank would have eventually been his targets again. Next time, Bruce might have had better luck.

Instead, Bruce was dead, and the nightmare was over. Now they had the aftermath to survive.

The ER doc was a cautious soul who wanted to keep an eye on Alex and Frank, given her concussion and his blood loss. She admitted both of them, which didn't thrill Alex for a couple of reasons. First, she wanted to have a long, private talk with Frank, something that wasn't happening with all the nurses, doctors, and cops hanging around.

Especially the cops. Two agents from the South Carolina Law Enforcement Division—also known as SLED—had already been by to grill her about every last detail of the incident. As was standard operating procedure in South Carolina whenever a cop shot anyone, the sheriff had asked for SLED's help. Ranger had three dead cops on his hands. The last thing he needed was to create the impression of a conflict of interest.

As it was, Frank had been put on paid leave pending the results of the investigation—more a matter of SOP than because anybody thought the shooting was unjustified. Bruce had, after all, left his blood all over Diane Gaffney's murder scene. That would prove he had indeed done the killings, as soon as the DNA results were back.

Then of course, there was Diane's bullet in his thigh, which the pathologist had already recovered during the autopsy. Ballistic tests would be done on both the sergeant's weapon and the rifle the Crime Scene Unit had recovered from Bruce's car.

In the meantime, the media had gotten their teeth into the case and were doing their usual gleeful job blowing an already bad situation out of proportion. The fact that Harrison High's legendary Coach, his wife, and daughter were involved only poured gasoline on the fire. The sheriff had been forced to post a deputy on the door to ward off reporters.

Alex was making a point of avoiding the Internet, though she'd taken calls from Cal, Cap, and his wife, respectively. All three said they were glad it was over, but were shocked Bruce had been behind Ted's murder.

"You keep your head down, PoPo," Cal told her. "It's probably gonna get a little nasty for a while, but—"

"Hey, we survived Bruce, baby. After damn near taking a bullet, a few bitchy Tweets don't rate more than a yawn."

"Good for you, hon." He hesitated, then added more seriously, "But if you need someone to talk to, I'm here for you."

Alex had thanked him sincerely, then promised to visit as soon as her duty schedule allowed.

"What are you going to do about Frank?" Mary Rogers asked now, her tone hesitant. She and Alex's father had planted themselves in Alex's hospital room, apparently determined to ride herd on visitors, whether they were her brothers or her cop coworkers. "If he does ask you to marry him, I mean."

"Ahh, that was the blood loss talking, Mom. He didn't mean it."

The Coach gave her a long, thoughtful look. "Yeah. Because most guys jump through plate glass doors when there's a jerk with a gun waiting to shoot them."

"Frank's a compulsive hero, Dad. He was awarded a Silver Star fighting in Afghanistan, for God's sake. He'd have come to anybody's rescue the same way. Especially given that a fellow cop and her family were the ones in danger."

"I was looking in his eyes when he said what he did, Alex. Yeah, he might have been a little woozy, but he meant every word."

"And I thought you said he was an abusive jerk."

"Abusive jerks don't risk getting killed to save somebody else."

"Your father and I were talking about this," Mary told her. "We don't pretend to understand your . . ."

"Love life?"

"That's one word for it." The Coach shook his head. "But you were right when you pointed out you're a grown woman. I don't ask your brothers what they do in their bedrooms . . ."

"Mostly because we don't want to know."

"Right back atcha, Mom."

"Point is, we think he does love you."

"Dad, I've only known the man a week. And given that we've been under fire most of that time . . ."

"You get to know somebody pretty well when somebody's been shooting at you," the Coach observed.

"Sweetie, you love him," Mary told her quietly. "I saw the look on your face when you realized how much he was bleeding. That's not the look you get over somebody you're just . . . dating."

Alex gave up trying to put up a front. "Look, I care about him, but . . . my judgment when it comes to men may not be the best. First Gary, now Bruce . . ."

"You haven't been with Bruce since high school," Mary pointed out. "And you might not have dated him then if Amy and I hadn't pushed you two together. Maybe if we hadn't—"

"This whole mess would have ended exactly the same way," the Coach told her tartly. To his daughter, he added, "The point of us sticking our noses in your love life is that we didn't want you to hesitate to do what makes you happy because of us. We'll support you whatever decision you make."

"Not sure my big brothers will agree with you."

"You let me handle your brothers."

Alex smiled. "Thanks, Dad."

Mary stood and put a hand over hers. "Sometimes you have to trust your heart, Alex, even when your head's afraid."

"I hope I'm not the one you're worried about," Frank said from the room's doorway. "You never have any reason to be afraid of me."

"Frank!" Alex straightened against the pillows, a grin of pure delight spreading over her face. "I was about to come see you."

He limped in. He wore sweatpants and a MCSO tee, a dark blue bathrobe playing up the blue in his eyes. "Did the SLED agents give you a hard time?"

"No more than you'd expect." If her parents hadn't been watching, she'd have lured him in for a kiss. "You?"

"Hey, it was more fun than a fight with the Taliban. The conversation with Lieutenant Davis, on the other hand . . ." He exaggerated a shudder. "Never piss off a SWAT lieutenant. I'm lucky the sheriff likes me. I don't think Davis does."

"We'd be dead if you'd waited for them."

"Lucky for us, you didn't." The Coach straightened and held out a hand for his wife. "Mary, I'm getting hungry. Let's go find out if they've put out anything more appetizing in the hospital cafeteria."

"Yeah, good luck with that, Mr. Rogers."

Ken paused beside him on the way out. "Call me Coach, son. Everybody does." He offered his hand for a short, strong handshake, then guided his wife out the door, swinging the door closed behind them.

"Which is my cue for a kiss." Frank started toward her, only to break step. "Unless you don't want me to . . ."

"Oh, fuck that." Alex slid out of bed and went into his arms. His lips were ravenous, hot. With a soft moan, Alex forgot everything else and let herself melt into him.

God, he felt so good. So bone-deep delicious, hard and broad and strong. Moaning in need and delight, she kissed him, drinking at his mouth like a woman in the grip of deepest thirst. Kissed him until they had to draw apart to breathe.

"I can't wait to be alone with you again," Frank murmured against her hair.

"Yes," she said softly. "I want to make love to you." Stroking a hand down the length of his back, she added, "Gently. I don't think either of us will be up to sceneing for a while."

"No. But I don't need whips and handcuffs when it comes to you. You're enough for me all by yourself."

"That door does have a lock . . ."

He looked tempted, then shook his head regretfully. "I would love to, but given your concussion, I don't think you're up to it tonight." Stepping back, Frank grimaced as his weight came down on his injured leg. "And much as I hate to admit it, I'm not sure I am either."

"Well, there's always tomorrow." She led him toward the window seat. "But maybe we can spend a little time together tonight."

"That sounds like an excellent idea." He smiled down at her and sank onto the seat, drawing her down into his powerful arms.

With a sigh, she relaxed against him as he leaned against the wall. They'd survived. They'd saved her parents and stopped a killer despite the odds.

Tomorrow they'd celebrate.

Getting out of the hospital through the lurking phalanx of reporters made Alex feel like a Cold War spy in a Tom Clancy novel. Her parents volunteered to act as decoys while Ben Tracy gave Alex and Frank a ride home; both were under orders not to drive for a couple of weeks.

They gave Alex's folks a five-minute head start before taking the elevator down. When the three of them got out, the Coach was holding forth in the lobby, doing the hail-fellow-well-met act he'd perfected over decades as a high school football coach. Dad had learned how to talk to the media about everything from embarrassing losing seasons to winning state championships. Being held hostage by a killer cop wasn't exactly in Ken's wheelhouse, but from the sound of it, he was holding his own before the dozen cameras pointed in his direction. Including those from all the major national news services.

Frank's hand landed in the small of her back, pushing her gently down the corridor. "Don't look back," he murmured. "You'll turn to a pillar of salt."

Alex swallowed a giggle and hurried after Tracy's broad shoulders. All three of them were in civilian clothes, but that might not keep them from getting caught. The local sports reporters knew Alex by sight, having watched her grow up cheering her father from the stands. Hopefully they were too enthralled with the Coach's account of the ordeal to spot them escaping.

The three cops strode down the corridor to the hospital's huge revolving doors and out into a gray October day. Leaving the redbrick building, they headed across the street to the parking garage where Tracy had left his car.

Which was when a slim blond fairy of a woman stepped out of the shadow cast by one of the garage's support columns. "Hi, there, Alex. Good to see you're alive and well despite the asshole's best efforts."

"Hi, Cassie." Alex smiled. She supposed if they had to be ambushed by a reporter, they could have done worse than Cassie York.

"Back off, Cassie." Glowering, Tracy pushed into the pixie's personal space and loomed there, emphasizing just how much bigger he was than the reporter. She didn't look intimidated in the least. "Leave these folks alone. They just got out of the hospital, for God's sake. And why aren't you inside with all the other piranhas?"

"Because I'm not a piranha." Cassie smiled, cheerfully refusing to be offended. "I'm more of a dolphin kind of person."

"Riiiiight. Because it's not like I've got your teeth prints in my ass, or anything."

"I wish." Cassie laughed wickedly, then considered Alex, head cocked. "Bruce was a sad guy, wasn't he?"

The girl was a hell of a lot better informed than your typical blogispheran. Then again, the Yorks had specialized in knowing where all the bodies were buried in Morgan County for the past century and a half. *The Morganville Courier* had been a weekly newspaper since the city was just a couple of mill villages, three churches, and five or six bars. Five generations of the York family had operated it until it had gone under in the great print apocalypse.

"Yeah," she admitted. "He was. A vicious killer who kidnapped my parents and tried to strangle me to death, but he was also a little sad."

"I found the story we did on the deaths of Greer's parents nine years ago." Cassie's clever eyes narrowed thoughtfully over the cell phone she was using to record the conversation. "Your folks were involved, too. Did he blame you for what happened? According to the story, y'all were dating back then. Were y'all going together more recently, too? Was he jealous?"

"No, I wasn't dating Bruce. He wasn't my type."

"Which speaks well of you. Greer's daddy was a white supremacist," Cassie continued, still digging away with a terrier's determination. "Was Greer?"

"I didn't think so until yesterday. Pretty sure the sheriff didn't either." Alex sighed. "Greer never said anything overtly racist or homophobic in my presence."

"How long did you two work together?"

"Two years. I thought he was doing a good job of putting everything behind him." At least until he'd snapped and beaten Gary to death. Apparently that had been when he'd just given up trying to be anything other than the killer his father had raised.

"I wonder if it had anything to do with Gary Ames being beaten to death back in September. Another friend of yours, I gather?" Cassie asked thoughtfully. "Have y'all tested Bruce's Maglite for DNA, Ben? You did tell me you thought it could have been a flash the killer used."

"Shit." Tracy's glowered at her. "We haven't released anything about the flash, Cassie. You keep that out of the story until it goes official."

"Hey, I've got more than enough stuff as it is." The blogger turned her phone toward Alex again. "What would you like to say, Deputy?" The humor had drained from her voice, and she sounded almost gentle.

Hell with it. Cassie had already put most of the story together. Might as well give her a quote—especially since Alex had something she wanted on the record. "Greer killed two damned good cops who had done absolutely nothing to deserve it. It's satisfying to know I fought him using hand-to-hand techniques Ted Arlington taught me. Otherwise I couldn't have kept him from killing us all until Frank could break in and shoot him."

"What do you think triggered all this?" The look in the reporter's eyes said she definitely had her suspicions.

Alex paused a long moment. "I don't know for sure—the only one who could have told us is Bruce, and that assumes he'd have told the truth anyway. But I think he let his father's expectations twist him until he broke. And then he started killing." She slanted a smile up at Frank. "If Deputy Murphy hadn't stopped him, he'd have kept killing. Frank saved lives, and he almost lost his own doing it. He's what a cop should be."

Cassie looked delighted, as if she was already getting an idea where she'd use that quote. "Deputy Murphy—"

"Cassie, quit trying to take advantage of people who aren't up to fighting you off," Tracy said sharply, glowering at the pixie. "The department spokesman will give you a statement. That's going to have to be enough."

"But—"

"That's *enough*, Cassie," Frank rumbled in his big bad Dom voice.

The reporter looked up at him, her eyes going wide. "Oh. All right, then." Turning her attention on Alex, she gave her a bright smile. "Glad you're okay, Deputy Rogers. We need all the good cops we can get." Turning, Cassie tucked her phone into her coat pocket and loped out of the garage, probably hoping to ambush Alex's parents before they got away.

"That woman thinks she's Lois Lane." Tracy sounded disgusted, but there was a note in his voice that made Alex wonder if there was more to his antipathy than the usual cops-hate-reporters dynamic. "Let's get out of here." He stomped off toward his car.

Alex and Frank followed. "Good job with the Dom voice," she murmured.

"Works every time." Frank grinned.

Alex grinned back. She was looking forward to listening to him use that voice to her in the very near future.

B en Tracy brooded as he drove them to Frank's house in his trooper-bait red Corvette.

"I wish to God I'd realized the son of a bitch was the killer before he had a chance to do this to you. Or Diane. She'd been so sure he'd try for her at Rose's—and she was right in the end. All week long, I had the SWAT team around that restaurant, ready to take him out. Never showed up. Then we caught a murder that diverted us, and that's when he went after her."

"Probably monitoring radio traffic," Alex said.

"Bastard," Tracy said bitterly. "She'd started to get kind of embarrassed to call us out here, as if she was afraid we'd believe she was exaggerating her danger. I kept telling her that after what happened to Ted, after everything the bastard painted on Ted's car, it was obvious he'd try for her eventually. Too goddamned bad I was right."

"Ben, I hate to say it, but Diane bears some of the responsibility," Frank pointed out. "She didn't call for backup when she should have. I know if she'd called me, I certainly would have come out to back her up, on duty or not."

"Any of us would have," Tracy agreed. He brooded a moment. "But at least she got the bastard. Not bad considering that she was under fire at the time."

"That's why he went after us," Alex said. "He knew that bullet meant he was caught. The minute they dug it out of him, he'd be done."

Tracy smiled grimly. "At least you kept him from killing anybody else."

"Don't do this to yourself, Ben," Frank said quietly.

The detective stiffened. "What do you mean?"

"The ultimate responsibility for Diane's death lies with the bastard who killed her." He took a breath and let it out. "I've blamed myself for a friend's death for a long time, but the reality is that I'm not God, and nobody but God could

have saved him." He looked at Tracy. "Don't blame yourself
for not being God, Ben."

He looked back at the road. "Of course not."

Alex and Frank exchanged a *Yeah, right* look.

A rm in arm, they watched Ben drive away. "It's going
to take him a while to get over this case," Frank murmured.

Alex sighed. "Now, there's a club with a lot of members."

"Yeah." He draped an arm over her shoulders. "But I
can think of a thing or two that'd make *me* feel better."

She smiled wickedly. "And me, too, I hope."

"Could be, could be." He turned her toward the house, and
they strolled up the walk together toward the front door. "And
since we're both on paid leave, medical and otherwise, we've
got plenty of time to experiment."

Frank unlocked the door and moved to key in the alarm
code before the system's warning beep could get any more
obnoxious.

"You do realize," Alex said, "that between your stitches
and my head, we're going to have to take this thing slow?"

Frank smiled wickedly. "Slow is one of my best things."

"So's fast and hard." She walked into his arms for a kiss
that took its time—lips, tongue, and teeth getting into the
act with nibbles and swirling strokes and lots of brushing
touches. When Alex finally drew back, they were both
breathing faster. "In fact, I've yet to find anything you don't
do well."

"Oh, stop," he deadpanned. "I'll get a swelled head."

Alex slid a hand down his flat belly to the bulge in his
jeans. "Feels like you already have."

"You're a bad, bad girl, Rogers."

"That I am, Murphy." She took hold of the bottom of
her T-shirt and slid it up, teasing. "Wanna see?"

"That depends." His grin was as toothy as a tiger's. "Are
you going to handcuff me to a chair this time?"

"We agreed there'd be no bondage today, remember?" She pulled off the shirt and tossed it aside. "We're going to try something really kinky—van-il-la." She enunciated each syllable of the word with a certain wicked relish.

He eyed her lace-clad breasts with approval. "And if anyone could find a way to make vanilla kinky, it would be you."

They undressed each other slowly, careful of one another's injuries. Frank murmured and kissed each of hers as he found them, gentle brushes of his lips against swollen bumps and bruises, blue with old blood. His hands felt exquisitely gentle as he touched and stroked. For all his dominant's chivalry, Alex had never realized how sweet he could be, how tender.

Alex stroked him just as carefully, just as sweetly, though most of his stitched-up injuries were hidden under layers of gauze. Exploring the hard ripples of muscle beneath smooth skin and gauze and soft hair, she realized she'd craved this tenderness, too. Particularly after they had almost lost everything that mattered. For all he seemed so big, so powerful, he was as vulnerable and human as she was.

They could have died so many times yesterday. She remembered the sight of Bruce, lying on his back, staring with empty eyes at the ceiling, just as Ted had stared at the sky the week before.

The thought made Alex shudder. Reaching up, she caught Frank's big head in her hands, her thumbs playing over the cuts he'd collected crashing through that glass door to save them. He could have lost an eye. The shard that cut his thigh could have slashed the femoral artery. It would have all been over.

With a tormented groan, Alex's lips opened against the velvet of his, her tongue swirling deep to stroke. He groaned into her mouth, the sound ragged with need.

"So close," she groaned. "We came so close . . ."

"Don't think about it," he whispered back, and his fingers

found her nipples, tugging and stroking and giving her something else to think about.

She ran a hand down his torso along the ripples of strong abdominal muscles. Traced a circle around his navel. Dropped lower to wrap around the hard column of his cock. For a moment she just held it, feeling his pulse beat beneath the thin skin.

"Nice to see the transfusion did its job," he joked.

"It certainly did." She used her grip on his cock to steer him backward to the couch. When he sank down, she nudged between his thighs, bent, and tasted him, savoring the cream at the tip of his cock.

"Are you sure . . ." He broke off to swallow. "Are you sure you should be doing this?"

She lifted her head and pushed him down lightly on the cushions. "I'll be gentle." The smile took on a wicked edge. "Just lay back and enjoy it."

Alex had sucked off men before, of course. For that matter, she'd sucked off Frank before. But this was different. She remembered what he'd said to her father. *"If the Archangel Michael had personally taken my order for the perfect woman, she wouldn't be as perfect as Alex."* Even half-drunk from blood loss, he'd sounded dead serious. Had he meant it?

Had he meant it when he'd told her father he intended to marry her?

She shut the thought away. Maybe he had, maybe he hadn't. That wasn't what was important now. All that mattered was being with him in this moment. As if it might be the last moment of their lives, the last time they were together. Because it could be. If yesterday had taught her one thing, it was that nothing was ever guaranteed.

She didn't intend to lose this moment.

Alex engulfed his cock and suckled fiercely, then drew her mouth off him. Slowly she ran the tip of her tongue the length of the great vein that ran along his cock, tracing lazy patterns until she heard his breath speed up.

"Wait," he said, pulling her up. "Across my mouth." The

touch of Dom snap in his voice wound her body tight in delicious reaction.

They rearranged themselves, Alex kneeling astride his face as she bent to lick his cock, alternating tongue strokes up and down the length of his shaft, with pauses to suckle the velvety head.

She had no intention of trying to deep-throat him— that much violent activity was sure to trigger a migraine that would have brought the play to an uncomfortable end. So instead, she sucked hard, wanting to make him feel it even as he worked her with fingers and lips and wicked tongue, working over wet flesh in a slick, sweet dance.

Pleasure rose in bright lace patterns, so pure and intense Alex could almost see the glow behind her closed lids. She licked and suckled him even harder, wanting to share the purity of her pleasure like a gift of frankincense and myrrh. A thing of precious, ancient magic.

Alex had lost track of the number of times they'd made love in the past week. How many times had he driven her to orgasm, made her call him Master, made her beg? No man, Dominant or otherwise, had ever affected her the way he did, right down to the core.

Yet none of those exquisite experiences with him had hit her like this one, even careful and gentle as it was. Was it just how close they'd come to dying? Some combination of neurotransmitters and hormones, flashing through the brain and blood, there and gone?

It didn't feel like that.

It felt more like a newborn's cry, like the warm touch of the Coach's hand, or the brush of her mother's lips. Something that made the soul reverberate to possibilities beyond sex and lust.

At that thought, Alex felt an orgasm rising in a sweet bell-like peal through her bones, her flesh. Gasping, she suckled him, fighting to hold on.

"I'm about to come," Frank gasped. "Stop, I want in you!"

"Yes! Yes, all right, wait!" Shivering, Alex drew away,

moved to straddle him, and guided his cock to her slick opening. Slowly, slowly, she sank downward, head falling back as he filled her and filled her. Until his balls rested against the lips of her pussy.

Bracing her hands on his muscled torso, Alex began to rise and fall, taking her time as she fucked him, sliding up, sliding down, until his head rolled back against the cushions as he groaned, the sound rich with sensuality and passion. "God, nobody's ever felt—"

"I know! God, I know!"

She was close, so close. Each thick stroke of that big cock wound the tension of her building orgasm tighter and tighter. He watched her ride him with his gunmetal eyes glazed, darkened almost to iron.

"Oh, God," she whimpered, "Oh God, I'm about to—"

"I love you," he chanted, "I love you!"

"Yes! Yes, I love you!" Alex came in an exquisite rain of warm light, softer than the ferocious orgasms she'd known before, yet sweeter, too.

Frank bowed under her with a sudden surge of effort that lifted her clear off the couch, as he reached a deep, groaning completion.

Panting, breathless, she collapsed on top of him. They clung together like survivors of a tsunami.

"Marry me," he said in a hoarse voice, stroking her hair with a hand that shook. "I know we've only known each other a week, but I'm not some kid in the first grip of infatuation. I know what I want, and I know what I need, and it's you. If you say no now, I'll ask you again later. If you need time, I'll give it. But—"

"Yes."

He stared at her as she cuddled into his warm, sweating strength. "Yes?"

"Yes." She grinned and sat back, enjoying the depth of his cock. "You're right, neither of us are kids anymore. I know what I need, and what I need is you."

Her big, bad Dom grinned up at her like a boy contemplating an endless Christmas morning. And dragged her down into his arms to kiss her until her head swam.

There'd be problems. There'd be drama. There'd be all the little disasters that were a part of life.

But as long as they had each other, they'd get through every bit of it.

From *New York Times* Bestselling Author
ANGELA KNIGHT

THE MAGEVERSE SERIES

MASTER OF THE NIGHT

MASTER OF THE MOON

MASTER OF WOLVES

MASTER OF SWORDS

MASTER OF DRAGONS

MASTER OF FIRE

MASTER OF SMOKE

MASTER OF SHADOWS

MASTER OF DARKNESS

PRAISE FOR THE SERIES

"A successful mix of magic, romance, [and] humor."
—*Publishers Weekly*

"Fantastic."
—The Romance Studio

angelasknights.com
penguin.com

M1659AS0315

Also available from
New York Times **bestselling author**

Angela Knight

THE TIME HUNTERS SERIES

JANE'S WARLORD

WARRIOR

GUARDIAN

"ENFORCER" FEATURED IN THE
UNBOUND ANTHOLOGY

PRAISE FOR THE AUTHOR

"If you like alpha heroes, wild rides, and pages
that sizzle in your hand, you're going
to love [Angela Knight]!"

—J.R. Ward, #1 *New York Times* bestselling author

angelasknights.com
penguin.com

Discover Romance

berkleyjoveauthors.com

See what's coming up next from your favorite romance authors and explore all the latest Berkley, Jove, and Sensation selections.

See what's new

~

Find author appearances

~

Win fantastic prizes

~

Get reading recommendations

~

Chat with authors and other fans

~

Read interviews with authors you love

LOVE
ROMANCE
NOVELS?

For news on all your f...
sneak peeks into th...
giveaways, an...

"Like" Love Alw...

 **LoveA...**